The Allotment Girls

Kate Thompson is a journalist with over twenty years'
experience as a writer for the broadsheets and women's
weekly magazines. She is now freelance, and as well as
writing for newspapers she's also a seasoned ghostwriter.
The Allotment Girls is her fourth novel.

Praise for Kate Thompson

'Poignant and moving'
Val Wood

'Hair-raising and gripping'
Daily Mail

'We love this nostalgic read
with friendship at its heart'
Take a Break

'Marvellous, full of gutsy characters
I immediately empathized with'
Margaret Pemberton

Also by Kate Thompson

Secrets of the Singer Girls
Secrets of the Sewing Bee
The Wedding Girls

The Allotment Girls

Kate Thompson

PAN BOOKS

First published 2018 by Pan Books
an imprint of Pan Macmillan
20 New Wharf Road, London N1 9RR
Associated companies throughout the world
www.panmacmillan.com

ISBN 978-1-5098-2225-6

1 3 5 7 9 8 6 4 2

A CIP catalogue record for this book is available from the British Library.

Typeset by Palimpsest Book Production Ltd, Falkirk, Stirlingshire
Printed and bound by CPI Group (UK) Ltd, Croydon, CR0 4YY

To my boys, Ronnie and Stanley
xxx

In memory of the Jarvis family:
Thomas, aged 39; Sarah, 39; Hannah, 16;
Mary Ann, 14; Thomas, 12; William, 10;
Louisa, 8; Alice, 5; George, 3;
Caroline, 2; and Elizabeth, 8 months

We are all gardeners at heart, and I believe if we were all gardeners in fact there wouldn't be any wars. But perhaps the fact that most of us are gardeners or garden lovers will help us to live cheerfully through these dark days, and build a sweeter and better world when the nightmare is over. I am sure it will, because the very essence of gardening consists of rooting out and destroying all the evil things, and cultivating and developing all that is good and beautiful in life.

'Dig for Victory', gardening correspondent and broadcaster Mr Middleton, *Listener*, 4 January 1940

Prologue

JANUARY 1897

It must be said, nowhere does a funeral quite like the East End. This one, taking place on a bitter Monday in January, quite surpassed anything the poor folk of the parish of Bethnal Green had ever before seen. Even in the depths of his guilt, he had to acknowledge this fact.

The entire funeral route was lined with thousands of people, a respectful crowd largely, all dressed in their best clothes and washed for the occasion. The sea of black bonnets, shawls and caps was chequered with the odd cluster of bright colour from the hats of assembled factory girls.

Even the weather had put on its funeral best, with scrawls of black cloud dirtying the sky and a rattling wind hammering the windows like fists. The police had been deployed in great numbers, but their presence was not required, he noted, as he tried to blend into the sea of faces.

He had never seen so many people before, sitting on walls, clinging to gas lamps and perched on sills, all craning their necks for a better view.

'Almost be worth being burnt to have such a handsome

1

turnout,' muttered a man in the crowd next to him, before his wife slapped him into silence. 'Wash your mouth out,' she hissed. 'The cortège is coming.'

A hush fell over the crowd. A painful lump lodged in his throat as the first notes of 'Dead March in Saul' drifted over the cobbles. The cortège was led by the Wapping Gas Workers' brass band, the dramatic clash of their instruments driving deep into his heart.

And then came the bodies. A mixture of horror and awe settled over the crowd. For once, no one was looking at the lavish wreaths or the magnificent black horses, resplendent in their rich purple plumes and velvets. All eyes were fixed only on the coffins, growing gradually smaller in size as they passed by.

'Just children,' wept the woman next to him, pressing a broad black handkerchief to her mouth in dismay. But to him they had names, and he murmured them quietly, like an undercover priest, as each coffin filed past.

Eliza, fifteen. Mary, twelve. Alfred, ten. Beatrice, nine. John, seven. Margaret, five. Marie, three.

By the time baby Emily's body passed him, he could no longer hold back his anguish, and a strange cry escaped him. In comparison to her parents' coffins, Emily's seemed absurdly small, and he longed to reach out and cradle her, to save her the journey into the cold, dark earth.

But they were already gone, one step closer to the closing scene of the mass burial that would be discussed in every public house in the borough for months to come.

And then came the mourners. And how! Conveyances of all descriptions, filled with anyone who had a connection to the dead. Mourning carriages, hansom cabs, broughams and even three omnibuses, willing to take passengers, mainly women it had to be said, to the final resting place for a shilling each way.

This was less of a funeral, he thought wryly, than a day out. But you could hardly blame East Enders. It was, after all, their generosity, sparked by an appeal from the vicar of St Bartholomew, that had paid for this whole funeral. Rumour had it they had arrived at the undertaker's to leave their subscription by foot and on trap, some from as far afield as Romford and Chingford.

He hadn't expected to see her, but suddenly he caught a flash of that unmistakable red hair, as rich and deep as brandy, between the broad black handkerchiefs fluttering at a coach window.

'Pol!' he called before he could stop himself.

The handkerchief slid away and their eyes met as the coach paused. Her face was as pale as eggshell. The look between them hung suspended in the frozen air.

Love. Grief. Guilt.

Oh, Polly. What a thing we did.

The coach jolted and moved off. She was gone from sight, the foot mourners quickly swallowing the gap in the cobbles behind her coach. He would not see her again for another forty-four years.

PART ONE

One

Liverpool

Everyone in Liverpool would always remember where they were the night the Matchy copped it. The colossus of a factory, where Bryant & May had been making matches for over forty years, was reduced to a smoking skeleton overnight, courtesy of the Luftwaffe. Somewhere between midnight and 1 a.m., incendiary bombs crashed through the roof into the top match room. Attracted to the flames, and demonstrating their usual ruthless efficiency, the German pilots soon came and finished the job off with five high-explosive bombs. Rumour had it the fires from the inferno could be seen in the night sky from as far away as North Wales.

The loss of a much-loved landmark – to say nothing of the loss of jobs – was enough to push already frayed nerves to breaking point.

'Fuck you, Hitler!' Pearl heard her neighbour Rita roaring into the smoky sky. Not a single woman down her turning told her to mind her mouth. Rita had supported

7

her entire family at the Matchy for the past forty-five years and was still reeling from the death of her eldest at Dunkirk.

Pearl felt Rita's pain, but for her that hellish night when the bombs had screamed from blood-red skies didn't signify the end. It was the beginning. She packed light and by the time the All Clear drifted through the smoky streets, she was already locking up and leaving. Just a few clothes, a photograph or two, her insurance papers, ration book and identity card hastily thrown into a carpetbag. No time for goodbyes. She didn't want anyone asking awkward questions.

Moving fast and stepping over puddles of filthy water, she turned the corner of Violet and Linacre Road. The local corner shop was rubble, and beyond that the match factory still smouldered. Curiosity drew her to what remained of the Matchy and she walked as far as she could before an ARP warden frantically signalled at her to step back.

Pearl stared up in dismay as a bleak dawn bled over the Diamond Works, flakes of soot settling on her face like snow. It seemed hard to believe she had been here on the line just yesterday afternoon, packing matches. It was as if a giant iron fist had come punching down through the clouds and smashed the factory to smithereens. The great weight of five tons of heavy metal match machinery had crashed through four floors and lay blackened and waterlogged in the scree of rubble. A stench of cordite and burning wood hung in the air, and charred bricks vomited out from the blackened entrance. Had the bombs dropped a few hours earlier . . .

Pearl shuddered. This was no time to dwell on the past.

Instead, she hurried off, head down, heels clicking on the pavement. Dodging bomb craters and crunching over a river of broken glass, she patted her coat pocket to check the letter was still there. Not that she needed it. She knew the address by heart: Millie Brown, 6 Parnell Road, Bow E3.

Pearl knew it was a risk turning up on the doorstep of a woman she had never met, but Millie was her last hope. Her only hope. One hour later, Pearl disappeared into the billowing clouds of smoke at Liverpool Lime Street Station, and officially vanished. Later, Rita and her other neighbours would conclude that poor Pearl had been killed in one of Liverpool's worst raids.

SATURDAY, 10 MAY 1941

On the morning of her twenty-first birthday, Millie Brown woke with a jolt and immediately sensed danger in the cool, stale air. She lay still as stone under the counterpane as her eyes, gritty with tiredness, adjusted to the gloom. A thin band of light slid in under the blackout blind. Millie made out the angular silhouette of her husband's face. She couldn't see his eyes in the darkness, but she knew he had been watching her sleep.

'All right,' she murmured uneasily, pulling the coverlet over her thin nightie. 'What a night. Wanna brew?'

She wasn't expecting him to shower her with birthday wishes. He didn't disappoint.

'What's your game?' With a sudden jerk, he leapt from his easy chair and ripped down the blackout blind. As their

9

bedroom flooded with light, she blinked, dazzled, but when her vision cleared, she saw what was dangling from his finger.

Bugger!

They hadn't got back from the air-raid shelter until gone 4 a.m., and it must have fallen out of her bag when they had finally stumbled in, half mad with exhaustion. Fumbling for her cigarettes from the bedside table, she decided to brazen it out.

'Well, it ain't a bloody banana, Curly,' she snapped, inhaling deeply before blowing a long stream of smoke from her nostrils. 'It's a diaphragm, if you must know.' She smiled coldly. 'You might know it better as a Dutch cap.'

'Where d'yer get it?'

'Sympathetic pharmacist down the Roman give it me under the counter,' she replied derisively. 'She does a good line in sheaths if you're interested.'

'Don't get saucy with me, Millie,' Curly warned, eyes flashing dangerously. 'I've had it up to here with your lip. I warned you when we got hitched, I wanted a son within the year.'

'And I told you that with Jerry bombing the hell out of us night after bleedin' night, this ain't the right time to be thinking about bringing a baby into the world. Did you see them poor nippers down the shelter last night?'

'I ain't accustomed to waiting this long to get what I want, Millie, war or no war,' he said steadily. Without taking his eyes from hers, he slid a razor blade from inside his jacket pocket and slowly drew it through the centre of the rubber, leaving a gaping slit.

'No more gadding about after work with those daft

cows,' he added, plunging his blade into the rubber and drawing a second slit through it. 'You answer to me. Your husband.'

Millie shook her head and stared out over the bomb-shattered chimney pots of Parnell Road, anger fighting off her tears.

'In name only, pal,' she muttered, drawing heavily on her fag.

'Maybe so, but you belong to me now. You owe me nippers, at least five. Once you've got a baby in your belly, it'll calm you down. Like taking the knackers off a dog, see,' he said, running the edge of his razor along the hem of his blue serge jacket, before replacing it. 'I want you in confinement by the end of this year,' he spat, tossing the remains of the slashed rubber cap onto the bedpost.

I'd rather lick the floor of a barber's than bring a child of yours into the world.

Millie kept those thoughts to herself, of course. Instead, she tore her gaze away from the window and stared in disgust as her husband, Curly 'Razor' Brown, turned his back on her and started combing his hair back with pomade in the looking glass over the mantel. His shirt was pristine white, but his neck was so grimy you could have planted a row of spuds along it. His boots gleamed, but Millie knew fine well his feet were rotten. All top show, but then that was Curly all over.

Not a day had passed since they had married twenty-one months previously without her wondering how the hell she had ended up hitched to some oily two-bit villain from Whitechapel. She'd had such high hopes.

With her voice, striking looks and platinum-blonde hair,

she could have trodden the boards at any music hall in the East End. She'd been heading in the right direction, too. Aged sixteen, she'd ridden high up on a float as the freshly crowned Miss Poplar at the summer pageant, smile as bright as her crown. Aged seventeen, she'd got a job at the Bryant & May factory at the Fairfield Works in Bow, and on the day of her eighteenth birthday she had been named Miss Brymay in a company-wide competition. What a thing that had been! Her face, advertising Swan Vestas, smiling out from every Bryant & May billboard in the East End of London. She'd even made it onto the side of the number 8 that travelled from Bow to Bond Street. Her image, flashing through the streets of the West End! With the optimism of youth, she had been so sure it wouldn't be that long before she would join it, maybe get snapped up by some Bond Street modelling bureau, work as a mannequin . . .

Except, none of that had happened.

Three years on, the billboards had faded and she was still a match girl, living in a bomb-shattered terrace, married to a man whose nickname would be ridiculous if it wasn't true. Curly denied razoring Walter Edwards in broad daylight in Watney Street Market, but there had been too many witnesses and he'd dined out on his reputation ever since.

Millie could still recall the day they had married at St Stephen's church in Tredegar Road in Bow. It had lodged in her memory like a fish bone in the gullet. The heat had been stifling that August day, causing even the pork pies laid out on the buffet table to sweat greasily and the silver-sprayed arum lilies in front of the altar to wilt.

It had felt like all of Bow had turned out to witness her misery. Millie trussed up in farthingale frills, and so much corsetry she felt as if she were wearing a straitjacket not a bridal gown. Curly fancying himself quite the natty dresser in a sharp suit, a quarter-inch of cuff on show, and his black hair slicked so closely to his scalp it looked like it had been painted on with a tar brush.

My God, it had been a terrible affair from start to finish. Her mother, Gladys, a right old gin-lizzie at the best of times, was pie-eyed on black market booze before the ceremony had even started, wobbling about the place in a musty-smelling squirrel fur and too much make-up. She'd blamed her unsteadiness on her afflictions, of course. Usually, Gladys wore an old pair of patched-up hobnail boots with holes cut out for her bunions, but in honour of the wedding, she'd squeezed her lumpy feet into a pair of pawn-shop heels.

Millie's older brother had slunk down in his seat as she walked up the aisle, looking as guilty as a dog who'd defecated on the hearthrug. She ought to have hated him – it was his fault she was in this mess in the first place – but Jimmy was spineless, as much a victim as she was in many ways.

When the insincere speeches had finished and the wedding breakfast was cleared away, the men had gathered round the makeshift bar to get down to the serious business of drinking. Gladys had used the opportunity to offer some motherly words of advice.

'Put that lip in! You got a face on you like the back end of a turkey,' she'd mumbled, a fag end glued to her bottom lip. When Millie had turned her chair the other way, she'd become even nastier.

'Do you think I loved your father when I married him?' she'd slurred, hissing port fumes over Millie. ''Course not. I was even younger than you, but I had to do my duty, just like you will tonight. Least you got a job to escape to. I had Jimmy hanging off my tit within the year and . . .'

Millie had risen abruptly and stalked outside before she could be subjected to any more. She'd imagined it couldn't have got any worse. Wrong again. The wedding day paled into comparison next to the night. In a small boarding house somewhere outside Clacton-on-Sea, she had lain like a lump of cold meat underneath Curly as he pumped away on top of her, engulfing her in fumes of tobacco and cologne, and beneath it all, the hot marshy odour of his sinewy white body. As she'd lain, pinned, in the hot, close darkness, she'd hated herself for allowing it to happen. Afterwards, he had rolled off her with a guttural grunt before falling asleep. Desolation had rolled over her in waves as she'd dabbed at Curly's sticky spendings with a hankie.

Four weeks later she'd been thrown a lifeline. The smell of roasting dinners scented the sunlit cobbles on a sleepy Sunday when the news broke.

'. . . this country is at war with Germany,' came the sombre voice that crackled from every wireless down Parnell Road. Overnight, Millie watched as someone's husband, sweetheart, brother or father became a soldier. Even her weak-willed brother Jimmy marched off to be turned into a man at last. Everyone except Curly, who'd been granted a reprieve via a forged medical certificate from a dodgy doctor he knew down Brick Lane. But for Millie, at least it meant the chance to continue working.

Bryant & May had been stockpiling raw materials in the build-up to war, so there had been no dislocation in output. In fact, production had increased to meet the demand caused by the boom in smoking. And now they were officially making matches for the British Army, it would be unpatriotic of her to leave. Well, that's what she told Curly anyway.

Her job, her friends and her under-the-counter contraceptive . . . Those were what kept her going in these dark days! But now one of those was hanging in shreds from the bedpost. Bleak thoughts, sharp and vicious, began to unravel inside her. She could do most things: whiten his step, cook his tea, doll herself up to look like the perfect wife, but bear his child? Never.

'Right,' grinned Curly, pocketing his comb and snapping her back to the present. In dismay, she saw he was tugging down his braces and – oh Christ, no! – unbuttoning his flies.

'Curly, I ain't got time,' she pleaded. 'I've gotta be at work in half an hour. The hooter's gonna go any minute now.'

'S'right,' he leered, 'won't take long. We got a bit of lost time to make up for, ain't we?' He smiled grotesquely, revealing a scattering of rotten stumps. Millie closed her eyes as he lowered himself down on top of her and swallowed a scream as he fumbled with her straps.

'Get off, Curly, please,' she cried, struggling under the weight of him. 'I told you, I ain't got time.'

'When you gonna learn to be a proper wife?' he grunted,

yanking up the hem of her nightie and pawing at the flesh on her thigh. Finding a strength she didn't know she possessed, Millie jerked her knee hard into his crotch, sending him crashing back onto the bed with a deep groan of pain.

Two

'Oi, Annie, don't forget your sarnies! I've done your favourite, bloater paste!' Elsie's voice rattled up Blondin Street like a klaxon.

'Nan, I've told you, I get a decent dinner at the work canteen!'

'I know, my darlin' girl, but I don't trust the food at that factory,' Elsie replied, bustling up the cobbles to meet her. With one hand she slipped the parcel into Annie's bag, and with the other, started picking imaginary bits of lint from her olive-green work overalls.

Elsie Trinder was a sixty-year-old force of nature and had been involved in Annie's upbringing since her mother had died. Hair as white as meringue and eyes as black as coal, Elsie was what you might call the poke nose of Blondin Street. *Nothing* escaped her. Annie often joked that her nan was a one-woman intelligence unit and if Churchill had taken her on, the war would be over by now.

Unfortunately, though, her feverish mind never seemed to stop imagining ways in which Annie could meet with a grisly death, which, during the Blitz, meant she was working overtime. She also had an unhealthy preoccupation with Bryant & May, the factory which paid Annie sixteen shillings a week to pack matches.

Annie's gaze travelled up over the rooftop of number 22 to the leaden skies beyond. There it was. A great, dark, smoking mass, the largest and most notorious factory out-side of the docks, easily identifiable by its two gigantic red-brick water towers that rose starkly into the heavens.

It didn't really matter where you were in Bow, you could see those twin towers brooding over the landscape. They all lived in their shadow and Annie had the queerest feeling that the old building was groaning with secrets and ghosts. She knew it had a chequered past, but times had changed since that fateful year when Jack the Ripper stalked the streets and striking match girls changed the course of history. The problem was, her nan hadn't moved with those times. Raised in the Victorian East End, her hopes tar-nished by brutal poverty, she chose not to forgive. Or forget.

Sighing, the old woman reached up and stroked her granddaughter's cheek. 'Darlin' girl, you could end up get-ting the phoss, or worse . . .'

'Nan,' she warned.

'. . . you could get a job anywhere. The cocoa factory over at Bromley, even Spratt's has got to be better than being a match girl, surely?

'But what am I saying?' she scolded herself. 'It's war. There's a whole new world out there now for girls like you beyond the sweatshops and sculleries. Join the services, experience a bit of life beyond Bow.'

'Please, Nan, won't you let it go?' Annie pleaded. 'You're talking fifty-odd years ago, and times have changed. Bryant

& May have the best facilities around, ask any of the girls in the match room. There's a doctor, dentist, library, social and sports clubs, and lots more besides. I'm in the Union of Women Matchmakers now, a fully signed-up member of the Match Girls' Club,' she added proudly. 'We form a committee just to take a pee these days, Nan,' she joked in an attempt to lighten the mood.

'Yeah, and we know whose blood paid for all that,' Elsie muttered darkly, ignoring Annie's stab at humour.

Annie sighed as she pushed back a bramble of red curls that refused to sit under her green hairnet. When it came to Bryant & May, she and her nan would *never* see eye to eye. Her work on the top match floor was the only bone of contention in an otherwise close and loving relationship, so, out of respect, Annie held her tongue.

The war was not being kind to the Trinders. Annie's father, Bill, Elsie's only son, was being held at a prisoner of war camp, captured just a few months into the hostilities; Annie's two younger sisters had been evacuated to Suffolk; and they were eight months into the worst aerial bombardment the country had ever endured – with the East End of London slap bang in the bombers' sights!

Night after relentless night Bow had copped it. Annie was finding it exhausting enough going on only a few hours' sleep a night, and she was just seventeen! She took in the broken veins on her nan's plump cheeks, the patched lisle stockings gathered in soft pleats around her sturdy ankles, and felt a rush of love. She'd always imagined her nan to be invincible, but now . . .

The piercing shriek of Bryant & May's steam hooter sounded.

'Oh, 7 a.m., there she blows,' Annie grinned. 'I gotta go, Nan. I'll just go and knock for Rose.' Bending down, she planted a soft kiss on Elsie's cheek. 'Have you remembered I'm going to the baths with the girls after work? Then I'm on fire-watching duty tonight, so I'll be back late.'

'The cheek of 'em to expect girls to do it!' Elsie said over the noise of the hooter.

'I volunteered, Nan,' Annie insisted. 'When the siren goes, please come down Bryant & May's shelter. I'd feel so much better knowing you were there.'

Elsie shook her head and stifled a yawn. 'Not tonight, darlin' girl. I don't think I've slept a wink all week. I'll take my chances in my own bed.'

'Nan, that's not—'

'No buts,' Elsie insisted, resting her arms over her enormous corseted bosom. 'Take more than Jerry to finish this old girl off.'

Annie went to protest further, but she was interrupted by the door next to theirs opening. Her best pal, Rose Riley, lived in rooms on the top floor of number 20. They'd grown up together, tearing up and down the cobbles of Blondin Street, and shared everything except looks. Annie was tall and rangy, as pale as a Swan Vesta, with a halo of copper curls and an impudent grin. Rose was quite a different creature. Her skin was smooth and nut brown – unusual for a girl from Bow – and she had almond-shaped eyes as blue as harebells. Her crowning glory was her lustrous dark hair, which fell all the way to the base of her spine.

Rose was adopted and knew nothing of her ancestry, but the girls had overheard the muttered comments. Not that Rose had ever dared broach the subject of her real parents with Maureen, her thirty-five-year-old adopted mother. No one entered into conversation with Maureen Riley unless it was absolutely necessary. Last time someone got into a doorstep debate with Rose's mother, she'd ended up with a fist – wrapped in a straightened-out wire kirby grip – smashed clean in her face. Once they'd experienced Maureen's DIY knuckleduster, they rarely came back for more. Her father had been a bare-knuckle boxer, you see, and the apple hadn't fallen too far from the tree, which made the differences between her and her gentle adopted daughter all the more stark.

'Hello, Annie, Mrs T,' Rose said.

'How's your mother, Rose?' Elsie replied. 'How did she like them raids last night, eh, dear?'

'Not so good, gone back to bed. She's got one of her heads on her. She reckons we're in for a bad one tonight, her knees are aching something rotten.'

'Never mind her bloody knees,' Annie protested, aghast. 'What on earth's happened to your hair?' Rose's long hair had been plaited and rolled into tight coils either side of her head.

Rose patted her hair defensively.

'Mum thought it more hygienic if I were to wear it permanently up. Means I don't have the bother of brushing it every night.'

'Oh, Rose, please tell me she ain't sewn it up!' Annie cried.

'Yes, but it doesn't really hurt,' Rose insisted. 'Honestly, it's quite practical when you think about it, especially if we're going to be spending every night in the shelters.'

'I thought we'd done away with the workhouses,' Annie

fumed. 'What next? Will she have you trussed up in corsets, chiselling out your teeth to save the cost of the dentist?'

'Well, bless me, your mother's a practical woman,' Elsie said lightly, shooting Annie a silencing look. 'Now, you best be on your way or you'll be late. I'll drop your mother in a bit of stew later, Rose, and a poultice for her knees.'

Annie didn't know why her nan always defended Maureen so. In the seventeen years they'd lived next door to her, Elsie had always treated her with such kindness, defending her to the neighbours. It was a peculiar friendship, and not just because Elsie was twenty-five years older. Maureen was as gruff as Elsie was garrulous.

'Come on,' Rose said, slipping her arm through Annie's, 'your nan's right. Millie'll be waiting, and there's a prayer meeting in the yard later so we can't be late.'

Elsie gripped Annie's face and planted a big lavish kiss on her cheek. 'Love you, darlin' girl. Stay safe tonight.'

With the hooter ringing in their ears, they made their way up the cobbles.

Annie walked in silence next to Rose, her nan's earlier words playing on her mind. Could she really leave Bow? She gazed up the length of the long narrow street and tried to define what it was she loved so much about the place.

The street was much like any other respectable East End terrace. The fronts went straight out onto the cobbles, blackened from centuries of heavy industry. The backs were all crowded little yards hung with washing, a shanty town of home-made rabbit hutches, meat safes and pigeon lofts.

The place was looking a little shabby now. Rose and Maureen's was missing its chimney stack since the Works boiler blasted through it after the factory took a hit, and number 28 was missing altogether.

'That used to be the best-turned-out house on the street,' Rose remarked as they walked past. 'I miss the O'Sullivans. Do you remember when we was nippers, her window ledge during the processions?'

'Not much.' Annie smiled nostalgically as she remembered the white lace at the curtains, the ledges festooned with crucifixes and candles. The Catholic processions were long gone now, of course, as was the heart of the community. No more old ladies shelling peas into their apron laps, or crowds of kids playing high jimmy knacker and tin can copper.

Today, sandbags obscured the snowy white steps, blackout blinds in place of lace. The cheerful yellow backyard dahlias had long since been replaced with cabbages. There was little beauty or sentiment to be found anywhere in the East End now.

Annie felt a strong tug of protectiveness. This old place was still her home, it was more than just blackened bricks and decaying mortar, it was where she belonged.

At the end of the street, where Blondin met Old Ford Road, Millie wasn't in her usual spot, having her morning smoke outside the tram shed and making eyes at the conductors. The girls settled down to wait, dodging the army of workers weaving their way to the back entrance of Bryant & May.

Annie squinted her eyes against the sea of match girls as they streamed past in their green tunics and matching green hairnets. What a tribe! With thousands employed at the factory, they staggered the start times, but the 7 a.m.

shift was still like kicking out time at a football stadium. The noise of it all was tremendous – shouts, laughter and the crunch of glass underfoot doing little to drown out the relentless hooter.

'Where is she?' asked Rose worriedly. 'Mum'll scrag me if I get my wages docked for being late.'

Then they spotted her. Swaggering along Old Ford, fag end stuck to her painted lips, gas mask bashing against her leg. Annie had to laugh. Only Millie could manage to make a tabard and hairnet look glamorous. The vivacious blonde didn't so much walk as wiggle, heels clipping on the cobbles.

They were an unusual trio of friends, Annie reflected, but since they'd all been placed together on the match-packing station, they had decided that if they were going to be stuck together ten hours a day, they might as well enjoy each other's company.

Married Millie was a few years older than them and Annie's heart had sunk when she'd realized she and Rose were going to be working with such a worldly-wise woman. As well as being the factory pin-up, Millie had a mouth on her. But instead of lording it over them, she had shown the girls nothing but kindness. All right, she could be a bit brassy, with a laugh as dirty as a drain, but she was pure gold where it counted.

'Morning, cock,' Millie called, a smile blossoming over her face. 'How's your luck?'

'Nice lie-in, was it?' Annie teased.

For a fraction, Millie's smile slipped and, as she drew closer, Annie noticed the deep shadows under her eyes.

'Oh, Millie, I was only pulling your leg. You and Curly had a quarrel? What's he done now?'

'What, apart from being born?' Millie retorted, angrily crushing her cigarette beneath her heel. 'Let's not ruin the day by talking about that waste of space.'

'Wait a mo,' Annie said, tugging her back. 'Me and Rose clubbed together, got you something for your birthday.'

'You remembered?'

''Course, couldn't rely on you to tell us, could we?'

'Happy Birthday, Millie,' Rose said shyly, pulling out a small package. 'It's not much, but we hope you like it.'

'Oh, girls, you shouldn't have wasted your money,' Millie scolded, but as she unwrapped the tiny phial of violet water and a small bar of her favourite Turkish Delight, she looked genuinely touched.

'This is the nicest thing anyone's ever given me,' she smiled, hugging them both.

'Did Curly give you anything?' Annie asked, instantly regretting the question.

'Only another reason to hate him,' Millie snapped. 'Come on, let's go. That hooter's going right through my bleedin' skull.'

As the three friends neared the black wrought-iron factory gates, the foul stench of phosphorus hit them in a cloying wave, with the undercurrent of another, ranker stench, which nearly made Annie retch.

Millie sniffed the air and put on her telephone voice. 'Matches mixed with cordite, a most delightful aroma, wouldn't one agree?'

Annie giggled. 'One would! Certainly clears the passages all right.'

Millie's gallows humour masked the unsavoury truth of it. No one talked about the smells of the Blitz. Annie missed the aromas of her East End, which used to roll over the Stink House Bridge in pungent waves. The tang of the offal factory mixed with the scent of boiling sugar from Clarnico hung like a soupy cloud over Blondin Street, but she loved it . . . Now all they could smell was the bitter stench of war.

As they neared the gate, a commotion from the other end of Old Ford Road drew Annie's eye. A huddle of people stood round what looked to be the number 8 bus.

'Oi, Millie,' called out a frizzy-haired match girl named Sandra.

Pushing their way through the crowds, they saw that the bus had obviously got caught out in last night's raid, and was lying half in, half out of a bomb crater. The metalwork was crumpled beyond repair, but it was the fire-scorched advert on the side of the bus which turned Annie's stomach.

A beautiful blonde with red lips and a red polka-dot scarf jauntily knotted round her neck was elegantly lighting a cigarette under the heading *SMOKERS PREFER SWANS*. Except, half of the advert was waterlogged and the blonde's face was gently drooping off the side of the bus.

'I don't believe it,' Millie gaped. 'That just about puts the tin bloody lid on my morning. I'll never get spotted now, will I?'

'Never mind, Millie,' Rose said, putting her arm round her as the three friends stared at Millie's one claim to fame. 'I expect there'll be other opportunities after the war.'

'Doubt it. You'll be on the scrap heap by dinnertime,' said Sandra cheerfully.

Millie glared at Sandra, a muscle in her jaw jumping.

'Come on,' said Annie gently, pulling her friend away. She could see Millie was trying very hard to put a brave face on it, but the bus, combined with whatever had happened between her and Curly earlier, had clearly rattled her. Usually Millie's wiggle became more exaggerated the closer they got to the factory yard, where the burly men of the sawmill worked on the ground floor. But she walked in silence, impervious to the admiring glances.

Close up in the yard, the factory looked even more imposing. Steam tractors – which collected the enormous tree trunks off the barges on the nearby River Lea and shunted them up the Old Ford Road – rumbled past them, belching clouds of greasy black smoke. There, the timber was stacked thirty feet high, a strange horizontal forest of aspen poplar and Sitka spruce felled from the Bryant & May estate in Ballochyle, Scotland. Annie always got a little thrill as the rich scent of freshly cut wood wafted across the yard to greet them. Close your eyes and you might be in the middle of a forest, not the congested heart of the East End.

At the very far end of the yard stood the handsome offices, enclosed behind a high red-brick wall, where the management and office staff worked, with their own separate entrance and canteen which, rumour had it, had polished wooden floors and sauce served in a silver jug.

Hard at work already, teams of strong men – and women – were busy transferring the logs into the sawmill. After two years, Annie still found it spellbinding to think of the process that transformed a rugged log on the ground floor, to millions of polished gleaming matches on the top floor.

Once the boys in the sawmill had roughly cut a log into smaller billets, it would go up a floor to the peeling room.

Annie had seen it once, a machine which slowly revolved the log, slicing off a long thin veneer of wood which the peeling boys ran along a counter, like a tailor might a bolt of satin. Then into the cutting room, where the veneers were guillotined into splints, before being boiled, rolled and polished in vast drums, and finally blown helter-skelter up large pipes into the top match room, where they would at last be turned into matches.

As they walked past the sawmill, ready to climb the black metal staircase that zigzagged up four floors, Millie paused, a queer look on her face.

'I feel like one of them flaming logs,' she muttered, blue eyes icy cold in the light of the stairwell. 'Turned over, sliced and diced until there's nothing left but a splint. That's exactly what I am. Like a Bryant & bloody May match.'

Three

Two years now, she, Annie and Millie had been working here in the top match room, and Rose had only just got used to the intense noise of production. The entire top floor of the factory clanked and rattled under the weight of forty tons of machinery and half a dozen solid lumps of brass, around which groups of girls sat on a raised dais, singing along to the wireless as they worked. Above their heads ran a complex system of revolving wheels and conveyor belts, which carried the matches around the enormous tiled room, impregnating them in a bath of paraffin wax, before dipping their heads into a smelly chemical solution of potash and phosphorus. The matches were dried by fans before finally ending up in the packing machines.

Sixty million matches a week passed over Rose's head. She felt as if she were in a permanent race to keep up with the conveyor belt. Deft fingers worked with such speed and precision, straightening, folding, picking up the inner, pushing on the outer case before passing them onto the next girl to pack them into dozens, then dozens into grosses, and grosses into cases. There was no time to sit and stare.

At least it gave her little time to dwell on the war, or her mother's increasing paranoia. Rose could scarcely bear to think about last night's 'incident', as she had taken to calling them. After the All Clear had sounded, she and Maureen had returned home. Rose was desperate to get some shut-eye before work, but, suddenly, Maureen had rounded on her, accusing her of flirting with boys in the Bryant & May shelter.

Rose had tried to protest, explain she'd only been playing cards with Billy from the peeling room, but Maureen was having none of it. Rose shuddered as she worked, remembering the vitriolic look on her mother's face as she yanked her in front of the mirror by her hair. Eyes narrow with anger, mouth as tight as a white-knuckle fist, she had grabbed great handfuls of Rose's hair.

'I saw you, girl,' she'd seethed, 'flicking your hair about, huh? Giving him the glad eye?'

'M–Mum, you're hurting me,' Rose had whimpered as Maureen had plaited her hair so tight her scalp throbbed.

'The problem is, my girl,' she'd muttered, ignoring her daughter's protestations, 'you're just like your mother. She couldn't keep her eyes off the boys neither, huh? That's what got her into trouble.'

Rose was seventeen now, growing into her looks, her body and beauty flowering, and with it, Maureen's control had tightened. Rose was desperate to know more about her real mother, who she was and why she had left her, but she knew better than to ask for fear of what it might unleash.

By the time Maureen had sewn Rose's hair into a tight coil, dawn was bleeding over the chimney pots, and the fire inside her had dissipated.

'It's bad enough you work with that Millie,' she'd sighed. 'She's nothing but a trollop with a filthy tongue, but while you're under my roof, you behave, hear?'

'I will,' Rose had promised.

Maureen's tight white fingers had moved fleetingly to her temple.

'I'm going to bed, you've brought on one of my heads.' She'd paused at the door, her voice soft and sour. 'I suppose it's not your fault. It's bad blood. Your mother's bad blood coming out.'

Sitting at the conveyor belt, Rose's mind worked as fast as her fingers, the matches a blur beneath her hands. Perhaps Maureen was right? Maybe she was infected somehow with badness? Could she have inherited that streak which sent her real mother off the rails? It was possible, surely?

'I said, are you all right, sweetheart?' Millie's voice jolted her from her reverie. Rose flushed. She hadn't even realized Millie was talking to her.

'Sorry, I was miles away.'

'That's all right. Dreaming of boys, was yer?' Millie winked from the other side of the conveyor belt. 'What about that nice Billy from the peeling room? I saw you two chatting last night down the shelter.'

Rose didn't know how she did it. Millie was the only person in the top match room who could keep up an endless flow of conversation while her small, dexterous fingers darted seamlessly. Annie often joked that Millie was the only person who could go on holiday and come back with a sunburnt tongue!

'S'right, Rose,' Millie went on, 'it's perfectly normal to

have a sweetheart at your age. I did. Remember Frankie
from the sawmill?'

'I do,' Annie piped up from across the dais, grinning as
she pressed down the outers. 'New Year's Eve social at the
Match Girls' Club, us lot singing "Auld Lang Syne", while
you two was seeing in the New Year another way.'

'You're a caution, you are!' Millie screeched. 'We was
only having a little kiss on the bowling green. Anyways, can
you blame me? I was footloose and fancy-free back then
and he was a right dish.' Millie fished out a broken match
and tossed it under her station. 'Poor chap . . .'

The rest of the sentence went unspoken. Rose had seen
Frankie Butler's name in the Brymay magazine for September 1940, in a company roll call of honour of all the factory
boys who had signed up and were now either deceased or
missing in action. In fact, most of the burly men who
staffed the heavier industries on the floors beneath them
had gone, to be replaced by ex-workers hastily called out of
retirement. Even the Bryant & May fire brigade was mainly
staffed by men who'd last fought fires when Zeppelins
loomed over London.

'Anyway,' Millie said, changing the subject. 'What I'm
saying is, we're living in uncertain times. Grab your happiness where you can find it, I say, before Billy's called up.
You don't want to end up like me.'

The bell rang for dinner at 11.59. The match machines
shut down automatically with a deep shudder and Rose
breathed a sigh of relief. Forty-five precious minutes off
the line.

All the girls rose stiffly, stretching out aching limbs,
eager at the thought of what grub awaited. You could get a

decent hot dinner off ration and the girls wolfed it down. Yesterday's dinner was all Rose's dreams come true! Roast pork, potatoes, cabbage and gravy followed by gooseberry tart and custard, all for 6d. Some of the match girls still legged it down the Roman for pie and mash, but Rose preferred the canteen, where you could also browse and borrow books from a mobile library.

'I'll catch you later, girls,' said Millie, ripping off her hairnet. 'I said I'd meet Mum outside the gates. I forgot yesterday, plus I've got to do a bit of shopping for Curly's tea.'

'Tell me you ain't still giving your mum a share of your wages,' Annie said, gobsmacked. 'You're married now. You don't even live at home any more!'

Millie shrugged. 'What else am I gonna do? With Jimmy away, if I don't contribute, it means my younger sisters go without.'

'Yeah, well, don't be late, will yer?' remarked a passing foreman. 'Sir Clarence has called a prayer meeting in the yard straight after dinner. Some special guests an' all.'

*

Millie waited until the floor was nearly empty before walking to the factory windows. The great sprawling metropolis was laid out beneath her. Up here, the steam tractors that made their way from Bryant & May's wharf to the back gates of the factory looked like children's toy cars. The River Lea coiled its way through the industrial heart of London like a thin grey snake, the midday sun glittering off its grimy surface, until it joined the suck and swell of the Thames at Bow Creek. Dozens of smoking factories clustered at the edges of the river, with an endless flow of barges offloading raw goods and material.

The ugly reminders of war were everywhere. Silver barrage balloons bobbed like bloated fish. Down on Old Ford Road, Millie recognized with a lurch what was clearly a bomb disposal squad, driving as fast as it dared, flanked by outriders with flashing red lights, in the direction of Hackney Marshes. Such a tiny thing from this height, yet it contained something that could blow them all to kingdom come. Ugly trenches tore through what used to be the Bryant & May tennis courts and netball pitches on the other side of the railway tracks, right next to the site of the Gilbert Bartholomew Memorial Girls' Club.

Annie had teased her about her midnight smooch there with Frankie, but Millie hadn't let on how much she had liked him. Her mind ventured back to New Year's Eve, when, on the stroke of midnight, Frankie had grabbed her hand as silver balloons cascaded down from under a giant Union Jack and pulled her outside, where he had proposed. Why had she said no?

Millie fought off bitter tears. She knew why. Because, vain fool that she was, she had selfishly believed she could do better than a boy from the sawmill, that someone, or rather something, more glamorous was on the horizon.

Millie closed her eyes and leant her forehead against the windowpane. How stupid she felt now. Had she said yes to Frankie's proposal, she could never have been forced into marrying Curly. Now, Frankie was missing in action and the Girls' Club was rubble, flattened by a high explosive on the first night of the Blitz. She turned and clocked out. As she neared the back gates, she recognized the bulbous figure of her mother leaning against the wall in a frayed housecoat, slapping the toe of her bedroom slippers against the cobbles.

'Took yer time, didn'cha?' Gladys Trotter sniffed, scratching idly at a stain by her left breast.

'Here you go, Mum,' Millie said, fighting back waves of irritation as she slipped a brown envelope into her mother's apron pocket. 'Make sure you get the girls down to the baths today, will you? And pay off what you owe at Harry's.' Gladys had so many goods on tick, it wouldn't be long before the grocer stopped extending her credit.

'Oh, and make sure you get Dad's good suit out the pawnbroker's for tomorrow. Curly wants you over to ours for your dinner,' she added, 'and he don't want the neighbours talking.'

Gladys snorted, her eyes gleaming slyly from the fleshy folds of her face.

'I couldn't give a tinker's fart what your neighbours say. Besides,' she hesitated, tapped the side of her florid nose, 'you wanna spend less time poking your nose into my business and start looking after your own affairs.'

'Meaning?' Millie snapped, stepping aside to let a group of match girls pass.

'Meaning, my girl, if you don't keep that husband of yours happy, there's plenty what will.'

Millie shook her head, exasperated. She didn't have the energy for her mum's nonsense today.

'I'll see you down the shelter later, Mum,' she sighed. 'And get them girls down the baths.'

She went to walk off but, as an afterthought, paused.

'It's my birthday today, Mum, can you believe that, eh? Twenty-one years since you gave birth to me.'

Gladys rolled her eyes and took a deep pull on her fag. 'Yeah, and blow me if my undercarriage ain't never been the same since.'

'Bye, Mum,' Millie sighed.

Clutching her ration book, she hurried in the direction of the Roman Road, the main shopping thoroughfare in Bow. As it was Saturday, it was also market day and the street was busy with housewives queuing for what little goods there were to buy.

Before the war, you could get anything you liked from this narrow, vibrant street, from a nice blouse to tripe and onions, the stalls so densely packed you could walk on shoppers' heads from one end to the other.

The amount of goods and services that used to be on display was bewildering.

Eight butchers, confectioners, corn chandlers, oil shops, bakers, tobacconists, gramophone makers, drapers, milliners, a smashing eel and pie shop, costumiers, pubs, pawnbrokers . . . Even a young cripple boy pushing a barrow around the streets selling packets of Mazawattee tea. All had done a roaring trade with the locals and factory girls.

'All right, girl, got a nice bit of fish for your old man's tea,' called a gruff voice over the chatter from the market. Millie looked up to see Benjamin Malin, the fishmonger, lingering on the doorstep of his shop. A smile twitched at the corner of her mouth. She had always got a kick out of the names of the shops in Bow. Aside from old Mr Malin the fishmonger, there was the aptly named Leon Light-stone, the local physician, portly Hubert Eatwell the confectioner, who was his own best advertisement, and not forgetting dear old Lilly Bonnet, the mealy-mouthed mil-liner. She often wondered if they had gone into their chosen professions simply because of their names. Only Lamb & Sons, the fishmonger at number 616, purveyors of the best whitebait around, didn't fit in, but then he was a quiet rebel . . . Like her.

'Not today, ta,' she called back to the fishmonger. 'I'll get strung up if I come home with no meat for his tea!'

Sighing, she passed the former headquarters of Sylvia Pankhurst and her East London Federation of Suffra-gettes, where Annie's nan, Elsie, used to buy jumble from their stall to help fund the cause. Skirting a stall selling cooked crackling, she crossed the road to avoid passing Curly's club. How remote did the cause of women's rights feel from her own life today?

Now, the whole street looked a little like she felt, lack-lustre and shabby, with not much to offer. She glanced up at a sign over the top of Lily Schindler's confectioner's. *Owner is a British Subject.* Survival and suspicion were the currency that flowed through the Roman these days.

The bell over the top of the butcher's door tinkled as she pushed it open and Millie took her place at the back of the queue.

'Mrs Brown,' called the butcher from behind his marble counter. 'I know you'll be in a hurry to get back to the fac-tory, step this way.'

The woman in front of her tensed, her feathers clearly ruffled.

'Ta, but it's all right, honestly,' Millie replied. 'I'll wait my turn.'

'Not at all, Mrs Brown, I won't hear of it,' he insisted, wiping his hands on his apron before reaching under his counter. Before she knew it, the butcher had come out into the shop front and was slipping a brown waxed package into her handbag.

'Couple of pork chops, my dear,' he muttered under his breath. 'With my compliments to Mr Brown.'

The woman in front whirled about. 'Fair shares all round,' she protested.

Every housewife in the butcher's was glaring at Millie, and she could hardly blame them. It was excruciatingly uncomfortable. She had to get out. As she hurried to the door, she overheard voices, loud and taunting.

'Curly's wife. You know, the fella what owns the club up the top of the Roman. Dark hair, eyebrows that meet in the middle . . .'

'You know what that means, don'cha?'

'Yeah . . . born to hang . . .'

The door banged shut and Millie ran down the Roman as fast as she could, dodging market stalls as she went. As she ran, angry tears streaked her face. Never in all her life had she felt so miserable and trapped.

It was always the bloody same, wherever she went. Being Mrs Curly Brown earned her certain privileges, even in wartime, like being served first in the tobacconist or the way her ration book was waved away. His reputation was like poison, seeping into everything.

Her heart was still ragged in her throat when she reached the turning into Parnell Road. Past the Hand &

Flower pub, with its taped-up windows, her tears blinded her and here she collided with a smartly dressed young woman.

'Millie? Millie Brown?' ventured the lady.

Millie looked her up and down. She didn't recognize her and, judging by the look of her, she was selling something, insurance policies most likely. 'It's not a good time, love,' she muttered tightly, stepping inside her door and slamming it shut behind her.

Once inside, she undid the top button of her coat and breathed out slowly. Once her pulse had slowed, she focused on the noises of the house. There was a queer muffled banging. The barrel-makers at the top of the road, maybe? No, they'd be on dinner by now. Besides, it was coming from upstairs, a strange rhythmic thudding sound. Surely no one would be daft enough to break into their house?

Without taking off her coat or gloves, she clutched her handbag and inched her way silently up the narrow creaking staircase. The knocking noise grew louder, more frantic, as she drew closer to the bedroom door. What was it? Maybe a pigeon had got stuck in the chimney breast, or was flapping about at the window?

Millie gripped the door handle and flung it open, bracing herself to see clouds of soot from the stricken bird.

What she saw instead was her husband's bare white arse bobbing up and down, his sinewy limbs coated in sweat.

Curly leapt round in shock. 'Jesus, woman!'

The naked woman underneath him yelped and pulled the sheet over her head, but not before Millie had got a look at her face. Betty Connor, an usherette from the Old

Ford Picture Palace. She'd seen her last when Betty had shown her, Rose and Annie to their seats for the Saturday afternoon matinee of some slapstick comedy or other. Millie had the queerest sensation that her own life was rapidly descending into a farce.

'So this is what you get up to when I'm at work, is it?' she said coldly.

Curly recovered himself quickly, stretching back luxuriantly against the white sheet, flaunting his nakedness, black eyes narrowed in spite.

'Well, what'cha expect, Millie?' he said blithely, reaching out to light up a cigarette. 'When I don't get it off my own wife, I gotta look elsewhere.'

Smoke curled slowly from his crooked mouth. 'Betty here's a nice bit of skirt, very obliging an' all.' He tapped the body still hiding under the bed sheets.

Millie felt her stomach heave. She had to get out of here. Out of this room that stank of sex and cigarette smoke.

'Get back to your lousy tart, Curly,' she snapped, fishing into her handbag, 'and while you're at it, have these an' all.' She flung the flaccid pork chops at him with all her might.

'Happy bleedin' birthday to me,' she muttered as she clattered back down the stairs. Twenty-one and she could feel her youth draining away.

Four

The important visitors were causing quite a stir at Bryant & May. Everyone from management to match girl, typist to fireman, was sandwiched between a giant stack of timber and the water tower. Now that the smoke from last night's raid had cleared, it had turned into a fine spring afternoon. Fat loafy clouds drifted lazily overhead. The yard was drenched in crystalline sunshine, but the towering pile of tree trunks cast the workers into shadow.

Presiding over them all, on a raised platform draped in the Union Jack, was their chairman, Sir Clarence Bartholomew. Standing either side of him were important-looking men in suits and uniforms. The chairman cleared his throat into the microphone and the sound reverberated around the yard. Annie stifled the urge to giggle.

'I would like to thank you, every loyal member, from office to factory, to those felling timber in far-flung lands, for your loyalty, your fortitude and your bravery in this time of peril.' He shuffled his notes. 'During the past eight months we have lost one hundred and eighty-one working hours. The destruction of our Diamond Works in Liverpool on Thursday night comes as a blow, but means we must double our efforts . . .'

Annie switched off; the statistics were bald and didn't even begin to come close to the heartache and exhaustion they all felt. Instead, she stared up over the chairman's head to the factory's smoking chimney. It was nothing short of a miracle the Fairfield Works hadn't taken a direct hit like the Diamond Works. After the first night's bombardment, the six-foot lettering of *BRYANT & MAY'S MATCHES* had been removed from the front of the factory, but there was no disguising the twin water towers, which loomed like Valhalla over the East End.

'And now for some brighter news,' announced the chairman. 'As you know, since the Battle of Britain, we have been busy fund-raising so that we might present the Royal Air Force with funds sufficient to purchase a Spitfire, to be christened *The Swan*. Our efforts have been valiant. Thanks to generous contributions from the directors, managers and foremen of the company's several Works – right down to a comptometer operator who I believe raffled her stockings for six shillings during an air raid – we have at last achieved our goal!

'I have here a letter from the Minister for Aircraft Production, Lord Beaverbrook, who says, and I quote, "There can be no better example of the determination of the people of Great Britain and the Empire to overthrow a barbarous foe than your gift. Your Spitfire will shortly join the squadrons, and in the glory of its achievements, you will all have your share."

'Would you please welcome representatives of the Royal Air Force, as they step forward to receive the cheque on behalf of the RAF. These two brave pilots will be playing a pivotal role in the air offensive against the Luftwaffe, so let's be sure to show our appreciation.'

Flashbulbs popped as a thunderous round of applause went up around the yard. Annie strained her head over the crowd to catch a glimpse of two handsome boys in blue stepping forward on the podium.

'Strike a light!' muttered a match girl from behind Annie. 'I'd have taken me stockings off for him an' all. Handsome bugger, ain't he?'

'Not much,' Annie giggled. 'What do you reckon, Millie?' She nudged Millie. 'Millie?'

But her friend was staring into the middle distance, looking even more miserable now than she was before dinner.

'Oh, Millie, are you gonna tell me what's biting you?' she whispered. 'And don't just tell me you're tired neither. We're all tired. This is something else.'

'Leave off, Annie,' Millie muttered. 'I just got a bit of a headache is all.'

'Let's go down the baths after work, then I'll treat you to a nice cup of tea down Mandy's if there's time before moaning Minnie starts up.'

Millie looked up and smiled weakly.

'You're a pal, Annie Trinder. I don't know why you put up with me.'

'Nor do I, you're a bloody nuisance.'

'Cheeky cow,' Millie grinned, poking her in the ribs.

'That's better,' Annie chuckled.

'Silence, girls,' hushed the Welfare Superintendent, Mrs Frobisher, from the row behind.

'Sorry,' Annie mouthed.

The elderly widow – who had lost her husband in the

Great War – could be a bit formidable at times, but her heart was in the right place. It was this slightly buttoned-up lady who insisted they get their free daily dose of cod liver oil and malt in the gargle queue in the Welfare Room, and gave them an aspirin when they had the curse.

Annie sighed and tried to focus on what the chairman was saying, but her mind kept straying back to her nan's fierce mutterings. If only she would come round to Annie's job, see what a plum position she had landed. She could understand if Elsie had been one of those involved in the strike, but to the best of her knowledge her nan had never even worked at Bryant & May. Elsie would have been just seven when the strike broke out, so her protectiveness towards their plight seemed at odds with her anger.

Annie didn't mean to be disrespectful to her proud pre-decessors. She doubted she could walk a mile in the shoes of the striking match girls of 1888, but that war was over. And now they were busy fighting a fresh one.

*

By the end of the shift, Millie had a pounding head, not helped by images of a naked Curly and Betty. When the bell rang at 5 p.m., Annie was up on her feet sharpish.

'Come on, let's get cracking if we want to make it to the baths.'

'Listen, girls, you go on ahead,' Millie replied. 'I'm gonna go and get an aspirin off Mrs F. My head's splitting.'

Annie frowned.

'Hmm, you're ever so pale, Millie. All right, well, make sure you catch us up.'

Millie made her way to the Welfare Room in the office block adjoining the factory, breathing in great gulps of cold sooty air. It tickled her that despite its smarter surroundings it was still as chilly as the factory. Once she'd got her aspirin, she walked past the typists' room on the first floor, smiling at the sight of all the office girls with their feet plunged into boxes filled with hay to keep warm. She wished they could do the same. Chance'd be a fine thing. One spark next to all that hay and they'd go up like a funeral pyre!

Her walk took her past the Bryant & May dentist, and Millie shuddered slightly as she caught sight of the old leather chair in the centre of the tiled room. Rumour had it that the dentist's room was haunted. She wouldn't have been surprised. Crowds of poor match girls had been treated there over the years for the dreaded phossy jaw, the condition which had killed and disfigured so many. Suffering on a level like that was bound to leave its mark in some deep-rooted way.

Hastening her step along the gloom of the chilly corridor, she didn't see him until he loomed up out of nowhere. His barrel chest smacked into her with such force, she dropped her handbag. A cracking noise, and the air filled with the pervasive scent of violets.

'Oi!' she yelled. 'Mind yourself!'

'Oh, I'm terribly sorry, I'm such a clot,' said the man, apologizing profusely as he bent down and scooped her bag off the floor. Millie could tell by the dark stain spreading over the bottom of her bag that her phial of scent had smashed. Could this day get any worse?

She took in the man's blue uniform. RAF. For a moment,

she was confused, then a vague memory of seeing him earlier at the chairman's presentation stole through her mind.

'Well, I hope you keep a better lookout when you're flying our Spitfire,' she snapped, 'otherwise we're all in trouble.'

The man's eyes shone with amusement.

'Halifax, actually. I'm destined for Bomber Command.'

He pushed back his blond hair and extended a hand.

'Trainee Pilot Samuel Taylor.'

The cut of his tunic made his shoulders seem unnaturally broad. She instantly thought of Curly's pale white chest.

Millie went to reply, but a queer thing happened. The smell of violets rose up to meet her, its sweet, cloying scent so pungent it permeated everything. Her brain felt like it was trying to crack out of her skull, and nausea rose up inside her like an uncoiling snake. She clutched the tiled corridor walls and squeezed her eyes shut.

'Miss? Are you all right?'

The corridor shrank and images of dentists' chairs and Curly's clammy white limbs danced tauntingly against her retina. She felt the stranger's hand, warm and steadying against her arm, and the floor seemed to slide gracefully from beneath her. Then, darkness swallowed her whole.

*

'Fruitcake or fruitcake? Take your pick, love, 'cause I ain't got nothing else.'

Millie looked from the bored expression of the waitress

at Mandy's Coffee Rooms to the RAF chap sitting opposite her in the small empty cafe.

'She'll have the fruitcake,' he said, smiling smoothly at the waitress, 'and I don't suppose you have any more sugar? The lady here's not feeling too well.'

'You'll be lucky, darlin', don't know if you boys in blue have heard of it, but over here in the East End we got this funny thing called rationing.'

'I'd be so grateful, miss,' he said, with a bright smile.

The waitress softened. 'Go on then. On the counter. Spoon's on the end of that string.'

She bustled off, but not before shooting him a little backwards glance.

Millie's rescuer came back with the tea and pressed it into her hand.

'Now drink,' he ordered.

Shakily, Millie sipped at the strong, sweet tea. It was horribly stewed and made with condensed milk, but it was bringing her back to her senses.

'I don't usually go around fainting on strange men,' she said, feeling grateful that she wasn't wearing her hairnet.

'I don't usually go around smashing into ladies,' he grinned back, pulling out a packet of Black Cat cigarettes from his uniform pocket and offering her one. His eyes never left hers as he fished around for a lighter.

'What's your name, miss?'

'Millie, Mrs Millie Brown,' she replied, gratefully taking the light and inhaling deeply. 'I'm sorry to trouble you,' she added. 'I expect you'll be needing to get back to wherever it is you come from. I'm pretty sure it ain't the East End.'

'No trouble at all, ma'am,' he reassured her. 'I'm on leave. Don't have to be back at base until tomorrow. I was only accompanying a pal of mine in the RAF to this ceremony today. It's all good publicity, or so we're told. Though I'll confess, it's nice to get out in the real world.'

The waitress returned, setting the thin slither of fruitcake – that arguably contained very little in the way of actual fruit – down on the table between them with a clatter. Millie pushed it away.

'When was the last time you ate?' Samuel frowned. She cast her mind back and realized with a jolt that she hadn't eaten anything since a bit of bread and drip before going into the shelter the previous evening.

'Last night,' she admitted. 'It's been a queer old day.'

He immediately summoned over the waitress, ordered Millie a ham sandwich, another piece of fruitcake and a fresh pot of tea.

'Must be my birthday,' she joked and he smiled, staring at her curiously.

Millie stubbed out her cigarette and started to eat, aware of those intense eyes of his studying her face as she chewed. Now her head was clearer, she could see he was impossibly handsome. His broad shoulders, the thick, wavy blond hair, the way his smile lit up every part of his face . . . He seemed larger than life in this small, dingy cafe sandwiched between the match factory and the tram sheds. Samuel Taylor had a quality about him that belonged to wide-open spaces. He even smelt of the countryside, a sweet, smoky scent of woodchips and windfall apples. He didn't belong here, in the mean, sulphurous stench of her world.

'You know, I recognize you from somewhere, Millie,' he said thoughtfully, 'but I can't place where.'

Millie picked up the last crumb of fruitcake with her finger, before taking another cigarette and lighting up. 'Gentlemen prefer Swans?' she said coyly, gazing up at him from under her lashes.

'Why yes, of course!' he exclaimed. 'I saw your poster in the reception at Bryant & May. Miss Brymay 1938.'

'That's me. Or rather, was me,' she replied.

'So you're famous! How does it feel to be a pin-up?'

Millie shrugged. 'Hardly a pin-up. Besides, that's all behind me. I'm an old married woman now.'

'It oughtn't to be behind you. If you were my wife, I'd want to show you off in every nightclub in town.'

'Curly – that's my husband – he don't really approve of that sort of thing,' Millie sighed. 'Truth be told, he hates me working, but he can lump it. Bryant & May are part of the Match Control Board now. War work, ain't it?

'You could say war's been good for business,' she added drily.

'Smoking and war are inseparable,' he acknowledged, tapping his ash into a small tin ashtray. 'Certainly helps me deal with all the hanging about. Anyway, I think it's terrific you match girls are doing your bit.'

'Sweet of you to say, Samuel, but I hardly think packing matches is doing much for the defence of our country.' She thought of his role in the Royal Air Force and realized what a very different war he was having to Curly. 'You fellas are the brave ones.'

'I disagree.' His gaze drifted out from the steamy windows of the cafe to the hazy spring skies above the railway line opposite. Somewhere in the distance the wireless crackled seductively. Vera Lynn singing 'Yours'. The potency of the lyrics wrapped Millie's insides into a tight knot.

'The RAF go up there, into the line of fire, because they choose to,' Samuel insisted. 'You girls here in the East End, why, you're getting bombed every night and you've no weapons with which to fire back.'

'I hadn't thought of it like that,' Millie replied, following his gaze. She stared at a cotton-wool cloud scudding across the sky until it disappeared behind a silver barrage balloon. There was a moment's silence and when she looked back, their eyes met over the tabletop. Samuel smiled softly, intimately, the corners of his mouth creasing into dimples, and Millie had a sudden urge to touch his face. His gaze held hers until her lashes fluttered and fell.

And then he did something that, later, Millie would analyse over and over again. The tips of his fingers brushed hers across the Formica tabletop. Something passed between them. Her fingers twitched and she jumped, sending tea skidding across the table.

'Oops-a-daisy,' Samuel grinned, grabbing a napkin and mopping at the spillage.

Millie cocked her head and started to laugh. 'Oh, that's tickled me pink.'

'What's so funny?' he asked, amused. Millie didn't like to tell him she was laughing because 'oops-a-daisy' was something she would never hear Curly 'Razor' Brown utter.

Instead. 'Nothing, you're just sweet, is all.'

'And you're very pretty, Millie Brown . . . *is all*. Especially when you've got cake crumbs on your cheek,' he teased, brushing them away.

Millie glanced up to see the waitress cast a knowing look their way and felt her face scorch. But their laughter broke the spell and, encouraged by Samuel, Millie opened up, telling him more about her work in the top match room, her friends, the dreams she once had of being on stage . . . He listened, nodding his head, asking her questions, but, astonishingly to Millie, seemingly content to let her talk.

In turn, he told her about his life before the war, and Millie found herself fascinated by the details. Turned out Samuel had been a gardener, with a promising career working for the Earl of Frampton at Highstanton Park in Sussex. She listened spellbound as he told her how he had just returned fresh off the boat from nearly two years in Canada, training with the British Commonwealth Air Training Plan.

'So you see, I'm not even a proper pilot with a squadron or crew yet,' he confessed.

'So, if you don't mind my asking, what the hell were you doing at the ceremony today?'

Samuel laughed and took a sip of his tea. 'Good question, Millie. I was just keeping my pal, a fighter pilot, company. My CO granted me leave to come. I think he thought it would be good for me to come to the East End, see the effects of the Blitz first-hand. I've been shielded from it in Canada. Us sprogs need toughening up, check we're not LMF.'

'LMF?'

'Lacking moral fibre,' he replied.

Millie had read about how the RAF had selected Britain's brightest and best young men in the air offensive against Germany. Looking at the sheer physicality of the man sitting opposite her, combined with his youth and brains, she doubted he was deficient in that way.

'So, what next?'

'Next I get sent to an Operational Training Unit, then a Heavy Conversion Unit.'

'Then what?' asked Millie, intrigued to hear the details of a life so different to her own. Despite living less than two miles from the docks, she had never set foot on a boat, much less sailed across the Atlantic.

'Well, presuming I make the grade, then I'll be taking the war to the enemy.' Almost imperceptibly, he sighed.

'You miss your garden?' she asked.

'You have no idea,' he said, tracing a complicated pattern through the crumbs on the tabletop. 'I'm proud to be in the Royal Air Force, but gardening is my first love.'

'Why?'

'Because I work hand in hand with nature, under the direct supervision of the Great Architect, or at least that's how my father put it,' he grinned, lighting another cigarette. 'Soil was as rich as fruitcake on the earl's estate – there was nothing I couldn't grow.'

He shook his head as he slowly exhaled a stream of lazy blue smoke. 'My God, I was green when I first volunteered, though. I knew nothing of warfare. I didn't even like to tread on the worms when I dug. But we are living through extraordinary times. One adapts.'

'And was that hard for you? To adapt?' Millie asked, cradling her cup, the thick orange tea long since cooled.

'As a gardener, I'm used to filthy conditions, so it made

the transition to service life pretty easy,' he said with a wry smile.

'You should chat to my friend Annie. She wants to start an allotment in the grounds of Bryant & May, but what's the point when the skies come crashing in every night?'

'She should,' Samuel insisted. 'The Government's desperate for Victory Diggers. Two million households growing their own now, apparently.'

'In the suburbs maybe, but here in the East End we ain't got room to swing a cat in our backyard, never mind start an allotment,' Millie scoffed. 'Besides, can't see the management agreeing to let a match girl dig up their bowling green.'

'They may not have any choice,' Samuel replied smoothly. 'All employers are being encouraged to find vacant land for their employees, or lease it to their local councils for allotments. Bryant & May would have to yield to a request to do so. Carrot a day keeps the blackout at bay, and all that.'

'Yeah, and if you believe that, you'll believe anything!' Millie quipped. 'I nearly got mowed down crossing Bow Road after dark the other day. "Didn'cha see the white arrows?" Annie asks. Never mind the arrows, I didn't even see the bleedin' Indians!'

Samuel rocked back in his seat with laughter. 'You're a hoot, Millie Brown. I've never met anyone like you before.'

'You mean, you've never met anyone as common as me before,' she grinned, lifting one pencilled eyebrow.

'No,' he insisted. 'I was going to say, anyone I feel I can talk as honestly with. Listen here, I don't suppose . . .'

At that moment, the waitress loomed over them. 'I hate

to break up the party, but I'm closing now, otherwise Jerry'll be joining us for tea.'

In alarm, Millie looked out of the window and realized that the blackout blinds had already gone up at the Caledonian Arms on the corner. Passers-by were picking up their pace, eager to get close to a shelter as darkness crept up the street.

'Oh, my days,' Millie gasped, clamping her hand over her mouth. 'I was supposed to be meeting my pals at the baths. They'll be worrying about me.'

'And what about your husband, won't he be worrying about you?' Samuel said, settling the bill.

Millie snorted. 'Curly? The only thing he'll be worried about is his precious club.'

Concern washed over Samuel's face. 'Will you be all right?'

She nailed on a smile. 'Me? 'Course. Tough as boiled brisket, me.'

Standing up, Millie extended her hand, feeling strangely vulnerable. She was back to her old gold–plated self, but Samuel had seen beneath the wiggle and the giggle. He had glimpsed her fragility and her truth.

'Thank you, Samuel, for coming to my rescue. And good luck. With everything,' she said, suddenly oddly formal as she picked up her coat from the stand. 'Where'll you go now?'

'Well, I was supposed to be meeting my pal at the Lyceum, but I'm hellish late now,' he said, stealing a glance at his watch. 'But who cares, I've had a much nicer time chatting to you, Millie Brown.'

'Can't think why,' she said as he helped her into her coat.

'I'd far rather be kicking my heels up West than drinking stewed tea in the East End.'

She went to do up her buttons, but suddenly Samuel placed his hand over hers.

'So what's stopping you, Millie? Come with me. To use the old biblical injunction, let's "eat, drink and be merry, for tomorrow we die". Nothing would bring me more pleasure than to take you dancing.'

Looking back, Millie wondered what she would have said to his proposal, and more importantly, what she would have done, but she never got the chance. The siren set up its awful, stomach-churning wail and brilliant incendiaries began to light up the skies above their heads. The path-finders had already arrived. Tonight, life had other plans for Millie Brown.

Five

Annie had been so focused on not spilling the cups of tea laced with rum on her walk to the top of the 136-foot water tower, she'd scarcely realized what a height she had climbed. But as she stepped out of the hatch onto the top of the tower, the breath caught in her throat. The wind whipped her red curls around her face, dizzying her, so that, for a moment, she clung to the heavy steel door. Two firemen in tin hats sat with their backs to her, huddled under thick coats.

When she got her bearings, Annie gazed about her, her green eyes wide with awe as she took it all in. For the first time in her life she was looking down on her East End, instead of always being in its shadow.

The eastern quarter of the city, with its jumble of narrow passages, shambling courts and dismal smoking terraces, gradually gave way to the vast stone monoliths of the City of London, all of it veiled beneath a heavy blackout. Not that it mattered. A full moon hung in the cloudless night sky, bathing all of London in a glittering silver sheen.

There were more planes than Annie had ever seen in her life, darting through the searchlights. Flares blossomed and in the distance the city was surrounded by a fierce orange glow. London was afire!

For a moment Annie was mesmerized, until a hollow thump, followed by a slithering noise, snapped her from her stupor.

'Christ al-bleedin' mighty!' yelled one of the firewatchers, whipping round and noticing her for the first time. 'Looks like Bow Church's copped it. As for you, love, what the hell are you doing up here without your battle bowler?'

Annie handed them the mugs, then patted her head. 'My tin hat, I forgot it!'

'Here, take this, love,' replied the older fireman in a gravelly voice, handing her his helmet. Annie reckoned he must have been sixty if he was a day, wiry too with a shock of silver hair. He had the grey, hollowed-out look of the sleepless and his face was a patchwork of lines and wrinkles. But it was a kind face, Annie reflected, warm and well lived-in.

Bright button eyes gazed out at her inquisitively as he slurped his tea.

'That's better. You don't 'alf remind me of someone I used to know. Any road, we're getting a right hiding tonight,' he remarked. 'We've had five incendiaries on the roof already and another's made a right mess of the powerhouse. Mind you, look at the City.'

All three of them turned and stared in the direction of St Paul's Cathedral, cloaked in grey swirling smoke.

'Reckon we're in for a rough night,' remarked the younger fireman. 'Full moon. Low tide. Think you can handle it, grandad?'

'Don'cha worry about me, boy,' he chuckled, draining

his tea. 'I was fighting fires while you was sucking jelly babies. Ted's the name,' he said, giving Annie a bone-cracking handshake. 'Pleased to meet you, love, and thanks for the tea, but why don't you get back downstairs to the shelter now, eh? It's getting a bit hairy up here.'

Just then, the wind changed direction and there was an eerie lull in the noise of the raid. For the briefest of moments, all they could hear was the sound of singing, drifting up through the darkness.

Run, rabbit, run, rabbit, run, run, run . . .

The voices sounded queer and echoey in the dark. Shivering, Annie bent down and picked up their cups.

'Thanks, Ted. I'm Annie. I'll keep the tea coming and—'

'Get down,' Ted yelled, yanking her to the floor of the water tower just as a vivid orange flash lit up the tracks over the railway line.

There was a roar, a whoosh, followed by the sound of hundreds of factory windows blasting out.

'Bloody hell, it's caught in Blondin Street,' shouted the younger fireman over the shattering of glass. 'Incendiary just whistled clean down a chimney.'

'Watch your language in front of the lady,' Ted scolded, but Annie scarcely registered it. With her ears ringing, she staggered to her feet and looked down into the abyss. Later, she would dwell on the strangest sight she had ever seen in her life. A herd of cows, with their tails on fire, streaming down Fairfield Road, but in that moment nothing was more important than reaching her home. The fire had already taken hold of the roof . . . Right over Elsie's bedroom.

'My nan!' she screamed, pointing to the burning house. 'She's in there.'

*

Nearly 160 feet below where Annie was standing, huddled in Bryant & May's vast basement shelter, Maureen and Rose Riley heard the muffled bangs and crumps of falling masonry from up above.

'I said as much,' Maureen muttered thinly. 'The moment my knees started up, I knew we was in for murders.'

'Let's try to stay positive, shall we, Mum?' Rose replied, staring enviously at a larger family group gathered round a bunk on the other side of the shelter, drinking tea and keeping their spirits up by singing 'Land of Hope and Glory'.

'Rose, come and join us,' called a match girl she recognized, singing along, with her feet swinging over the edge of the bunk.

'It's not a church hall, love,' Maureen spat back, her breath pooling in the cold air, 'some of us are trying to get some rest.'

'Mum, please don't be rude,' Rose hissed, mortified.

'Well, I can't bleedin' stick it. It's bad enough being cooped up here as it is without being stuck with the jam and Jerusalem set. Where's their bloody God now, huh? They keep on with that racket, I'm gonna clump her one,' Maureen sniffed, pulling a blanket tight around her reedy shoulders. 'I ask you, we're hiding in a basement while our houses get bombed. Where's the sodding hope and glory in that?'

Rose didn't reply. Instead, she cast her eye over the mass of huddled bodies, desperately trying to see if she could spot Millie. Unease nagged. She and Annie had waited for ages outside the baths for her and when the sirens sounded, she had hoped to find her here. She'd seen her mother, Gladys, and even Curly – jumping the queue on the way in – but Millie was nowhere to be seen.

'I said, where's their God now, huh?' Maureen grumbled, interrupting her thoughts.

'I don't know, Mum,' Rose whispered, wishing the ground would open and swallow her up. Maureen licked a bony finger and plastered back a strand of hair that had escaped from her plait. She was even more tense than usual tonight and Rose was wary of saying or doing anything to inflame her. She'd spotted Billy from the peeling room on the way in, giving her the glad eye, but she'd turned her head away, ignoring the hurt look on his face.

Just then there was an enormous bang, a collective gasp. The room flickered and plunged into darkness before the emergency lighting kicked in.

A voice nearest the shelter door piped up: 'The railway's got it.'

'Nah,' called another. 'Reckon the water tower's been hit, look at the leak.'

The heavy brick walls seemed to bulge, then a slow trickle of water began to drip from the ceiling. For a moment, Maureen's mouth dropped open in fear, before quickly regaining its customary sour tuck.

'I ain't staying here to be drowned!' she shrieked. 'I'm off.'

Casting aside her blanket, she stood sharply, grabbing Rose's arm and a small case with her valuables.

'Come on.'

'Mum, no!' Rose pleaded, gripping the edge of the bench. 'Let's stay here. See, it's just a little leak, they're dealing with it.' She pointed to a team of wardens busy digging holes into the basement floor with pickaxes for the water to escape through.

'She's right, love,' remarked the man next to them, 'you're still a lot safer in here than you are out there.'

'Oh, shut up, you're grating on my last nerve,' she muttered, and then she was off, heading towards the exit, dragging Rose behind her. At the shelter door, the officious ARP warden was having none of it.

'Can't open the door during a raid, mother, rules is rules.'

Maureen's eyes narrowed as she delved into her coat pocket. From the corner of her eye, Rose swore she saw metal, or was it wire, wrapped round her knuckles. In a flash, Maureen had the warden's testicles clenched tight between her bony fingers, as she leant in close to his face.

'Don't you "mother" me, sonny Jim,' she hissed. 'Now open the fucking door.'

They were out in less than five seconds flat, and Maureen was off like a ferret, her thin body remarkably agile as she tore down the yard in the direction of the front gates to Fairfield Road. No longer cushioned below ground, the noise outside was tremendous, and Rose blinked, bewildered. She'd gone down into the shelter in darkness, and seemed to have emerged into the brightness of noon. Shimmering white spangles of incendiaries exploded like fireworks above their heads. On the other side of Fairfield Road she could make out the flash of fire beyond the roof-tops, and smoke rose from the chimney of a house in Blondin Street.

'Mum,' she panted, skidding to a halt. 'The railway tracks have gone up, and just take a look at our street. Please, this is madness.'

Maureen whirled round and Rose reeled back. Her eyes seemed to be on fire, burning balls of hate, until Rose realized it was simply the glow of the fires reflected in them.

'Please, Mum,' she said softly, trying to keep her voice low and calm. 'Let's just get back in the shelter . . .'

Maureen's fingers slackened in hers and, for a moment, Rose thought she had reached her.

'Please, Mum, I don't want to die,' Maureen snarled, mimicking Rose in a voice of pure poison. 'You're just like that woman.'

'What woman?' Rose said, swamped with confusion and despair.

'The woman what gave birth to you. She was a coward an' all. Threw herself in the Thames at Shadwell, drowned herself 'cause she couldn't take the shame, leaving me to pick up the pieces.' She was ranting now. 'Well, I ain't no coward. And if I'm dying, it's in me own home.'

Maureen turned and marched towards the giant gates to the Works, her wiry body silhouetted by the fires raging from the rail tracks beyond.

Rose stood and stared in disbelief, her body rooted to the spot until, suddenly, she almost seemed to re-enter herself.

'What do you mean? Come back!' she cried. When she

reached the entrance to the Fairfield Works she hurled herself past the night guard stationed at the gatehouse and stood alone in the deserted street, frantically scanning left then right. But it was as if her mother had vanished, snuffing herself out like a light.

'Get to safety, girl!' yelled the guard from behind the gatehouse. She glanced back, struck dumb with terror. Inlaid into the brick wall of the gatehouse was a terracotta panel of beasts clutching flaming torches.

For a moment, Rose wondered whether she hadn't come face to face with Lucifer himself. The streets glittered with a sea of broken glass, hurting her eyes, and suddenly the ground beneath her feet seemed to tremble. She listened over the pounding of her heart; what on earth was that noise?

Out of the darkness and smoke, clattering and skidding on the cobbles, was a sight Rose would never forget.

Ten, no maybe twelve cows, charging down Fairfield Road, some with their hides on fire, others with their tails blazing. Wild with fear, they charged towards her, hooves battering and sparking on the cobbles, nostrils flaring in panic. Ellis Griffith's dairy at number 44 must have taken a hit.

The sight plucked at her heart, and in desperation she flattened herself against the wall of the burning box factory opposite as the cattle charged past her in a frenzied stampede.

As the avalanche of hot bricks came raining down on top of Rose, crushing her, what hurt most was the knowledge that if she died now she would never discover what else Maureen knew about her mother.

Six

'All right, tough girl, I know you're made of steel, but I should still like to get you to safety,' Samuel said over the wail of the siren as he ushered Millie out of Mandy's cafe. 'Where do you usually shelter?'

'In the basement of Bryant . . .' A hollow boom ricocheted up the street, followed by a choking cloud of dust and smoke.

The explosion deafened Millie and, for a moment, there was nothing but perfect silence, the street coated in grey mist . . . After a few seconds everything came to life. The clanging of bells and screams snapped Millie out of her stupor.

'Christ alive! They're not hanging about tonight,' Samuel said shakily. 'Looks like the rail tracks have been hit. Quick.'

Gripping her hand tight in his, Samuel led her up the street, running as fast as they dared, until they reached the safety of the railway arches. He pushed her against the dank wall of the arch, shielding her from the street. Pressed against his body in the darkness, Millie could feel his heart going like the clappers. The speed of the raid had clearly taken him by surprise. But then, she supposed, this was all new to him.

Staring up past his broad shoulders at the fantastical night sky, Millie was stunned. Great clusters of planes swarmed through the darkness, more than she'd seen in eight months of bombing. The sky was lit up like a magic-lantern show. Oddly, though, she didn't feel scared; in fact, something about the situation was charged, erotic even.

Her breath, her blood, her pulse . . . Everything seemed to be rushing and she was acutely aware of the buttons on Samuel's uniform digging against her flesh, her back brushing against the rough brick wall of the railway arch.

'Are you not scared, Millie?' he ventured, his breath hot on her cheek. The scent of him filled the rank darkness of the archway: clean, warm skin, mingling with tobacco and cologne.

'No. I'm fatalistic,' she whispered. 'Are you?'

'Yes,' he admitted. 'It feels strange to me to be down here on the ground.'

As he spoke, she was aware of how close his mouth must be to her own. Just inches away. All it would take would be for her to reach up on her tiptoes and tilt her head to find his warm lips in the darkness.

But suddenly, outside on the street, came the sound of running footsteps. A woman lit up by moonlight streaked past, face grimly determined, and Millie recognized her as Rose's mum, Maureen. Why wasn't she down the shelter? The thought was blown out of her head when from some-where up above a terrific noise started up and she felt Samuel's thighs tense.

'Oh, there goes Big Bertha. Go on, girl, give 'em some back!' she yelled.

'Sorry, w-what, who?' he stuttered over the racket.

'Big Bertha's the anti-aircraft gun,' Millie explained, 'up on the railway siding.'

A clattering of shells rained down around their feet.

'Buggered if I'm getting killed by our own. Come on,' she yelled, yanking Samuel back out onto the street.

They ran back the other way, hearts galloping. The sights were astonishing. The gutters ran with water, soot and oily rainbows. From nowhere came a herd of cows – *cows!* – streaming past them, their tails on fire. They careered around the corner, out of sight, and Millie and Samuel could do nothing but stare after them. Further up the street, the box factory burnt fiercely. It was bedlam.

'Millie, we have to get to shelter,' Samuel urged. 'Where's the nearest?'

Even in the midst of such confusion, at the back of Millie's mind nagged the thought that she mustn't turn up at the Bryant & May shelter with Samuel. Curly would be there. Never mind the fact that she was alive, he couldn't have stood the loss of face.

'There's a public shelter on Old Ford Road, we can get there through Blondin Street.'

Cutting through the street where Annie and Rose lived, Millie was amazed to see Annie herself pelting up from the other end of the street, her red hair pasted to her face.

'Annie!'

'Millie!' they gasped as one.

'It's Nan,' Annie blurted, face wild with fright as she

pointed to her house, fire leaping and billowing from the chimney. 'I . . . I think she's still inside.'

Annie turned the handle, but the door was wedged shut.

'Bloody door!' she cursed. Over the past eight months, the whole street had been rattled that many times in its foundations that the wood had swollen and the door often jammed in its frame.

'Stand back,' Samuel ordered. He forced the door with his shoulder and disappeared into the smoky hallway. Annie shot Millie a questioning look, but there was no time to explain as they followed him into the house. Samuel grabbed a stirrup pump from the base of the stairs and took them two at a time, the girls close behind.

They found Elsie huddled in the corner of her bedroom in her salmon-pink housecoat and curlers, as if she was just turning in for the night. Fire had already claimed one wall and was making light work of the eiderdown, flecks of red-hot cinders floating up into the fierce heat of the room. Decades-old paint was bubbling and blistering on the walls. Another ten minutes, and this room would be incinerated.

'Nan!' screamed Annie, through the shimmering haze of heat. 'What you playing at? We gotta get out.'

The old lady looked up, eyes glazed, and Millie could see she was paralyzed with fright. Her arthritic fingers kneaded and twisted the hem of an old shawl.

'Come on, Els,' she soothed. 'Let's get you out of here, shall we?'

'I can't leave,' Elsie wept, 'it's my fault.'

Annie shot Millie a look, before turning back to Elsie.

'What you talking about, Nan? 'Course it's not your fault. We've been bombed.'

'I can't . . .'

'Nan!' Annie howled as a rafter from the roof creaked and, with a terrible wrenching roar, crashed from the ceiling onto the burning bed.

Millie's heart smashed against her ribs and, sobbing, she turned away, unable to look. When she turned back, she saw Samuel disappear into the smoke. In one swift move he had gathered Elsie in his arms, scooped her up and was making his way through the room towards them.

'Get out!' he shouted, struggling under Elsie's weight. 'The roof's going to come down any second.'

As Samuel staggered past, Millie suddenly realized how old and vulnerable Annie's nan looked, being carried in his arms like a baby. Elsie's housecoat had ridden up and, to her dismay, Millie saw her thighs were a rough patchwork quilt of scars. Lines of milky tissue criss-crossed her flesh like a snail trail. The image was a fleeting one, like a flash of fire, but it stopped her in her tracks.

'Millie!' Annie bellowed behind her. 'What you waiting for? Let's get out of here!'

Heat. Noise. Chaos . . . How they all made it out of that burning house alive was nothing short of a miracle, but they burst onto the street, spluttering. Samuel didn't stop until he had carried Elsie further along the road and gently set her down on the cobbles. Taking off his coat, he wrapped it round the old lady and Annie crashed to her knees beside her nan, sobbing with relief.

'Wait here,' he ordered Millie, 'I'm going back to check the houses either side.'

Neither of them spoke. All three sat huddled in shock as they watched Samuel bound off back towards the burning buildings.

A minute or two later he re-emerged, guiding Maureen up the street.

She was livid as she batted his hand away. 'This bloody idiot soaked my sugar rations.'

'Maureen!' gasped Millie. 'Never mind your sugar, where's Rose?'

*

Groaning, Rose tried to move her body, but she was completely pinned down, encased in a tomb of darkness. She coughed and her throat burnt as brick dust and phlegm spooled from her dry lips.

'Help me . . .' she whimpered into the darkness, but her words were no more than a croak. Strangely she felt no pain, but she was so cold. So cold and numb, her brain felt like it had been encased in ice. The stench of gas was unholy. It would be just her luck to survive being buried alive, only to be blown to bits. *Come on, Rose,* she scolded, trying to wiggle her toes. *You're going to make it out of here.*

Events were foggy. The last thing she remembered was running after her mother; the cows, then the walls of the box factory had come tumbling down on her. How long she had lain here unconscious, of that she had no idea, but, somewhere in the distance, she heard the clanging of ambulance bells, the muffled shouts of rescue workers. Help was there, she just had to summon it.

The night guard at the gates to Bryant & May, he had

seen her running past. People saw her leave the shelter, and surely her own mother would have raised the alarm by now?

'Help!' she cried again into the impenetrable darkness, feeling a prickle of panic as her head began to spin. Her voice sounded thin and reedy, like an old woman's. Her mouth was caked with dust. She moistened her lips and tried again. This time, it sounded even weaker, and Rose realized it might be better to conserve her energy in trying to stay alive. Somewhere above, the rubble creaked and groaned, and a shower of loose bricks and mortar bounced down around her, caking her in yet more dust. Rose barely dared to breathe for fear of upsetting the tons of rubble precariously suspended over her prone body.

After the first couple of hours she lost track of time, and hope began to slip away. From somewhere way above, a thin shred of grey permeated the darkness. Dawn was breaking. Now she could see her surroundings better. She was trapped in a thin, airless tunnel, the only thing saving her from being crushed alive a giant beam that had fallen across what looked like a shattered staircase. Covering her legs were broken chairs, timber and plasterboard. Her mouth and nostrils were now so choked with dust they had swollen and her tongue felt like a mattress in her mouth.

Rose began to think of all the things she would miss. Splashing about with Millie and Annie at the Bryant & May swimming lessons at Romford Baths every Wednesday afternoon . . . Needlecraft and keep fit lessons at the Match Girls' Club . . . The firm's annual beano down to Bideford in Devon . . . But mostly, she realized with a pang, she would just miss her friends.

She was sweating now; a cold, slippery sheen which covered her face, melting the brick dust into a claggy paste round her mouth. In silent surrender, Rose closed her eyes. Thoughts rushed at her, woolly and disjointed, but somehow she knew it wouldn't be long. She forced her mind back to her last company outing with the girls. Soft sand between her toes . . . White sails patching a pale blue sky . . . Millie larking about in a Kiss Me Quick hat . . . She wanted to die with bright and happy thoughts in her head.

From somewhere nearby she heard a noise and her eyes flickered open. It was a scrabbling. She cried out and the noise stopped abruptly. She whimpered in despair. It was just a mouse or, more likely, a rat. But wait. There it was again. The scrabbling noise grew stronger, more frantic, and dust began to shower down on her from the beam above. A scuffling, a digging, and, hold on . . . Was that a bark?

Summoning every last shred of breath in her body, Rose cried out again. A second later, a small, damp black nose burst through the rubble behind the beam, followed a second later by a white furry paw.

Rose stared incredulously as the tiny Jack Russell wriggled and pushed his way through the wreckage towards her, crawling on his belly through the tunnel, and began to bark frantically.

'All right, fella, all right, I'm coming,' rang out a voice from above. 'Let me just fetch my shovel.'

As the tiny dog began to lick her face, Rose sank back in relief, tears streaming down her cheeks.

*

That little dog stayed right by her side until the rescue workers and a team of wardens had pulled her free from the rubble, blinking into the light of a smoky Sunday morning.

Lying on a stretcher on the pavement outside Bryant & May, an ambulance worker tending to a gash on her leg, she sipped a cup of hot sweet tea and stroked the velvet-soft ears of the miniature Jack Russell. He sat patiently by her side, his white fur matted with grime, brown eyes gazing at her.

The rescue worker who had finally pulled her clear from the rubble wandered over and crouched down beside her, cocking his tin helmet back.

'You was in a bit of a pickle there, eh, love?' he said, with masterful understatement.

'I don't know how to thank you,' Rose replied shakily.

'Don't thank me, pet. It's all down to this little fella.' He reached out and ruffled the dog's head.

'He was scrabbling at the rubble until his paws bled, that's what alerted me.' He gestured to a propaganda poster, plastered a little way up from Fairfield Works. 'Dig for Victory,' he read out loud. 'He certainly did that all right. Jack Russell terriers are at home underground, probably thought he was chasing rabbits down a hole. So, he yours, is he, darlin'?'

'Why, no,' she replied, confused. 'I thought he was yours, a rescue dog?'

He shook his head.

'No, love, nothing to do with us. We just found him scampering over the rubble.'

The nurse looked up from her bandage.

'Could be something to do with Battersea Dogs' Home maybe?' she ventured.

'Battersea?' frowned the rescue worker. 'I doubt it, it's miles away.'

'No, she's right,' Rose exclaimed. 'They have an East London branch, right here on Fairfield Road. Number 69.'

'It wasn't bombed, but he could've escaped, probably got scared by all the racket,' said the nurse wearily. 'Last night was a bad one.'

'Well, wherever he's come from, I reckon he's yours now,' the rescue worker remarked. 'You know what the Chinese say?'

'No,' Rose said, her head swimming with tiredness. 'I don't know any Chinese. My mum doesn't let me go to Limehouse.'

The nurse smiled kindly. 'If you save someone's life, they belong to you. You become their responsibility.'

The little dog barked and began to lick the dust from her cheek.

'Think that rather settles it, don't you?' chuckled the nurse. 'He's yours. Or rather, you're his.'

Rose reached out and gently tugged his ears. Solemnly, he placed a paw on her chest and she chuckled, her laughter quickly dissolving into a spluttering cough.

'We're stuck with each other, little pipsqueak.'

'He's that all right,' smiled the rescue worker, wearily hauling himself up. 'What a little smasher.'

Never had the idea of having someone to love – and to love her back unconditionally – seemed so appealing. She knew Maureen would kick up a right stink, but she would find a way to keep him. In all the confusion and pain of last night, Maureen's scornful revelation and her terror at being left, one thing stood out clear and true in the smoky dawn. This dog had brought her back from the dead.

'Time for you to be checked over at the London,' announced the nurse, as she finished the bandage and signalled for Rose to be lifted into the back of the ambulance. 'Just to make sure there's no lasting damage, though by the looks of you I'd say you're a very lucky young lady.'

'Please, sir, will you keep him at your station?' Rose pleaded with the rescue worker. 'Just until I'm discharged.'

'Go on, then,' he laughed. 'I'm off shift now, but I'll take him back and give him something to eat and a drink. Come and collect him when you're fit and ready.'

Scooping up the dog, *her* dog, Rose kissed his silky ears and nuzzled his neck, before passing him over to the rescue worker.

'Hang on, what yer gonna call him?' he asked.

'Pip. His name's Pip.'

*

Samuel insisted on walking Millie back home after the All Clear sounded over Bow at 5.57 a.m.

What an unholy night of chaos and destruction. They had all been drinking steaming mugs of tea from a WVS van when news reached them that Rose had been dug out from a collapsed building on Fairfield Road and was now being treated in hospital. In her exhaustion, Millie couldn't fathom why she hadn't been down the shelter at Bryant & May, or with Maureen at home, but no matter, she was alive and miraculously unscathed, as was Elsie. Thanks to Samuel.

They walked slowly into Millie's turning, both of them reluctant to reach the point where they needed to say their goodbyes. Smoke from the many fires that had raged all night mingled with the early morning mist drifting up Parnell Road. Despite the hour, the women of the street were already out, sweeping up the glass and bashing their mats. Millie knew the sight of her being escorted home by a chap in air force blues would keep them in gossip for weeks to come. Let them talk!

'What you did, it was very brave,' she said, sneaking a look at his face as they walked. 'Elsie would've died had you not rescued her. Definitely not LMF, I'd say!'

Samuel shrugged, his blond hair streaked grey with dust, his face doughy with exhaustion. 'Anyone would've done the same, Millie.'

They reached her doorstep, and Millie glimpsed a dark shadow pass against her bedroom window.

'Not everyone.'

They faced one another and an awkward silence fell between them.

'I guess this is it then,' Millie murmured. 'Sorry it wasn't quite the night off you had planned.'

Samuel took her hand in his and gently pressed his lips to her knuckles. His eyes lingered on her face, drinking in the sight of her.

'Who cares? It's been a pleasure getting to know you, Millie.' He paused. 'I'll be honest; I've been having doubts, serious doubts, about whether I'm cut out to be in Bomber Command, whether it's the *right* thing to do . . .' He hesitated. 'But after what I witnessed last night, those doubts have passed.'

'Maybe it was meant to be then, you coming here.'

'Maybe. Tell you what, I also have a terrific respect for the women on the Home Front now.'

'You're sweet, Samuel,' she replied, flushing as she remembered the unwholesome thoughts that had gripped her in the brick archway last night. He was staring at her so intensely that, absurdly, she wondered if he hadn't somehow read her mind.

'Can I write?' he blurted. 'As a friend, I mean. I know you're a married woman, but it's just nice to hear about other people's lives.'

'I'm sure you got no end of nice WAAF girls to pass the time with,' Millie replied.

''Course, but it's not the same as talking with you. You're different, Millie.'

His face was so blackened with grime, it made his eyes seem all the brighter. They were beautiful, pale blue and flecked through with tiny threads of gold, which shone in the swirling dawn mist.

'If you like,' she gulped.

Millie glanced up nervously to her bedroom window; she had the strongest sensation she was being watched.

'I shall, thank you, Millie,' he beamed, straightening up. 'And tell your friend Annie to get that allotment up and running. Gardening's good for the soul. Clears the mind.'

'If you say so . . .'

A thud sounded from inside.

'Look here. I have to go. So long.'

On impulse she reached up on her tiptoes and kissed his cheek, before vanishing inside.

Seven

Rose might have been buried alive on Saturday, but by Monday morning she was back on the line packing matches. London had taken a right battering that night. Annie had read in Elsie's *Daily Mirror* that the Luftwaffe had taken advantage of the full moon and the low ebb tide to start over two thousand fires in the capital. One thousand five hundred poor souls to add to the death toll; legions in mourning.

In light of that, Annie supposed that Rose was one of the lucky ones. Apart from a nasty gash on her right leg, she seemed otherwise unhurt, but Annie had misgivings about her hasty return to work. How could anyone go through such an ordeal and come out unscathed? No doubt Maureen's concern over the loss of her wages had something to do with it. 'You sure you're all right, Rose?' she asked again. 'You're very pale. Why don't you get yourself down the Welfare Room and get Mrs Frobisher to look you over?'

'Quite sure,' Rose insisted. 'Doctor at the London declared me fit for work.'

Annie doubted the doctor had the first clue of the long hours and the conditions that she was expected to return to.

Lift, check, press. Lift, check, press.

With every matchbox she helped to assemble, Annie felt as if a little piece of her brain was sailing away down the production line. She was proud of earning a wage and loved the perks of the job, but at times she struggled to see what she was really contributing to the war effort. Didn't help that it was also perishing up here on the top floor of the factory. No sooner had the glaziers been in and replaced the shattered windows than Jerry had come round and blasted them all out again. The wind was whistling in through the cracks, and Annie's fingers were so cold they were like claws.

'You still haven't told us what you were doing out in the middle of the raid, Rose,' Millie remarked. Annie glanced up.

Millie wasn't faring much better than Rose, and was sporting a cracking shiner round her left eye. Annie bit down her anger. Her friend was making light of it, claiming she collided with a lamp post during the terrible events of Saturday night, but Annie had her suspicions.

'I told you, Mum got scared when she thought the water tower had taken a hit and insisted on leaving the shelter,' Rose replied. 'In all the confusion, we got separated. Anyway, never mind about that, I'm so excited, girls. I'm picking up Pip from that rescue chap after work.'

When the girls had visited her in hospital yesterday afternoon, they were stunned when she told them that it was a stray dog who had helped to alert the authorities and dig her out. Annie had heard of some queer things happening in wartime but this took the biscuit.

'I can't wait for you to meet him,' Rose gushed, 'he's a

little smasher. I stopped in at the butcher's on the way to work, persuaded him to give me some leftover bones, and Ralph from the peeling room's digging me out some old hessian sacking to make into a bed for him.'

'I'm thrilled for you, sweetheart, but—'

'What about Maureen?' Millie finished off. 'No disrespect to your mum, but I don't really have her down as an animal lover. Besides, I'm not actually sure you're allowed to keep a pet dog, are you?'

Annie didn't like to say it out loud, but they'd all heard rumours of the secret pet burial ground in East London.

Unfortunately, Millie – who had never been one to tiptoe round a subject – wasn't quite as subtle.

'They say there's eighty thousand dead cats and dogs laid to rest at the start of the war, buried somewhere round here,' she announced.

'That's dreadful,' gasped Rose, her head snapping up over the conveyor belt. 'How could anyone put their pet down just 'cause war's broken out?'

'Listen, girl,' Annie said softly, 'I dare say no one *wanted* to, but if it's a choice between feeding a child and a pet . . . ?'

'Exactly! And what are you going to do about feeding him, Rose?' Millie pressed. 'Tinned dog food's harder to come by than fresh meat.'

Rose's jaw clenched as she worked. 'I'm keeping him and I'll find a way,' she said firmly. 'He saved my life. I can't very well turn him out on the streets, can I? I'd given up all hope when . . . when . . .'

She started to cough, her slender shoulders shuddering and her face blanched of colour.

'Oh, don't upset yourself, sweetheart,' Annie cried. Millie held up her hand and the foreman was over in a flash.

'Permission for Rose to leave the line for a minute, sir.'

He whistled over to a girl manning the safety machine to take her place.

'Minute only.'

Gratefully, Rose scurried off to fetch a glass of water and Annie and Millie exchanged a look.

'Poor Rose,' Millie muttered. 'Can't see Maureen taking well to having another mouth to feed, can you?'

'Unlikely,' Annie admitted. 'She's more likely to skin him and serve him up for dinner.' It was gallows humour, but the pair couldn't stop their laughter.

'And what about you?' Annie said curiously. 'Want to tell me more about Samuel? Aside from the fact that he's a handsome bugger, my nan thinks he's a hero for putting his life on the line.'

Annie was surprised to see a deep flush of colour rise up under Millie's tunic. She had never seen her cocksure friend actually blush before.

'Yeah, well,' she muttered. 'He certainly deserves a medal all right. Poor chap was only on leave when he got tangled up with us.' The conversation drifted into silence and, out of nowhere, she started to hum a Vera Lynn song.

'Millie?' said Annie, astonished. 'Anything you want to tell me?'

'Me?' said Millie, looking up briefly from the line, blue eyes the picture of innocence. ''Course not.'

'Millie,' Annie went on in a low voice, 'you'd be playing with fire if you went there. You know that, right?'

''Course I know that,' she snapped, pressing down firmly on an outer case. 'You think I've forgotten who I'm married to? He was just nice, is all, treated me like a proper lady. Makes a pleasant change.'

Millie blinked and an angry tear broke and slid down her cheek, dissolving the pan stick she'd used to cover her black eye.

'Curly did that, didn't he?' Annie said softly.

Millie nodded.

'Word got back to him that I'd been seen in Mandy's with an airman. I tried to explain there was nothing to it, that we'd got caught up in the bombs, but he weren't having none of it. Said I'd made a show of him.'

'But that ain't fair, Millie,' Annie gasped.

'What's fair got to do with it?' she flashed back. 'Life ain't bloody fair.'

'Why don't we go to the pictures tonight?' Annie said, tactfully changing the subject. 'We could all use some cheering up. Who knows? We might even make it to the end before the sirens go.'

It was a rare night when the red light hadn't gone off halfway through the picture to let them know the enemy was near. Though by some act of what Annie could only conclude was a miracle, last night they'd managed their first full night in eight months without any bombs, which had given London a much needed break to repair the previous night's damage.

'I do hope Jerry hasn't forgotten us,' Millie quipped, dabbing briefly at her eye with a hankie. 'Go on, then, why not? I'll sort Curly's tea, then let's make a night of it.'

She laughed drily. 'Might even serve the old bastard cat's meat pie.'

*

When the final hooter rang out over the neighbourhood, the girls went back to Blondin Street while Rose headed off to pick up Pip, promising to meet them at the pictures later.

'I've got to nip to the shops, so I'll just see if your nan needs anything fetching,' said Millie, cutting down Annie's turning with her.

As they walked, the street was filled with the sounds of industry, folk hard at work repairing the damage to their homes. The comforting, primitive sound of someone hammering wood in a backyard echoed up the cobbles. The scent of washing and stew drifted through open windows.

Most of the houses on this terrace, which abutted the Fairfield Works, were owned by Bryant & May. The management had wasted no time in rehousing Annie and Elsie, even allowing them to store what spare furniture they had managed to salvage in the factory dance hall.

They paused for a second outside the sodden shell of Annie's old home. Pinned to the door frame was a note.

We are bombed, but far from beat.
'Cause we've only moved in, over the street.

Annie shook her head in bewilderment. Her nan never failed to astound her. In many respects, Elsie Trinder was a proper East End girl, as tough as old boots, and yet, something about the strangeness of her behaviour on Saturday night, when they'd found her cowering from the fire, didn't sit right. 'It's my fault,' she'd said. What had she meant? Annie had never before seen the slightest crack in her nan's tough veneer. She was the street matriarch, the unofficial community leader, the one the neighbours called on when a baby needed delivering, a rent collector needed sorting or there was a dead body to lay out. Elsie held no truck with self-doubt or introspection. She had always been far too busy raising her grandkids and running the house to go in for any of that malarkey.

Annie turned and gazed at her nan, hard at work outside their new home further up the street, as if seeing her for the first time.

Elsie was seemingly back to her old self, bashing a rag rug against the front of the house while singing 'Dear Irish Boy' to herself in a sweetly quavering voice.

'Nan, you must have been at it all day,' Annie exclaimed as she poked her head inside number 33. In the space of a day, she had transformed the deserted house with some good old-fashioned elbow grease. The coconut mats in the passage had had the dust bashed out of them, the step had been scrubbed and whitened with a hearthstone and windows were polished between the blast tape.

'Darlin' girl,' Elsie smiled, wincing as she straightened up and rubbed the small of her back. 'And Millie too, what a treat! Come on in, I'll put the kettle on.'

'I'll do it, Nan,' Annie insisted, 'you look done in. Why don't you sit down?'

'Sit down?' she scoffed. 'I ain't got time for that. Now then, Millie, you and yours all right, dear?'

'You know Mum. If it ain't her bunions, it's her back,' Millie grimaced. 'I ain't stopping. I just wanted to see whether you needed anything fetching from the shops.'

Elsie wasn't listening; she was staring up at Millie's eye.

'Oh, love,' she sighed, delicately touching her face. 'He wants stringing up. Parsley-water eye bath'll fix that. I'll make you one.'

'Please don't go to any bother, honestly, I'm fine,' Millie insisted. 'I'm such a silly sod, bashed into a lamp post Saturday night.'

'Really? Talking of Saturday night, any word from that nice young pilot?' Elsie remarked, clearly not taken in by the story. 'Give you a kiss on the hand, dear, did he, when he left? How d'ya like that, eh? Now that's a gentleman for you.'

Annie rolled her eyes. Who needed jungle drums when you had East End gossips?

'He's not a pilot yet,' Millie replied quickly. 'Now what do you need from the shops?'

'Pennyworth of pot herbs and two penn'orth of bones, if you don't mind, dear,' Elsie replied, raking about in her purse for some coppers. 'And tell the butcher to leave the meat on. I got a stew on the go.'

Sure enough, a giant pot was bubbling away on the black-leaded stove. Elsie took her lead from the Jews and could make delicious food out of nothing. Her bone marrow and barley stews were cobbled together from sixpence. Thrift was nothing new to this old girl. She knew without even stopping how to dispatch a chicken or render dripping.

'Smells delicious,' smiled Millie, taking Elsie's money.

'Nan'll be through those bones, teasing out every last

scrap of marrow with her knitting needle,' Annie grinned, kissing her nan's head affectionately.

'Right, I'm off,' said Millie, turning back to the street. 'Oh Lord, watch out. Someone's dander's up!'

Maureen was marching up the cobbles, mouth as tight as a gnat's chuff. Annie thought about retreating out to the yard, but Rose's mum had already spotted her.

'All right, Maureen dear, you just finished work? Expect you'll be wanting a cuppa,' called Elsie.

'Where's my Rose, huh?' she demanded, ignoring Elsie's offer of tea and glaring at Annie and Millie.

'Sorry, Mrs Riley, she was, er, where was she going again, Millie?' Annie blustered.

'Went to see a man about a dog?' Millie smirked.

Maureen surveyed her coolly.

'You got some brass, girl, talking to me like that . . .'

Elsie laid a placating hand on her arm.

'Come on in, Maureen. I got the place straight now, so come and have a cuppa while you wait for your Rose. No sense in being gloomy now, is there, dear?'

Maureen glared at Millie, but eventually allowed herself to be led inside by Elsie.

'Dunno why you bother, Els,' she grumbled. 'Jerry'll be back tonight to mess it all up again.'

'I'm not letting my standards slip 'cause of Hitler,' Elsie replied, pushing back a stray lock of her white hair. 'Now come on in. If you don't fancy tea, I got a drop of porter. Shall I rustle up some bread and drip? I can do it quick as a wink.'

Annie turned to Millie, rolling her eyes. 'I'll meet you outside the bug 'ole later.'

Millie had not moved five yards when a young lady approached them from the other side of the street.

'Sorry to bother you, but . . . it's Millie, isn't it? Millie Brown?'

'Bleedin' hell,' Millie muttered under her breath, 'it's like King's Cross Station round here tonight.'

'Yes, darling, what can I do for you?' she said, turning to face the lady with a bright smile. ''Ere, I know you, don't I? You was outside my house the other day. Well, I really don't need anything, thanks all the same. I get all my policies through Bryant & May.'

*

Pearl felt confused. Mind you, she'd felt confused from the moment she stepped off the train at London Liverpool Street Station two days previously. London was a huge and bewildering city to wash up in. She'd already tried talking to Millie once outside her home, but received short shrift. After hiding out for the duration of the raid in the basement of the boarding house she was staying at, she'd tried knocking again, only to be told by an offhand chap she assumed was Millie's husband that she'd probably find her here. Millie looked like a woman at the end of her tether, and Pearl was beginning to think she'd made a huge mistake turning up here in Bow unannounced. She was running out of money and hadn't had a proper wash in days.

'I'm not selling anything,' she said, trying to keep the note of desperation from creeping in. 'Please, Millie, I've come a long way to see you. It's Pearl. Pearl O'Hara. Your pen pal. I'm a Diamond Girl, from the Matchy . . .' her voice trailed off. 'Well, I used to be at any rate, before it got bombed.'

'Pearl!' Millie exclaimed, flabbergasted. 'I'm so sorry, darlin'. I thought you was trying to sell me something.'

She turned to the surprised-looking redhead standing next to her.

'Annie, this is Pearl,' she said excitedly. 'Remember, the girl I write to through the factory pen pal scheme?'

The redhead gazed at her curiously.

'Of course, I know you. We played you once in the inter-factory netball game, March '39, weren't it? Diamond Works v Fairfield Works.'

'That's right,' Pearl replied, smiling shyly. 'You thrashed us.'

'Lovely to finally meet you in the flesh,' Millie said. 'But you're an awful long way from home, Pearl. What brings you here?'

'Well, that's just it. I don't have a home no longer,' she said. Pearl had never really told a lie in her life, white lies yes, but not whoppers. 'You heard about the Matchy?'

Millie sighed. 'We did, the Chairman announced it on Saturday. So sorry, darlin'.'

'Well, my rooms copped it too,' Pearl continued. 'I got no job, no home, no prospects up there any more. I thought I might try my luck down here, see if you would maybe speak for me, about getting a job?'

She hesitated. 'I know we've only been writing a year, but I feel like I know you, Millie, and I don't really know where else to turn. Being a match girl's all I know.'

'Well, 'course I will,' Millie replied, squeezing her arm.

'I'll take you up the factory tomorrow, but, well, I don't mean to be funny, but talk about outta the frying pan, into the fire.'

'You might've been safer in Liverpool,' agreed her pal. 'I'm Annie, by the way.'

'Hello, Annie,' she smiled, 'and, yeah, I know that. But, well, I've always fancied coming to see the bright lights of London.'

'Well, I really can't see you having a problem getting a job in the factory, but I can't offer you a place to stay at mine, I'm afraid,' said Millie. 'Curly, my husband, well, he ain't exactly landlord material.'

'Oh.' Pearl felt crushed.

'Well, that's all right,' Annie piped up. 'I'm sure we can make a bed up for you here, long as you don't mind sharing with me? You ain't married, or got a sweetheart?'

Pearl shook her head. 'Oh, no,' she said emphatically. 'It's just me.'

'Well, that's settled then. I'll check with Elsie – that's my nan – but I can't see her having a problem with it, as long as you don't mind contributing.'

'Absolutely, I'll pay my way,' she replied.

'Well, come on in, then,' she beckoned. 'And welcome to Blondin Street.'

Pearl hated lying to the match girls, who, despite all they had been through, had just greeted her so warmly, but as she was shown into the spotlessly clean terrace, she felt light-headed with relief.

*

The search-and-rescue chap had done a smashing job look-ing after Pip for Rose. He'd washed and brushed his white and brown fur, found him a collar and lead and the little terrier had been thoroughly fussed over by everyone at Post B in Southill Street, Poplar. In fact, he seemed so at home curled up asleep on a blanket in front of a flickering fire that Rose wondered if he'd be better off there.

At the sound of her voice, Pip's eyes snapped open and he scampered over. His little tail was going nineteen to the dozen as he leapt up and down in excitement, paws scrab-bling on the ancient brown linoleum floor.

'Hello,' she grinned, scooping him up in her arms. Pip lunged at her face, showering her with wet kisses, his warm little body rolling over and wriggling in excitement.

'You want a tummy tickle, do you?' she chuckled.

'We're going to miss this little fella,' said the chap who had dug her out from the ruins, 'but judging by that greet-ing, I'd say his place is with you.'

He handed Rose a bag.

'We had a whip-round at the station, all clubbed in for some dog biscuits. Should last you a little while.'

'You're so kind,' Rose replied, touched at their thought-fulness.

'Just one thing we noticed, love. He goes berserk if any men come near him in heavy boots. Don't know what hap-pened in his past, but I reckon he's been on the receiving end of a good kicking at some point, poor little pint-size.'

As Rose walked back in the direction of Bow, the little Jack Russell trotting happily at her feet, she felt a fierce protectiveness tug at her heart. Pip was a rescue dog with a shadowy past, of which she knew nothing.

'Just like me,' she whispered, crouching down to stroke his ears. 'Two misfits together, eh, boy?'

Cutting down Fairfield Road, she spotted Pip's old home, the Bow branch of Battersea Dogs' Home, and felt a twinge of guilt. Pip had escaped and now she was just claiming him as her own. At the very least she ought to tell them where he was.

Pushing open the door of the kennels, she called out into the gloom.

'Hello?'

A boy's head poked out from over a kennel door.

'Are you missing a dog?' she asked, gesturing to Pip.

'Sorry, miss, all the dogs have gone. They moved 'em all back to Battersea soon as the bombs started.'

'Looks like they may have left one behind,' she replied.

'Poor little chap,' he grimaced. 'Afraid he can't stay here, though. I'm renting the kennels now, set up a pig club with my brother, John,' he said proudly. 'I'm William, by the way,' he grinned, extending a grubby hand.

'Rose. I work over the road at Bryant & May,' she said, returning his smile. 'A pig club, eh? I'll be sure to remember that.'

Outside, Pip gazed up at her from the sooty cobbles. All of a sudden, he tipped back onto his hind legs, his big brown eyes imploring.

'All right, all right,' she chuckled. 'Stop laying it on thick. I shan't leave you here. Looks like you really could use a new home now, my forgotten little stray.'

Back in Blondin Street, Rose pulled the piece of string through the letter box and unlocked the door, before climbing the stairs to their rooms.

'There you are.' Maureen loomed up through the darkness of the passage, a guttering candle in her hand, a shawl draped round her bony shoulders. Rose jumped.

'Mum, you gave me a fright.'

'Where you been, huh?' she said gruffly. 'I've been searching all over for you.'

'M-Mum, this is Pip. He helped lead the rescue workers to me on Saturday night. I don't reckon as I'd be alive if it weren't for this one. I . . . I thought it'd be nice to keep him, you know, give him a home.'

Maureen made a strange noise in the back of her throat, as if she were clearing phlegm.

'Oh, you did, did you? Well, if you think he's staying under my roof, you got another think coming.'

Rose felt Pip's body tense in her arms, his tiny chest beginning to tremble.

For pity's sake, she had been buried alive. Buried alive! And Maureen had not mentioned it once . . .

'Under your roof?' she scoffed. 'We ain't even got a roof, Mum.' She gestured to the gaping crack where the Works boiler had damaged the chimney stack. Rose stared about her, as if seeing their lodgings for the first time. A single bulb cast a pallid light. It wasn't a home. It was a hollow heart. The rooms were dark, dingy and smelt of mildew.

A freezing fog had crept in through the roof and was slowly licking its way around their ankles.

Her tea, a piece of flaccid tinned tongue slung on a plate, sat atop a table fashioned from a couple of old orange crates. She thought longingly of Annie's, of the fire that always crackled in the grate and the permanently whistling kettle, the delicious smells of suet and sizzling bacon that laced the air.

Here, Maureen's misery and sourness seemed to ooze from the distempered walls.

'Don't get saucy with me, you ungrateful little madam,' Maureen seethed. 'You see fit to lay your head here night after night. If it weren't for me, you'd be in a home.'

Rose's head buzzed like a hive of clashing wasps. How many times was she to have this thrown at her?

'I wish you'd never taken me in!' Rose cried. In a fit of pique, she ripped the ties from her plaits, allowing her long dark hair to escape down her back.

'I don't need your protection any more. I'm seventeen now.'

A brilliant lance of pain seared through her cheek, stunning Rose into silence. She felt her flesh grow hot and red where Maureen had struck her.

Tears blinding her, she hugged Pip tight and clattered back down the stairs. Maureen's acid tongue ran after her.

'That's it, run! Takes a stray to know one!'

Rose ran to the only place she could think of. Elsie's. Growing up, Annie's nan had treated her more like a daughter than Maureen ever had. Elsie took one look at her tear-stained face and ushered her up the passage into the light and warmth of the kitchen.

'Oh, Rose, dear, whatever's happened?' she asked, settling her by the fire with a cup of tea.

'I don't get it, Elsie, why does she hate me so much?' Rose wept, her tears seeping into Pip's warm fur. 'Why did she bother taking me in when she clearly doesn't want a family?'

'She loves you in her own way, dear,' Elsie said quietly. 'It's hard for your mother to express herself. Her life's been a struggle, but trust me, she cares deeply for you.'

'She don't love me, Elsie, she resents me.'

'She *does* love you. Why do you think she's so protective over you?'

'I don't know,' Rose said miserably, 'but I can't go back there now, can I? She won't let me keep Pip, and I ain't turning him out on the streets.'

Elsie looked at the little ball of fur curled up on her lap.

'Well, we can't have that now, can we, dear?' she smiled, gently picking Pip up. 'You're a lovely little fella, ain'cha? Tell you what. I've already given a bed to one poor homeless creature tonight. What's one more? Go and meet the girls at the pictures and then go on home to your mum afterwards. Make your peace. This little fella can have a home here and you can visit him whenever you want.'

Speechless with gratitude, Rose flung her arms around the elderly lady.

'Thanks, Elsie, I owe you.'

'Give over, dear,' she chuckled. 'You're gonna crush poor Pip.'

'Elsie,' she asked quite suddenly, 'did you know my mum? My real mum, that is.'

The old lady looked thoughtful in the firelight, her callused hands slowly trailing through Pip's fur.

'I did, dear,' she admitted.

'Please, tell me more,' Rose begged.

'She had a beautiful soul—'

'How did you know her?' Rose interrupted. 'What colour was her skin? Was she dark, like me?'

Rose knew it was too much, too fast. But the questions that had simmered away inside her for so long refused to be silenced.

Elsie held up her hand. 'Please, dear Rose, don't ask me no more.'

A sudden gust of wind howled down the chimney, making the coals hiss and flare. Even the rafters of the old house seemed to moan and sigh.

'Just let it be, dear girl. Let it be.'

*

Every seat for the 7 p.m. performance of *The Road to Zanzibar* at the Old Ford Picture Palace was taken, except the one next to Millie.

'Where's Rose?' she asked.

Annie shrugged, her fingers delving into a paper bag and pulling out a sweet, before passing it onto Pearl.

'Search me. Sure she'll be here soon enough.'

The picture house was packed with Bow factory girls, all chatting away over the newsreel shown before each film, and passing sweets around. No one seemed to bother to watch the Ministry of Information propaganda segments any more. Who wanted more daily reminders of what they should and shouldn't be doing to aid the war effort?

Eight months now they'd been bombed senseless, with the exception of one night at Christmas. All anyone wanted was the escapism of sitting in the snug dark warmth of the picture house, watching glamorous Hollywood idols with beautiful clothes and white smiles. With any luck, they'd get to see Bing Crosby kiss Dorothy Lamour under a silver

African moon before the siren sounded. But first, they had to sit through some man with a plummy accent extolling the virtues of growing your own.

'Dig for Victory,' he was saying. 'Let this be the slogan of every able-bodied man and woman capable of digging an allotment in their spare time. I appeal to you – lovers of this great country of ours – to dig, to cultivate, to sow and to plant.'

A photo of a smartly dressed lady in a fawn suit and low heels digging with a spade in Kensington Gardens flashed up. Millie stifled a yawn. The girls in the row in front – Clarnico sweet packers by the looks of them – were paying even less attention, instead giggling and pointing to a couple of suited men who'd just walked in.

'I wouldn't mind getting to grips with his able body,' whispered one, as the whole line of girls fell about.

'Keep it down, will you?' Annie hissed. 'Some of us are trying to watch.'

'Yeah,' Millie chipped in impishly. 'Not everyone wants to hear your gutter talk.'

'Hark at who's talking,' the girl spluttered. 'You match girls got right potty mouths on you.'

'Like gardening, do you?' Pearl asked Annie, amused.

'I'd love to have a go, yes,' Annie admitted, her face animated in the glare from the screen. 'Make a change from packing matches all day. I've helped my nan plant a few dahlias in the backyard, but I don't really know the first thing about crop rotation and all that malarkey.'

'I'd be happy to help,' Pearl said. 'My dad has an allotment. Taught me a thing or two.'

'You want to stop talking about it, Annie, and just do it,'

said Millie, who'd left off sparring with the Clarnico girls and was waving to Rose as she walked in.

'But how?' Annie protested. 'The only spare land's at the factory, and I can't see them letting me dig it up, can you? Besides, I wouldn't even know where to start.'

'All employers are being encouraged to find vacant land for their employees, or lease it to their local councils for allotments,' said Millie, getting out a nail file. 'Bryant & May would have to yield to a request to do so.'

Annie stopped sucking her sweet and stared at her.

'Someone swallow a dictionary?'

Millie laughed out loud as she filed the edge of a broken thumbnail.

'What's the joke?' Rose asked as she settled herself down.

'Annie here's come over all green-fingered. She's going to start up an allotment at work,' Millie replied.

'Oh, you should,' Rose enthused. 'I've always fancied having a go at that. Anything to get me out the house.'

'Take it your mum didn't warm to having a pet dog then?' Millie asked sympathetically.

'What do you think?' Rose groaned.

'Well, that's settled then,' Millie said. 'We're gonna speak to the bosses, set up our own match girls' allotment.'

Millie became aware of a commotion behind her. The suited and booted men who had entered the picture house were weaving their way up the line behind, causing a fuss.

'Move it, pal, this seat's mine.'

She turned round to see Curly lowering himself into the seat directly behind hers. With a smirk, he pulled out a cigarette and gestured to the usherette for a light. Betty

Connor was by his side in a heartbeat, whispering something in her ear as she obligingly lit his cigarette.

But Curly didn't take his eyes off Millie's face.

'All right, love,' he said mockingly, blowing a blue plume of smoke into her face. 'Thought I'd come and keep an eye on my wife.'

Millie turned back round and stared hard at the screen, hot, painful tears blurring her vision.

Eight

Maureen Riley was wrong about Jerry returning that night, or even the one after. In fact, apart from a delayed-action bomb exploding in the Bryant & May wharf quite suddenly one dinnertime – sending a sheet of golden flame billowing up the River Lea – all had been quiet, comparatively speaking. The bombs had finally stopped dropping and four weeks on from the 'Hardest Night', as they were now calling it, the match girls were daring to hope that might be it. The Luftwaffe had turned their attentions east to the Soviet Union and had begun bombing the Russians.

Back in the East End of London, summer was blooming over Bow. Millie's black eye had faded, thanks to Elsie's home-made remedies: a parsley-water eye bath and infusion of dried flowers for a sad heart. Rose's leg was healing, and she had quietly returned home to Maureen, the dutiful daughter once more.

Annie had been hard at work, doing her research, and had requested a meeting with the Works Manager and Mrs Frobisher, the Welfare Superintendent, on their dinner-break, about getting their allotment up and running.

As for the newcomers, Pearl was settling in well at number 33, as was Pip. The Liverpool lass was very reserved, but Annie had to admit, it was nice to see their little group swell to four, well five, if you included Pip. With her soft voice and gentle manner, Pearl was a calming influence on Millie. Annie was impressed to see how well she knew her way around the machinery, too, having worked identical ones at the Diamond Works, and how she too had learnt to lip-read to get round the terrific noise of the top match room. Not that you needed it with Millie.

'Oh, bleedin' buggery balls,' Millie groaned loudly. 'I just remembered it's my turn manning the match machine after dinner.'

All of the girls were given different jobs and rotated to stop boredom creeping in. The most dreaded of all, though, was standing at the conveyor belt in silence for hours on end to check that no splints went astray and accidentally clogged the whole system. One tiny match not being where it should could cause mayhem. On really hot days like today, or if the machinery broke down, the matches would spontaneously burst into flames, which was nothing short of a disaster with so much paraffin and phosphorus about.

'I'll take your turn, Millie,' Pearl offered.

'Really?' she exclaimed, fishing a cigarette out from her cleavage.

'Yeah, 'course, I don't mind a bit,' she said, a shy smile spreading across her pale cheeks. Annie knew she herself was on the thin side, but Pearl was ever so slender. Her skin was luminescent and she had a frail, fragile quality about her that seemed at odds next to Millie's diamond-hard glamour. Give her a few more weeks, Annie thought with a smile. Few more plates of her nan's bread and drip, and she'd soon fill out.

The bell for dinner sounded.

*

Annie had been told she was allowed to bring a friend along to the meeting with the Works Manager.

'I'm just here as your wingman, all right, Annie?' Millie said as they paused outside his office. 'This is your show!'

'Right,' said Annie nervously, clutching a Dig for Victory leaflet she'd picked up from the Town Hall and fanning her face with it. It was cracking the cobbles outside, making it even harder to keep her cool.

Seated across from the elderly man – his predecessor had been called up at the start of the war – and Mrs Frobisher, Annie's mind went blank.

'My pal here wants to start an allotment,' said Millie, nudging her.

'An allotment, here at Bryant & May?' said the manager, leaning back in his chair to reveal a large sweat stain under each armpit.

'Yeah, that's right,' Annie ventured.

'Where?'

'I was thinking of two possible sites. Where the Girls' Club used to be, in the recreation grounds off Wrexham Road, and another one where the bomb fell in the yard, at the back of the office block.'

The foreman looked out of his office window at the very site where Annie had suggested and roared with laughter.

'That's a cracking wheeze, that is.'

'Please, sir, I ain't joking,' Annie said, crossing her legs in annoyance.

'But it's a bombsite, girl.'

'I know that, sir, but over in Bethnal Green, they're starting allotments all over the place in the grounds of old bombsites. They call themselves the Bethnal Green Bombed Sites Producers' As—'

'I don't give a monkey's if they've found a way to grow bananas,' the manager interrupted, 'this is a business premises. Besides, look at all that debris. I should like to see you try and clear that, never mind grow veg on it. That's a man-size job, that is.'

'But we could try, couldn't we?' Annie said quietly.

'No point,' he sniffed. 'Soil is key. You ain't even got any topsoil there. The ground'll be as acidic as anything 'cause of the cordite.'

'Oh, bugger the cordite!' Millie exclaimed. 'Ain't no filth you can't grow 'taters in. 'Sides, this factory has a legal obligation to allocate spare land for use as allotments. Ain't you heard of Dig for Victory?'

The Works Manager bristled in annoyance.

'And you are?'

'Millie Brown, match girl and Miss Brymay 1938,' she replied, jutting her chin out. 'Me and my pal here are members of the Match Girls' Club. It's been instilled into us, the virtues of a good sense of citizenship. What's Digging for Victory in a factory allotment if not that?'

'Am I being lectured in citizenship by a potty-mouthed match girl?' he spluttered, smoothing down his tie.

Annie groaned inwardly. This was not going according to plan.

'I think she might have a very good point there, actually,' piped up Mrs Frobisher. 'I back these girls' plans wholeheartedly. I think the factory should be seen to be participating in the Government campaign. The Ministry of Agriculture has announced it wants an extra five hundred thousand allotments by the end of this summer. Don't you think we should be doing our bit at Bryant & May? We have three acres of ground, after all.'

'The Cultivation of Lands (Allotment) Order, 1939, empowers councils to take over unoccupied lands for allotments,' added Annie, finding her voice. 'I think it would be better to volunteer to cultivate the bombsites ourselves, before it's forced upon us.'

The Works Manager peered at her and blew his cheeks out.

'I don't know what this world's coming to. Match girls . . . gardening? Whatever next. But very well, I shall talk to the chairman about it.'

Mrs Frobisher showed them to the door. 'Well done, girls,' she whispered under her breath. 'Please, Millie, in future, watch your language.'

'Sorry, Mrs F,' she said contritely.

*

'Silly old arse,' tutted Millie as they returned through the reception area to the factory canteen. 'Who's he think he is?'

'You were terrific in there,' sighed Annie. 'I was like a wet rag.'

'No you weren't,' Millie admonished.

'Where do you get your front?' Annie asked.

'My nan Nelly! Also, marriage to a toerag'll help you tough anything out,' she joked. 'But seriously,' she added, taking Annie's chin and lifting it up, 'hold your head up high, girl. You're as good as any of them.'

'Thanks, Millie,' Annie replied, her rumpled red-gold curls shining in the dazzling June sunshine. 'I'll remember that.'

Millie's bright smile faded, and Annie turned to see what she was staring at. Pinned to the noticeboard, next to progress updates on Bryant & May's employees called up to the forces and factory sewing bees, was a glossy black and white photograph of Samuel Taylor. He was standing on the podium beside the chairman and the Spitfire pilot, above a report of the RAF's visit to the factory. He looked so dashing in his uniform, so purposeful and new, buttons glinting in the sunshine.

'How's your nan?' Millie asked quickly. 'Has she got over the shock of the fire?'

'Nan? She's a game old bird. Now the bombs have stopped, she seems almost back to her old self.'

Annie sighed as they left reception and crossed the yard. 'It's been tough on her mind. Dad being taken prisoner of war really hit her hard, and I know she hates being parted from my sisters, even though I try to tell her the country-side's the safest place for 'em. She doesn't just worry about us, either, she worries about everyone down the bloomin' street.'

'Don't kid yourself, girl,' Millie laughed. 'She rules them cobbles.'

'You're probably right there. She was up half the night

delivering Mrs Ramsey's baby at number 9. She was only coming back in as I was leaving for work this morning.'

'Don't her legs bother her?' Millie asked.

'Her legs?' Annie replied, puzzled.

'Yeah, I noticed, on the night of the fire when Samuel picked her up, she's got scars all over her thighs.'

'Think you must be mistaken, Millie,' Annie frowned. 'Her back's shot to pieces, but there's nothing wrong with her legs.'

'If you say so, only I could've sworn—'

Millie pulled Annie to one side to avoid a steam tractor piled high with timber lumbering up the yard. 'Oh, never mind. Come on, I'm famished, let's get some grub.'

*

Pearl walked back across to the factory floor after dinner and, for the first time in years, felt an unfamiliar feeling wash over her. Safety.

Annie and the girls were terrific and her new landlady, Elsie, was an absolute gem. She had been made to feel so welcome here in Bow. Pearl had heard such terrible things about London, especially East London, but gazing out over the wide-open windows at the sea of bobbing barrage balloons and smoking chimneys, she finally felt at home. Liverpool and all its memories were behind her now.

Pearl felt as if she had shed all the dreadful components of her life but kept the parts she loved. Like working at Bryant & May. Everywhere she looked, steel wheels kept turning and dozens of machines revolved. Thousands of matches kept appearing, as if out of a conjuror's hat, and before her eyes grew a box, every single second. Work gave her such a sense of purpose, when all else had threatened to destroy her.

She took up her place, safety-watching to check for rogue splints. So intent was she on her duties, she didn't hear him at first.

'Wotcha, love. I know that face. Nice to see someone else from the Matchy's washed up here.'

She glanced up to see the face of a messenger boy she vaguely recognized from the Diamond Works.

'I wondered if I'd see anyone else down south,' he grinned, leaning in conspiratorially. 'Feels like a foreign country down here, doesn't it?'

'Can't you see I'm busy?' Pearl snapped. She was aware of Millie, Annie and Rose gazing over in curiosity.

'Suit yourself,' he huffed, 'I was only trying to be friendly!'

Pearl's legs started to tremble as the lad stalked off across the factory floor. Why had it not occurred to her that there would be other workers here from the Matchy? Angry tears pricked her eyelids, blurring her vision.

'Pearl . . . Pearl . . . The button!' She didn't hear Millie's voice over the drone of production. In fact, it wasn't until the smell of burning filled her nostrils that she realized a splint had caught fire.

'Oh, fuck!' She slammed her hand down on the red button to stop production, but it was too late. The match had already set fire to the ones either side and the fire was spreading like falling dominoes up the conveyor belt.

'Didn't you bloody see it, girl?' bellowed the foreman,

sprinting to the other side of the floor to activate the sprinkler system.

Within minutes, you couldn't see your hand in front of your face. A thick curtain of choking smoke filled the entire floor.

'Annie!' Pearl cried, whirling round and round. The smoke was disorientating. She couldn't tell up from down.

'Keep calm,' bellowed a male voice. 'Fire brigade's on the way.'

Pearl fell to her knees and crouched down as close to the floor as possible, like she'd been taught at the Matchy. The smoke was so dense, the smell of phosphorus so pungent, it felt like a blanket smothering her.

The sprinkler burst into life, and she could feel cold water running down the back of her hairnet, drenching her tunic. Then hands were lifting her up.

'You're all right, love. Let's get you out into the yard.'

As the smoke cleared, she saw firemen, dozens of them, escorting dazed-looking match girls from the floor. No one panicked, as they filed in an orderly fashion down the stairs and out into the yard. Their calm, exemplary behaviour only served to make Pearl feel more wretched.

As she passed into the yard, she gasped great lungfuls of air.

Four fire engines were parked nearby – Bryant & May's own fire brigade – and teams of firemen were tackling the fire on the top floor as clouds of grey smoke billowed from the open window.

A deep shame engulfed her. This was her fault. Her mind simply hadn't been on the job. A match girl could have died because of her.

'Pearl . . .'

She turned to see Millie, Rose and Annie running up the yard towards her.

'What have I done?' she asked, trembling.

'Oh, come here, darlin',' Annie soothed, pulling her into her arms. 'You ain't done nothing that many a match girl before you ain't done. This sort of thing happens all the time.'

'That's right,' added Millie. 'That's why they've got two bloody great water towers and a fire brigade here.'

Pearl was shaking so much, she couldn't reply.

'It's not like you set fire to the match, is it?' Rose soothed, patting her hand.

'B–but I wasn't concentrating,' Pearl stammered. 'I didn't spot it immediately.'

'All right, girls, production's over for today. Clock out then head off home,' shouted the foreman. 'New girl, we'll have words tomorrow.'

'Come on, pet,' said Annie. 'Don't mind him. Let's all go back to mine. Reckon we can talk Nan into an early tea.'

The girls clocked out and grabbed their coats and bags, but as they reached the bottom step, a fireman was heading back up to the top floor.

'Oh, hello, it's Ted, isn't it?' grinned Annie.

'That's right, good memory, and you're Annie, ain'cha? You brought us tea that night the whole of bloomin' London was set on fire.'

'How you finding your new job?' she asked.

He shook his head, but his quick eyes were gleaming.

'Come out of retirement and join Bryant & May fire brigade, they says. It'll be a nice quiet job for you, they says

. . . I ain't stopped fighting fires since I bloody got here!' A wide grin spread over his weather-beaten old face to show he was only joking.

'Is it bad up there?' Pearl asked, passing her hand across her mouth nervously.

'Nah, don't worry, love,' he winked. 'We'll have it cleaned up by tomorrow.'

'See you around, Ted,' Annie smiled, and then, as an afterthought, 'Oh, Ted, we're hopefully starting up an allotment, here in the grounds of Bryant & May. How do you fancy helping out?'

'An allotment? Here?' he asked, raising one eyebrow. 'Why, what a smashing idea, love. I'll see if I can rope some of the lads in the brigade into helping out.'

*

By the time Rose and the girls had left the back entrance of the factory and turned down Blondin Street, Elsie was already near the top of the road, clutching Pip to her voluminous chest.

'Oh, thank the Lord!' she gasped, making the sign of the cross over her apron. She let Pip down and he tore up the cobbles and leapt into Rose's arms. 'Woah, boy,' Rose laughed, as he smothered her face with kisses.

'I saw the smoke from the top windows,' Elsie panted. 'I thought the whole factory was on fire.'

'Calm down, Nan,' Annie soothed. 'It was only a rogue splint, nothing to worry about.'

'Nothing to worry about?' she screeched. 'Look at the state of you all!'

Rose realized they made quite a sight, their tunics sodden.

'Oh, my girl, you have no idea.' Elsie trembled. 'I do wish you wouldn't work there, it ain't safe to work with matches.'

'Nan, let's not start this up again,' Annie said firmly. 'Me and the girls are dying for a cuppa and some dry clothes.'

''Course you are, come on in, all of you,' Elsie said, ushering them in over the doorstep.

After a cup of tea and a change of clothes, the girls laid their wet tunics over the fender in front of the fire. Gratefully, Rose sank down into an easy chair and Pip hopped up onto her lap.

'How's Pip been, Mrs T?' Rose asked, as Elsie bustled about the tiny kitchen fixing their tea.

'Good as gold, love,' she called back, lifting the lid on a steaming pan and giving it a gentle stir. 'He's smashing company for me when Annie and Pearl go off to work.'

Hearing his name, Pip pricked up one ear and stared intently at Rose.

'All right, boy,' she smiled, scratching behind his ear. 'I'll take you for a walk once I've had some tea.'

'Nan cooks as if she's feeding the five thousand,' Annie joked, raking a towel through her tousled hair. 'What we got?' she asked, dropping the towel and lifting the lid on the pan with a hiss of steam. 'One of your famous stews?'

Elsie batted her hand away. 'Liver and onions if you must know, and pick that bloody towel up, girl, or else you won't get your sweet for afters.'

'Did someone say sweet?' asked Millie, coming into the

kitchen from the lav in the yard. A mischievous grin flashed over her face. Gathering her into her arms, she waltzed Elsie round and round the tiny kitchen. 'Goodnight, sweetheart,' she crooned, 'till we meet tomorrow . . .'

Elsie tipped her head back and shrieked with laughter, her chest heaving like a blancmange. Pip leapt off Rose's lap and jumped up at the pair of them in excitement.

'Get away with ya, you daft little article,' she cackled, grabbing the range handle for support. 'You're a flamin' caution, you are! Look, you've set the dog off now.'

Rose turned to Pearl, giggling. 'Don't worry, they're always like this.'

Annie meanwhile had unearthed a box from the meat safe in the yard and was peering in with her eyes all aglow.

'Oh, hello, what we got here?'

'Mr Rosen who runs the baker on Old Ford give it me, to say thanks for lighting his fires earlier,' Elsie said, still fanning herself down with a tea towel.

Annie turned the box round to reveal the most perfect-looking cakes and pastries. Rose immediately felt her mouth start to water.

'Mrs T lights all the Jewish people's fires for them on the Sabbath,' she explained to a puzzled-looking Pearl.

'That's right,' grinned Annie, reaching her hand into the box and pinching a pastry. 'Nan's what's known as a Sabbath Goy.'

'Why must people be so quick to put a name to things?' Elsie grumbled, sinking her comfortable frame down into a chair next to Pearl. 'I respect the Jews, unlike some, and I see no barrier in colour or religion. Lord knows, we wouldn't be having this war if more people were a little more tolerant.' She patted the edges of her frayed arm-chair. 'Live and let live, I say.'

Pearl nodded. 'All sorts of folk make up this world.'

'That's right, love, and surely you must have experi-enced the same prejudices in Liverpool?' said Elsie. 'You're a working-class community close to the docks, same as us.'

'Liverpool people are proud, like you cockneys,' Pearl agreed.

'So, if you don't mind me asking, don't you miss it?' Elsie asked. 'Don't get me wrong, we love having you, dear, but don't you miss being with your people?'

Rose watched in fascination as Pearl's colour rose, as if her cheeks were stained with cochineal.

'I . . . I miss me mam and dad,' she admitted. 'They live a little way out of the city, but I needed work, simple as that.'

'But there must be dozens of factories in Liverpool,' Millie pressed. 'It ain't a crime. You can admit it!'

'A-admit what?' Pearl said defensively.

'You was in pieces when that messenger from the Matchy came over to say hello earlier. You've done a moon-light flit, ain'cha?' said Millie, sympathetically. 'That's why you didn't want him recognizing you. It's all right, love, trust me, it goes on here all the time.'

Millie casually smoothed down her stockings. 'Most of my childhood was spent flitting.'

For a long time, Pearl sat in silence, picking at a flap of skin by the side of her thumbnail.

'Yeah,' she whispered eventually. 'Something like that. My dad was in an accident a few years back and he weren't able to work, and what with the Depression and all . . .

Times have been tough . . .' Her voice trailed off and she looked so anguished that Rose wondered if she oughtn't go to her and comfort her, but Elsie beat her to it.

'Oh, my dear girl,' she soothed, giving her an enormous cuddle. 'Ain't no shame in being poor.' It was a gentle understanding, born of poverty, but Rose couldn't shake the feeling there was more to the story than Pearl was letting on. But no matter. The girl was entitled to her secrets. God knows, Rose herself had plenty.

Four weeks on from being buried, Rose had told no one of the nightmares that plagued her, of so many hands clutching at her clothing, dragging her down into a dark, unknown place. Or the vice-like headaches that started a few weeks ago. Neither had she told the girls about her walks with Pip down to the river basin at Shadwell. The same place where the woman who had given birth to her had thrown herself into the dark, swirling waters.

A part of Rose was changed forever the night she was buried alive, and that was something she would have to deal with. But at least she had Pip now. She couldn't explain how his love was healing her, but he was like a part of her now, always there. Never questioning or criticizing, just accepting her unconditionally.

A deep silence stretched over the room. The only sound was Pip's tail softly thumping on the aged wooden floorboards.

'Blimey, it's like a morgue in here,' Millie chirped eventually.

'Yes, let's all cheer up,' said Elsie, heaving herself up from her chair and patting Pearl on the hand. 'Rose, be a dear and lay the table, would you? Set one more place an' all. I've invited your mother. She's coming over soon as she's finished her shift at the cafe.'

'Oh, great,' Annie sighed. 'That'll really cheer us up.'

'Mind your manners,' Elsie scolded.

*

Twenty minutes later, Elsie was just serving up when Maureen swept in like a cold wind, headscarf tightly knotted round her thin face. Rose fussed over her mother, taking her coat and getting her settled at the table with a glass of porter.

Maureen raised the glass to her lips and took a deep drink.

'What's that dog doing here, huh?' she said, turning on Rose. 'Thought I told you you couldn't keep it.' Pip slunk under Rose's chair.

'It's all right, Maureen dear,' Elsie soothed, as she ladled a spoonful of steaming gravy over Maureen's plate of liver and onions. 'I said to Rose I'd keep him here.'

'Yeah, well,' Maureen snapped defensively, her lips as thin and sharp as a razor. 'I got enough on my plate. Twelve-hour shifts I've been putting in down the cafe.'

'Course you have, dear,' Elsie soothed, handing her a fork. 'Go on, dig in. You must be shattered.'

Rose felt a deep ache press down on the sides of her skull, and from somewhere under the table, Pip pushed his wet nose into her palm.

But Maureen was just getting going. Chewing loudly on a piece of liver, she swallowed, wiped the side of her thin mouth and looked triumphantly at Millie.

'You'll never believe what I heard down the cafe earlier.'

'What's that, dear?' Elsie asked, tucking her napkin into the top of her apron.

'Betty Connor, you know that usherette from the Old Ford Picture Palace. Well, she's only in the family way.'

Nine

July blazed through Bow like a shimmering arrow. The stagnant air over the greasy waters of the River Lea was green with flies and hot with the scent of coal dust. Bombsites all through the district were already sprouting great drifts of ripe willowherb, pushing through the cracks, helping to heal and hide the ugly scars of war.

Thankfully, Double Summer Time had been introduced. Longer daylight hours meant Annie could begin her allotment plans in earnest. To her astonishment, the chairman of Bryant & May had thought her idea a splendid one and not only agreed to allocate her the two bombsites she had requested, but also placed funds at her disposal to help develop them. But even with Bryant & May's full backing, getting a Dig for Victory allotment off the ground was an overwhelming task.

'What are we supposed to do now, Annie?' Rose asked, as they stood in the eerily quiet yard early one Sunday morning, dressed in dungarees with a couple of spades they had begged and borrowed. 'I don't know one end of this spade from the other.'

Annie sighed. It was a good question. It was all well and good Churchill instructing the nation to put their garden on war service when the soil was rich and full of humus, but it was an altogether different task when it entailed the transformation of a bombsite!

Some fellas from the council's Heavy Rescue Service had cleared away the masonry and rubble, but the curmudgeonly Works Manager was right. The ground beneath was covered in slivers of broken glass, bricks, shrapnel and scree.

'Well,' said Annie, consulting the *Dig for Victory Leaflet No. 1* she had got from an exhibition down Poplar Town Hall. 'I guess we, um, well, you know, dig.'

'Right you are, Annie,' Pearl said. She dug her spade into the ground, immediately hit a brick and turned her ankle.

'Arghh . . . flaming hell, that hurt!' she cried, hopping about on one foot.

Rose looked at Annie and grimaced. 'Perhaps this is a man's job?'

'That's rot, Rose, and you know it,' Annie replied crossly. 'We just need to put our hearts and our backs into it. Now, where's Millie? She ought to be here by now.'

'Need any help?' called out a voice.

'Ted!'

Marching up the long yard, accompanied by four other off-duty Bryant & May firemen, was Ted, the fireman she'd met on the last night of the Blitz. He'd made good on his promise to help.

'You ain't gonna get very far doing that, girl,' he chuckled. 'What you need is these.'

He held up a dustbin lid pierced with holes, and started shovelling great piles of earth and rubble into it.

'If you sift the earth through this you'll soon get rid of all the glass and shrapnel.'

'You're a genius, Ted,' Annie cheered, and unable to help herself, she planted a kiss on his cheek.

'Grandad's too old for all that, but I'd happily take a kiss off you,' winked a younger fireman.

'Shut your cakehole,' Ted said cheerfully, chucking him a key. 'Now go and get some more tools and some gloves for the girls from the station.'

He turned to the girls, his lovely craggy old face squinting against the bright summer sunshine.

'I won't lie, girls. This is going to murder your backs, wreck your hands and give you calluses on your calluses, but you'll never sleep as well in all your life. Let's get sifting, then we gotta dig. And when we're finished digging, what we gonna do?'

'Get a cup of tea?' Rose asked hopefully.

Roaring with laughter, Ted hitched up his braces and grabbed a spade.

'Nope. We're gonna do some more digging.'

Annie and the girls set to work, sifting and raking through the debris until their hands were black. Even Pip joined in, scampering about, sniffing eagerly and pausing every now and again to dig furiously.

Even when she was working in the top match room, Annie found it impossible to keep her thoughts from ticking over, but something about working out here in the fresh air allowed her mind to roam gloriously free. She was astonished when she realized two hours had passed by in the blink of an eye.

It was amazing how quickly the ground transformed

itself with the help of five firemen – and a dog. As they worked, Annie was stunned to see what the earth revealed, the deeper they dug. All manner of queer treasures were plucked from the ancient soil beneath the yard of the match factory, revealing the area's rich history.

Oyster shells, pottery, stirrups, a set of false teeth, a clay pipe and the remains of a corset lay piled in a heap to one side. Pip even unearthed a piece of old crinoline.

'Well, I'll be,' Ted remarked, digging his spade into the ground with a grunt and leaning against it. 'These works used to be a crinoline factory before Bryant & May took it over in 1861.' He paused and, mopping his brow with a hankie, his gaze was drawn up to the very top of the water towers.

'Grandest factory for miles,' Annie said proudly.

Ted's eyes narrowed, squinting against the midday sun.

'Yeah, and we know whose blood paid for that,' he muttered. '1888. The match girls went on strike and outside these works, Jack the Ripper stalked the streets,' he muttered angrily. 'You'd think there was no other year in history that counted!'

'What do you mean?' Annie asked.

'Folk think the girls' victory saw an end to the suffering of match-makers, but you mark my words, girls, there's hidden tragedies here, buried way deeper than that bit of crinoline.'

His battered old face darkened, but his eyes gleamed brightly like glass.

'Are you all right, Ted?' Annie asked softly.

'Oh, don't listen to me, love,' he sighed, pocketing his hankie. 'I'm nothing but a silly old fool raking over the past.' He picked up his spade and dug it into the ground with a defiant grunt.

'Are you from Bow yourself, Ted?' Rose asked.

'Me? Nah, love. Bethnal Green born and bred.'

'Have you always been a fireman?' Pearl asked.

He nodded. 'Apart from a spell in my grandad's market garden in Kent when I turned seventeen.'

'Why did you leave the East End?' Annie questioned.

'Blimey, the Spanish Inquisition ain't got nothing on you girls!' he chuckled. 'Circumstances required it, shall we say. In the finish, though, I couldn't keep away.'

'You can take the boy out of Bethnal Green . . .' Annie laughed.

'Quite so, Annie,' he replied with a grin. 'And so I landed up back here as a fireman and that, as they say, is what made a man of me.'

A wry grin spread across the old man's cheeks, black earth creasing into the fissures and cracks of his face. 'Forty years fighting fires, thought I'd seen all there was to see with the first war, and yet, here we are again. Jerry obviously don't want us to retire. Ain't that right, Walt?'

One of the older firemen looked up from his spade and nodded.

'Don't reckon so, Ted, no. Do you know, during the last war, the lads in the peeling room found 120 bullets in the butt end of a piece of Belgium poplar that had been delivered to the yard.' He shook his head, either through dismay or horror.

'That was a horrible reminder of the fate of our boys in those trenches. I never thought I'd live to see the day when war itself would come to our doorstep.'

Annie gazed at the old firemen, their hearts freighted with the history of the past. They – much like her dear old nan – had seen too much. Ted and his pals, Elsie . . . They were all too long in the tooth to be fighting fresh wars.

Suddenly Ted's whole face lit up, chasing the sadness out.

'Soil!' he exclaimed, crouching down and scooping up a handful with so much care you'd have thought he'd struck gold.

Their collective sifting and digging had at long last paid off. It might have been untilled, poor and three feet beneath the surface, but it was at least earth in which to start sowing fresh seeds. Pip started to snuffle his wet nose through the damp soil, sneezing noisily, to the laughter of all.

'This looks like a lark, can anyone join in?' trilled a voice from behind.

'There you are, Millie!' Annie exclaimed. 'Whatever are you wearing?'

'What I always wear on a Sunday,' she replied with a shrug.

Millie was head-to-toe glamour, in a pair of improbably high, peep-toe, cyclamen-red suede heels, a skirt that looked like it had been sprayed on and pencilled-in seams up her legs.

'Sorry I'm late, girls,' she blustered. 'Only I was painting my nails. Right, where shall I start?'

'Do you think that's appropriate, Millie, for digging?' asked Rose.

'Yes,' she said defensively, grabbing the nearest spade. 'That's the problem with this war, femininity's going out

the window. You can't tell the hes from the flamin' shes. I
don't mean to be rude, girls, but look at the state of you!'

Annie went to protest, but Ted laid a hand on her arm
and winked.

One hour later, Millie's seams were sweaty smudges
down the backs of her calves, she'd kicked her shoes off and
had resorted to prodding the earth with a hand trowel.

'My nails are ruined,' she moaned, 'and this ground's
hard as rock. Is anything gonna grow here?'

'Potatoes will,' Annie reassured her. 'War Ag fella up the
Town Hall said they yield a good return for small outlay in
money. They just need a lot of double-digging, or "bastard
trenching" as he called it.'

'Certainly bloody that all right,' Millie huffed, plunging
her trowel into the earth with venom. Suddenly, the ground
seemed to tremble and a moment later, a great plume of
water burst from the soil, showering Millie in a filthy
stream.

'Arrgh, help me!' she screeched as the water sent her
cannoning backwards, so she was sprawled on the earth.
Rivulets of muddy water ran down her cheeks, streaking
her make-up.

'She's hit a water pipe!' Ted yelled. 'Walt, run and turn
it off at the mains.'

'Right you are, boss.'

When the water finally slowed to a trickle, Millie tried
to get to her feet but promptly slipped back over into the
muddy swill. Pip leapt on her chest, barking furiously and
licking her face.

The sight was too much. Annie couldn't speak for the
tears of laughter rolling down her cheeks.

'Oh, Millie,' she gasped. 'You don't half look a state!'

Millie clambered to her feet with as much dignity as she could muster.

'I declare the Match Girls' Allotment open,' she announced, bobbing down into a curtsy. 'Now, where can I get my hands on a pair of flaming dungarees?'

Match girls and firemen alike broke into riotous applause and wolf whistles, and Annie realized that the allotment was going to change them all. What she did not know, then, was just how deep and profound those changes, when they came, would be.

As the laughter died down, Annie realized that Ted's smile had slipped. He was staring up the far end of the yard with an unreadable expression. Intrigued, she turned and followed his gaze . . .

'Tea for the workers?' beamed Elsie, setting a flask down onto the ground. She busied herself unpacking giant slabs of seed cake from a brown waxed-paper parcel. 'You must be famished. Millie, whatever's happened to you, dear? You look like you've been rolling in the mud and . . .' Her words trailed off as she locked eyes with Ted.

The emotions that passed over the old woman's face were quite extraordinary. Joy and shock turned to sorrow, then something altogether darker, as if someone had walked over her grave. Elsie's hand flew to the collar of her apron and she took a step back.

'P-Polly?' Ted asked tremulously, wiping his dirty hands down the front of his trousers. 'Polly from Dixie Street? It never is . . .'

With what seemed like an immense effort, Elsie seemed

to recover herself and, picking up the flask, began to busy herself by pouring tea into chipped enamel mugs.

'Sorry, dear,' she said briskly. 'You've got me muddled up with someone else.'

'Really, only I'm sure . . .'

'Quite sure. Never heard of no Polly, I'm afraid. I'm Elsie, Annie's nan.'

Ted took a step back. 'I apologize, Elsie, I must be mistaken. You look just like a lady I used to know. I'm Ted, I've just started working here as a fireman. I'm helping your Annie out, to get their allotment off the ground.'

'Nice to meet you, Ted,' Elsie replied, her mouth pressed into a tight smile. 'Very decent of you to help the girls out, I'm sure.'

Elsie stayed and chatted for a while as they drank the tea, but something about the joyous atmosphere had evaporated in the oppressive heat.

Ten

The next day in the canteen, Rose was giving a particularly tasty piece of suet and bacon pudding her full attention, but Annie had other ideas. After their successful first day in the allotment, the redhead was fired up, her green eyes gleaming with tenacity.

'Now, girls,' she said, rooting around in her bag and producing a plethora of pamphlets and books which she slammed down on the table with a thud. 'This is everything I've collected so far on Dig for Victory. I had a cuppa with Mrs Frobisher yesterday afternoon, and together we've come up with a plan of attack.'

'Blimey, Annie,' Millie said, winking at the girls. 'We're starting an allotment, not manning the trenches.'

'But that's the point, Millie,' Annie protested. 'The more I've learnt, the more I see *this* is our way of fighting back. More food grown here will relieve ships from convoy duty.'

Her face darkened. 'The first year of the war we lost eight hundred tons of food at sea, thanks to the Nazis. Last year, twenty-two thousand tons!'

'Imagine all those lost souls,' said Rose quietly, finding she had lost her appetite. 'To say nothing of all that waste.'

'Exactly,' said Annie. 'Churchill says food wins victories as surely as gunpowder.'

'But this isn't just about food, is it, Annie?' Pearl said perceptively.

'No, Pearl.' Annie sighed. 'I don't know about you girls, but after all we've been through this past year, I feel like all we've done is hide in basements and make matchboxes, while . . .'

Her anger deflated like a balloon and, to Rose's dismay, Annie began to cry.

'My dad's a prisoner of war, I ain't seen my sisters in over a year. My family's been torn apart and I feel so bloody useless.'

'Oh, Annie,' said Millie, reaching her hand across the tabletop and squeezing her fingers. 'I'm sorry, I didn't mean to poke fun at you.'

'Nor me,' said Rose. 'I think it's a smashing idea, and we'll all support you in any way we can. Won't we, girls?'

'Too right,' said Millie. 'We'll make it the best bloody allotment the East End's ever seen.'

Relieved, Annie talked them through the plan she'd fleshed out with Mrs Frobisher. After her morning of digging, Annie had gone to Vicky Park to watch a practical demonstration by an adviser from the borough's horticultural committee at a model allotment. She'd come away brimming with ideas.

Their allotment was to be a registered war charity, affiliated to the National Allotments Society and run by a committee led by the chairman of Bryant & May, Mrs Frobisher, the head of Fairfield Works and Annie. All the produce they grew would be sold to raise funds to support relief organizations, including the Next of Kin Prisoners of War Club run by St John's Ambulance, the British Red Cross and the Women's Voluntary Service.

'Anyone else want to sit on the committee?' Annie asked.

A silence fell over the table.

'We trust you to deal with that side of things, Annie,' Millie remarked, jokingly flexing her biceps. 'You be the brains. We'll be the brawn.'

'Very well. Just think, me, a match girl, on a committee, alongside the chairman,' Annie breathed. 'I hope I don't get tongue-tied at our meetings.'

'What do I always say?' Millie asked.

'Hold your head up?' Annie ventured.

'That's right,' Millie said. 'You're as good as any of them.'

'If not better,' Rose smiled.

'Thanks, girls,' grinned Annie. 'It's so exciting, there's so much to learn. I don't even know where to start,' she gabbled, pulling out more paper from her bag. 'Here's our objectives.'

Rose began to read and quickly felt her head start to swim.

To promote the interests of allotment holders and gardeners.
To cooperate with any committee set up by Government, local authorities and other bodies to further the interests of allotment holders.
To ensure good management of land.
To protect the allotment from damage, trespass and theft.
To take part in the national effort and Dig for Victory.

'We'll develop the site in the yard behind the office block into a ten-rod allotment, and the other one on the site of the old Girls' Club at the recreation ground will be bigger, twice the size.'

Annie was excited now, scarcely pausing for breath. 'We'll have to build a potting shed, a tool shed – oh, and start developing a compost heap at both sites.'

'Where will we get the seeds from?' Pearl asked.

'Seeds, seedlings, fertilizers and insecticides can be bought cost price from the Allotment Subcommittee of the LCC Allotments Council,' Annie remarked, looking pleased with herself.

'I'm sure Woolworths sell Cuthbert's seeds for 1d a packet,' Rose added.

'And how will we divide our time between the two sites?' asked Millie. 'It's quite a trek from the yard to the recreation ground.'

'Easy,' Annie grinned. 'Mrs Frobisher's bagged two bikes from the factory cycling club. They're only rattly old sit-up-and-beg affairs, but it'll mean we can zip between the two sites.'

'Annie, this is great and all, but it's an awful lot of work for four girls,' Rose added cautiously. 'We can't expect Ted and his men to always spare time to help us out.'

'Aah, but we won't be on our own, Rose,' Annie replied. 'Mrs Frobisher'll be asking for volunteers from the factory, local businesses and schools. Also, she's looked into it and, apparently, there's something called a soldier-gardener scheme, which means trained gardeners in units can be detailed on their leave to work in Dig for Victory schemes.'

'Nice, we'll have a bit of muscle about the place,' Millie said, raising one eyebrow.

'Behave, you,' Annie said, poking her. 'Also, the Ministry of Agriculture have formed the Young Farmers' Club, and might be able to send a chap with a bit of know-how to help out. As long as they're photographed for a propaganda piece.'

'Sounds like we won't be short of helping hands,' Pearl said.

'Or men!' added Millie, grinning slyly. 'On the subject of which, look what I found pinned to the noticeboard this morning.'

Rose groaned inwardly. She knew that smile usually meant trouble.

Millie pulled out a letter from her tunic pocket and, clearing her throat, began to read.

'We are two sailors desperate to hear from girls. We neither of us receive any mail whatsoever, unless it's an income tax form. As you may well imagine, it's not very pleasant to sit on the mess deck, watching other chaps read letters, while we have to make do with copies of the Daily Mirror—'

'Millie,' Annie interrupted, 'we're supposed to be talking about the allotment, remember!'

'Yeah, yeah, let me just finish this,' Millie replied, returning to her letter.

'To get down to brass tacks, we would appreciate letters from girls, preferably unmarried and, if possible, girls

who are not on the top line to be married, especially if their blokes are big. Here follows a short description. Modesty is the best policy. Alfie, 23. Grey eyes, brown hair, fresh complexion, no false teeth. Val, 22 years old, hazel eyes, fair hair, used to belong to the Wolf Cubs. If you write, we promise to use your matches. Here's hoping. Cheerio.'

Millie finished and clutched the letter to her tunic. 'How can you ignore that? Poor Alfie and Val.'

'Count me out,' Annie replied, 'I'm going to be far too busy with the allotment.'

'Me too,' Rose added. 'I've got Pip, and he's the only man in my life.'

Millie rolled her eyes. 'Honestly, Rose dear. You can't marry a dog!'

She turned to Pearl.

'How about it?'

'How about what?' she asked, draining her cup of tea.

'Writing back to one of these chaps. You never know where it might lead.'

'I'm not really interested, thanks all the same, Millie.'

'But you've kissed a fella before, surely?'

''Course! But . . .'

'Hand up the jumper?'

'Millie!' Rose scolded. She did love Millie, but there were times when her volubility went too far.

Pearl's mouth tightened.

'Just leave it, will you? I told you, I'm not interested.'

She scraped her chair back from the table.

'I'm gonna get a book out the library before the dinner bell goes,' she muttered. 'I'll see you upstairs.'

Millie looked at the girls, wide-eyed, as Pearl swept off. 'What did I say?'

'Pearl's a bit sensitive and sometimes, Millie, you're about as subtle as a brick,' Rose remarked.

She shrugged. 'I was only trying to do her a favour.'

'Do you think there's something a bit, well, odd about Pearl?' Annie asked, lowering her voice. 'She's a terrific girl and all, but I've lived and worked alongside her now for nine weeks and I still don't really know anything about her. She's not had a scrap of mail from her family neither.'

'I've been her pen pal for ages, and she never gave nothing away in her letters,' said Millie. 'I get this queer feeling, like we're not getting the full story.'

'Girls,' said Rose softly. 'Pearl's lost her home. It took real guts to come here and leave behind her life in Liverpool. She's shy, that's all. I think we need to show her some compassion.'

'But she never says anything about her life in . . .'

Annie's voice was drowned out by the bell. The room filled with the clatter of chairs being pushed back as hundreds of match girls readied themselves to return to their stations.

Sandra paused by their table, surrounded by a cluster of her mates. Sandra and her pals worked on Safety Matches – the housewife's favourite – at the other end of the top match floor. As Rose and the girls worked on Swan Vestas – the smoker's favourite – a division had sprung up between them, with each group feeling slightly superior to the other.

'All right, girls,' Sandra said, with a sly smile. 'What's all this about you starting an allotment? Never had you down as green-fingered, Millie.'

Millie's eyes narrowed. She still hadn't forgiven Sandra for her bitchy remark when she'd spotted her advert on the bombed bus.

'You should join us, Sandra, bit of fresh air do your complexion the world of good, love.'

Sandra's eyes glittered.

'Maybe I will,' she said beadily.

Sandra went to move off but as an afterthought added: 'Perhaps you should spend more time at home keeping your husband satisfied, then he wouldn't need to go to the fleapit so much.'

'Meaning?'

'Meaning Betty Connor's obviously giving him something you can't.'

'Why, you little . . .' Millie was on her feet in a flash, ripping Sandra's hairnet off and a fistful of her blonde hair with it.

The fight was over before it even began. Annie and Rose pulled Millie off and the elderly canteen manager hauled Sandra off the floor.

'For pity's sake, girls,' she said wearily. 'I didn't come out of retirement to break up fights! Show some respect. Our ancestors went on strike back in 1888 to fight for the right to this canteen, and here's you lot, fighting in it like cats in a courtyard.'

An embarrassed silence fell over the group.

'Sorry,' mumbled Millie.

'Me an' all,' said Sandra.

'Anyone wanna make a complaint, take it down to Mrs Frobisher,' she ordered, pointing at the door.

Millie and Sandra both shook their heads. A strict code of honour between the match girls meant that neither would ever make a complaint against the other. The only thing dented was Millie's pride. As they made to leave the canteen, Rose spotted Pearl watching from a distance, clutching a library book between her fingers, her face slum white.

*

When the hooter rang at 5 p.m. Millie couldn't face joining the throngs of match girls streaming up Old Ford back in the direction of the Roman Road. Instead, she made her excuses and slipped down to the canalside.

The walk home was longer this way, but after the racket on the assembly line and her bust-up with Sandra, she needed peace and quiet to think. Pulling a cigarette from behind her hairnet, she lit up and inhaled deeply. The late afternoon sunshine was warm and syrupy, seeping straight into her bones, better than any medicine Annie's nan could give her.

As she walked, she gazed at the oily film on the surface of the water and her thoughts turned to her husband. The humiliation she had felt over Curly's affair paled in comparison with the knowledge that everyone knew he'd been playing away. She hated that her inadequacies as a wife were being discussed on every street corner in Bow. Now it was common knowledge in the factory. She hadn't discussed it with Curly. What was the point?

Since his affair with Betty had begun, he was home less and less now. He'd never kept regular hours at the best of times. Often he didn't come home at all, and that suited Millie just fine. It was saving her a job, after all. What hurt the deepest was the knowledge that her youth was passing her by. Soon, she'd be an old woman getting her long-service medal at Bryant & May.

The Blitz, as dreadful as it had been – and Millie would never admit to this in public – had in some queer way provided a flash of excitement, the potential for change. Now it was over and they were back to the same dreary old routine: grey bread, powdered egg and dehydrated meat. Perhaps Annie was right to get them growing their own. Food was so scarce now, Millie barely recognized the anonymous lumps that ended up on her plate. Everything was mock these days: mock apricot flan, with carrots instead of apricots; mock cream made with marge and cornflour . . . Nothing on earth was as fraudulent as her marriage, though. In fact – and the thought made her laugh as she tossed a stone into the canal with a splash – her wedding had been the marital equivalent of powdered egg. Fake, quick and tasteless.

Millie stared at the ripples spreading over the surface of the water. What if she'd married someone she actually cared for? How different would things be now? Samuel's beautiful face danced painfully through her mind. He had come in and out of her life so fast, she half wondered if she hadn't dreamt him up. He'd never written, but then, had she really expected him to? She stared up into the delphinium-blue skies as if she half expected to see his Halifax fly overhead.

Flicking her fag butt into the canal, Millie sighed and headed for home. Back in Parnell Road, she was just letting herself in, only to find a woman was already opening the door. Curly was showing her out. She must have been in her fifties, dressed sensibly in a headscarf and lisle stockings despite the fierce heat. Not Curly's usual type.

She froze when she spotted Millie.

'I'm . . . I'm very sorry, Mrs Brown,' she mumbled, before turning and scurrying up the street.

'Betty's mum?' Millie sighed, shutting the door behind her. 'Sorting out your dirty business, I presume?'

Curly lingered, his dark eyes fathomless in the gloom of the passage.

'You know then? About the baby?'

''Course I know,' she said with a hard, bitter laugh. 'The way you've been carrying on, you might as well have announced it on the front page of the *Advertiser*.'

Curly shrugged.

'What's it to be, then?' Millie spat, unbuttoning her summer coat. 'Hatpin Bella or off to visit an auntie in the countryside for nine months? Poor cow.'

'Neither . . .'

Millie inhaled sharply. 'You can't mean . . .'

'She ain't getting rid of no son of mine.'

'But . . . but then?'

'I've come to an agreement with her mother, see. Betty lies low, then when the baby comes, the whole family are moving to Essex. Starting over. Her married sister'll pass him off as hers, so there's no talk, and I get to visit Betty and the baby whenever I like.'

Millie felt cut to the heart.

'But how do you think that makes me feel? W–what will people say? I'll be a laughing stock!'

'I don't care,' he said coldly, lighting up a cigarette. 'Next month we'll have been married two years, Millie, and you haven't given me a son yet. You ain't lived up to your side of the bargain. In fact,' and here he started to laugh, 'I should do you for breach of contract.'

'What's it matter now?' Millie replied, staring at a piece of flaking plaster on the wall behind Curly's ear. 'You'll be getting your son and heir soon enough.'

'Oh, no, no, no, Millie. It ain't the same. I want a legitimate son.'

'Don't make me laugh,' she scoffed. 'You wouldn't know legitimate if it came up and slapped you round the face.'

She moved away but Curly pulled her back, shoving her forcefully against the wall of the passage and forcing the breath from her lungs.

'You really are a piece of work, Millie,' he said, his fingers twisting tighter round the neck of her tunic. 'I ought to jollop you until your arse bleeds.'

A dull rage crept up inside her.

'Go on then!' she bellowed. 'Do it! Bloody do it! I dare you! Give me a black eye to match the other one you give me, see what folk round here make of that. Plays away *and* beats his wife.'

Curly released his grip and stepped back.

'Do you know what you are?' she hissed, mustering her last shred of strength.

Curly took a deep suck on his cigarette, amused.

'Enlighten me . . .'

'You think you're a twenty-four-carat villain, but you're

nothing but a common street tough from Whitechapel. You ain't got the guts of a flea.'

'Is that right?' he said slowly. 'Well, *you* think 'cause you're from Bow that you're a cut above.' His black eyes narrowed in spite. 'Well, let me tell you, sweetheart, you might have had your face on the back of the number 8 when I met you, but you were still a match girl. And you still are now. Only older.'

A rapacious leer spread across the bones of his cheeks. 'You ain't off the hook. I want a baby, Millie. And you're giving me one.'

With that, he grabbed his jacket, turned and walked out. Trembling, Millie stood on the doorstep and watched as he walked down the length of Parnell Road. He had a swing to his walk, a cocky strut that marked out the territory as his own. In that moment, she wished him dead.

'Monkey talks, bullshit walks,' she muttered under her breath, before slamming the door.

Eleven

For the rest of that long, hot, sultry summer of 1941, the girls worked harder than they ever had in their lives, hands growing tougher and arms more muscled with each passing day. Elsie propped them all up with mugs of strong tea and slabs of home-made cake.

Their efforts were paying off, though, and gradually the allotments were beginning to take shape. The ground had now been completely cleared on both sites, and Pearl was surprised to find how much she sought sanctuary in the hard labour involved in the constant double-digging of the ground.

The girls weren't at it alone either. All over the land, allotments were springing up in the most unusual places, from railway sidings to rooftops, but Pearl only really cared about theirs. The Girls' Club allotment, as they had christened it, was the bigger site. Annie had such grand plans for it, including a chicken run and rabbit hutches. But it was the second, smaller, site in the factory yard, nestled against the warm, south-facing brick wall of the adjoining office block, that Pearl loved best. She and Annie often came here at 6 a.m., to put in an hour of digging before their morning shift began.

'I love this time of the day,' said Annie, echoing her friend's thoughts as they gazed out over the still and misty yard.

'Beautiful, all right,' agreed Pearl, filling her nostrils with the scent of poplar wood and creosote. The sky over the factory was brilliant, striated with bands of palest lemon and peach as a new day dawned over Bow.

Annie blearily pulled her unruly bramble of red curls back with a headscarf and handed Pearl a paintbrush. Ted had made a fence out of scrap to surround the allotment, and Annie wanted to get a second coat of creosote on it before the hooter went.

'Ted reckons we're nearly ready to start sowing some winter crops,' Annie remarked as they set to work. 'But Nan reckons we need to dig in more compost first.'

'Your nan and her compost!' Pearl laughed as she painted.

They both glanced over to Elsie's compost heap, which lay gently steaming in the morning mist. The elderly lady had taken it upon herself to be the unofficial queen of compost at both sites. Scarcely a day had passed when she hadn't turned up at the factory with a smouldering bucket in one hand and a shovel in the other.

Nothing escaped Elsie's eagle eye. Tea leaves, horse and cattle dung, feathers, cuttings of hair swept from the floor of salons, even spent hops from Truman's Brewery . . . They all went into the mix, and each day the heap crept a bit higher.

'I think your nan's right, mind you,' Pearl said, slapping away an insect. 'When you've got no proper topsoil, triple-digging and laying in lots of compost is the only way to make sure the ground's properly aerated. We gotta make the soil nice and rich if we want anything to grow.

'Tell you what, though,' she added. 'We won't half get some lovely tomatoes up against that brick wall next summer if we put the work in now.'

'You know an awful lot about gardening, Pearl,' Annie remarked.

'Told you, my dad used to have an allotment. I used to help him out when I was a little girl,' she replied.

'Tell me about your family, Pearl. I hardly know a thing about your life back in Liverpool.'

Pearl shrugged. 'Not much to say, really. Dad hasn't worked since his accident at the docks so Mum does what she can, dressmaking and so on, to get by.'

'Don't you miss them?' Annie probed.

Pearl felt her fingers tighten round the brush and willed back the tears.

'Everyone's parted from someone they love at the moment,' she said quietly.

'Is there a sweetheart somewhere?' Annie ventured.

'No,' she said sharply, standing up and wiping her hands down the front of her dungarees. 'I think that should do it. I'd kill for a brew before we start work.'

'All right, let's leave it for now,' agreed Annie.

Once inside the loo, Pearl locked the door and leant heavily against the cold tiled wall. She wished Annie hadn't brought up her mam and dad. She had been carrying round their letter in her pocket for days now, since it had arrived at the factory. It had been delivered along with her wage packet last Friday.

Sighing, she pulled the crumpled letter out of her

dungarees pocket. It was senseless to read it again, but like picking at a scab, she couldn't resist.

Dear Pearl,

Your dad and I are writing this letter in the hope it might reach you. We telephoned the Welfare Department at Fairfield Works, pleaded with them to tell us whether you're working there. But staff records are confidential, apparently, so we've resorted to writing this, in the hope that you are working there.

Your dad and I have written to every factory we can think of where you might get work. Because in our hearts, we know that you're alive. We know that it's you who sent the parcel of money. We've visited your lodgings, scoured every inch of it for clues as to where you went. I've sat in your bedroom for hours, trying to imagine what was going through your mind the day you vanished.

My darling girl. We understand your reasons for leaving. We know you felt you had no choice. We don't blame you.

There is no easy way to tell you this, but your dad, he has aged so much since your disappearance. He barely leaves his bed now. The accident, the doctors say, is what's causing it, but they say he'll be lucky to survive another year. Come home, dearest one, I beg of you. No harm will come to you here.

Your devoted Mam
xxx

Pearl closed her eyes as two tears squeezed beneath her eyelids and slid down her cheeks. Tears for the parents she knew she would never see again, for despite her dad's ill health, she knew she could never return home. Not now. Not ever. It wouldn't be fair to tangle them up in her mess.

'Pearl, love, you nearly ready?' Annie's voice echoed round the lavatory.

'Coming,' she replied and, scrunching the letter up, she flushed it down the toilet.

*

Friday evening after work, and instead of dressing up in her glad rags, Millie was changing into a pair of dungarees and pulling back her platinum-blonde hair into a cherry-red scarf.

'I might have to dress like a fella,' she grumbled, pulling out a tube of red lipstick her mate at the Yardley factory in nearby Stratford had slipped her, 'but it don't mean I have to look like one.'

Annie laughed. 'Lipstick? Seriously, Millie? For digging in compost!'

'You wanna try it, Annie,' she replied, painting on a thick slick of carmine red and blotting it with some loo roll.

'Red's a bit risqué, ain't it?' Rose replied as she washed her hands with a slither of Sunlight soap.

'That's the one good thing about this war, Rose sweetheart,' Millie said, popping her lipstick back in her purse and snapping it shut with a shrug. 'If I'd worn this shade before, I'd be called a slut. Now I'm patriotic.'

Annie laughed at her friend's chutzpah, as Mr Rosen

would call it. Despite living with a spiv of a husband, and being neglected by her blousy mother, or perhaps because of it, Millie was irrepressible.

'Come on. Miss Frobisher wants to introduce us to two important visitors at the Girls' Club site.'

'Who?' asked Rose, as she finished drying her hands on the roller towel.

Annie shrugged. 'Search me.'

Outside in the yard, a heavy summer downpour was bashing the bricks, and streams of demob-happy match girls ran down the yard, coats and cardigans pulled over their heads.

Millie kicked off the brake on one of the rattly old boneshakers on loan from the factory and raised her voice over the still-shrieking hooter.

'Right, who's going backy with me?'

'You can't be serious?' Pearl laughed.

'Come on, hop on,' Millie urged. 'It's a ten-minute walk to the Girls' Club.'

'I'm game,' Annie laughed, grabbing the handlebars of the other bike and getting on. 'Rose, you get on the back of mine.'

'You're a case, Millie Brown,' Rose giggled as she swung her leg over and wrapped her arms round Annie's slender waist.

Soon all four girls were speeding along the yard on the bicycles, dodging tractors and strong men hauling timber, with the wind ruffling their headscarves. After the heat in the top match room, it was the most glorious feeling of freedom. The fresh summer rain speckled Millie's cheeks and a mad rush of spontaneity gripped her.

'Millie!' Pearl yelled from behind. 'What you playing at? Put your feet back on the pedals!'

But the match girl was in no mood to play it safe.

Tipping her head back, she rang the bell and whooped into the wind. The gatehouse flashed past and Millie just about made out the shocked faces of the girls on Safety Matches.

'Swan Vesta girls coming through!' she hollered, frantically ringing her bell. 'Make way!'

Sandra's face was a picture as she stumbled back to avoid them, landing in an indecorous heap in the gutter.

'Sorry!' Millie called over her shoulder, not looking sorry at all.

They jolted out onto the cobbles of Old Ford Road, narrowly avoiding a street hawker and a man delivering goods to Baggots the drapers. The sight of four match girls in dungarees on bikes caused a stir outside the tram shed.

'Oi! Give us a lift, girls!' whistled a driver.

'You'd never get your leg over!' Millie hollered back, blowing them a kiss. Four kids chased them in hot pursuit before finally giving up.

'Did you see Sandra's face?' yelled Annie from behind. Her red hair had broken free from its swaddling and was billowing around her face likes flames. 'I thought she was going to burst a blood vessel.'

'Yeah, she was well jibbed,' Millie cackled, pumping the pedals faster.

'Slow down,' Pearl warned. 'We're about to go under the, rarrghhh . . .'

They whizzed under the smoky railway arch, skidding over the rain-soaked cobbles, just as a huge steam train thundered overhead hauling tons of matchsticks from the factory.

Pearl closed her eyes as Millie blazed past the Bryant & May wharf to a fanfare of wolf whistles, past the shocked face of the guard on the warden's post, straight across the bowling green of the recreation grounds, before skidding to a halt before a small group assembled at the allotment.

'You're barmy,' Pearl laughed. 'I'm soaked.'

'You're soaked?' Millie laughed throatily, dismounting and flapping her trouser leg. 'Look at me. I'm so wet, the rain's running out the arse of my trousers!'

'Millie,' Mrs Frobisher scolded. 'What did I say about your language? We have visitors.'

For the first time Millie noticed the two men standing either side of the Welfare Superintendent.

An earnest, fresh-faced man in a tweed jacket, and standing the other side . . .

'Samuel!' she breathed in astonishment. 'Bugger me! Sorry, Mrs F. B–but what are you doing here?'

The effect of seeing him standing in front of her was so overwhelming, she didn't know what else to say. Instead she threw her arms around him.

'Millie,' he laughed, when he had finally disentangled himself. 'That was some entrance.'

'You clearly remember Samuel Taylor of the RAF from his previous visit,' Mrs Frobisher remarked, looking perplexed.

''Course we do,' Annie beamed, stepping forward to shake his hand. 'Samuel here rescued my nan on the last night of the Blitz. He's an absolute hero. But what are you doing back?'

'Mrs Frobisher wrote to my CO asking whether there were any trained gardeners in our unit who might like to assist with Bryant & May's allotment on their leave.'

He shrugged. 'I get six days or so, every six weeks. This ought to be the perfect respite from dummy runs and learning Morse code, so here I am.'

There he was indeed. A shining six foot one of impossible vigour. It had been sixteen weeks since Millie had last seen the trainee pilot – not that she was counting – and he was even more handsome than she remembered.

She scarcely registered being introduced to Tom Beckton, from the National Federation of Young Farmers, or the knowing look which passed between Annie and Rose. Samuel was back. And nothing else mattered.

*

By the time the rain dried up and the warmth of the early evening sun burnt through the clouds, the ground was steaming and the air was ripe with smells. The ground wasn't the only thing hotting up. Rose caught Annie's eye and knew she was thinking exactly the same thing.

Ted had come over to meet the new recruits and was listening with interest as Samuel crouched down in the middle of the allotment.

'Do you really think you'll get anything to grow here, Samuel?' Ted asked. 'This place took a high explosive on the first night of the Blitz. I dread to think how toxic the earth must be.'

'Took me years to get the soil right in my old garden down in Sussex, so don't expect miracles,' admitted

Samuel. 'But with a little love and care, vegetables ought to grow here all right.' He rubbed the blackened ball of his thumb lovingly across the earth. 'Handled right and treated with a little love and tenderness, anything can flourish.'

He glanced up at Millie, his golden face bathed in late summer sunshine and the air between them shimmered. He might have been addressing the group, but his eyes were all for Millie. Rose looked away, embarrassed.

'Samuel's right,' Tom replied, oblivious to their obvious chemistry. 'We'll help you all we can, but what's really important is making sure we plant to provide vegetables all year round, not just in the summer months. The Ministry of Agriculture keeps stressing the importance of avoiding a glut of summer vegetables and harvesting nothing in the lean winter months. I've got a copy of their cropping plan,' he grinned enthusiastically, producing a pamphlet from his trouser pocket. 'It's perfect for a plot this size.'

He glanced over at Rose and smiled shyly. She smiled back, and at once his cheeks coloured. Standing next to Samuel, Tom looked like a boy, though Rose guessed he must be around eighteen.

As they started digging, she found herself falling into easy conversation with the shy young man.

'Where are you from, Tom?'

'Bideford in Devon, don't expect you'll have heard of it,' he replied.

'But of course I have,' she grinned, looking up from her spade. 'We went there with Bryant & May on a company outing one summer. We all got a free bucket and spade and a marzipan fish. I dropped mine under the seat of the charabanc, though . . .

'Funny what you remember,' she added, feeling suddenly foolish. 'Still, the rest of it was glorious. I should never get enough of living by the sea, and all that space.'

'Afraid farmers don't get much chance to go bathing, Rose,' he replied stiffly. 'Too busy working on my father's farm.'

'Must be hard work.'

He shrugged, suddenly looking very self-conscious. 'I should have liked to join the RAF, like Samuel, but farming's a reserved occupation, so I'm having a very soft war.'

'Farming's very important, I'm sure,' Rose said reassuringly.

'Not much to tell the grandkids, though, is it?' he said ruefully. 'Still, at least I get to come to places like this and help out. I've been doing my bit over in Bethnal Green too – they're getting something going called the Bethnal Green Bombed Sites Producers' Association.'

'Bet that's a bit different to what you're used to,' Rose said.

'I should say. I'm hopeless in cities,' he grinned, pushing back a mop of sandy hair. 'I miss my Betsy something rotten, too.'

'Is Betsy your sweetheart?' Rose asked.

Tom started to laugh. He had a lovely laugh, rich and infectious and, for the first time, he seemed to forget himself.

'Good grief, no! She has breath that could strip paint and she's forever weeing on my mum's rug. Betsy's my sixteen-year-old Jack Russell,' he explained, seeing Rose's confused expression.

'Oh, I've a Jack Russell too!' she exclaimed. 'Pip. He's smashing. I found him. Or, rather, he found me.'

'I should love to meet him, Rose.'

'Oh, but you should,' she replied, glancing up from her digging. 'Hang about, I've an idea. Where are you staying?'

'I'm only here for another week, and I'm lodging with a landlady down Bow Road.'

'Annie!' Rose called across the allotment to where her friend was deep in conversation about crop rotations with Ted and Samuel. 'You know Elsie's cooking for us tonight. Do you think she'd mind one more?'

''Course not, and you're more than welcome too, Ted. And you too, Samuel.'

'You sure your nan won't mind?' Ted asked cautiously.

'Not a bit. She loves a full house, and she's doing beans and barley, which'll always stretch.'

'Handsome! Count me in,' Ted replied. 'That's proper grub to take the wrinkles out yer tummy, that is.'

'Sounds lovely,' Samuel chuckled as he dug his spade deep into the earth, 'but I promised I'd help out at the evening soup kitchen my lodgings run.'

'Millie?'

Millie cast a sideways glance at Samuel, admiring the strong curve of his back as he worked. 'I oughtn't to, really.'

*

When the sun started to fade from the sky, the small and disparate group of allotment workers downed tools.

'Reckon we can safely say we've Dug for Victory,' Ted puffed, rubbing his battered face with the heel of his hand.

'Dug for Victory?' Millie laughed, stretching out her back. 'Dug for dear life, more like. I'm bloody exhausted.'

'You sure you won't join us, Millie?' Annie asked.

'Your nan'll have enough on her plate feeding you lot,' she grinned. 'You go on. I'll knock for you in the morning.'

'Cheerio,' Samuel called to Ted, Annie, Rose, Pearl and Tom as they gathered their things together. They made their way across the former recreation grounds in the direction of the warden's post that straddled the factory grounds and connected it to the street beyond. As the group faded from earshot, Millie realized how quiet it suddenly was, the only sound the warden's Ferranti wireless crackling into the inky blue evening. The air was so soft and still. The outline of the factory's water towers loomed in the hazy dusk, beyond them countless barrage balloons swaying gently over East London.

'Listen,' Samuel said gently, touching her shoulder. She jumped, goosebumps shivering over the naked flesh on her forearms.

'"Yours",' she whispered, turning to face him.

'They were playing this in the cafe, the evening we met,' he said, looking down into her eyes. 'Millie?'

'Yes?'

'I hope you don't think I'm forward offering to help out on your allotment, especially after you never replied to my letters.'

He paused, searching for the right words.

'I understand why you didn't. You're married, it wouldn't have been appropriate and I didn't mean to put you in a difficult situation. Only . . .'

Millie's heart gave a sudden twist in her chest.

'Only, I had to see you again.'

'I didn't get any letters, Samuel!' she cried. 'I promise.'

The information hung between them like a grenade. There was no need to expend too much energy attempting to work out where the letters were, but she didn't want to bring the spectre of *him* into the intimacy of this moment.

Samuel's eyes, so gentle, shone with hope.

'I'd have written back,' she whispered.

'I had a feeling. Please don't go, Millie. Not yet. Will you walk with me a while?'

They took the turning out of Wrexham Road and walked in the shadows in the direction of Samuel's lodgings in Bromley-by-Bow. The streets were silent and serene, blanketed in the gauzy twilight. A soft mauve light deepened to indigo over the jumble of factory chimneys, as if someone had draped the gritty urban landscape with a silken cloth. It was a beautiful summer's evening. Millie tore off her headscarf and a gentle breeze caught her glossy blonde curls.

'This is a bit different to the last time we were together,' he said.

'There's a lot that's changed since we last saw each other,' she remarked, thinking of how her husband had knocked up an usherette!

'I'll say. This church took a hammering,' he remarked, pausing outside the dark remains of Bow Church.

Millie nodded. 'The same night we met. I don't think I'll forget that night as long as I live, will you?'

But Samuel didn't answer; his attention had been caught by a handsome bronze statue of William Gladstone in the churchyard. Blunt against the greening bronze, the statue's right hand was painted red.

'Why's someone done that?' Samuel asked, puzzled at the strange act of vandalism.

'East End legend.'

'Do tell,' he replied, smiling. 'I love a good story.'

'Bryant & May financed this statue as a gift back in 1882,' Millie said, kicking the plinth with her boot. 'Well, I say gift, but it was the match girls who funded it. Each girl had a shilling docked from her wages to pay for the statue. Some say their wages went towards the water fountain outside the station, others this thing.'

'Democratic,' Samuel said wryly.

'Exactly,' Millie nodded. 'Rumour has it at the unveiling some of the girls cut their hands with stones and bloodied the statue in protest. They scrubbed it off, but it keeps getting painted red, even to this day.'

'Who does it?'

She shrugged. 'There's a lot round here who won't forgive or forget the way women used to be treated at the factory. A lot of the old-timers who remember the strike do it in tribute.'

Samuel nodded. 'Aah, the infamous match girls. Ted was telling me all about their strike earlier . . . seems the memory of it lingers.'

'Yeah, well, I suppose he would be old enough to remember it,' Millie replied.

'He was seven years old or so, says he saw the striking women marching down the Mile End Waste, singing songs and holding their banners.'

'Then he'd have seen my nan, Nelly,' Millie said proudly. 'Family folklore has it she was on the strike committee. I could believe it an' all. Proud Irish woman, she was. She and her kind were exploited something rotten, but she knew how to fight her corner.'

'Was it really that bad?' Samuel asked.

'And worse . . .' she snapped. 'Match girls like me working for a bloody pittance. Girls getting laid off the moment they showed any sign of getting phossy jaw. Imagine the bones in your jaw putrefying and crumbling until your face is all but falling off . . .' She tailed off and choked back an angry sob.

'I'm sorry, Millie,' Samuel whispered, laying a gentle hand on her shoulder. 'I didn't mean to upset you.'

She drew in a deep breath.

'It's all right. I think I'm more upset that I never asked my nan more about it while I had the chance,' she replied. 'When you're young, you don't care about the past and then by the time you realize how important it is, there's no one left to ask questions of.'

'Tell me what you know of Nelly,' Samuel asked, sensing how important her nan was to her.

'I don't remember that much, she died of the dropsy when I was a nipper.' A proud smile suddenly lit up the match girl's face. 'I can still see her now, mind you, in my mind's eye. Velvet hat pinned on her head like a clam shell, all proud and upright with a feather on top.' Millie laughed like a drain. 'Do you know, I once saw her knock a man out with one punch.'

'Tough lady!' he exclaimed.

'She had to be.'

'So that's where you get your fighting spirit from!'

'Well, I certainly didn't get it from my mum,' Millie spat. 'She never raised so much as a finger to save me from

Curly. My nan Nelly would never have stood by and let it happen.'

'Hang on, Millie,' Samuel frowned. 'What are you saying? You never wanted to marry?'

'It's complicated, Samuel,' she muttered, folding her arms. 'Forget I said anything.'

Samuel glanced up at the reddened hand of the statue that loomed over them.

'Some stories can't be rubbed out, Millie. I'm a good listener.'

Millie narrowed her eyes and stared past the statue, into the gloaming.

'Quick,' she said suddenly, grabbing his hand and pulling him away. 'Don't turn around, just walk. Fast.'

'What is it?' he asked, bemused, as they strode quickly away from the church.

'It's one of Curly's cronies. He can't see me with you. Run!'

With her hand still clutched in his, they ran as fast as they could along the Bow Road, ducking under Tom Thumb's Arch, pelting through the maze of streets and factories until, finally, they paused outside the ruins of another church.

'What if he comes this way?' Samuel asked.

'In here,' Millie urged, breathless with exhilaration.

Pulling him into the damp darkness of the ruined church, Millie was aware of her shallow breath and thumping heart. She looked down at her naked fingers, pale and slender, entwined through his, and realized she had stepped over an invisible line.

Wordlessly, they walked down what remained of the aisle,

past a sycamore, whose winged branches rose up to the gaunt skeleton beams. Moonlight flooded in through the roofless church and the jagged walls rose starkly into the heavy indigo sky.

'How strange this place is,' Samuel whispered, staring in wonder at the bracken, moss and wild plants that blanketed the pews like a ghostly green carpet.

An elderberry tree smothered in black, juicy berries rose up behind the lectern, and some starlings, which were nesting in the font, took fright at the intruders and flapped into the night.

'It's beautiful,' he murmured, tracing his hands through the fronds of a fern. 'There must be dozens of varieties of ferns and herbs here. The spores must have been carried from Epping Forest in the wind.'

The potent smell of fungus and something altogether richer and earthier permeated the fecund darkness.

'It's like another world,' he breathed. 'What is this church?'

'St Stephen's,' Millie said, gazing about her.

'Hard to imagine brides gliding down this aisle, right where we're standing.'

Millie suddenly turned to him, her face haunted in the ethereal light.

'I did.'

'You mean . . .'

She nodded slowly. 'This is where I married Curly. One month before war broke out.'

She stared down at the mosaic of grimy tiles on the floor, at the willowherb pushing its way up through the cracks.

'Did you ever love your husband?'

'No,' she confessed.

'So why marry him?'

Something about the hushed atmosphere in the church was compelling Millie to speak the truth. 'I had to,' she said quietly. 'Jimmy – that's my older brother – got into debt. Bad debt at Curly's spieler . . . Gambling club,' she added, sensing Samuel's confusion. 'Stupid sod never did know when to call it a day.'

She gulped, pushing back the tide of angry tears.

'Curly said he'd waive the debt if I agreed to marry him. He'd had his eye on me for years, apparently.'

'B-but that's awful! How could your mother permit it to go ahead?'

Millie shrugged.

'What did she care? Jimmy's debt wiped clean. Daughter married off. One less mouth to feed. It was a win-win situation for her.'

'What kind of a mother could allow that?' he gasped.

'One who's as sharp as a butcher's knife. Besides, it didn't really matter what she said. I had to do it. I knew exactly what would happen to Jimmy if I didn't.'

Angrily, she kicked a stray stone, which ricocheted against the wall, sending a flock of pigeons roosting in the tower soaring into the heavens.

'Millie, I-I really don't know what to say,' Samuel said softly.

'What can you say? What can anyone say? My chump of a brother gets in over his head, and I have to pay the price.' She snorted. 'When it comes to Curly, everyone has a price attached.'

'It's just so . . . so wrong. Your family sacrificed you to some sort of racketeer!'

Millie was about to fire back a smart comment about how most women's lives are ones of sacrifice, but found she couldn't. Because all of a sudden, Samuel's hands were on the straps of her dungarees, pulling her body towards his chest. The flesh of his fingers was tilting her chin upwards. In the darkness, his warm mouth found hers.

Right there in church, under a lustrous summer moon, he kissed her tenderly and all of her anger, her fears and frustrations melted to nothing.

Twelve

Annie swore her nan had rigged up some sort of radar from number 33 Blondin Street.

'Good. You're home,' the elderly lady remarked as she flung open the front door before Annie's hand had even touched the handle.

'Be a treasure and run this up to Mrs Donnelly at number 16,' she ordered, pressing a warm pot at Annie. 'She can't pay her rent this week and she's been seen picking up specks down the Roman.'

'Specks?' Pearl asked.

'Bits of bruised fruit and veg from the market floor,' Ted said, stepping out from behind Annie.

The smile froze on Elsie's face.

'You don't mind, do you, Nan?' Annie asked worriedly. 'Me inviting Ted and this young chap, Tom, for tea? I know it's an ask, Nan, but they've been ever such a help to us on the allotment today.'

Elsie recovered herself quickly, but her smile was guarded. 'Any friend of Annie's is a friend of mine,' she replied, throwing open the door. 'I've your mum over too, Rose dear, but I dare say we'll all squash in.'

'Thanks, Elsie. I've brought my tea rations and a bit of salted butter I'd been saving,' Ted said, holding up a bag.

Inside the warm, tumbledown terrace, Elsie served up a meal cooked with love. Bean and barley soup, which had been simmering away for hours, and fish, which Maureen had brought, smoked over wild garlic and rosemary that Elsie had found growing on a railway siding. Sweet was a slither of honey cake.

'Every mouthful is like a velvet kiss,' Tom sighed, casting a sideways look at Rose, who blushed, her dark eyes sparkling in the firelight.

'A velvet kiss indeed,' Elsie chuckled, leaning back in her chair expansively. 'How do you like that, Maureen dear? The boy's a poet.'

Maureen was busy hoovering up cake crumbs with a bony finger.

'I'd say the boy should be doing his bit for king and country, huh,' she grunted, 'instead of eating other people's rations. What are you, one of them conscientious objectors?'

'A farmer actually,' Tom mumbled, flushing.

'Mum!' Rose scolded, looking mortified.

Annie's heart went out to her friend. 'There's manners,' she muttered under her breath, avoiding her nan's reproachful gaze.

'I'll make tea,' Maureen said, glaring at Tom as she scraped back her chair.

'So tell me, Elsie, how does an Irish woman end up cooking like a Jewish bubbe?' Ted asked, tactfully changing the subject. 'That was the best meal I've eaten in years.' He patted his tummy and smiled, his face as brown and craggy as a walnut in the firelight.

Elsie stilled in her chair and surveyed him carefully. A tarry block in the fire popped, spitting out a red-hot ember onto the hearth.

'How do you know my family is Irish?'

'Aren't most in Bow?' he said, meeting's Elsie's direct gaze. 'Besides, look at your Annie here. Hair as red as fire, and pale as a matchstick.'

'Oh, you should have seen Nan when she was younger,' Annie gushed. 'Her hair was a beautiful deep red, the colour of brandy, weren't it, Nan?'

'Hush, dear,' Elsie replied, laying a hand over Annie's.

'Is that right?' Ted asked, his gaze soft and curious.

A look, fathomless, passed between them.

'Ted started at Bryant & May in the fire brigade three months ago now, didn't you, Ted?' Annie said as Maureen returned with the tea tray.

'And why do you feel the need to work for them?' Elsie remarked in a queer voice, as she began to pour from a giant pot.

'You don't approve of the factory?' he asked.

'To be frank, I don't like Annie and the girls working there, no.'

'Nan . . .'

'They don't remember the way it used to be, but I do,' Elsie insisted, setting the teapot down with a quake. 'And so does Maureen.'

'That's right,' Maureen said gleefully. 'Girls with putrid abscesses, swollen jaws, disfigured faces . . .'

'I still remember the glowing piles of fluorescent vomit

when the factory girls used to clock off,' Elsie said, rubbing her legs in agitation. 'I'm surprised you don't recall, Ted, seeing as you're from the East End of old.'

'Times change,' Ted replied softly. 'People change . . . Don't they, Elsie?'

Elsie said nothing, just traced her finger in a complicated figure through the cake crumbs.

'Besides, they need firemen now, even ones as old as me,' he joked.

'Well, we're all very glad to have you there, aren't we, Rose and Pearl?' Annie interjected.

Pearl nodded. 'We'd never have got those two allotments ready without Ted and his boys.'

'I'm happy to help, girls. Talking of which . . . Elsie, I've got a load of wood I've salvaged from the bombsites and I've been drying it out at the station. Make lovely kindling. Would you like me to run some up to your friend Mrs Donnelly?'

Elsie looked up. 'Why, that'd be lovely, thank you.'

'Say nothing of it,' he grinned, standing up wearily. 'We none of us know when it's our turn to starve.'

Ted looked reluctant to drag himself away from the cosy room.

'I can't tell you how much I enjoyed this evening, Elsie,' he said, holding his cap over his heart and lingering by the door. 'An unexpected pleasure.'

Elsie coloured. 'You're welcome, Ted,' she replied, her voice high and strange.

Once Ted had left, Annie watched her nan, intrigued, as she cleared the table, humming to herself. Something had passed between Elsie and Ted this evening. Annie had a queer feeling that there had been another deeper, unspoken narrative taking place.

She wasn't the only one observing. Maureen was watching Elsie like a hawk and when she went to take the plates through to the scullery, Maureen followed.

As Pearl, Tom and Rose sat by the fire, playing with Pip, curiosity drew Annie to the door of the scullery.

Working in the terrific noise of the top match room meant that Annie had become surprisingly adept at lip-reading. Which is how she was able to decipher perfectly what Maureen mouthed to Elsie.

It's him, ain't it?

Her nan paled as she lit the fire under the copper.

Hush. Remember our agreement.

Maureen turned and Annie stole softly back, unseen, into the parlour.

When Maureen came back into the room, Rose was standing, buttoning up her coat.

'I'm just taking Pip for a quick walk, Mum, I won't be long.'

Tom was on his feet. 'Mind if I join you, Rose?'

''Course not,' she smiled. 'I should be glad of the company in the blackout. Last time I nearly ended up in the Lea!'

Maureen groaned suddenly and groped for the wall.

'What's wrong?' Rose gasped.

'It's one of my heads,' Maureen whispered, with a theatrical shudder. 'I shall need to go straight home before it takes hold.'

Rose looked apologetically at Tom. 'Another time?'

'I'll take Pip out for a walk if you like, Rose?' Pearl offered.

'Thanks, Pearl, you're an angel,' Rose smiled.

When everyone had left, Annie found her nan in the scullery, her hands immersed in warm soapy bubbles.

'Nan,' she said softly, pulling her hands free of the butler sink. 'Leave that, I'll do it.'

Ever so gently, she dried Elsie's hands with the tea towel before taking a jar from the cupboard. The ointment was the only thing that gave her any respite from her arthritis. As Annie worked the thick grease deep into her fingers, she looked at her nan's hands. The skin was so thin over her knuckles, like parchment. Turning them over, she traced her fingers along the white scars that trailed her palms.

'How did you get these, Nan?'

'These hands tell a tale, dear girl, each blemish another chapter of my story,' Elsie replied wearily. 'But not for now.'

'But if not now, when?' Annie blurted. Elsie looked up, a flicker of annoyance crossing her face.

Annie knew she had overstepped the mark, but Elsie was an old woman now. Her past was cloudy. Annie knew nothing of her life as a young woman; where she was born even. And what 'agreement' did she have with Maureen?

'Well, tell me this, Nan,' Annie persisted. 'Why is Maureen such a poisonous toad to poor Rose? Showing her up like that in front of Tom earlier. I could've throttled her.'

'She speaks her mind, dear, always has,' Elsie replied stiffly.

'No. She's got a venomous tongue!' Annie protested. 'I don't even get why she took Rose on.'

'Annie,' Elsie chided, pulling her hands away in exasperation. 'You don't know how Maureen's struggled. Used to take Rose to work with her under her skirts at the sack factory down Cable Street, just so she could feed and clothe them both!'

Elsie's eyes met hers in the still of the scullery. Annie knew them to be darkest brown, but in that moment they were as black as pips.

'It hasn't always been honey. She's had a hard life,' she muttered.

'Haven't most women in the East End, Nan?' Annie replied searchingly.

Elsie closed her eyes. 'Annie, just drop it, will you? I'm worn out.'

''Course, Nan,' Annie replied, feeling suddenly guilty. 'You go on up to bed, I'll see to the fire.'

Elsie creaked up the stairs, shakily clutching the banister, and Annie sank down in front of the fire, her mind still swirling. Ted, Elsie, Maureen and the match factory had a deeper connection than any of them were letting on. Her nan was hiding something, of that she was now sure. The question was what.

*

Outside, Pearl breathed in the damp, coal-scented night air and strode purposefully towards the factory, Pip trotting along by her side. At the gates to the recreation ground, a warden shone a covered torch in her face.

'Halt. Who goes there?'

'Pearl O'Hara. I work here, sir. I'm one of the girls working the allotments. I'm such a clot, I left my bag here earlier. Can I fetch it?'

'Go on then,' he said, waving her through.

Being careful not to stumble in the trenches in the dug-up tennis court, she made her way to the Girls' Club allotment. Standing on the edge of the damp earth, which they had spent so many weeks now digging over, she decided it was time. Earlier, Samuel had said they were finally ready to start planting and no more deep digging was required, so it was as safe a hiding place as any.

A strong breeze swept over the grounds, bringing with it the rank, sour smell of the river. Shivering slightly, Pearl pulled her wedding ring from her pocket. Crouching down, she pushed it deep into the earth, before brushing more soil over the top. Pip gazed at her, his head cocked to one side. Pearl raised one finger to her lips, before patting his silky head.

'Our secret, boy.'

'Oh, do tell.'

The man's voice in the darkness took her entirely by surprise and Pearl leapt to her feet.

In the moonlight, his face glowed like an apparition.

'C-Curly, what are you doing here?'

'I've come to see if I can find my dear wife, who ain't come home yet.'

Curly walked closer to her, and Pip started to growl.

'Was she here this evening?' he demanded.

Pearl thought back to her last sighting of Millie as they'd all left, chatting intimately with Samuel.

'Um, er, briefly.'

'Not that briefly. She left her gas mask here,' he said, pulling the box from behind his back. 'Leave in a hurry, did she?'

'I wouldn't know,' she mumbled.

Curly stared at her for what felt like an age, his gaze cold and unflinching.

'Don't worry. I won't put you on the spot. I can see she ain't here. But *you* are.'

He smiled slowly and Pearl could see his brain working overtime. Unfortunately for Pearl, Curly had an unerring instinct for corruption. He could smell out trouble like a pig sniffs out truffles.

'You gonna tell me what you just buried down there, sweetheart?'

Pearl was so frightened, she stepped back with a shudder.

Curly looked amused. 'I ain't gonna hurt you, love. I just wanna know what you buried.'

Pearl shook her head.

'Suit yourself,' he shrugged, rolling up his shirtsleeves. Pearl hadn't dug it as deep as she thought she had, as a minute later she caught a flash of gold.

'Well, well, well,' he tutted, his thick eyebrows knotting together. 'A wedding ring. I'm assuming it's yours. I don't have you down as a villain. So the girl from Liverpool don't want no one' knowing she's married. Fancy that!'

'W-what do you want?' Pearl choked.

'I want to be friends, Pearl. That's all. I won't tell no one you was here today, if from time to time you'll oblige me. You've given me a little idea, see.'

'I-I don't understand.'

Curly's smile crept further. 'I'll be in touch . . .' With that, he swaggered his way back across the recreation ground before turning round and sauntering backwards. 'Ta–ta, friend.'

Thirteen

By the last day of his leave, Samuel had transformed both allotment sites. Together with Tom, he'd scoured every bombsite in the area and salvaged anything they could find of use. Cold frames had been fashioned out of old iron bed frames, and buckled bicycle wheels lashed together to grow pumpkins against vertically to save space. Old timber had been transformed into a handsome potting shed and tomato frames, and there was even a chicken run made from old wooden packing cases. Rusting tin bathtubs had been earmarked for herbs and flowers, and Elsie's ripe compost breathed new life into the soil.

A Union Jack flag fluttered patriotically from the top of the shed, and in the shadow of a sycamore tree Ted had cobbled together a makeshift bench from a couple of wooden pallets where the girls could sit and drink their tea in peace.

It might have been a little higgledy-piggledy but it was their space, and Annie adored it. Who'd have thought two glorious green allotments could be found nestled snugly in the grounds of a choking match factory! She could hardly wait for their shift to be over so they could tear down to either site. Millie seemed just as eager as she, though she suspected for different reasons.

'You and Samuel seem very close,' she mentioned when their shift ended and they got changed in the loos. She stood behind Millie as she helped to tie her hair back in a headscarf in front of the cracked toilet mirror.

'He's going tomorrow, Millie, and I'd hate to see you hurt. And what about Cur—'

'Please stop,' Millie interrupted. 'Samuel's a friend, is all. He understands me.'

'Just be careful, Millie, you know what Curly's capable of.'

At the Girls' Club allotment, Samuel was stripped to the waist, hammering a piece of wood, the late summer sunshine dappling his naked skin. All four girls stopped, stunned into silence.

'There's a sight for sore eyes,' Millie said eventually and Samuel looked up, his blue eyes sparkling with amusement.

'Sorry, girls,' he grinned, picking up his shirt. 'Few of us chaps have been digging up some ground next to the runway back at the unit and we always go shirtless. I forgot where I was for a moment.'

'Don't mind us,' Millie breathed, hardly able to tear her gaze from the contours of his muscles.

'You've been busy,' Rose smiled, looking about the allotment.

'Me *and* Tom,' he corrected. 'We've been planting Vegetables of National Importance.'

'Blimey, what are they when they're at home, then?' Millie asked.

'It's a grand way of saying root veg,' Samuel chuckled.

'You know, potatoes, carrots, parsnips, beets, swedes, all your basic root crops, and some lovely Ormskirk Late Savoy cabbage, much tastier than your normal stuff.'

'Sounds delicious,' Pearl said.

'Why now? I thought you wanted to wait a bit for the soil to settle in,' queried Annie.

'I did, but then I realized it's a full moon, always better to plant then.'

'Full moon?' Annie remarked, her eyebrows shooting up. 'You sound like Nan! She swears a full moon sets all the expectant mothers off labouring.'

'I don't know about that, Annie,' Samuel grinned, doing up his shirt buttons. 'But I do know it makes the soil richer in nutrients and more resistant against weeds.'

'Talking of weeds, according to my *Dig for Victory Leaflet No. 16* we need to "Blitz the Bugs",' said Annie. 'There's corrosive sublimate for clubroot, lead arsenate paste for sucking bugs—'

'Good grief, no,' Samuel interrupted. 'I know I'm unconventional in my thinking, but that stuff's the devil's own work for destroying nutrients and taste. Besides, this is an industrial area. You start spraying for potato blight round here and there's a risk of cumulative chemical damage.'

'You know best, Samuel,' said Millie, impressed.

'So what are we supposed to do?' Annie asked despondently.

'Well, I've seeded marigolds between rows of potatoes to stop beetles, lemon balm around the carrots for slugs. Half a potato stuck on a stick and buried into the ground will attract the wireworms. There's lots you can do to wage war on bugs, beyond spraying poison about. See this,' Samuel added, tapping a line of string over the rows where he'd sown carrots. 'Painted with creosote. It will easily see off carrot fly.' He gazed about the garden with satisfaction.

'You really love all this, don't you?' Annie remarked.

'Gardening, not flying, is my first love,' he smiled. 'You should see my seed cabinet at home. I only wish I had it here with me now.'

'You've done more than enough,' Annie insisted. 'I don't know how we'll be able to thank you.'

'It's me who should be thanking you,' he replied. 'At OTU, it's constant fighter affiliation exercises, evasion techniques and hauling clapped-out old kites off the tarmac.'

The girls looked as if he'd just spoken in double Dutch.

'Hard work,' he added. 'To be here, working British soil, well, it reminds me of everything I need to fight for and to protect.'

His gaze was directed firmly at Millie, and Annie's mind flashed to her earlier warning.

'I think I get what you're saying,' Pearl remarked. 'War's so destructive, and gardening's all about renewal.'

'Exactly, Pearl,' he said, smiling warmly. 'The two are antithetical.'

'If I knew what that meant, I'd be agreeing with you,' Millie chipped in. 'But I'm just a dumb blonde.'

'Anything but dumb,' Samuel replied, holding her gaze softly.

'Where's Tom?' Rose asked. 'I thought he wasn't going until tomorrow?'

'Don't worry,' Samuel replied. 'He's over at the other site, sowing winter crops. In fact, tell a lie, here he is now.'

'Not the bearer of good news, though, I'm afraid,' Tom sighed as he hove into sight. 'Afraid the tools we left at the other site have been stolen. A draw hoe, shovels, spades, forks, hand trowel, that nice galvanized watering can and a trug basket. They took the lot.'

'Oh, the rotten bastards,' Annie moaned, kicking her boot against the ground in frustration. 'I gave Nan the last of the funds this morning to get some chicks. I'll not get more now.'

'Why don't you ask Ted if he could donate any spare tools from the factory fire brigade?' Samuel suggested.

'Don't worry, Annie,' Pearl said soothingly, 'we'll think of something.'

'You know, Rose,' Tom remarked thoughtfully, looking at Pip. 'Jack Russells make excellent guard dogs.'

'Look at the size of him,' she laughed.

'I know, but he's got one heck of a bark on him and he's very territorial. Who's not to know he's a great big savage in the blackout?'

'I'm not sure,' Rose frowned, scooping Pip up and stroking his ears.

'I could build a kennel for him over at the yard allotment, if you like?'

'It would solve the problem of where to keep him,' she admitted. 'Elsie's been ever so sweet letting me leave him at Blondin Street, but I don't want to take advantage of her kindness.'

'That settles it,' said Annie. 'I'll check with the Works Manager, but I can't see him objecting.'

'Right, come on, you lot,' Samuel said, picking up a sack by the shed. 'I want to teach you how to fertilize the crops, it'll need doing regularly.'

'But there's a waiting list for fertilizer,' Annie objected.

'Which is why Tom and I have collected wood ash and soot,' he grinned, tossing the bag at her. 'Perfect substitute. And when we're done with that, we're going to plant out comfrey herb. Reeks to high heaven, but when steeped in water it makes an excellent liquid fertilizer.'

'Absolutely,' Tom agreed. 'And remember, we feed the earth, not the plant.'

'It's not what you know, but who, eh, Annie?' Millie remarked, with a playful wink.

They worked in companionable silence until the sun sank down over the water towers, a giant misty ball streaking the skies vermilion pink.

'Time for the workers to down tools,' sang a cheery voice through the gathering dusk. 'I've got fish and chips.'

'Nan,' beamed Annie. 'Are you ever a sight for sore eyes!'

Elsie laid out an old picnic blanket on the ground, while the workers washed their hands at the standpipe the Metropolitan Water Board had installed.

'Cor! Wish I was having tea with you lot again,' said a big, bluff voice behind Annie.

'Ted!' she grinned, drying her hands on the front of her dungarees. 'Why didn't you tell us you was coming over?'

At the mention of Ted's name, Elsie's head snapped round.

She began busily brushing down her apron skirt. 'Never mind, there's plenty to go round.'

'Very kind of you, Elsie, but I'm just off to do the night shift. Besides which, I can't avail myself of your kindness again. That tea you cooked was smashing.'

'Oh, it was nothing,' she flushed. Was it Annie's imagination or was her usually formidable nan behaving like a giddy sixteen-year-old?

'For you,' he said, handing Annie a box. 'It's only an old primus stove, but I thought you could leave it here so you can brew up while you're working the allotment. There's a little bit of tea and some stera in there. Couldn't get no sugar, I'm afraid.'

'Oh, Ted, how thoughtful,' she exclaimed.

'Isn't it?' Millie agreed, chucking Ted's weathered cheek. 'Don't know why you never married, you'd have made someone a lovely husband.' She winked at Elsie. 'Still, never too late, eh, Else?'

'Give over, you daft sod.' Ted blushed, swiping her with his cap.

'I'll stay for a cuppa then I'd best be off,' he said, settling himself down on the rug next to Elsie.

They ate fish and chips straight from the newspaper, the paper dark with grease and vinegar. After the back-breaking work of the day, no food had ever tasted so good.

'If they ever rationed fish and chips, I swear to God I'd wave the white flag there and then,' Millie groaned, polishing off the last chip and licking her fingers.

'None of that defeatist talk, you,' Samuel teased. 'Besides, come wintertime, with any luck you'll be pulling the tastiest veg you've ever eaten straight from the earth with your bare hands.'

'No feeling like it on earth, is there, Samuel?' Tom remarked.

'Certainly isn't,' he grinned, stretching out his long legs and leaning back against the sun-warmed boards of the potting shed. 'How's the old poem go?

'The kiss of the sun for pardon
The song of the birds for mirth,
One is nearer God's heart in a garden
Than anywhere else on earth . . .'

He looked directly at Millie as he spoke, and when he finished gave her a smile that almost stopped her heart.

'That's beautiful, Samuel,' she replied.

Feeling like she was intruding on a private moment, Annie glanced over to where Elsie was sitting tearing up the old newspaper into strips.

'What you gonna do with that, Mrs Trinder?' Pearl asked.

'Why, it's going on the compost of course, dear.'

'These youngsters haven't got a clue, have they, Else?' Ted chuckled, as he drained his tea.

But Elsie wasn't listening, she was reading from a slightly chip-stained piece of newspaper.

'I don't believe it,' she tutted. 'Says here there's been a spate of bag snatches and pickpocket binges down Chrisp Street market. Dozens of people have lost clothing coupons, ration books, money and . . . Oh, no! that really is too much!' she gasped.

'What is it, Nan?'

'One old boy even had all his medals from the Great War stolen.'

Ted's face darkened. 'These villains want hanging. That'd stop their filthy crimes.'

'First our tools, now this,' Rose said worriedly.

'Is it me or are we seeing more of this since the war began?' Annie asked.

'I read that shopkeepers lost more to looting during the Blitz than to Jerry's bombs,' Samuel remarked.

'So let's hope for a swift end to this war so as we can all get back to normal,' Ted said, rising to his feet. 'Right, I'm off. Cheerio, all.'

'I best be off too,' Elsie said. She took Ted's hand, as he helped her to her feet.

'Rose, do you want to show me where you want Pip's kennel?' Tom asked.

*

Before long, all the workers had scattered, leaving Samuel and Millie alone once more at the allotment.

'I better not stay too long,' Millie said. 'Curly's getting suspicious about where I'm going after work.'

'Come,' said Samuel, holding out his hand. 'I want to show you something. Just quickly.'

They walked once more through the streets in the direction of Bromley-by-Bow, making sure this time to stick to the quieter back roads, their footsteps falling softly into step as they passed under the shadow of a viaduct.

Row after row of smoking, soot-stained terraces stretched out, housing communities, until now, untouched by time.

'This street was known as incubator alley,' Millie remarked. 'You couldn't move for the prams, carts and kids.' She smiled nostalgically. 'Us East Enders grew up on the streets.'

'Same in the countryside, except the fields were our playgrounds,' Samuel replied.

'Funny when you think about it, but all the kids who lived down here could be playing in the fields you grew up in,' Millie remarked, looking at the deserted street. 'It's like the Pied Piper's come and lured them all away.'

'War's turned everything topsy-turvy, hasn't it?' Samuel agreed. He turned suddenly, looking her full in the face. 'I adore children. One day I hope to have a whole brood.'

'I dare say. Easy enough to be fond of kids when you ain't got none.'

He smiled curiously.

'Do you not want children then?'

'What, and find myself tied to the kitchen sink?' she muttered defensively. 'No, thank you very much.'

They continued their walk in silence until they reached a handsome red-brick building, covered in ivy.

'What is this place?' she asked.

'My chance to show you something of the history of the East End,' he said mysteriously. 'Come on.'

Samuel swung open the door and they were assailed by a fug of warmth in the blacked-out room. Trestle tables heaving with urns of soup lined a large wood-panelled room.

'Kingsley Hall. My lodgings,' he explained as they wove

their way through the crowded room. 'A place which helps feed and clothe the poor in the community. It's also a rest centre and shelter now. Run by Muriel Lester, a pacifist who supported the suffragettes.' He paused. 'Have you really never heard of it, you being from Bow?'

'Come to think of it, I have,' Millie replied. 'My mum was always too proud to come to places like this, though. "I ain't having no daughter of mine have Sally Army soup",' she scoffed, mimicking Gladys's voice. 'She'd rather sell me off to the nearest villain.'

They passed a dining room and a space for worship until they came to a dark winding staircase.

'My room is up here.'

Millie hesitated. 'Samuel . . . I . . .'

'Don't worry, I promise I'm not about to try and ravish you. We're not all the heavy-drinking playboys the public would have you believe.'

At the top of the stairs, he led her outside onto a terrace. Lines of rooms opened out onto a wide balcony. Someone had planted containers full of flowers and vegetables, which trailed prettily over the balcony railings, perfuming the night air. Millie spotted sweet peas in a patriotic blaze of red, white and blue, and an old bathtub bursting with rosemary, comfrey, mint and thyme, even tomatoes growing in an old orange box. It was the most unusual little garden she'd ever seen.

Samuel looked at her face and smiled.

'A little green oasis up in the sky, isn't it? This is my room,' he nodded. 'But look. This is what I brought you up to see.'

Reverently, he opened a door onto a sparsely furnished

room next to his. The room contained the barest of necessities, a mat in place of a bed, a wicker chair and rush matting on the floor.

'Mahatma Gandhi stayed here when he visited in 1931,' he breathed. 'He could have stayed at some swanky West End hotel, but he chose to make the East End his home. Don't you think that's wonderful? They've preserved his room. Apparently, at six o'clock each morning, after his prayers, he took his walk along the canal, talking to workmen and factory girls on the way.'

'Fancy that,' smiled Millie. 'Bet he turned a few heads in his loincloth.'

Samuel burst into laughter. 'You do make me laugh, Millie.'

They walked to the balcony edge and stared in silence, back in the direction of Bow, bathed in the milky light of the full moon.

'Why've you brought me here?' she asked. 'It weren't just to show me that, was it?'

'Because I want to give you another perspective on your life,' he explained. 'You don't have to accept the injustice of your marriage, Millie. You're too young and too beautiful to let hatred blacken your heart.'

She stood before him, her sultry curves hidden beneath baggy dungarees, her face bare of make-up.

'When will I see you again?'

'I wish I could say, Millie,' he sighed. 'I'm still in training, which makes it easier to get leave, but things are gearing up all the time. I've seen so many men pulled out of our base in Lincolnshire early. Crews are coming faster and faster from training. Bomber Command is gathering in strength.'

'You don't think this war is going to end anytime soon, then?' she ventured, realizing how naive she sounded.

He shook his head.

'For me, it's just beginning.'

Millie nodded, and felt a powerful emotion grip her heart at the thought of him flying over enemy lines.

'I'll do everything in my power to come back to you,' he insisted, drawing her tenderly into his arms and kissing the top of her head, 'and maybe, together, we can find a way out of your mess.'

'When do you go?'

'First light.'

A fierce longing swept through her. Her fake marriage, her reputation . . . it was war, what did any of that matter now?

Impulsively, she pushed her body against his broad chest, snaking her hands up and under his shirt. Stroking the warm naked flesh on his back, she began to kiss, slowly and sensuously along the curve of his neck, tasting the sweet saltiness of his skin.

His body responded instantly and, groaning, he crushed his lips against hers. Surrendering to the moment, Millie moaned softly as he gathered her up and moved towards the dark doorway to his bedroom.

But then, abruptly, he stopped.

'We mustn't,' he breathed, resting his chin on the top of her head and trying frantically to damp down the sheer lust crashing through him.

'I–is it me? Do you not fancy me?' she whispered, feeling an annihilating disappointment.

'Christ, no!' he said, drawing back and gripping her face in his hands. 'You're incredible, Millie, beautiful, astonishing . . . I've never wanted anyone so much in all my life, but . . .'

'But what, then?'

'You're not mine. And until I've worked out a way to make you mine, we can't.'

Reality fell like a damp cloth on an ember. She touched his cheek, then turned so he couldn't see her tears in the moonlight.

'Stay safe, sweetheart.'

*

'Look at that full moon,' Tom remarked as he sat side by side with Rose on an old wooden bench in the yard allotment at Bryant & May.

Pip had fallen asleep on Tom's lap as he gently stroked his slumbering body, and even though she knew she was hellishly late home, Rose didn't have the heart to move him.

'Beautiful, isn't it?' she murmured, her long sooty eyelashes sliding down as she scuffed the ground with her boot.

'Like you, Rose,' Tom said, unable to meet her eye.

'Don't talk daft,' she mumbled. 'I can't hold a candle next to Millie. Plain as a pikestaff, me.'

'Well, I think you're smashing, Rose. Ought I be able to write to you? When I get back home?'

'That'd be nice,' she replied.

Rose dared a sideways glance at his face and quickly looked back.

Tom smiled. Then he slowly slid his hand along the bench. Rose drew in a big breath and moved her hand to meet his. There they sat, hand in hand, silent, save for the sound of the distant rumble of steam tractors and the buzzing of insects.

When it became too late for Rose to ignore, she reluctantly stood and woke up Pip.

'I'll write, Tom,' she mumbled, wondering whether she ought to let him kiss her.

'And I'll be waiting, Rose,' he replied, too shy to stand. 'Might even send you a marzipan fish.'

A soft breeze ruffled her hair, bringing with it the sweet smell of poplar sap. Rose turned and ran up the moonlit yard, feeling as light-hearted and happy as she could remember in years.

*

Back in Parnell Road, Millie let herself in and crept quietly along the darkened passage to the kitchen.

Please let Curly be at his club.

After her encounter with Samuel, she was emotionally wrung out and could do without a fight.

'You're home, then,' said a voice from the darkened parlour as she passed the door.

'Bleedin' hell! You gave us a fright,' Millie gasped, as she snapped on the light. 'Why you sitting here in the dark? And what's with the bags?'

'I'm going away.'

'Where?'

'To stay with Betty and her family. They're moving to Essex earlier than planned.'

'But why?' she asked, flabbergasted. 'I don't see you staying in to rub her feet. And what about your club?'

'It'll look after itself for a while. Besides, things are getting hot round here.'

Millie went to reply, but decided she'd rather not know what he'd been up to. He strode to the looking glass over the mantel and combed back his patent-leather hair. Curly was suited and booted, all rigged out in a sharp new suit – Max Cohen, looking at the cut of it. She stared down dully at her muddy dungarees.

'They're after me for ARP duty as well.' He laughed contemptuously. 'Me? In a tin hat, I ask you!'

'What exactly have you done to stop Hitler?' she asked waspishly.

Ignoring her question, Curly pocketed his comb and bent down to pick up his bags.

'I'll be back, Millie. We still got unfinished business. And in case you're thinking you can be sneaking around behind my back, I got my people here.'

Bending down, he pecked at her cheek and gave her backside a painful squeeze at the same time.

'Clean yourself up, eh, love? You look a fright. Ta-ta.'

The front door shut behind him and Millie fell back against it, overwhelmed with relief.

*

Four streets away, Rose was also letting herself in after her chaste encounter. She paused in the blacked-out street and, ever so slowly, pulled the key through the letter box.

Maureen was on an early shift at the cafe tomorrow. With any luck, she'd have already gone to bed. Just in case, Rose tiptoed past the tiny darkened parlour to her attic room. She slipped in and stripped off her clothes in the darkness, hardly daring to breathe for the sound it would make.

'The problem with this war is that everyone's standards are going the same way as their knickers.'

Maureen's reedy voice filled the darkened chamber.

'Mum!' Rose flinched, hugging her arms about her naked chest. Maureen was sitting in an easy chair in the corner of the room, her long, bony fingers beating a tattoo against the frayed arms.

'I'm . . . I'm sorry I'm late. I was working at the allotment.'

'This is how it all begins,' Maureen said in a queer voice, rising slowly and pinning Rose's hands to her sides, leaving her breasts cold and exposed.

'M-Mum, what are you doing?' Rose trembled. 'I'm cold, please, let me put my nightgown on.'

'Why?' Maureen said icily. 'If you carry on cavorting with that farmer, you're gonna end up naked anyhow, may as well get used to it, huh.'

Rose's eyes, dark as treacle, widened in horror.

'Oh, yes, I saw you and 'im. Holding hands at the allotment.'

'It was innocent, Mum, I swear it,' Rose pleaded.

'Trust me, girl, when it comes to men, it's never innocent,' she sneered, pulling a pair of scissors from her apron pocket. 'One minute you're holding hands, the next you're peddling your fanny like that slut Millie. She was dragged up, not brought up, but I shan't have that life for you, huh!'

Rose saw the flash of steel and gasped.

'W-what are you doing?'

'Preserving your innocence, so you don't follow in the footsteps of that whore.'

'Millie's not a whore,' Rose protested.

'Not Millie. Your mother.'

Quick as a flash, Maureen lunged, grabbing a fistful of Rose's long, lustrous hair in her hand and severed it with the blades. She chopped savagely, jerking Rose's head as she worked. The clock on the mantel ticked loudly and the heavy silence seeped around the room, as Rose's hair drifted to the floor. When at last Maureen had sheared her hair so that all that remained was an uneven, boyish crop, she stood back.

'You are never to see that boy again,' she ordered, thrusting the blades of her scissors in Rose's face. 'No kissing and keep your hand on your ha'penny. Understood?'

Rose nodded, mute with despair, staring hard at a milky bloom of damp on the gravy-coloured wall.

Maureen looked her up and down, gave a satisfied nod, then swept from the room, flicking her shawl like a whirlwind. With an anguished sob, Rose fell onto her battered horsehair mattress, drawing the coverlet around her naked body.

*

For a fleeting moment, Pearl thought she was alone at the Girls' Club allotment, then a smartly dressed figure emerged from behind the potting shed. A thick bank of cloud had passed over the moon, casting the allotment into darkness, until a match crackled into flame, illuminating his face.

'Good. You got my note,' he said, drawing deeply and flicking his match on the ground.

'How did you get in, Curly?'

'That useless old boy on the warden's post. Eyes closed, listening to "A Nightingale Sang in Berkeley Square".'

Curly laughed nastily. 'Bet a pigeon or two's shit there an' all. Anyway, I sauntered straight past.'

Pearl shook her head, wondering how on earth someone as lovely as Millie could wind up married to such a rotten creep.

'What do you want?'

'I've buried something behind the potting shed and I need my *friend* to make sure no one goes poking around back there. Digging up something that's not their business.'

'And if I refuse?'

Curly stepped closer. So close she could smell the pomade greasing his hair back, the rank odour of Players tobacco on his breath. There was something so evocative about the smell, catching at her nostrils, awakening memories she thought she had buried.

'Then I tell everyone you're a liar,' he said, pulling her wedding ring from inside his jacket pocket. 'That you've run away from your husband.'

Pearl stood rigid in a cloud of blue smoke.

'Does your husband know you're here?' Curly murmured, taking a deep suck on his cigarette.

She remained silent.

'Thought not, and if you want it to stay that way, you keep quiet. You and me got an agreement, ain't we, Pearl? I'll keep your secret, you keep mine, yes?'

Pearl nodded, a surge of impotent despair crawling up her spine.

'I'm going away for a while, but I'll be back. Make sure no one goes round the back of the potting shed, and I'll make sure none of my associates pay any visits to Liverpool.'

He laughed with dark relish, shaking his head as he ground his cigarette butt into the freshly dug earth.

'Dig for Victory, don't you just love it!'

With that, he melted into the darkness.

PART TWO

PART TWO

Fourteen

'The Queen's coming here? To Bryant & May? Pull the other one, it's got brass bells on,' Millie scoffed.

'I can assure you, Mrs Brown, it's perfectly true,' the chairman replied, amusement shining in his eyes.

'Sorry, sir,' she babbled. 'Only, well, it's bloody marvellous is what it is, ain't it, Annie?'

Millie nudged Annie.

'Oh, it certainly is, sir,' she replied. 'May I ask why?'

'Her Royal Highness visited Bethnal Green last month. Did you see it in the newspapers?'

The girls nodded. You could have hardly escaped the fact. The Queen's trip to visit the allotments dug out of the ruins of Bethnal Green's bombsites, accompanied by the Mayor, a Pathé film unit and other hoi polloi had caused quite the stir! Especially when a goat had tried to eat Her Majesty's handbag.

'Our neighbours in Bethnal Green are doing some outstanding work for the Dig for Victory campaign,' he went on. 'The Bethnal Green Bombed Sites Producers' Association has only been going for fourteen months, but they have four hundred members growing vegetables on thirty bombed sites in the district. It's the talk of London.'

He paused to pick up a copy of *The Times* newspaper and read out loud: 'Thousands of shirkers might feel ashamed of themselves if they could see what people are doing in Bethnal Green. This experiment shows that with hard work and relatively little money, even East Enders can make their contribution to food production . . .'

'Even East Enders? Cheeky sods!' Millie squawked, until Mrs Frobisher laid a silencing hand over hers.

'Let the chairman continue, please,' she chided softly.

'Naturally, this makes very good propaganda material and—'

'You're keen for Bryant & May to get in on the act, sir,' Millie grinned, casting him a sly wink.

'Well, I wouldn't have put it quite like that, Mrs Brown, but I'm certainly not averse to showing off the fine work that's being achieved at Bryant & May. Now, I have it on good authority Her Majesty will do us the honour of a visit next spring.'

'Next spring,' Annie gasped.

'That should give you ample time to make sure the allotments are looking their best. The Palace is particularly interested to see how we are producing vegetables alongside matches. Rumour has it she will be accompanied by the Minister of Agriculture, who will be handing out Certificates of Merit.'

'This is your big chance, girls, to show the allotments off to the whole country,' beamed Mrs Frobisher. Annie had never seen the usually composed factory matriarch so enthused.

'Indeed. You are a credit to the factory,' added the chairman. 'I'll admit, Miss Trinder, I had my doubts when you first approached me with this idea. I couldn't see how you could possibly grow vegetables from a bombsite, but, well, you've done it.'

'We've done it, sir,' Annie corrected. 'Without Ted and the other firemen, and of course Samuel Taylor from Bomber Command, it would never have got off the ground.'

'Aah, of course, and what word of our special volunteer?'

A silence fell over the room. Millie fiddled with her wedding ring.

Mrs Frobisher coughed. 'The last we heard, sir, was that Mr Taylor's squadron was involved in Bomber Command's campaign over the Ruhr. We are all praying for news of his safe return. He has been a tremendous support, and so kind in giving up his precious leave to help the girls.'

The chairman sighed and looked out of the taped-over windows.

'Sacrifice is nothing new to Bomber Command. Such brave chaps, taking it to the enemy night after night. He'll be in my prayers.

'One last thing,' the chairman added as they made to leave. 'It's this afternoon you'll be selling vegetables by the Old Ford Road gate?'

'Yes, sir,' Annie replied. 'I believe there's a queue forming already.'

'Good. I've arranged for a photographer and reporter from the *Daily Express* to come along and take photographs and interview you all for their Monday edition, which coincides with the launch of National Allotment Week. We'll show everyone it's not just Bethnal Green Digging for Victory!

'I think that concludes our committee meeting.'

*

Outside, a syrupy July sunshine bathed the cobbles and Annie smiled, still glowing under the chairman's praise. When they had started the match girls' allotments two summers ago, she had scarcely been able to look the chairman in the eye, but now things were changing for the better.

Allotment fever had gripped the East End. Residents who had dared to stay had created idiosyncratic vegetable plots from old baths, canes and packing boxes, and it filled her heart with pride to see vegetables nurtured in such unexpected places. Gardens now bloomed in the most curious of locations: marrows grew on top of Anderson shelters, tomatoes on factory window ledges and haricot beans in place of hopscotch in school playgrounds. Every street was growing their own, but it was the allotments in the grounds of bombsites which Annie found most affecting. Where old houses had been blasted away, gardens, chicken coops and rabbit hutches had been hastily constructed, the greenery incongruous amongst the rubble and fire-scorched buildings.

There was such poignancy to seeing plants blossom where human life had ended. To Annie's mind, fresh green shoots provided a more fitting tribute to their dead than a slab of granite.

But it was their allotments, here at Bryant & May, which

gave Annie a purity of purpose she had never once felt packing matches.

As she and Millie left the main office building and entered the yard, she felt the familiar leap in her breast.

Two years ago it was indescribable, a filthy rubble- and glass-filled bombsite. Now, broad beans, beetroot, lettuce, marrow, onions, peas and potatoes grew in neat lines. The tomatoes here were as spectacular as Pearl had predicted they would be, loving both the south-facing brick wall of the office block and the rich loamy mixture of Elsie's compost. Annie breathed deeply, filling her nostrils with their comforting, earthy tang.

Samuel had told them that wherever you reclaim the land, wildlife would return. He was right. Birdsong rose above the rumble of steam tractors, and bumblebees drowsily feasted on the drifts of rosemary and lavender he'd insisted on planting in the old bathtub. Pip dozed in a patch of sunshine outside his kennel. All was contentment and peace.

Up above sounded the comforting tones of Mr Middleton, as his regular programme, *In Your Garden*, drifted down through the open window. On warm days such as these, the typists on the first floor kindly turned up the wireless and threw open the windows so that they might have music and entertainment while they worked.

'Now come, look over my shoulder and let us look through this catalogue together,' said the broadcaster conspiratorially. 'Shall we start with flowers?'

'Ooh, not much,' Elsie replied, from where she was bent double, thinning onions.

'Nan,' Annie chuckled as they drew closer. 'He can't actually hear you.'

Elsie straightened up with a groan and a flash of pain crossed her face.

'You all right, Mrs T?' Millie asked, reaching out to steady her.

'Good as gold. Don't fuss, dear. Now, what news from the committee meeting?'

'Well, you won't believe it, but we're only getting a visit from the Queen next year,' Annie said. 'Apparently, she was so impressed with what she saw over in Bethnal Green, she wants to come back and see ours.'

'That's smashing news,' Elsie exclaimed, clapping the dirt off her old chamois gloves.

Rose and Pearl looked up, surprised, from where they were carefully going down the lines of lettuce, feeling each heart with the back of their knuckles.

'We better get it looking its best,' Rose said. 'Millie, any idea when Samuel might next be getting leave? We could use his advice on crop rotation.'

Millie shook her head and turned away quickly.

'You've seen the papers,' she muttered as she picked up a hoe and began vigorously working her way down the lines. 'It's anyone's guess.'

A heavy silence descended and Annie felt her heart ache for her dear friend. Samuel's effect on the allotment was plain for all to see. His love of natural methods ensured they had the most luxuriant leeks, succulent carrots and a garden strangely free of slugs. But the mark he had left on Millie's heart ran far deeper.

Since he had graduated from dropping letters over

occupied France to bombs over Germany, they had seen less and less of him. Millie was still keeping up the pretence he was just a good friend, but if it wasn't love, then she was a Dutchman!

'I expect he'll have been involved in that battle over Happy Valley. I was reading about it only this morning,' Elsie remarked. 'Whole cities on fire.'

The Allies were making great strides in all theatres of war, but it was the crews of Bomber Command who were thrilling the British public with area bombing of German cities.

'Do you think it's right, so much suffering?' ventured Rose. 'I'll never forget what it felt like to be buried. It's not something I would wish on any human being, German or otherwise.'

'Even more reason, dear girl, why it's about time they got a taste of their own medicine!' Elsie shot back. 'It's the poor bombers who I feel sorry for. Young men, sent off to their deaths in an unmarked grave over Germany . . .' She tailed off. 'Oh, Millie, I'm sorry.'

Millie's lips were drawn in a tight white line across her face as she hoed. She didn't need to know the cold calculus of death in Bomber Command to know Samuel's chances of making it out alive were slim at best. She'd had just a handful of visits over the past year and a half, with gaps between each growing achingly longer as he worked towards the end of his training. He had been on active service now for two months, three days, with not a word.

'Let's change the subject, shall we, Elsie?' she murmured.

'Good idea,' Annie said. 'We'll have to get going in a bit

anyway, they'll be opening the gates to the public soon for the vegetable sale, and I want to have the trestle tables set up.'

'Need a hand?' piped up a voice.

'William!' Rose smiled as Pip sleepily climbed to his feet and scampered over, wagging his tail.

William, the lad who ran the pig club from the kennels on Fairfield Road, ambled his way over, clutching a galvanized bucket, helped by Ted.

'I found this one wandering about the Works with a bucket full of pig muck,' Ted said.

'Ooh, not half, I'll have that for my compost,' Elsie said, her face lighting up.

'You're the only woman I know to get excited over pig poo,' Ted said, gazing at her affectionately.

'You may mock!' she scolded. 'But you want yer garden to feed others, you gotta feed it!'

'Nan, you know they've brought in National Growmore Fertiliser now?' Annie remarked. 'Save you lugging your bucket after every passing animal.'

'I don't trust that stuff. Artificial,' she sniffed, as she began forking the pig droppings onto the heap. 'Besides, I promised Samuel I'd keep it going.'

Elsie's compost heap had become something of a fixation, dinned in by wireless talks and a well-thumbed Dig for Victory pamphlet. Now it was like a giant cauldron of smells, so ripe and fertile, Annie wouldn't be surprised if it didn't just walk off by itself!

'Anyway, never mind my compost, how's your club going, William, my lad?' Elsie asked.

'Terrific, Mrs Trinder. Got three lovely sows from

Essex, nice and fattened up. For every three I have slaughtered, I have to give one to the Ministry, then the rest I send to be butchered. Everyone in the club gets a share.'

'Stick me down to join up,' Elsie said. 'It's been a long while since I had a nice pig's trotter.'

'Ooh, I'd do anything for a bacon sarnie right now,' Annie said, feeling her mouth water.

'You leave it to your nan,' Ted said. 'With her thrift, she'll use up every part of the animal bar the squeak.'

Elsie flushed. 'Money's short and appetite's large. I'm obliged to be thrifty! Now, William dear, how old are you?'

'Fourteen, Mrs Trinder,' he replied politely.

'Didn't fancy the countryside?' Ted asked.

'No, sir. They evacuated me to Oxford but I got the first train back to London. The East End's my home.'

'Good for you, boy,' Elsie said approvingly. 'This war's making a man out of you.'

William cast a long, lingering look round the allotment, glancing admiringly over to where Pearl had finished with the lettuce and was now busy staking tomatoes. A few tendrils of her wavy black hair had escaped and curled softly down her slender neck as she worked.

Annie smiled. She could hardly blame the lad. Pearl was a handsome-looking woman. In the two years she'd been living with them, her nan had managed to feed her up a treat. The waiflike girl who first turned up from Liverpool was all curves and sun-kissed skin now.

'Right,' William said. 'Best get back to my pigs.'

'Thank you, dear,' Elsie replied. 'I'll be over to the kennels later with my money.'

'Funny, ain't it?' Ted remarked, with a lopsided smile.

'Pigs in kennels, rabbits on the roof. Life's full of surprises, ain't it, Elsie, old girl?'

'Shut up, old man,' she scolded, but her aged face was transformed, her smile radiant. Annie watched them laughing over what felt like a private joke. This feeling that her nan was hiding something had taken hold, like an itch in the back of her mind that demanded to be scratched.

*

Half an hour later, the vegetable sale was in full swing. The girls could hardly keep up with the scrum of housewives jostling outside the factory gates for the best pick. Pearl glanced over to where Millie was holding court, her platinum-blonde hair gleaming in the sunshine. A photographer from the *Daily Express* was clicking away, his lens firmly trained on Millie.

'Come and try Bryant & May's best veg!' she hollered over the line. 'We got Painted Lady runner beans, some lovely Tom Thumb lettuce! Oh, hello, Mrs Richards, how about some nice radishes? French Breakfast. Nice and spicy, you've never tasted anything like 'em.'

'French Breakfast?' exclaimed the stout elderly lady. 'Sounds a bit naughty.'

'Never know, might put a bit of lead in your Alf's pencil,' Millie winked.

'I'll take a bagful!' she said quickly.

'That's the spirit,' Millie grinned, tucking the radishes into her string bag.

'How long have you been Digging for Victory at the Fairfield Works?' asked the reporter over the clamour.

'Two years now,' Annie said proudly. 'Two allotments we dug out of old bombsites, and both are thriving.'

'That's right,' interjected Mrs Frobisher. 'All the money goes to support relief organizations, and the people of Bow know that when they buy their vegetables from us, it's not been at the expense of sailors' lives.'

Pearl listened from her end of the trestle table, where she was selling bags of tomatoes, silently praying the reporter or photographer wouldn't venture near her.

She didn't notice him until his face loomed up in front of hers.

'I'll take two bags!'

She jumped, sending a bag of tomatoes rolling over the cobbles.

'Butterfingers. You don't want to lose your grip, do you, Pearl?'

'Curly,' she muttered weakly, glancing nervously to where Millie was laughing with the reporter. 'Does Millie know you're back?'

'All in good time.'

Pearl's eyes strayed to the other side of the street, where a young woman was jiggling a smart Silver Cross pram in the shade of the tram shed.

'You've brought Betty and the baby back with you?' she gasped in disbelief, staring at the blonde-haired toddler, who was stuffing a chubby fist into her mouth.

'Free country still, ain't it? Betty's visiting her auntie, and I'm back on business.'

He leant in closer. 'On the subject of which, I shall need you to meet me at the allotment later.'

Pearl closed her eyes. For months now, she had been free

of Curly's pernicious blackmail. She had almost allowed herself to forget whatever he had buried behind the potting shed. A dull ache of despair tightened like a band across her chest.

'No, Curly,' she said with more defiance than she felt. 'Just leave me alone.'

His gaze hardened and then, to her amazement, a smile crept over his face.

'John Brunt.'

'W-what did you say?'

'John Brunt. Your husband. I've been doing some digging of my own. I even know what regiment he's serving in.'

Casually, he picked up a raspberry from a punnet and popped it in his mouth. 'One phone call is all it takes. Expect he'd like to know where his wife's got to.'

In the concentrated silence of the moment Pearl's heart was beating so loudly, she was surprised no one else could hear it.

'What the hell are you doing back?' Millie exploded. 'And how dare you bring that tart with you!'

'Hello, love, miss me?' Curly replied smoothly, as if he'd just popped out for a pint of milk.

Pearl looked at her tormentor. The mask never slipped from Curly, because there was no mask. Beneath the piercing eyes and the patent-leather hair, he was cunning and shrewd as the day was long.

'You've got another think coming, pal, if you think you're coming home,' Millie muttered.

'Too late. Betty's going back to Essex tonight and I've

already moved my stuff back in,' he snapped. 'It's my house. You're my wife.'

'B-but why now?'

'Betty prefers the countryside now, reckons the East End's a hole, so she wants to stay in Essex, but me, I prefer to be where the action is.'

Teasingly, he reached out and tugged the top button of Millie's blouse.

'So I ain't going back with her. Besides,' he said, lowering his voice, 'I'm bored of her, she ain't a patch on you in the sack, Millie.'

'Oh, piss off, Curly,' she said loudly, slapping his hand away.

All around, conversations tailed off. Sensing a juicy story, the reporter's ears had pricked up and he was watching intently.

'Give me a couple of bags of them tomatoes,' he ordered, pulling a wad of notes from his pocket.

'No!' she said, crossing her arms.

'What's up, Millie? You don't like the colour of my money?'

'Do you know people laugh at you behind your back?' she yelled, anger heating her cheeks. 'They know the only way you could get a wife is through winning a dodgy card game.'

'Stop making a fool of yourself and give me two bags of tomatoes, or—'

'Or what?' Millie challenged, her shrill voice silencing the crowd. 'You'll give me another smack round the face?'

'Millie, you go and serve the customer at the end, I'll deal with this,' said Mrs Frobisher firmly.

'We are limited to one 1lb bag per customer,' she said, coolly surveying Curly. 'That's 1s 8d, please.'

Curly's smile was mocking as he handed over his money, and to Pearl's disgust she realized he was actually enjoying this.

'Now please be on your way,' said Mrs Frobisher. 'We don't want any trouble here, Mr Brown.'

'Don't worry, I'm going. Just one last thing, though.'

In a flash, he waved the photographer over and moved round the side of the table next to Pearl.

'Can I have my photo taken with this lovely match girl?'

Pearl recoiled from his touch. 'No . . . no, I don't think so,' she stuttered.

'Don't be daft, this is your moment,' grinned the photographer.

Taking his cap off, Curly slung his arm round Pearl's shoulder and grinned broadly as the photographer raised his Box Brownie.

'These girls deserve a medal for all they're doing for the Dig for Victory campaign,' he told the reporter. 'Poor husbands forgotten at home, homes abandoned and all for the national effort. Put that in your paper.'

Fifteen

Four days later the girls waited outside the back gates to the factory, dressed in their dungarees and clutching an assortment of tools.

'This is a touch, ain't it? Getting an afternoon off work!' Annie announced brightly.

'I know,' Rose agreed, still stunned that the factory bosses had said they could leave early to take part in the Allotment Week parade through the city, ending at Victoria Park. 'They must've been pleased with that write-up in the *Express*.'

Millie pulled a copy of the paper from her satchel and scowled.

'They might be, but I ain't! How the hell did he manage to muscle in and get his ugly mug on the front of the paper?'

Under the headline *Sparky Match Girls Dig for Victory* was a photo of a beaming Millie posing in front of the gates to the Fairfield Works. A smaller photo, buried in the text, showed Curly with one hand clamped around Pearl's shoulder.

'Locals show their appreciation for the Match Girls' green fingers,' she spat, reading out the picture caption.

'I'd like to shove those tomatoes right where the sun don't shine.'

'Just put it away, Millie,' Pearl groaned. 'I can't bear looking at it.'

'Yeah,' said Annie. 'This ain't about Curly. This is about the allotment, and all our hard work.' Her green eyes shone fiercely under the halo of copper curls. 'This is our big chance, girls, to show what we're made of. The Queen's coming to visit us. Us!

'Millie, you promised we'd make this the best bloody allotment the East End's ever seen!'

'Sorry, Annie, you're right,' said Millie, shoving the paper back in her bag. 'Let's not let that toerag take the shine off it.'

In the distance, a dull thud echoed off the cobbles, followed by the clash of brass. Pip's ears pricked up and he began to bark.

'Oh, look, girls!' Annie cried. 'There's a band accompanying the march.'

Moments later, the girls joined the march and were caught up in the spectacle and jubilation of the Dig for Victory celebration.

There were allotment groups from all over the East End, marching in their wellies, pitchforks and spades proudly held aloft. Children clung to the tops of gas lamps, housewives in aprons stood on their steps applauding, even locals spilled out of the many pubs to whistle as they marched past.

'This is terrific!' Rose exclaimed, gazing up, wide-eyed, at the home-made bunting fluttering overhead.

Soon the march had turned left into Blondin Street, and

Rose smiled as she caught sight of Elsie and all the neighbours gathered in a great gaggle at the end of the road.

'There they are!' Elsie whooped, waving a Union Jack flag furiously overhead.

'I'm proud of you girls!' she shrieked, before putting her fingers between her lips, sending an ear-splitting whistle up the street.

'Nan, stop it, you're embarrassing us,' Annie scolded, but Rose could see she was secretly chuffed to bits.

Rose glanced over to her doorstep, to see if Maureen was standing outside. The door was shut. She caught a glimpse of her mother's face, pale and disapproving, behind the net curtains.

The march was a long one and by the time they reached the Royal Exchange in the City of London, Rose's feet were numb in her boots. Her spirits lifted when she saw the enormous crowds gathered at the busy intersection.

'Look at that,' cried Annie. A gigantic banner had been slung across the pillared facade of the imposing building.

Dig for Victory!

A Ministry of Information Crown Production Unit was standing underneath the banner, filming them as they marched past.

'The rallying cry of "Dig for Victory" has been heard and obeyed all over the country,' cried the reporter over the cheers. 'By jove, these plucky girls have even recruited a dog!' The camera swung round towards them.

'Come on, girls!' Millie was breathless with excitement as she hauled them all in front of the camera. 'I always wanted to be famous.'

'No, Millie, I really don't . . .' Pearl protested, but it was too late, Millie had her firmly by the arm as the reporter pressed his microphone under their noses.

'Where are your allotments, girls?'

'Bryant & May, we're the match girls of Bow,' said Millie proudly.

'How terrific! Channelling the esprit de corps of the original match girls, no doubt.'

'That's right,' Annie grinned. 'I'm Annie, this is Millie, Pearl and Rose.'

'And not forgetting our best victory digger,' Rose added shyly, holding Pip up.

'Marvellous stuff.' He turned back to the camera.

'What about that then? Chaps, take note. Don't be shown up by four girls and a dog. Put your garden on war service.'

Millie was jubilant as they rejoined the march.

'Just think, girls. We might end up in every picture house in the country! I always wanted to be on the big screen!'

At the entrance to Vicky Park, the crowds intensified as the march came to an end by the allotments. Kids ran shrieking through the trees with toffee apples, and bright sunshine dappled the grass. So many evacuated children were home again now the bombs had stopped. It was a gratifying sight.

'I'll go and get us some lemonade, I'm parched,' said Millie, putting her pitchfork down in relief.

Rose sat down to wait, her back against the railings to the lido, while Annie and Pearl chatted to a horticultural inspector.

She gazed at the glittering waters of the lido, which she,

Annie and Millie had used all the time before war broke out, and which now supplied the fire service. Suddenly Pip was straining against his leash, jumping up and down and yapping excitedly.

'What's up, boy?'

A shadow fell over the grass in front of her, then a familiar face hove into view.

'R-Rose? It's me, Tom Beckton, from the Young Farmers' Club. Do you remember me?'

'Of course I do,' she said, feeling guilt and joy in the same moment.

His smile faltered. 'Only, you never wrote. Did you not get my letters?'

Rose climbed to her feet, brushing the grass off her dungarees.

'I-I never got any letters.'

'But I wrote,' he protested, 'lots of times.'

Rose sagged. 'I believe you. They must've got lost in the post.'

Tom looked confused, but not without hope.

'That's the war for you, but, well, I'm here now and . . . Oh, Rose, I can't tell you how good it is to see you again! Say, what happened to your hair?'

Her fingers leapt to the ends of her hair; twenty-two months and still it hadn't grown much past her shoulders.

'Cut it off. It's a danger round the machines at work,' she lied, the blood rushing awkwardly to her cheeks.

'You're still just as pretty,' he said, blushing. 'Listen, I'm down for a few days, helping out with Allotment Week. Mayn't I take you to the pictures, Rose?'

'I don't think it's a good idea,' she muttered, picking Pip up.

'Oh,' he replied, crestfallen.

A silence fell between them as Pip looked from one to the other.

'Can I buy you a lemonade?'

'My pal's getting me one.'

Tom stared at her, dejected, and Rose wanted to cry out.

'Okey-dokey. I'll, er, I'll go then, shall I?'

She nodded, squeezing back tears.

He turned to leave, but stopped and fished something out of his pocket.

'I was hoping I'd bump into you today, so I bought this.'

He pressed something into her fingers then turned and hurried off through the crowds.

Rose looked down. In her palm lay a small pink marzipan fish, wrapped in tissue, the colouring beginning to bleed in the hot sunshine. In that moment, she felt torn open. She had feelings for Tom. Strong feelings. She opened her mouth to call him back, but Maureen's voice cut through her thoughts.

You got bad blood in you.

Maybe that's why she'd so readily held hands with Tom in the yard that evening. It surely wasn't normal to want him to put his arms around her, put his lips on hers . . . was it? Maureen had told her where kissing led, what it had done to her mother.

'Oh, Pip.' She stifled a sob and buried her face in his warm fur. Why was life so confusing?

*

Millie strode through the noise and sunshine of the park, towards the lemonade tent, enjoying the feel of a cool breeze against her neck. She rolled up the sleeves of her jade-green blouse, and decided if nothing else she would give herself an afternoon off from worrying about Samuel.

Suddenly, a tall compelling figure in blue stepped out in front of her and the breath left her lungs.

'Oh God!' she gasped, her hand leaping to her mouth. He touched her elbow gently and the tears streamed silently down her cheek.

'I'm sorry,' Samuel whispered, his breath hot in her ear as he steadied her trembling arm. 'I didn't mean to surprise you like this. I went to the factory and Mrs Frobisher told me you'd be here. I have a few days' leave.'

She closed her eyes, totally unable to form a coherent sentence.

'I've been reading all about the bombing campaign in the papers,' she whispered eventually. 'I thought you were dead.'

'So did I. Listen, let's get away from here. Can you escape?'

She nodded and they slipped away from the crowds.

As they strode quickly from the noise of the park allotments, she stared up at his face. Millie tried to hide her shock. He was the same handsome, blond-haired, blue-eyed poster boy for the RAF, but something had altered since she last saw him. More than just the dark smudges under his eyes, or even the grey pallor of his skin. Gone was the newness, the shininess of him; he had an exhaustion about him that went beyond mere tiredness.

They walked quickly to the furthest reaches of the park,

into the shade of a bank of plane trees, and only then did Samuel pull her into his arms.

Without saying a word, he kissed her hungrily as his hands closed round her waist. The first time Samuel had kissed her in the ruins of the church, it had been with such tenderness, reverence almost. This was different – a passionate urgency that left her senses reeling. He'd brought the smells of his base with him: cigarettes, rubber and oil.

Finally, he let her up for air.

'Sorry,' he sighed, pulling her headscarf off and gently running his fingers through her hair. 'You must think me an animal! I've been waiting to do that for a very long time. I didn't even have time to shower properly. The minute I found I had leave, I hitched a lift to the train station.'

He cupped her face and kissed her again, softer this time, slow and deep, his fingers probing the naked skin of her neck.

'You've no idea how many times I've dreamt of this moment.'

They sat under the spreading canopy of leaves and Samuel pulled a picnic and a slightly frayed blanket from his kit bag.

'All I could grab from the mess on the way out. A WAAF prepared it for me for the journey, but I wanted to wait and save it to eat with you.'

The picnic might have been begged and borrowed, but it looked like heaven to Millie's eyes. Slices of wholemeal buttered bread, damson jam, boiled eggs, a slither of chocolate and, joy of joys, an orange!

'Wherever did you get that?' she exclaimed.

'We get them on base, along with extra rations of butter

and eggs. Margaret, that's the WAAF I mentioned, she makes sure to always keep one aside for me.'

Millie felt an ugly prickle of jealousy.

'She fancy you, does she?' she muttered, picking up the orange and rolling it between her fingers.

'I don't think so,' he laughed. 'She bosses me like a little brother, but secretly I think she feels sorry for me.'

'Oh,' Millie mumbled, feeling foolish.

'Come on, let's eat. I'm famished.'

As they tucked into the picnic, Millie was all questions about his first two months on active service. She discovered the food was 'plentiful', the base 'a Nissen-hutted mud lake' and the WAAFs 'jolly'.

'It's my crew who keep me sane,' he added, as he chewed thoughtfully.

'How's that?'

'Well, we're a mixed bag. Not a tribe so much, like you match girls, but they're my comrades.' He paused. 'I don't know, Millie, it goes beyond friendship to something deeper . . . I'm not explaining myself terribly well, am I?'

'Go on,' she coaxed, sensing he needed to talk.

'It's like we have a telepathic understanding of each other.' He smiled wearily. 'Talk about superstitious, though. Frank, my Australian navigator, insists on listening to "Waltzing Matilda" on the mess gramophone before each op and Billy, my rear gunner, you ought to see his turret by the time he's finished decorating it with charms and rabbits' feet.'

He sighed and traced his fingers through the dust. 'Billy's a good kid, eighteen and only just got married when we got pulled out of OTU early. He's with his wife now in

Bethnal Green, just up the road. Belated honeymoon.' A smile suddenly creased his face. 'We went on a crew binge together, he taught me a few songs . . .'

'I can imagine,' Millie grinned, arching one eyebrow.

Samuel yawned and leant back against the grass, kicking his long legs out as he peeled the orange.

'And you, what lucky charm have you got?' Millie asked, stroking his forehead.

'I don't need one, I've got you,' he grinned sleepily, taking her fingers and pressing them to his mouth.

In that moment, it suddenly seemed very important that he had something, some sort of talisman to remind him of her. But what could she possibly give him? The old Millie would probably have given him a pair of satin unmentionables, but this one was shaped by her encounter with him. She dug into the pockets of her dungarees and pulled out a crumpled packet of marigold seeds.

'Have these, I was going to plant them round the potatoes to stop beetles, like you showed us, but I want you to take them with you.'

She bent down and brushed her lips softly over his. He tasted sweet this time, of damson jam. 'We can plant them together. When you come home.'

Samuel drew back.

'Millie, you really ought to know, you know there's every chance—'

'Don't.' She pressed her finger to his lips and slipped the seeds into his pocket. 'I'm not stupid, I read the papers, but I don't want to hear it.'

He nodded. He didn't really want to tell her either. How could he even begin to describe the sensation of flying through that great wall of flak surrounding Essen? The astonishing conflagrations of fire, aircraft plunging out of the night sky into the glowing red core of the burning city beneath . . . How could he explain that he didn't just sense the hand of the Grim Reaper, he walked in his shadow every single day?

But he was alive now, and with some of the greatest pleasures a man could have in life, a knockout girl by his side and warm sun on his face.

He broke off a segment of orange and handed it to Millie.

She bit into it and giggled as the juice ran down her chin.

'What does it taste like?'

'Try for yourself,' she said teasingly.

'Very well.'

Quick as a flash he flipped her back, so her blonde hair fanned out over the grass, and kissed the juice from her soft pink mouth.

'This is going to sound terribly corny, Millie,' he sighed, 'but I've seen stars and sunsets that'd make you believe in God; the Alps by moonlight . . . But nothing, I swear, is as beautiful as the sight of your face against the grass.'

He kissed her once more.

'*You* are my reward for staying alive, Millie.'

'And there was me thinking it was a plate of bacon and eggs after debriefing,' she quipped.

'I'm serious, Millie. I'm in love with you. I-I think I fell in love with you the moment I first laid eyes on you.'

His confession hung in the still summer air between them.

She smiled dizzyingly, then held him in her arms until his eyelids flickered shut. As he slept, diagonal pillars of sun began to creep over the park, casting a gentle peach hue over his face.

'And I'm in love with you,' she whispered, tracing her fingers along his jawline, over the faint dimple in his chin, trying to commit every detail of his face to her memory.

After an hour, he woke.

'Damn! Did I fall asleep?'

She nodded.

'What time is it?'

'Close to 7 p.m.'

'Do you have to get home . . . to him?'

Millie shivered, feeling suddenly cold.

'I'm all yours.'

'Good,' he said, clambering to his feet and draping his coat round her shoulders.

'Where are we going?' she asked hesitantly, as he linked his fingers through hers. 'Only, I have to be careful.'

'Sadler's Wells Ballet is performing in the park tonight. I bagged us a couple of tickets to *Swan Lake* earlier, only sixpence each.'

Millie smiled. 'Don't worry, I don't think we'll bump into Curly there. Ballet's not really his scene.'

In truth, she didn't really think it was hers either – she'd far rather have gone dancing. But if it meant a few more precious hours in Samuel's company, then she was game.

At the performance, she was stunned to see thousands of East Enders clustered on the scorched earth of the park.

'I think you'll enjoy this,' Samuel said. 'It's been getting terrific reviews up and down the country.'

Millie nestled into Samuel's arms and watched, captivated, as the first dancers appeared on the makeshift stage. She had never seen anything as thrilling as their grace and stamina. For two and a half hours, she snatched life back from the war.

As the last notes quivered over the fading dusk of the park, Millie almost felt moved to tears. Samuel watched her closely, enjoying the look of pure enchantment on her face.

'Breathtaking, isn't it?' he said, gently picking a blade of grass from her hair.

As they stood and began to gather their things, a passing street photographer paused, drawn by the sight of such an attractive young couple.

'Keepsake for you and your husband?' he asked, nodding at his Box Brownie.

Millie looked nervously at her wedding ring and back to Samuel.

'Why not,' he replied, without a second's hesitation.

Samuel paid the photographer and gave him the address of his squadron to send the photo to. 'A memento for me to keep.'

The photographer pressed his finger over the shutter release and they both smiled into the warmth of a perfect summer's evening.

'God bless you both,' said the photographer, shaking Samuel's hand firmly. 'Finish the job off, and then make sure you come home safe to this lovely wife of yours.'

When he was out of earshot, Millie asked him why he hadn't sent the photographer away.

'Because I liked pretending you belonged to me.'

'Why me, Samuel?' she asked, baffled. 'I mean, you could be off with your pals getting drunk in the mess.'

Samuel shrugged. 'Not my scene.'

'But even if I weren't married,' she persisted, 'it could never work!'

'Why?'

'For starters, imagine introducing me to your mother. She'll be reaching for the bug powder and locking up her silver soon as I open my mouth.'

'She's not like that.'

'Very well, I have dinner, you eat luncheon.'

'So we'll have picnics,' he grinned.

'Ha ha, very funny.'

'I'm not mocking you! If this war is teaching me anything, it's that class doesn't matter. In the finish, we're all just human beings.'

'Some of us more human than others,' Millie remarked.

'I'm serious. I'm convinced that when this war is over, we'll be a society of equals.'

She smiled at his optimism.

They had reached the park gates by now, time to go their separate ways: Samuel to his lodgings, Millie home to her husband. Streams of people hurried past them, back to hot cocoa and warm shared beds, she thought enviously.

'You know I can't get divorced,' she said quietly.

'There must be a way to prove your marriage was unlawful,' Samuel replied, under his breath. 'My pal, he flies Spitfires now, but before the war, he'd just trained as a lawyer.'

'So?'

'So if anyone can show you were coerced into that

marriage, it's him. Admittedly, I don't know much about the law, but even I can see you had no choice but to marry that man. If . . . if I survive, when the war is over, I'll do whatever it takes to find out, I promise.'

Millie smiled up at him, stroking her fingers slowly along the sweep of his jaw.

There were a lot of *if*s in that statement, and God knew the odds were stacked against them. But for the first time in years, Millie felt a fragment of hope.

'You have to believe me, Millie,' Samuel urged. 'I promise, I'll sort this mess out.'

'I believe you, but look here. I don't want charity.'

'Millie—'

'Hear me out. I've money of my own, a savings account with Bryant & May, three and half per cent we get on savings. I got nearly £100 in an account that Curly knows nothing about.'

'Clever girl,' Samuel smiled, looking impressed.

The evening was slipping away now, and on the horizon, an enormous silver moon was rising over the treetops. In the velvety light, Millie finally plucked up the courage to ask the question.

'How . . . how many more ops do you need to fly?'

'Millie, I don't think—'

'How many?'

'Twenty.'

'That many! I'd have thought your numbers would be higher.'

'Not every sortie counts,' he explained. 'Gardening runs, attacking targets over France . . . If we have to turn back because of weather, they only count as a third of an op.'

'That's bloody unfair.'

'That's exactly what Billy said, funnily enough. But listen, Millie, it really doesn't pay to play the numbers game.'

She nodded, trying desperately to swallow back her tears.

'If it makes you feel better, I'm a meticulous flyer and I don't take unnecessary risks.'

He could have said more, of course: that flying through flak barrage is like Russian roulette, that only one in six aircrews complete their first tour. Instead, he tilted her chin up and drank in the sight of her beautiful face bathed in the moonlight.

'One day, you will belong to me,' he vowed.

'Then you must stay alive, Samuel,' she urged, her tears breaking free. 'You must.'

*

'They must be here somewhere,' Rose muttered under her breath, as she searched through the chest in her mother's bedroom. She'd be back from her cafe shift any moment.

She flung aside some rather musty drawers. Nothing. Her foot creaked on the board by the bed and she realized it wasn't nailed down. It lifted up easily, and there they were. Tom's letters, dozens of them. Rose shook her head at the sight of his perfect looped handwriting. Words leapt up from the mildewed paper.

I think of you all the time . . . Yours, hopefully . . . Was it something I said or did?

She stuffed them back into their hiding place, unable to look at them a second longer.

In that moment she despised Maureen, hated her for taking her youth and nailing it beneath the floor. Then another letter caught her eye, the handwriting nothing like Tom's. She opened it and scanned the contents, her eyes growing wide with disbelief.

> *Civil Defence Post B have informed us of the bravery
> of your adopted dog, Pip, in digging you out from the
> bomb blast on Fairfield Road last month. Poplar
> Borough Council should like to award him for his
> tremendous bravery at a special civic awards ceremony
> for heroes of the Blitz. Please reply at your earliest
> convenience.*

The letter was dated June 1941 . . . Two years ago. Anger, hot and bright, sliced through Rose's head. It was an unspeakably wicked thing to do. In a queer way, she begrudged this more than she did the concealing of Tom's letters. How could Maureen?

Rose replaced the letters just as the front door downstairs banged shut.

'Mum!' she stormed out into the passage, but one look at Maureen's face stole her anger away.

'We are out of this dump, girl, I'm telling you. I'm done with the East End.'

Maureen unknotted her headscarf and lit a cigarette, deep lines puckering her mouth as she inhaled deeply.

'What's wrong?'

'They fucking sacked me is what's wrong,' she said, dark eyes flashing.

'What? Why?' Rose gasped.

'For refusing to serve a darkie. Bleedin' cheek of 'em. You should have seen him, Rose, straight off the boat, black as a Newgate knocker.'

She banged her fist against the table.

'It's a disgrace. I've lived in the East End all my life and I barely recognize the place. Nothing's where it should be no more.'

Rose's head was beginning to hurt.

'W-what do you mean?'

'You got Yanks in the street, wops in the park, girls in trousers . . . I mean, look at you lot marching through the streets earlier in your dungarees, carrying on like bloody suffragettes. I've never been so ashamed.'

Rose closed her eyes.

'Well, don't matter no more, 'cause we're leaving.'

Rose's eyes snapped open.

'What?'

'I stopped in at the Town Hall on the way home. Told 'em they're to stick our names down for relocation in the next round of slum clearance.'

'B-but, Mum! I can't leave Bow!'

'I fancy Dagenham myself,' Maureen went on. 'I don't much care, so long as it's away from here. You'll get a job round that way easy, I'll speak for you.'

'I have a job already, and friends, and a dog . . .'

'You'll make new friends. My mind's made up.'

'When?' she whispered.

'They reckoned it could be six months.'

'Mum,' Rose said slowly, her anger over the hidden letters now eclipsed by shock. 'I can't leave Blondin Street. It's my home.'

'You ungrateful cow.' Maureen jabbed a nicotine-stained finger in Rose's direction. 'I gave up the best years of my life to raise you and you're not even my own flesh. The least you can do is look after me in my twilight years.'

Sixteen

For Millie, her memories of the rest of that hot and torrid summer were illuminated in sound: the soft cluck and scratch of two plump new pullets; *In Your Garden* crackling over the allotment wireless; Vera Lynn reassuring a nation of sweethearts that they would meet again . . .

Samuel's declaration of love had filled her with bittersweet joy. She might be eighteen again, the same dazzling blonde who smiled out from the Swan Vesta billboard, when life had held such promise. Her affair with Samuel had given back the joy to her life that marriage to Curly had leached from her.

The allotment had become a womb, not just to Millie, but all the girls, nurturing and protecting them from the horrors of the war. The constant circle of sowing and harvesting, weeding and hoeing had kept nerves steady and minds occupied. So much so that by late September, as Samuel clocked up more stencilled bombs on his fuselage, Millie had almost begun to convince herself that it was possible.

She had seen him twice since that dreamlike July night in the park. Two precious visits in which he had arrived without warning on leave, bone-weary and haunted by whatever he had seen over the night skies of Germany. Each time he had thrown himself into the allotment, working with a feverish intensity, until his adrenalin levels returned to normal, and then . . .

Millie smiled as she looked up from the earth and gazed at the dark recesses of the potting shed, remembering stolen kisses amongst the seedlings.

'Wherever you are, dear, can I join you?' Elsie's voice cut through her tumbling thoughts.

'What? Oh, sorry, Mrs T. I was miles away.'

'I can see that,' Elsie said with a wink. 'Thinking of the pickling party, were you, dear?'

'Something like that,' Millie replied, returning to the winter spinach she was sowing with an enigmatic smile.

Thanks to the cloches Samuel had introduced to extend the growing season, combined with Elsie's magic compost and an exceptionally warm summer, they were overrun with fruit and vegetables. It had been Annie's idea for them all to go back to hers that evening and make up big batches of pickles, chutneys and jam. They were working as hard as possible to harvest the produce before the last of the light went.

'Mrs Frobisher told me that producing foods for the winter will go towards our Certificate of Merit,' Annie remarked, looking up from where she was carefully storing potatoes in pallets of dry earth. 'She even reckons we could get a visit next month from the Ministry of Agriculture to inspect both sites.'

'They're coming here?' Pearl asked, looking up suddenly over the top of the redcurrant bush she was pruning.

'Blimey,' said Rose. 'We better mind our Ps and Qs.'

'Yeah, we better had . . . Millie!' Annie said, shooting her a meaningful look.

'I'll be like a Girl Guide,' Millie grinned, feigning innocence.

'And I was wondering, do you think we should dig and sow something in that space behind the potting shed?' Annie said, straightening up and wandering over to where the back of the shed butted up against the wall of the recreation ground.

'I know it's a bit dark and damp, but apparently the inspector wants to check we're utilizing every spare inch of the allotment.'

'Good idea,' Millie said. 'Surely we could grow some more spuds back there – shouldn't take us long to double-dig it.'

'Funny,' said Rose, gazing down at the ground. 'Looks like someone's already had a go at digging it, the ground looks freshly dug.'

'You're right, dear,' said Elsie, peering into the dark space.

'Who's been back here?'

'Pip,' Pearl blurted, throwing down her secateurs and hastening over. 'I caught him digging something out of the ground only yesterday. I think it was a dead rat.'

'Urgh,' Annie grimaced, wrinkling her freckled nose. 'Perhaps we'll leave it alone.'

'I reckon,' Millie said, yawning suddenly. 'Don't worry. The rest of the allotments look smashing. That War Ag inspector better be prepared to have his socks knocked off, Annie.'

'She's right, dear,' Elsie said. 'You've all worked so hard, girls, I'm proud of you. If he's not impressed by this, well, there's no hope.'

The girls fell into silence at they looked out over the Girls' Club allotment, hazy in the pearlized light of dusk.

The inspector could never accuse them of not utilizing every spare inch. There were pumpkins growing vertically against bicycle wheel frames, lettuce and radish peeking out between stately lines of Home Guard potatoes and, Millie's favourite, blousy pink dahlias and drifts of lavender bursting out of battered old bathtubs.

Every sunny windowsill down Blondin Street was covered in tomato plants and cress. Even the warden was cultivating dwarf beans against his post and nasturtiums against the gate.

'I reckon 1943 will go down as the year Bryant & May burst into bloom,' Elsie chuckled, looking out over the blaze of crimson, salmon and yellow foliage spangling the earth.

'I'm worried about the flowers, though,' Annie said, chewing her thumbnail.

'Of all the things to worry about!' Millie laughed.

'You mock, but I read about a nurseryman who was fined £15 for cultivating tulips instead of cabbages. Rules is rules.'

'Oh, hang the rules,' Millie sighed. 'What harm is a bathtub full of flowers? Besides, it attracts the bees, and Samuel reckons you can even eat nasturtiums, so there!'

'Come on,' said Elsie, pulling an old battered shawl round her shoulders. 'Light's gone now. I promised Ted we'd meet him back at ours.'

They walked across the grounds in silence, and once they'd spilled out onto Old Ford Road, Annie hung back and tugged on Millie's arm.

'Millie. You and Samuel . . .'

'Oh, please don't start with that carry-on, Annie.'

'Do you know what you're getting into?' she whispered. 'What kind of pal would I be if I weren't looking out for you?'

'I know, and I appreciate it, Annie, sweetheart, truly I do, but I can look out for myself. 'Sides, the main thing is, Curly seems to have finally given up on me.'

'That don't sound like Curly,' Annie said worriedly.

'Honest. Now Betty's gone back to Essex, poor cow, he's busy chasing every bit of skirt going, and who cares? So long as he's not pawing me every night.'

She stopped, pulling Annie to one side as a truck bounced past next to the kerb with half the neighbourhood's nippers clinging to the running board.

'Samuel has a plan,' she whispered, her eyes gleaming with excitement as she waved to the kids. 'It'll all be fine. Trust me.'

*

Back in Blondin Street, Elsie was in her element, juggling great bubbling pans, stirring and wafting away clouds of steam.

She had the pickling party run like a military organization. Pearl was salting beans, Millie was sterilizing old glass jars, Annie was peeling onions and Rose was pretending to chop cauliflower and carrots to make piccalilli, but was secretly feeding Pip under the table. Every window in the tiny terrace had steamed over and the air was thick with vinegary smells.

'It's no good, I can't stop crying,' Annie said, blinking.

'Put your gas mask on,' Millie said. 'That horrible old thing's gotta be useful for something.'

'You're a genius. Oh, bugger it.'

'Language, Annie.'

'Sorry, Nan, but I just remembered I left it on my peg at work.'

'Borrow mine if you like,' Pearl said. 'It's in my drawer.'

Annie scampered upstairs to the room she shared with Pearl and, still blind from the onions, began groping around her drawer in the old wooden chest. She tugged at the box and pulled it out, but suddenly the lid flipped open. As her vision cleared, she saw it wasn't a gas mask after all, but a wooden jewellery box.

Inside, there were smelling salts, a sheet of soot-blackened newspaper, and a photograph . . .

'Oh, Pearl!' Annie gasped, her hand flying to her mouth.

It took her brain a moment to register that the bride in the small portrait was Pearl.

The queerest thing of all, apart from the realization that Pearl was married, was the portrait itself. It was grotesque.

Pearl was a striking bride, all right, her jet-black, wavy hair stunning against the ivory of her high-necked gown, but her expression was rigid, her fingers clamped round a small chalk-white bouquet. The portrait had been tinted, her cheeks painted with a pink dye, but the closer Annie looked, the more she was convinced that beneath the pale pink wash, her eye was bruised and blackened.

The groom stood tall and clean-shaven, an imposing figure in a serge suit and tight smile. The thing that struck Annie most was that, apart from the groom, no one was smiling. It might have been a stiff portrait from the Victorian age.

'What are you doing, Annie?' she muttered, guiltily putting the portrait in the box and carefully replacing it at the back of the drawer. Pearl's private life was just that, private. And if she had chosen not to tell them she was married, then there was obviously a good reason.

Downstairs, Ted was standing in the kitchen and her nan was clutching a bouquet of wild flowers that were wilting in the steam.

'Look at you, all rigged out!' Annie grinned, taking in the suit that was a little on the large side for his wiry frame and the freshly shined boots. Gone was the cheese-cutter cap, and his silver hair was shined to his head with pomade. Even the soot and earth, which was usually embedded into the calluses of his palms and pushed deep under his fingernails, had been scrubbed off.

'Tell your nan, will you, Annie?' he urged.

'Tell her what?'

'That's she's not too old to go to the pictures. I even got her favourite chocolate limes,' he said, patting his pocket.

'Ted wants to take your nan to see a flick at the bug 'ole, but she's not having it,' Millie chipped in.

'Oh, Nan, you ought to go!' Annie cried. 'When was the last time you let your hair down?'

'Don't be daft. At my age? Besides, look at me!' Elsie held out hands stained purple from chopping red cabbage. 'And I've still the jam to make.'

'We can do that, can't we, girls?' Rose said.

''Course we can. Go on out, Mrs T. You're always telling

us to enjoy ourselves, now it's your turn,' Millie remarked. 'But don't be getting fresh on the back row, Ted!'

It was just a joke, but Elsie paled.

'That's enough, dear, I won't have it in my own home.' She trembled. 'I'm a sixty-two-year-old woman. And you, Ted,' she snapped, thrusting the flowers back at him, 'are old enough to know better! We ain't kids no more.'

She tore off her apron and marched up the steps, leaving a cloud of disapproval behind her.

'Sorry, Ted,' Annie grimaced. 'I can't think what's got into her.'

'No, darlin', it's my fault,' he said, throwing the flowers on the kitchen table and rubbing a hand over his face. 'I should've known better.'

The door clicked behind him and the girls exchanged shocked glances.

'What a shame,' Millie sighed. 'You're never too old for love!'

'Clearly Elsie doesn't agree,' Pearl said, getting up and poking the coals in the hearth. 'Not everybody finds happiness through love.'

Just when Annie thought the evening couldn't get any more queer, there was a sharp rap at the door.

'Oh God, it must be Maureen,' said Rose, leaping to her feet. 'I'm late. She'll have my guts for garters.'

But when Annie opened the door, it wasn't Maureen Riley's face she looked upon.

'Samuel!' A flare of joy ran through her, but as he stepped into the passage, Millie froze.

'Whatever's wrong?'

*

Twenty minutes later they were sitting in a British Restaurant on Devons Road, where you could get a square meal for 9d, but it was a mistake. It was busy and the sound of chatter and scraping cutlery seemed to grate on Samuel's nerves.

'I oughtn't to be here,' he said, trailing a spoon through a bowl of watery soup. 'I was only supposed to visit Billy's wife in Bethnal Green, but knowing you were so near . . .' He glanced at his wristwatch. 'I shall have to try and get back to base tonight.'

'Sorry, I don't understand . . . Why've you been with Billy's wife?'

'Because he's dead,' Samuel replied dully. 'And I've just broken that young woman's heart.'

The awful story came out in fractured pieces. Samuel's squadron had been on their way home from an op to the big city, their nickname for Berlin, when they'd been caught by flak, engines so badly damaged they'd limped across the Channel before crash-landing at an emergency airstrip.

'There was no hope for Billy when we found him in the turret . . .'

Samuel squeezed his eyes shut. He saw the images so clearly, like a cinema spool unravelling. Aircraft corkscrewing to earth, cities engulfed in flames, Billy's brains leaking through the plane . . .

He opened his eyes, praying that the throbbing in his head would stop.

'I wanted to be the one to tell her,' he sighed, scrubbing his face, 'not some God-awful telegram. He was my responsibility.'

'How did she take it?'

At this he shook his head, and to Millie's horror she realized he was crying. Heartbroken, painful sobs.

'She's expecting a baby. H-he never knew.'

'Oh, Samuel, no!'

'Turns out he also lied about his age,' he said, pushing away his soup and lighting a cigarette. 'Quite spectacularly, actually. He was seventeen, Millie. *Seventeen!* Too young to die for his country.'

Millie felt the blood in her veins turn to ice.

'Can we get out of here?' he said eventually. Wordlessly, they walked to the only place they could both think of. The allotment. Outside, the night air was fresh and reviving. A bank of cloud covered the moon, so that there was just blackness, relieved only by the star-spangled vault above them. She felt his hand slip into hers and, as they walked, Millie had the queerest sensation she was walking on a path of no return.

Strange odours bloomed through the still night air. All day, the air over Bryant & May had hung heavy with the ripe stench of rotting carcasses from the nearby soap works, but now a gentle easterly blew in the scent of sugar and smoke from the Clarnico sweet factory.

'You could travel the world on the smells of Bow,' Millie sighed.

She felt Samuel's fingers tighten round hers.

'I'd rather stay right here.'

At the Fairfield Works, Samuel helped Millie jump over the wall. She landed with a soft thud on the earth behind the potting shed of the Girls' Club allotment.

They settled on the wooden bench outside the shed and he lit two cigarettes, handing one to her.

'Is the blackbird still here?' he asked, drawing deeply, the tip of his cigarette glowing in the dark.

'Yeah, he's made his nest in the branches of that tree,' she said, gesturing to a sycamore that had seemingly grown up from nowhere after the Blitz.

Samuel exhaled deeply, comforted by the nicotine and being amongst nature.

'If I die, I should like to come back as a blackbird.'

'Why?'

'Better a bird in the next life than a bomber in this one,' he said bitterly, a vein in his jawline jumping. 'Sorry, Millie,' he sighed. 'I didn't drag you away from your friends to come over all maudlin on you.'

Suddenly, the bank of cloud slid away to reveal a perfect waxing moon.

'I–I just needed to see you. My love for you is the only thing that makes sense to me right now.'

She could see his face, bathed silver in the moonlight, and felt a rush of longing.

The night was warm and still, lacing the allotment with an intoxicating fragrance. Lavender, roses and evening primrose still bloomed, bravely waiting for the first frost. Samuel rose and held out his hand.

The minute they were inside the cool darkness of the shed, Samuel turned and caught Millie in his arms, his mouth groping for hers.

In one swift move, he picked her up and her buttocks grazed the shelf, scattering seeds and earth everywhere. Their mouths barely broke off, their kisses urgent, as he tugged her blouse free from the waist of her skirt. His fingers slid over her flesh, stroking the curve of her back, circling her waist, unbuttoning the blouse.

Her fingers responded, finding the gaps between his shirt buttons, the hot skin beneath. The darkness was heightening her senses, making her blood rush. *The musky fragrance of rosemary and sage, the ripe tang of fertilizer, the feel of the sun-warmed wooden shelf scraping the flesh on her thigh . . .*

'Not sure this is allowed,' she joked weakly, as his hands toyed with the final button. 'The committee may terminate the membership of a member whose conduct is detrimental . . .' She inhaled sharply as his fingers teased open her blouse and the silky material slid over her shoulders and slithered onto the floor of the potting shed. Goosebumps spread over the naked flesh on her shoulders, and her skin glowed creamy in the dim light of the shed.

Samuel pulled back, his eyes drinking in the sight of her smooth white limbs and luscious mouth.

He shook his head, incredulous. 'You are perfect, Millie, so astonishingly beautiful.'

Her heart ached with exquisite love; never had she felt so exposed or vulnerable. Then she felt his breath tingling in her hair, his strong hands exploring her body and she felt her desire rise and swell.

'I-I thought you wanted to wait,' she murmured.

'I'm already on borrowed time,' he breathed, sliding his fingers round the back of her neck and drawing her closer.

The heat between them grew with every touch and as his fingers unclipped her garter and teased down her stockings, sex became not only inevitable, but impossible to delay a moment longer.

He broke off and gazed down at her, his eyes glazed with longing. 'Shall I stop?'

Millie said nothing, for there was no turning back now. Instead, she reached over and with a kick of her heel, slammed shut the door to the potting shed.

*

Annie yawned and padded over to the sash window. Drawing back the blackout blind, she peered out between the criss-crossed anti-blast tape. To her surprise, she saw dawn was breaking over the rooftops of Blondin Street. The factory chimneys smoked dreamily in the mist. Loose skeins of smoke hung in the street and, in the distance, the clanking of milk bottles echoed off the cobbles.

She had given up trying to sleep and, not wanting to wake Pearl, she had come downstairs and fixed herself a Bournvita, but her mind was like a ticking clock. The wedding photo had disturbed her more than she cared to admit. Why had Pearl left Liverpool and her husband? Was she in some kind of trouble? More importantly, should she tell her nan, or stay quiet?

Her mind grappled with all eventualities, but it always came back to the same thing – she had no right to be going through Pearl's belongings. Whatever the real reason was for running from Liverpool, Pearl had found safety and a sense of belonging here in Bow. Annie owed it to her friend to keep her secrets. And it wasn't just Pearl she feared for. As match girls and friends, they had always been so tight, but lately . . .

Millie was playing with fire; one look at her face when

Samuel had arrived at the house unexpectedly last night left Annie in no doubt that her dear friend had fallen head-long in love. And as for sweet Rose, the thought of her leaving Bow was simply unimaginable. Elsie had told her not to interfere, but how could she sit by and let her best friend vanish from her life?

Outside, the sun was rising, turning the sky a sallow yellow; even the clouds looked bruised. Maybe she was overreacting from a sleepless night, but a sense of impend-ing doom seemed to coat everything. Blondin Street looked the same, but everything felt different. Annie did not know it then, but all their lives in Bow had shifted key, and they were hurtling towards an uncertain end, ready or not.

The aged boards in the passage creaked and Annie turned.

'Morning, darlin' girl.'

Elsie blinked wearily and, pulling her housecoat about her, started to clear out the grate, filling the air with the musky smell of embers.

'You go on up and wake Pearl. I'll make you both a nice cup of tea before work.'

'Thanks, Nan.' Annie wandered over and kissed her nan softly on the cheek.

'What's that for?' Elsie smiled

'For being the best nan in the world. I know you miss Dad as much as I do, yet you never let on.'

'I pray for him every night, darlin' girl, but we have to get on with things.'

'You're right,' Annie replied. 'And I'm sorry about last night, pressuring you to go to the pictures with Ted . . .'

'About that,' Elsie said warily. 'I'd appreciate it if you wouldn't invite Ted round here no more.'

'But why?' Annie gasped. 'Ted's smashing. I . . . I half hoped you and he . . .'

'Oh, I know what you thought all right, madam. You always did have a warm imagination! Well, it ain't happening. There is no me and Ted. Never has been, never will be. You're not to invite him round here again.'

Outside, the factory's steam hooter sounded, signalling the end of the conversation.

Seventeen

Scrawls of black cloud dirtied the sky and a rattling wind sent dry leaves spiralling into the air when the inspector finally came to call on a filthy November morning. The first frosts had already arrived and seen off the roses and the last of the tomatoes. Even the sturdy root veg looked as if they were battening down the hatches for winter.

'I apologize it's taken so long to reach you,' remarked the man from the Ministry of Agriculture, holding on to his trilby hat for dear life. 'It's terrifically busy for allotments in the East End. Who'd have thought it? Hardly a blade of grass to call your own!'

'Patronizing sod,' Millie muttered under her breath. Annie silenced her with a swift kick.

'Not so surprising, East Enders have a long tradition of gardening,' said Ted smoothly, crossing his strong arms. 'Look in any backyard and you'll find chickens, rabbits and veg!'

Suddenly, an enormous gust of wind picked up the inspector's hat and sent it flying, to reveal a shiny bald head. It landed with a soft thud on the compost heap.

'Oops,' grinned Ted, racing after it and fishing it out. 'That compost is pretty ripe. Still, look on the bright side – might make your hair grow back.' His eyes glittered with good humour and everyone laughed . . . Except the inspector.

'Shall we press on?' he said icily, wiping the rim of his hat with a handkerchief.

Annie knew the moment she had shaken his hand that this wasn't going to go well, and five minutes into his inspection her suspicions were proved correct.

'Flowers!' the inspector remarked, staring in disbelief at a few hardy perennials still bravely clinging onto their blooms. 'This isn't a flower show. Nourishment is the point, young lady. Utility, not beauty.'

'We planted them to attract wildlife and bees, not to look pretty,' Annie protested.

'All the same, dig them up,' he ordered. 'Plant vegetables of national importance instead.'

As he stomped off, Annie felt territorial. Who was he to say what their allotment's purpose was? Since they had started it over two years ago, she had discovered an increasing appreciation of the natural world. There was such pleasure in unearthing a potato, seeing the first crop of beans or the blossoming of a blousy dahlia. Gardening was primal. For the first time ever, Annie was connected to the changing of the seasons, something she had previously only noticed by seeing what colour the sky was outside the factory windows. How could all that be condensed down into a food production unit?

After that, the inspector found fault in everything. The sunken container filled with beer to ward off slugs, which he unfortunately stepped in, was dismissed as 'nonsense'; the scattered eggshells also used to deter slugs, 'hocus pocus'; and the glistening bands of copper round the herbs to stop the snails in their tracks, 'bunkum'.

'It's a wonder you're not overrun with pests,' he snapped, scribbling furiously in a notebook.

Annie shot a look at Ted and the girls, all of whom were as grim-faced as she was, with the exception of Millie, who was in a world of her own, staring at a blackbird with a peculiar look on her face.

Then came the final straw. The inspector discovered that the remains of their potato crop was infected with blight.

'I-I don't understand it,' Annie stammered as he showed her first the infected tuber, rotten and spongy to the touch. 'This has never happened before.'

'One doesn't have to be an assiduous reader of Dig for Victory material to know that liberal spraying with fungicides is the only way to prevent an outbreak of blight,' he said piously.

'Samuel says there's a risk of cumulative chemical damage spraying in an industrial area,' said Annie, staring in dismay at the diseased potato.

'Well, whoever this Samuel chap is, he is misinformed,' he sniffed, tearing the sheet from his notebook and handing it to her.

'Samuel is only the gardener for the Earl of Frampton, is all,' snapped Millie, wrenching her eyes away from the blackbird and turning on him.

'Be that as it may, prophylactic measures need to be taken immediately to prevent this spreading. On that sheet, you will find details of the appropriate chemicals which need to be purchased.'

The list of chemical solutions swam in front of Annie's eyes.

'I'm afraid I shan't be awarding a Certificate of Merit today. Gardeners need to prove they are using their allotment to produce food in winter as well as summer. Quite clearly this is not the case here.'

He picked up his briefcase. 'I shall return next spring, and hopefully you will have implemented my suggestions by then. Good day.'

Everyone stared bleakly as he strode from the allotments, Pip running after him, nipping at his toes.

'Pip, stop that racket and come back here,' Rose ordered.

'What a disaster!' Annie wailed.

'Rotten sod,' Millie sniffed.

'Except we need that certificate,' Annie protested. 'The bosses have told us how important it is, especially if we're to get a visit from the Queen next year.' Suddenly she felt a crushing sense of disappointment.

'Ah well, the gods weren't on our side today, love,' Ted said, sliding an arm round her shoulder.

The wind blew a leaden cloud across the darkening sky.

'It's gonna tip down,' sighed Rose. 'Shall we all head in?'

'How about we pop back to yours, Annie?' Ted suggested. He pulled out a sheet of bloodstained newspaper from his bag. 'William sent one of his pigs off to be slaughtered and he only gave me a trotter. I know how much your nan loves them.'

Annie felt awkward.

'Sorry, Ted, she's still being a bit funny about seeing you.'

'It's been seven weeks now,' he mumbled, 'I thought she

might have come round by now. I . . .' He stumbled on his words. 'Well, I miss her.'

Annie studied his lovely, craggy face, as familiar to her now as the shrapnel-pocked factory wall – battle-scarred, but never beaten. Except now he looked crushed.

'She'll come round. Just give her some space.'

'No, she won't,' he sighed, removing his cap and wiping a hand through his grey hair. 'When your nan's made her mind up on something, she won't change it.'

The wind changed direction quite suddenly, bringing with it the stench of pig's blood.

Annie was about to question Ted further, when Millie shot past them, clutching her mouth. Seconds later, the sound of retching came from behind the potting shed.

'Millie, you all right, sweetheart?' Rose called.

When she emerged, wiping her mouth with a hankie, she looked wretched.

'Fine, must have been something I ate. I just feel a little peculiar.'

The whole day was turning out to be a little peculiar, Annie thought with a feeling of foreboding.

*

The next day, a Sunday, Millie didn't think it was possible to feel worse, but every time she bent over to dig out the diseased potatoes, she fought back waves of nausea and anxiety. She put it down to missing Samuel. It was like a form of sickness.

Every waking minute, her thoughts rushed back to him, taking over every corner of her mind. Usually working in the allotment allowed her blissful respite from herself, but since that last night together here, she'd found it difficult to think of anything else. The memory of his touch burnt through her like a fever. She loved him with a passion she had not thought possible. Her love – coupled with a fierce hope – was all that was keeping her going, willing him safe as he flew across the German skies. Well, that and the packet of marigold seeds she had given him as a good luck charm. How stupid she felt now – how the hell was a packet of seeds supposed to protect him from fire and flak?

Last night, at the pictures with the girls, a propaganda film had flashed up. She had watched the pilot climbing into the cockpit of a Lancaster, her eyes brimming with tears as the picture house filled with the throaty roar of the four Rolls-Royce Merlin engines.

'Our boys in blue risking their lives nightly to fly to the major cities of Germany, making good on Air Marshal Harris's claim to raze the Reich from end to end,' sang the commentator cheerfully. People had even started applauding, filling Millie with a crawling horror.

The days had bled into weeks. Seven of them to be precise, with no word. The changing season had mirrored her despair. Her fragile hope slipping further away as she watched the allotment flowers wither and curl, their petals rotting brown.

Millie stood up to stretch out her aching back, but as she did so her head began to spin, and for one awful moment she thought she might black out. She closed her eyes and clutched the side of the potting shed. In the sudden darkness, memories came rushing at her. *Their limbs entwined, pale as stone, lit up by the moonlight falling through the window, the intensity of Samuel's lovemaking, the way they had clung to one another after the act, neither daring to move . . .*

She tried to hold on to the memory but it was fading . . . When she opened her eyes, she could see Mrs Frobisher walking across the dug-up tennis courts towards the allotment.

'Why's Mrs Frobisher here?' asked Pearl. 'She's usually at church now.'

One look at her face, and Millie knew. She didn't need to see the piece of paper clutched in her hand, nor the look of bleakness etched across her usually cheerful face. Her unease turned to a volley of shrieks inside her head as Mrs Frobisher drew closer, her eyes fixed on Millie.

'I'm sorry, girls, but I have tragic news,' she began, her voice trembling. 'I've just received word from Samuel's squadron leader. His plane was shot down over France two days ago during a raid to Berlin. He's missing, not believed to have survived. I-I know you were all terribly fond of him.'

A hush fell over the allotment.

Rose's sobs, a distant hooter . . . all were silent to Millie as she looked around the group in bewilderment. The wind whipped her tangled hair around her face as she fell to her knees on the sodden earth. The grey November skies closed in over her head.

*

The letter arrived a few days later. One of three Samuel had written and left in his locker in the event he didn't come home. One to his mother and father in Sussex, one to his elderly grandmother and, unbeknownst to any of them, one to a married match girl from Bow. Mrs Frobisher had discreetly handed it to Millie in her office on a Wednesday dinnertime, leaving her alone to read it.

For a long while, Millie stood in the aching silence of the office, staring at his handwriting on the front, before ripping it open.

If you're reading this . . .

'No,' she whimpered, closing her fist over it. She couldn't bear to have the image of his last-ever words imprinted on her mind. She only wanted to remember the living Samuel, the one who'd made love to her like a man who knew his time on earth was brief, and believed in her. She had committed every moment of their time together to memory, locking it away like a precious jewel.

She tucked the envelope away, but as she did so, something fell out. A photograph. She blew out slowly, her hands trembling as she picked it up off the floor. It was the two of them, taken by the passing photographer when they were ambling through Vicky Park after the ballet. A sundappled evening with Samuel's hand snaked round her waist. She was squinting against the sun, but he was grinning proudly straight into the camera, both of them drunk on stolen kisses. Just four months ago, on a languid summer's evening, when anything had seemed possible. She could still hear his words.

One day, you will belong to me.

Now he belonged to the earth, the sky or the inky depths of the ocean. The terrible thought occurred to her: there would be no way she could attend his memorial, no chance to grieve publicly for her forbidden love, no full stop to her pain.

'Oh, Samuel,' she sobbed, feeling as if her grief was strangling her.

*

Over the coming days, Millie retreated into herself. She worked relentlessly in the allotment, digging out the diseased potato plants. That's where the girls found her on Sunday morning, one week on from his death, the rain driving against her face horizontally. Her gloves were two cakes of mud and she was soaked to the bone.

'Millie, please,' Pearl cried, 'you don't have to do this.'

'Pearl's right, you need to rest. Come over to Annie's and dry out,' Rose coaxed, gently trying to pull her to her feet.

'I don't want to rest,' she snapped, shrugging her off. 'Samuel would be horrified if he knew we had blight. Supposing they're wrong, eh? Have you thought about that? What if he comes back and sees this?'

The girls exchanged alarmed looks.

'What, you don't think it's possible?' she snapped, desperate for their story to continue.

'You've seen the matchboxes we pack with the fancy French labels on, it's so bombers who bail out have a disguise. Why, even now he could be hiding out in some French farmhouse . . .' She trailed off and went back to her work, driving her spade deep into the churned-up earth.

'Millie,' Annie said, crouching down beside her. The rain spattered off her head, soaking her hair from red to a slick of burnished copper. 'He ain't coming back. You need to face up to that, sweetheart. Maybe we could hold some sort of memorial service here, at the allotment?' Annie persisted gently. 'No one else need know.'

Finally, Millie looked up through her streaming hair, her blue eyes wide with fright.

'Soon everyone will know.'

'How?' Annie asked. 'It's only me, Rose and Pearl who knew about the two of you. Well, I think Nan suspected, but she won't say anything.'

'You don't get it. I'm . . . Well, I'm, you know . . .'

Shakily she dropped the spade and stood up slowly, resting her hand on her stomach. The enormity of what she was saying hit the girls.

'And before you say anything, I'm certain.'

'But what if you *have* got it wrong?' Rose blustered. 'I'm always getting my dates mixed up. It's the war, it's sending everything haywire.'

But Millie knew this wasn't simply a case of confused dates. Two missed bleeds, constant nausea, the bone-sapping weariness that thickened her limbs. She looked down at Pip, shaking with cold in the rain, and scooped him up, as much for comfort as anything.

For a while, all that could be heard was the drumming of the rain on the shed roof, and the screeching of a distant gull.

'W-what are you going to do?' ventured Pearl.

'It's sorted, or at least it will be. I've got an appointment, with a woman down Cable Street. This afternoon. The sooner the better to avoid complications.'

'Oh, Millie, no!' Rose cried. 'There must be another way . . .'

'So tell me,' she said angrily. 'What possible other way can there be for me?'

Silence.

'See. I'm not exactly brimming over with options, am I? I've made the worst mistake possible, now it's up to me to fix it.'

Even after the girls took Millie back to Annie and Pearl's and dried her off and forced sweet tea down her, she still couldn't stop shaking. Fortunately, Elsie was out at church, but she'd be back soon.

'I've got to go,' Millie said, hauling herself out of the seat and tying a headscarf over her blonde hair. 'If I'm not back in work tomorrow, cover for me, will you? Oh God, I feel like I'm going to be sick again.'

She rushed for the door, but Annie was on her feet in a second.

'You ain't going anywhere without us.'

'That's right,' said Pearl softly, taking her bag. 'You're going to need help getting home afterwards.'

'Thank you,' Millie sobbed, surrendering to her tears. Annie had never seen her so petrified and, suddenly, she too felt afraid.

'You're not alone,' she said, linking her arm through Millie's.

'That's right,' Rose smiled, tucking a wisp of her hair under the headscarf.

'Thanks, girls,' Millie replied tremulously, her eyes vast pools. 'Let's get this over with.'

*

The girls walked in silence down Cable Street, eyes darting nervously about. The rain had eased off and the narrow cobbled road was steaming. The air was soupy with sulphurous smells. The thick odour of garlic sausage and smoking fish, mingled with wet concrete, was making Millie gag. A sharp November wind cannoned down the street, cutting her face far sharper than any of Curly's razors could.

'Down here,' she said, jerking her head towards a dark passage that led to a tumbledown court, flapping with laundry strung from side to side. A curious smell of garbage and rotting meat pervaded the oppressive courtyard. Above, a vast sign: SMOKE PLAYERS 'NAVY CUT' CIGARETTES.

A small Jewish grocer was open for business, along with an assortment of other stores, the floors above crowded with rooms, housing God knows how many families.

Next to the grocer was an inconspicuous door. Millie coughed and adjusted her headscarf, her heart hammering out of control.

She glanced to her left. Playing in the gutter was a raggedy assortment of boys playing Gobs. Further up, two girls were carefully unloading an old pram piled with coke and bits of timber and scrap. One of the girls surveyed her curiously through huge black eyes. Behind them another pram, this one with an actual baby in it, tucked up under the blankets sound asleep. Someone had tied a piece of string from the wheel to the doorknocker to stop the pram blowing away. The detail plucked at Millie's heart. Deep in the tenements, and in the depths of poverty, someone had taken care to preserve and nurture life. And now she was about to destroy it because it didn't suit her circumstances.

The truth hit her like a hot wind. She had always imagined she didn't want children, but now she saw with perfect clarity that she did – or rather, she wanted Samuel's child.

'I've got to get out of here!' she cried, wheeling round and stumbling from the courtyard.

＊

Back at Annie's, and overwhelmed by the day's vicissitudes, Millie didn't even have the energy to hide her despair from Elsie.

'You're expecting, aren't you?' said Elsie, sitting down heavily opposite her at the scrubbed table. 'And I'm assuming it ain't Curly's.'

Millie went to protest but Elsie eyed her shrewdly. 'Don't play me like a tuppenny whistle, I know an expectant woman when I see one.'

Millie nodded. The girls stood behind her chair, flanking her protectively.

'Quite the council of war, aren't we, girls?' Elsie said, eyeing them beadily. 'Did you know about this, Annie?'

'She didn't know, not really, and certainly not about the baby,' Millie protested.

'Never mind that,' Elsie replied. 'What we gonna do about it?'

The room was filled with a heavy silence, the only sound the tap, tap, tap of Elsie's slippered foot upon the floorboards.

'I can't go through with it, Else.' The words came out of Millie in a shudder. 'I–I can't get rid of his baby, but what's the alternative? Disappear for nine months? But Curly . . .

Oh Christ! He'll come after me.' Her face was bone white and her hands started to shake. 'He'll kill me, he'll actually kill me.'

Elsie stood up creakily and walked to the scullery, where she poured a glass of cool lemonade and pressed it into Millie's hands, urging her to drink.

The drink was cool and sweet, settling her churning stomach.

'There is another way, dear girl . . .'

'Which is?' she asked warily.

The flames from the gas mantel played on Elsie's face, but her expression was unreadable.

'If you've got to stoop down to the gutter, for God's sake pick something up.'

Millie stared blankly. 'I don't understand.'

'Why must it be Samuel's baby?'

Millie set her glass down with a thump.

'You mean . . .'

'Pass it off as Curly's?' Annie gasped behind her.

Elsie nodded, her eyes as dark as midnight.

'But Curly ain't daft,' Millie cried. 'We haven't been, you know, familiar with each other in months. Besides, I must be at least eight weeks gone now, the dates won't tally up.'

'When a man wants something badly enough, he'll believe anything. Go home and make your peace with him.'

A heavy silence fell over the room. Millie felt a ring of steel enter her soul. Elsie was right.

*

The smell of frying mince hit Rose as she wearily climbed the stairs after leaving Annie's. Inside their rooms, Maureen was stirring a pan with one hand and smoking a cigarette with the other.

'I always said she was fur coat, no knickers,' she crowed.

'What are you talking about?'

'Millie and her artful ways,' Maureen sniffed, tipping her ash into a broken cup. 'Whose was it? Curly's, or that RAF chap she's been having it off with?'

Rose felt her cheeks colour.

'Did it work?' Maureen demanded.

'Did what work?'

Maureen shook her head.

'Don't come the innocent,' she sniffed, turning and pointing the wooden spoon at Rose. 'You forget I know everyone down Cable Street, worked down there, didn't I, huh? You was seen.'

Rose was mortified.

'Who . . . who . . .'

'What are you, a bleedin' owl?' Maureen snapped, her voice rich with scorn. 'Oh, don't tell me no more,' she said, turning back to her mince, 'I don't wanna know. Anyway, it'll probably end up at the bottom of the boating lake in Vicky Park, along with all the other unwanted war babies.'

Rose felt herself gag at the savagery of her mother's words.

'But this loose behaviour . . . This, my girl, is why we're leaving the East End.'

'Mum, not this again. I really don't want to . . .'

'Don't answer me back,' she ordered. 'I told you already.

We're done with the East End, and not a moment too soon by the looks of it.'

Rose stared at the warped floorboards.

'Tomorrow I'm going down the Town Hall again and I'm going to kick up a right fuss. It's a bloody liberty, is what it is. We're in a dangerous dwelling now,' she said, pointing to the jagged crack in the roof with her wooden spoon. 'We want relocating and if they won't, then we'll move anyway. I've an aunt in Chigwell who's got a spare room.'

'I—'

'My mind's made up.'

*

'What changed your mind?' Curly asked, shutting the bedroom door softly behind them and leaning back against it in case Millie had a change of heart.

'You know,' she muttered, peeling off her gloves and tossing them on the bedside table. 'I ain't getting any younger, and this war don't show any sign of ending.'

He stared at her for what felt like a very long time.

'I'm ready to be a mum, is all,' she said defensively.

Her top lip felt like concrete and she swore she could feel her heartbeat pulsing in her fingertips. God in heaven, he would see through it. How could he not?

'I knew you'd come round!' He pushed back off the door and walked slowly towards her, wetting his lips at the same time.

She closed her eyes, hearing the soft thump of his jacket landing on the counterpane, the creak of the floorboards as his hands gripped her waist . . .

She swallowed back bile. Oh God, how could she go through with this? How? It was such a betrayal to Samuel's memory, to all the intimacy they had shared.

'I'm going places,' he whispered wetly in her ear, as he fumbled with his fly buttons. 'They all want to work with me. Jack Spot, I'm in with all the Jews. I ain't Yidified. I'll even work with the Maltese. Now Sabini's been interned, I'll take over there.'

He was ranting now, his breath coming in hot rasps, emboldened by the prospect of what was to come.

'This is the start of something big, Millie,' he vowed, stepping out of his trousers and lowering her onto the bed. 'And I want you by my side for it all.'

Please, Samuel. Forgive me.

He was on her in a flash, so excited he didn't see the tears seep down her cheeks. As his bony hips raked across hers, she cried out in despair. He mistook it for a cry of pleasure and pushed deeper and faster, the veins on his forehead knotting together. As he came to a shuddering climax, Millie balled her hands into fists over the sheets, silently screaming.

Afterwards, neither moved, Curly replete, Millie full of self-loathing.

'Weren't so bad, was it, girl?' he grinned eventually, rolling off her and slapping her thigh.

'Tea?' she offered in a hollow voice.

'No, lie there,' he ordered, thrusting a pillow under her thighs. 'Let it take.'

'You think it'll work first time?'

He smiled smugly.

'Did with Betty. Ain't nothing wrong with my little fellas.'

As he bounded down the stairs, whistling to himself, she collapsed back against the pillows and stared out of the window. Outside a woman laughed. Loneliness and fear yawned in the fading light between the curtains. A slither of tarnished moon rose over the slate rooftops.

Suddenly a flutter of black landed on the windowsill. A blackbird.

Millie closed her eyes and felt a colossal wave of grief which she swore cleaved her heart in two. Samuel was everything that was gentle and handsome and good. Correction. Had been.

The only bright and good thing in her life had gone, and all that was left was rotten and sullied. All except one . . . Her fingers splayed over the cool flesh on her tummy. This baby – Samuel's baby – was all that mattered now.

*

Across the rail tracks, in Blondin Street, Annie had already turned in, exhausted by the emotion of the day, and Pearl was just about to do the same, when Elsie called her back to the fireside.

'Come and sit by me for a while, Pearl,' she said, her voice deceptively light. 'As it's a day of confessions, is there anything you need to share with me, dear?'

Pearl's heart stilled as she sat down next to Elsie.

'I know you ran away from Liverpool. I don't want to pry, but maybe I can help.'

Pearl's pale, slender fingers pushed back the mass of dark hair from her face as she stared into the dying embers of the fire. She was tired. So tired of being afraid.

'A trouble shared is a trouble halved,' Elsie coaxed.

'Where shall I start?'

'From the beginning, dear.'

As she emptied her heart by the fireside, Pearl hoped this would be an end to the story.

PART THREE

Eighteen

The fifth winter of the war had crawled in like a Limehouse fog, the coldest since it began, freezing lead pipes and turning the allotments into solid sheets of ice. There was little cause for merriment or cheer with the dawning of a new year, only weeks of back-breaking digging once the ice had thawed to keep the ground turned over. The girls were just heading there after work on a Thursday to discuss Annie's plans for crop rotation, when Millie suddenly remembered something.

'Oh, Mrs Frobisher wanted me to pop in and see her quickly. I'll catch you up.'

'Millie,' said Annie tactfully, resting her hand on her pal's swollen tummy. 'Why don't you get off home after you've seen Mrs F, and rest?'

'Rest! Whatever for?' she snapped. 'I'm not dying, I'm expecting a baby!'

With that, she turned on her heel and hurried in the direction of the main office block. Honestly, she did wish people wouldn't try to wrap her in cotton wool. At four months gone, she had never felt so well.

As she passed through reception, a familiar photograph pinned to the noticeboard drew her eye and she wandered over for a closer look.

'I don't believe it,' she gasped, unpinning the notice with a trembling hand.

My wife and I would like to pass our gratitude to the work-ers of Bryant & May for the letter and handsome wreath which was delivered to our home, in time for the memorial service of our son, Pilot Samuel Taylor.

Your kind words and thoughts come as a great source of comfort during this time of mourning. Samuel greatly enjoyed his time spent helping to develop the Bryant & May allotments during his leave, and wrote often to tell us all about his admiration for the match girls and the friend-ships he had formed. We hope one day to visit and see the fruits of his labours.

Making the decision to hold a service, in which we hon-oured our beloved only son's life was not an easy one, but in light of recent news, we felt it necessary as a means of accepting and coming to terms with our loss . . .

Tears streamed down Millie's cheeks as she turned on her heel and took the stairs to Mrs Frobisher's office two at a time.

The Welfare Officer was locking up her glass-fronted medicine cabinet and whirled round in shock when Millie burst through the door.

'When were you going to tell me about this?' Millie demanded, angrily brandishing the notice. 'Or were you just hoping I wouldn't see it? You had no right to keep news of his memorial from me.' Even though privately Millie knew there was no way on earth she could have attended, it still hurt to have been deliberately kept in the dark.

'Calm down, my dear,' she soothed, rushing over and guiding Millie to a chair. 'Please don't upset yourself, it won't do in your condition to be getting in a state.'

'It's a bit sodding late for that!' she blazed. 'Why didn't you tell me, and what do they mean, "in light of recent news"?'

'That's why I asked to see you,' she said, drawing up a chair and tenderly taking Millie's shaking hands in hers.

'There's no easy way to say this, but it seems that Samuel's navigator astonished everyone by turning up out of the blue last month at the home of his station commander.'

'What . . . ?' breathed Millie, flabbergasted.

'He escaped capture and managed to walk and bicycle across France, quite an epic journey by all accounts . . .'

'B-but surely that means there's hope for Samuel too,' Millie stuttered, feeling a brief jolt of joy.

'I'm afraid that is an extremely remote possibility,' Mrs Frobisher replied quietly. 'The navigator reported that after they were hit by flak, he and the rest of the crew bailed out. Only Samuel remained. I'm told it's protocol that the pilot is always the last to leave.'

'Protocol or not, Samuel would never have deserted his crew,' Millie said loyally.

'Soon after the navigator's parachute went up, he saw the plane hit the ground and explode in a fireball . . .'

Millie remained motionless.

'He didn't see Samuel bail out . . . so, so you see, my

dear, to cling to hope in those circumstances is, dare I say it, futile.'

Millie felt her anger deflate, to be replaced by an aching chasm of sadness. The last shred of hope, the hope that had sustained her these past three months, was now dead.

'And the memorial,' Millie whispered, 'why didn't you tell me? I'd have liked to have gone.'

Mrs Frobisher gazed at her, her expression full of compassion and pity.

'Oh, my dear, do you *really* think you could have turned up there?' she questioned delicately. She laid a tender hand on Millie's tummy. 'I think it would have been . . . inappropriate.'

'You're right,' Millie said, regaining her composure. 'Well, thank you for telling me.'

She wasn't aware of leaving Mrs Frobisher's office. Her body seemed to move of its own accord. All she could see was one image. Samuel pinioned by the G-force of his descent, desperately struggling to free himself as the burning aircraft corkscrewed to earth. She closed her eyes, but in the sudden darkness the ferocity of the flames just glowed brighter.

As she walked outside to the yard and hurried to the allotments, the icy air hit her lungs, causing her to gasp, but the blast of air acted like a wake-up call. There and then, Millie made a decision. If she allowed it to, this news could destroy her. She could not buckle and surrender. She had to survive this. For Samuel and their unborn baby. As the allotment hove into sight, Millie made a snap decision not to tell the girls. She couldn't stand to see their pity, for she knew it would cause her to cry. And she worried that once her tears began, they might never stop.

*

Annie was just in the middle of explaining her ambitious crop-rotation plan when Millie joined them at the yard allotment.

'There you are, Millie,' said Annie impatiently, looking up from her *Allotment & Garden Guide*. 'Everything all right?'

'Tickety boo,' Millie muttered. 'Mrs F just wanted to know if I'd had my extra ration of orange juice.'

Pearl noticed how pale Millie looked, but knew better than to probe.

'Good,' Annie replied. 'I was just saying how, on plot A, we'll have the green vegetables. Plot B is peas, beans, onions and leeks, and C, potatoes and root crops . . .'

Rose stifled a yawn with the back of her wrist.

'Am I keeping you awake?' Annie demanded.

'Sorry, Annie, I'm just so tired,' she replied, rubbing her face. 'Also, I can't stop thinking about *The Swan*.'

Earlier that day, the chairman had gathered them all in the yard to break the news that the Spitfire they had paid for had been shot down by enemy fighters while carrying out a sweep from Cassel to Hazebrouck.

'He was Samuel's pal,' said Millie, cradling her tummy. 'Poor bugger, just trained as a lawyer before war broke out. He was going to look into my marriage, see if there was any way . . .' She broke off, looking like she was fighting off tears. 'Oh, what's it matter now, anyway.'

'You quite sure you're all right, Millie?' Annie questioned.

'Yeah, don't worry about me, girl,' she replied, nailing on a smile. 'I'm gonna be fine. I have to be! Got this little one to think about now, ain't I?'

Rose smiled and reached out to touch Millie's burgeoning belly. She was over four months gone now, and Pearl couldn't remember when she last saw a woman suit childbearing so well. Mrs Frobisher had given permission for Millie to carry on working until she could no longer reach the conveyor belt, which seemed to suit her just fine.

'And Curly?' Pearl ventured.

'He's still buying it, if that's what you mean, ignorant chump! Even better, he's leaving me well alone. Thinks if we have sex, it'll harm the baby.'

'Can it?' gasped Rose.

'Don't be a nitwit, Rose,' said Millie loftily.

'And who will he harm when he finds out the truth?' Annie demanded angrily, picking up her pitchfork and turning the compost so Millie wouldn't see her expression.

Millie hugged her arms about herself defensively.

'He won't.'

Annie had made it perfectly clear she didn't agree with her nan's idea of tricking Curly into believing the baby was his, and used every opportunity to voice her concerns.

'How can you be so sure?' she asked, throwing down the pitchfork. It landed with the prongs sticking up in the air.

'You should pick that up, a good gardener takes care of their tools, as you're so fond of telling us,' Millie muttered.

'Sod the pitchfork, Millie,' Annie snapped. 'Have you forgotten who you're dealing with?'

''Course not. He's my husband, but like I keep on saying, what choice have I got?'

'But it's a lie,' Annie persisted. 'What'll you tell your child when he or she grows up? Daddy was a pilot you had sex with in the potting shed?'

Millie winced as if she'd been slapped.

'Annie!' Rose cried, appalled. 'How could you?'

'Oh, I'm sorry, Millie,' Annie sighed. 'That wasn't fair. But I'm only saying all of this because I care about you, and I'm worried.'

'I know you are, Annie, but trust me, this is the only way. Besides, show me a mother and I'll show you a liar,' she added sourly.

'And you don't need to end up like yours,' Annie replied.

'Pearl, what do you think?' Annie demanded. 'Sometimes I feel like you're the only voice of reason here.'

Pearl was grateful for the shadow of the factory walls, which plunged her face into darkness. She thought of the Curly she knew, the one who had wormed out her secret and turned it to his advantage. The man who had taken such pains to find out the identity of her husband and even now was using it to blackmail her into keeping quiet about the stolen goods he'd hidden at the allotment.

'He deserves everything he's got coming,' she muttered.

A tense silence fell over the chilly allotment.

'Who deserves everything he's got coming?' rang a voice out of the darkness. 'Not me, I hope.'

'William,' Rose grinned, grateful for the interruption. 'What are you doing here?'

'Just thought you girls might be in need of some more manure, especially as you're digging over. Courtesy of my old girls.'

'That's kind of you, William,' Annie smiled. 'But we

were just thinking about heading home, it's getting too dark to work now.'

'Plus it's freezing,' Rose added. 'And the skin on my hands is peeling off like paintwork.'

'I don't know, these southern softies,' Pearl said teasingly. 'Here, let me help yer, William.'

She could see the lad flush as he set down his wheelbarrow. Pearl smiled; she could tell he was soft on her and a little kindness went a long way at that age.

'You sure you don't mind staying to help?' Annie asked.

'You go on. We'll be fine, won't we, William?'

'Very well, I'll tell Nan you're coming. We'll wait for you before we eat tea.'

Pearl and William spent a companionable twenty minutes forking pigs' droppings onto the compost and chattering about this and that, before he picked up his wheelbarrow.

He hesitated, a stain of colour flooding his cheeks.

'I don't suppose you'd let me take you to the pictures tomorrow night?'

The question took Pearl by surprise.

'I'm chuffed, but don't you think I'm a bit old for yer? You're only fourteen.'

'Fifteen now, and I'm going places,' he said proudly. 'Got my own pig club, and I'm thinking of expanding.'

'Oh, William,' she said gently, suppressing the smile she could feel twitching at the corner of her mouth. 'One day you'll make some lucky girl very happy.'

'I shan't give up,' he vowed, picking up his wheelbarrow and pushing it out of the allotment. He turned at the gate and threw her a cheeky grin. 'You're everything a man could want.'

She smiled sadly.

If only you knew.

Once he'd gone, Pearl sat down on the bench, lit a cigarette and allowed her thoughts to wander. She shouldn't have said anything earlier about Curly. It wasn't her business. She had already told Elsie too much about her past. Not that she regretted it. It had felt good telling someone, and Elsie had been the right person to confide in.

An iron fist in a velvet glove, was Annie's nan, but still, Pearl had come here to make a clean break. As she smoked, her gaze travelled up the steep factory walls to the dark office windows above. All the secretaries who worked there had gone home, and, with a jolt, Pearl realized that with the exception of the guard on the front and back gates, she was all alone. Even the boys in the sawmill had clocked off. It was unnerving being alone in a place that usually teemed with people and noise. To see it deserted like this gave her the collywobbles.

In the distance, she heard an owl hooting. Out of nowhere, the blackout seemed to have swallowed Bow whole. Darkness oozed about her. The wind changed direction and the stench of something unspeakable drifted from the whalebone factory in St Stephen's Road, all the more potent in the darkness. It was time to get home.

Mashing out her cigarette, she stood up, and for a moment felt disorientated. Where was the path leading out of the allotment? The darkness of the tenebrous blackout was so heavy, it seemed to bleed into the factory walls.

Then she heard it. A rustle followed by a tapping. Something was moving through the allotment. Her heart began to pick up speed and, rummaging in her bag, she found a torch, its beam masked by tissue paper to comply with the blackout. It threw out a slim band of light as she cast it over the allotment, hoping to see a fox, or even a hedgehog. Nothing. Just damp black earth and beyond, the faint outline of a giant stack of logs.

Tap. Tap. Tap.

'William?' she whispered into the darkness.

Tap. Tap. Tap.

Someone was playing with her.

'Curly, is that you?'

Tap. Tap.

'Stop messing about.' Her breath billowed into the darkness like smoke.

Suddenly a conversation popped into her head and the memory made her smile in relief. Ted and some of the fire brigade reckoned that when they worked a night shift, you could tell the prostitutes patrolling down Fairfield Road looking for trade in the blackout, because they hammered tacks into their heels. That was it. Pip was fast asleep in his kennel; she could hear his faint breath nearby and if it hadn't woken him, he must be used to the sound. 'Daft cow,' she scolded herself. 'You'd think after five years of war, you'd be used to the blackout by now.'

Picking up her bag, she followed the faint beam of torchlight along the narrow path between the dug-up plots.

She reached the fence circling the allotment and breathed a sigh of relief as she pushed open the gate. She could run from here to the back gates of the factory, and then she was out on the street. But even though she'd opened the gate, there was something blocking her way. Groping with her hand in front of her she felt something cold and wooden. *Strange.* She shone her torch on it and jumped back.

It was a long wooden yardstick with the brush head pulled off and both ends lashed with leather. The breath froze in her throat.

No. No. No.

Her head started to spin. Panic bloomed in her chest. The coincidence was too much. She had never seen anything like it at the allotment. She had only ever seen it before in her husband's hand.

'Hello, Pearl.' The familiar voice was soft, cajoling almost.

His face drew up out of the darkness in front of her. No longer a memory, but the man himself. The dark muscled mass of his body edged closer until she could see the whites of his eyes, smell the sour scent of him even over the stench of blubber.

Later, she wondered why she hadn't run like the wind; could she have avoided the chaos and horror? But in truth, she knew she had been paralysed by fear, absolute mouth-parching terror, which allowed him to run his hands up her rigid body. Her flesh shrank.

'Oh, my Pearl,' he said in an awful whisper, gripping the collar of her coat. 'Why did you go and leave? You should've stayed, we could've worked it out, but you didn't, did you?'

Scream, Pearl, scream! The nightwatchman will hear you.

Her body betrayed her. Not a sound was uttered from her lips.

'I can't let that go, I'm afraid,' he went on, stroking her cheek. 'Silly, silly girl.'

Her voice, when it came, was a tight little whisper.

'How did you find me?'

'One of my pals saw you in the paper, selling tomatoes, outside Bryant & May. Said you worked here. Imagine my surprise that you'd left Liverpool without even telling me.'

He was drawing her closer now, his knuckles bunching the fabric of her blouse.

'Which is funny, 'cause everyone else seemed to think you died in the bombings. But I knew better, see.'

Sour spittle flecked her face as he pushed the back of her head so that their noses touched.

'You and me are connected. Soulmates until the end.'

The words fell like stones between them.

He pulled back abruptly.

'We're going home to Liverpool.'

A flicker of strength rose up inside her.

'This is my home now.'

A muscle jumped in his cheek.

'You. Are. My. Wife,' he said slowly, drawing out every syllable. 'You belong to me.'

She shook her head. Her defiance was enough.

Pearl whimpered as his fist smashed into the side of her skull, felling her to the ground with one blow. Through double vision, she saw him reach for the yardstick. His 'attitude adjuster', he called it.

She rolled into the foetal position, and it all came flooding back. Confusion. Straining muscles. Sobbing breath. A roaring in her head as he brought down the stick again and again on her prone body . . .

'That's for leaving,' she heard him say dimly as a searing pain streaked across her abdomen. The world was going dark and fuzzy now and she waited for the merciful moment when unconsciousness would come.

Suddenly, he pulled back and howled in pain. Pearl opened her eyes, confused. Pip had his jaws clamped round his ankle.

'Get this bloody mongrel off me,' he roared, pulling a blade from his pocket.

'No!' she rasped, struggling to sit up as he sliced the air around Pip's head. Then his hand locked round the dog's neck. She heard a whine as John's heavy boot smashed into Pip's ribcage, caught the flash of steel as he pulled back his knife.

Lurching to her feet, she threw herself at him. Her body made contact with his with a thud and he fell, landing with a heavy, wet-sounding grunt, followed by the rushing of breath.

For a moment, there was perfect stillness as he lay sprawled on the damp earth. A look of profound surprise crossed his features, and a minute later, a trickle of dark blood seeped from one nostril. Beneath his head protruded the prongs of Annie's discarded pitchfork.

Pearl's cry elongated into the night air, then the giant walls of the factory seemed to loom over her and buckle, as though the sky was caving in. Blackness.

*

When Pearl came to her senses, she was sitting by the hearth in Elsie and Annie's, covered in a blanket. A glass of brandy had been pressed into her rigid hand. She was trembling. Violently.

'Pip . . .' she groaned, as a red-hot poker of pain seared through her ribs.

'He's fine,' Rose whispered, cradling the little dog in her arms.

'What happened, Pearl?' Annie asked. 'You turned up with Pip as white as a wedding.'

'I-I can't really remember. Just that John . . . He found me. He . . . He was going to hurt Pip. He hit me, with the attitude adjuster.'

Rose's eyes widened. 'Who's John and w-what's an attitude adjuster?'

'Hush,' urged Elsie. 'Let her speak.'

'I-I pushed him. I think . . . he fell . . . and then . . .'

Her voice trailed off. She remembered running, and now she was here. Everything between was confusion and darkness. The words came out of her in a tremor.

'I think he might be dead.'

A silence stretched over the parlour before Annie broke it.

'Oh, Pearl, why ever didn't you tell us you were married?'

'Because I wanted to leave it all behind. When the Matchy was destroyed, John was away at army training camp. I hoped he'd believe I was killed that night in Liverpool.'

Suddenly she saw his face, cold and white against the bare earth of the allotment.

'I should've known he'd find me.'

Her mouth was a tight scarlet slash in the pale pallor of her face as the awful reality began to dawn on her.

'What have I done?' she whispered.

'I think the question is, what are we going to do?' Millie asked, looking tremulously around the group.

Elsie took charge.

'Annie and I will go back. Millie and Rose, you're to stay here and look after Pearl.'

'No,' said Pearl, groaning as she struggled to her feet. 'I'm coming. I have to see for myself.'

'Very well,' said Elsie, and, fetching her coat, she turned to a stricken-looking Rose and Millie.

'Don't answer the door to anyone.'

*

It was approaching 10 p.m. by the time Annie, Pearl and Elsie made their way past the night guard, who fortunately Annie had kept sweet with extra tomatoes last summer. How she managed to stay so calm when she told him they'd forgotten to lock the tools away was beyond her. She'd only seen one dead body before, and that was a dismembered torso strewn amid the rubble of a bombsite after the first night's bombing. No face. No identity.

How she hoped it was all a grotesque mistake. That Pearl had got it all wrong. That somehow John had picked himself up and even now was on his way back to Liverpool. But as they drew closer to the allotment, their breath ragged in the frozen night air, she saw the dark outline of a body slumped in the ditch she had dug earlier.

Annie swung her torch beam onto his face and a cry seemed to burst out of her. He didn't look like the man she had seen in the wedding photo. His face was like a wax-work, so still; the blood had frozen on his cheek, the pitchfork she had so casually discarded earlier appeared to be embedded into the back of his skull. His tongue lolled pink and lifeless from the side of his mouth.

'Oh my God,' she whispered, covering her eyes.

Pearl whimpered, turned a queer greenish-white and ran to the gate of the allotment where she threw up violently. Only Elsie remained calm, a look of resolute determination on her face.

Annie drew a shaky breath, and when Pearl returned, she turned to her nan. 'What . . . What'll we do? Ought we to call the police?'

'No,' said Elsie fiercely.

'But he was attacking Pearl, he'd have killed Pip,' Annie cried.

'Elsie, this is my mess,' Pearl protested. 'You go and I'll call the police. I'll tell them it was an accident.'

'Oh, my dear girl. Do you really think they'll see it that way?' Elsie said slowly. 'You've a lot to learn if you think you can just walk away from this.'

'But surely . . . we can't . . .' She pointed helplessly to the body.

Elsie's voice was sharp and queer in the flannelly damp of the night.

'You ran away from your marriage, led people to believe you were dead, and you expect people to believe it was an accident? Without a single witness save for a dog to back you up? Setting aside the fact that the army has lost a soldier. This is war, dear girl. You'll not be treated with compassion.'

'You're right,' Pearl wept, her face ash pale and wet with

tears. 'I'll hang. I'll bloody hang.' She started to quiver and sank down on the earth beside her husband.

'I'm sorry,' she said, placing her hand softly on his cheek. 'May God forgive me.'

Elsie pulled her to her feet and gripped her firmly by the shoulders.

'Stop that,' she ordered, shaking her. 'He was a monster and the world's a better place without his kind.'

Pearl nodded, like a child.

'Now, girls,' she said, turning to them both. 'We bury his body deep. Then we never speak another word of this again. It's done.'

Annie nodded with a feeling of utter unreality as Elsie turned to the shed and began to hand out shovels. And there and then, with fog licking their faces, they began to dig.

It could have been ten minutes, it could have been an hour, but finally the grisly job was done. His body was buried in the yard allotment. Slap bang in the middle of the East End's oldest factory, John Brunt was consigned to his final resting place. The gradual pull and suck of East End roots and microscopic creatures would slowly make him at one with the earth. The thought made another wave of panic begin to bloom inside Annie. What *had* they done? Her head was swimming with exhaustion and she was in a state of lassitude. It had been a night of cold, creeping despair. A night none of them would ever be able to erase from their minds.

Annie drew Pearl into her arms as she began to sob like her heart had broken wide open. Elsie simply stood and stared at the freshly dug and covered ground. Over Pearl's quivering shoulder, Annie gazed at the elderly matriarch. Maybe she was used to death, having laid out the bodies of countless dead in the neighbourhood over the years, but Annie couldn't fathom where she got her strength from. How she wished she could see into her nan's thoughts, but she was afraid to. Afraid of what she might see there. Thoughts, bleak and confused, swirled through her mind as they traipsed from the allotment, earth ingrained beneath their fingernails.

*

Over the next three days, Pearl smelt and saw death everywhere. It was in the lorries full of bones heading to the soap works, in the clammy stench of the whalebone factory. It hung like a dreadful reminder over everything, clinging to her hair and her skin. Every time she closed her eyes, the image of her husband's lifeless body was burnt onto her retina, dancing tauntingly through her mind.

On the fourth day, a Monday, she came down with a fever. Elsie took control once more, packed Annie off to work with instructions to tell Mrs Frobisher that she would not be in all week.

As Pearl's body burnt like fire, Elsie carefully drew back her shift and inhaled sharply as she saw the purple and black bruises that covered her torso like a grotesque tattoo. A sympathetic doctor was called.

'Four broken ribs, concussion and shock,' he declared. 'If it were anyone but you looking after her, Mrs Trinder, I'd have had her admitted to hospital immediately. You must bring down this fever,' he instructed, discreetly asking no more questions and waiving his fee.

Elsie tended to her like a new-born. No one was allowed in the room but she, with Annie banished to the parlour floor with Pip for comfort. She swaddled Pearl's body with cooling poultices, fed her tiny sips of bone broth and mopped her brow with cooling orange-flower water.

By Thursday, the fever had broken and Elsie wrapped her in blankets and threw open the windows. She allowed the girls to visit after their shift had finished.

'Ten minutes is all,' she ordered, as they nervously entered the room.

'Oh, Pearl,' said Rose, bursting into tears as she sat down gingerly on the side of the bed. 'We've been so worried about you.'

'Just a bit. How you feeling, sweetheart?' said Millie, clutching her lower back as she eased herself down into a chair by the bed. Annie hung back nervously in the door-way, her face pale against the smattering of apricot freckles over the bridge of her nose.

Pearl and Annie locked eyes, both of them bound by the unspeakable horrors they had witnessed one week previously.

'Please, come and sit down, Annie,' Pearl whispered. 'There are things I need to explain.'

Pearl found that once she started, the words tumbled out of her. This time, she left nothing out. She told them the real reason she had fled her home. She described the brutality she suffered at her husband's hands, and his sadistic mind games, in unflinching terms.

'I knew there was more than you were letting on,' said

Millie, shaking her head. 'I'm just so sorry we didn't ask more. We've let you down.'

'No,' Pearl protested weakly. 'I wasn't ready to tell anyone. Except your nan, Annie, she guessed.'

'I thought as much,' she replied.

'When did it start?' asked Rose nervously.

'Soon as we met. It sounds like a cliché but I just kept hoping he'd change, made excuses for his behaviour. The Depression made it worse. He got laid off at the docks. I felt so sorry for him, which is why I agreed to marry him.'

'And it still went on, even after you married?'

'The day we married, even, Rose,' Pearl said, almost in a trance, and Annie's mind wandered to the wedding portrait she had stumbled upon like a thief.

'But . . . but why?' Rose went on, struggling to comprehend.

'Because some men only feel alive if they're controlling women,' Millie interjected.

'Millie's right,' said Pearl. 'It was all about control. He beat me because he was angry, unemployed, sometimes just because it was Tuesday . . . Who knows, Rose? He's a sick man. *Was* a sick man.'

'Was there no one you could talk to?' Annie said, feeling a tear break and trickle down her cheek.

'It wasn't that simple. He used to have this stick, he called it his attitude adjuster. He used it whenever he felt I was getting too big for my boots. Kept one in every room in the house, so he didn't have to go too far to give me a beating.'

Pearl groaned as she tried to shift herself under the covers. 'It didn't 'arf do some damage.'

She drifted to some unknown place of horror in her head.

'He told me I was worthless and I believed him. Until I came here. Until I met all of you.'

Drawing in a big shaky breath, she turned to the girls. 'Working here at the allotment with you has been the happiest time of my life. I'm just so sorry you've all been caught up in this.'

The girls wrapped their arms around her, as firmly as they dared, as the tears splashed down her pale cheeks.

'Well, I think Elsie's right,' said Millie, drawing back. 'You didn't kill him. It was a dreadful accident.' She glanced round at the girls. 'Let this be an end to it. Pearl's suffered enough.'

Only Annie didn't look convinced. However you dressed it up, a man was dead and they had buried him in the allotment like a bulb.

The door swung open and Elsie walked in with a tray. The scent of chicken broth and fresh-baked bread filled the room.

'Yours is downstairs on the table, girls, go and tuck in.'

Annie looked at her crisp and capable nan, gently setting down the tray before plumping Pearl's pillow. The sharpness of her voice in the allotment was all gone now, no trace of the woman who so adeptly buried bodies and scandal.

Millie was just leaving when Pearl called her back.

'Please, Else, just five minutes,' she pleaded.

'Not a moment more, you need rest,' she said, quietly shutting the door behind her. Pearl had made up her mind to tell Millie everything about Curly, about the blackmail and the stolen goods he had buried in the allotment. She was done with secrets and, besides, what could Curly do to her now?

'What you choose to do with this information is up to you, Millie,' she said, when she had finished. 'But he's your husband, and you have a right to know.'

'Thank you, Pearl,' she said. 'I'm glad you told me.'

Nineteen

Millie had thought long and hard over Pearl's disclosure, and by the time the first wild bluebells began to push their way through the earth, she had formulated a plan.

It was the end of May and the alchemy of spring was working its magic. The dull brown earth had begun to warm and a blanket of green was spreading. The winter frost had been dissolved by sweet spring rains and everything was bursting into bloom, including Millie.

Seven months gone now, even she hadn't been able to persuade Mrs Frobisher to allow her to carry on working, so most days she came here, to the Girls' Club allotment. It was where she felt closest to Samuel.

This morning, a Saturday, she was out of the house at the crack of dawn, before Curly woke. She sat on the bench outside the potting shed, sipping on a cup of tea made on the old primus, and watched as the sun rose, streaking the sky pink and gold. A thin mist hung lightly over the allotment. In the branches of the tree overhead, a blackbird was building its nest. Millie smiled and gently patted her tummy.

By some unspoken agreement, Pearl never returned to the yard allotment on the other side of the factory grounds.

Instead she came here to garden with Millie, leaving Annie, Rose and Ted to sow the seeds at the other site, the site where even now John Brunt lay rotting.

Millie shuddered to think of his corpse becoming one with the earth. That night unspooled in her mind like some sort of horror picture come to life. Not one of them had dared speak of it again, let alone voice an opinion as to whether or not it had been the right thing to do. But it was too late now. Tight-lipped, Elsie had planted out runner beans over the patch where his body lay and shot them a look that brooked no argument.

No matter what else, in a queer kind of way Pearl was free now. Millie had experienced suffering at the hands of Curly, but nothing like the darkness and pain that poor girl had suffered.

'Penny for 'em,' sang Rose's voice through the mist, Pip trotting at her side.

'You don't wanna know, sweetheart,' she sighed, patting the bench beside her.

Rose's expression told her she already knew.

She sat down heavily, a vein pulsing in her forehead, and Pip jumped straight up onto her lap.

'I know we shouldn't discuss this, but the thing that happened. There's no way anyone will ever be able to find out?'

She searched Millie's face.

'Suppose the army or his family come looking for him, suppose someone saw him in Bow? What . . . what would happen to Pearl, to Annie and Elsie, and us?'

'Rose, you know we shouldn't speak of this,' she whispered. 'But you mustn't worry. Pearl was acting in self-defence. She saved Pip's life that night.'

'I know,' Rose sighed, running her slim brown fingers through Pip's fur. 'And I'm so grateful to her for that.'

Out of nowhere, she covered her face and began to cry.

'I don't want to leave Bow. It's going to break my heart leaving you all, and Pip.'

Pip snuffled his wet nose back under her hand, put out that she had stopped stroking him.

'Oh, Rose, you know what your mum's like. She'll most likely change her mind. She's never gone further east than Stink House Bridge, much less Essex.'

'No, Millie,' Rose said, looking up through long wet lashes. 'It's all set. Her sister's lodger moves out on Saturday, 15 July, and we're to leave that day and take the room. I don't even know where Chigwell is!'

Millie ran her hand along Rose's cheekbone and tilted her chin so their eyes met.

'Rose, you're nineteen now. Old enough to make your own way in life.'

Rose's blue eyes teemed with sorrow. 'It's not that simple, Millie. I owe her. She gave up everything to adopt me.'

Millie stared back at her, unable to comprehend the control that vile woman had over sweet Rose. Just then the hooter blasted out, calling the neighbourhood to work.

*

'Do you know what Mrs Frobisher wants to see us about?' Pearl asked as she and Annie clattered up the stairs to her office at dinnertime.

'Search me,' Annie shrugged.

The Welfare Superintendent cut straight to the chase.

'Girls, I had the Chief Inspector here this morning.'

Pearl felt a bright white light spangle behind her eyes.

'W-why?' stuttered Annie. 'Are we in some sort of trouble?'

'Don't look so guilty, girls. He's visiting all the factories this morning, warning us all to be on our guard.'

'Why?'

'Seems like the crime wave that Bow has been experiencing is on the rise. Weekly bag snatches down Chrisp Street market, pickpockets down the Roman and, last night, the box factory next door was broken into. It's reached unprecedented levels, and with the Queen's visit fast approaching, we have all been warned to be on our guard.'

'Right,' said Annie, swallowing hard.

'The night guard tells me you came to the allotment late one night in February, Annie and Pearl, something about forgetting to lock up tools?'

Both girls nodded bleakly.

'May I please remind you to be vigilant? Her Majesty's visit is two weeks today. The allotments are looking splendid, thanks to all your hard work, and I should hate for anything to put a stain on the visit.'

'Of course,' Annie mumbled.

'Are you quite well?' Mrs Frobisher asked, gazing quizzically at Pearl. 'You haven't been yourself since that terrible fever.'

'I'm fine.'

'You're terribly pale. I think you could use a dose of extra malt and cod liver oil,' she said, rising and reaching up to her medicine cabinet.

'No, really, I . . .'

But the medicine was placed in front of her.

She drank, shuddering as the slimy liquid slid down her throat.

'Her Majesty will visit the yard allotment first, before a tour of the factory, then luncheon with the chairman.'

Pearl coughed, choking on the medicine.

'Why the yard allotment?' she blustered. 'The Girls' Club allotment is far prettier, and we have the chickens there.'

'True, but the yard allotment is next to the factory, so not as far for the royal party to walk, and the picture opportunities are better there. Plus the runner beans are doing splendidly, and we should like to show them off, oughtn't we, girls?'

Pearl and Annie nodded in shock.

'Off you go then, girls, and remember, keep your eyes open for any suspicious activity.'

Outside, it was all Pearl could do to keep herself upright.

'Annie,' she hissed.

'Don't talk, just keep walking,' she muttered, striding down the corridor at great speed.

Pearl caught up with her at the end of the corridor and spun her round.

'I can't do this,' she whispered. 'I don't think I can keep this up.'

'But you have to,' Annie said helplessly. 'It'll all be fine. You'll see.'

In silence, they both stared out of the window. There, from the corner of the office block, they looked down directly over the yard allotment.

It had rained recently, but now the sun had come out. The ground was almost steaming as fresh green runner bean shoots curled their way out of warm, damp earth. Above them rose a column of speckled butterflies, dancing in the sunlight. The rotten stench of comfrey herb masked a more unsavoury odour.

'They know he's there,' Pearl whispered, her face as white as bone. 'How long before everyone else does?'

Annie bit her lip, speechless with fear.

*

Over the next fortnight, the anticipation over the royal visit reached a fever pitch. Bow was crawling with police, and every employee of Poplar Council was out in force cleaning the kerbsides and sprucing up the borough.

'I don't know why they bother, that'll only get painted over again,' Millie sniffed as she and Annie paused outside Bow Church and watched as two workmen scrubbed the red paint off the bronze statue of William Gladstone. 'Why can't they take us as they find us? There is a war on.'

'Yeah, but it's not that simple, is it, Millie?' Annie replied. 'It's about having pride in your neighbourhood, putting your best face on in spite of your troubles. You more than anyone should get that,' she grinned, turning to look at her old friend.

'Ha!' Millie laughed, rubbing her back. 'Look at the state of me. Ankles like bleedin' barrage balloons. Just as well Samuel ain't round to see the state of me.'

It was gallows humour, and they both knew it.

'I'm proud of you,' Annie said, tweaking Millie's chin. 'I know how much you miss him.'

'Well, I won't have time to soon when this little one puts in an appearance.'

She winced. 'He must have legs as long as Samuel 'cause he ain't half kicking about. Can we walk?'

Millie had taken to meeting the girls every day when they clocked off their shift for a stroll in the early evening sunshine. Annie's disapproval over her decision to pass the baby off as Curly's had not been mentioned again. Somehow, in light of what had happened, it had paled into insignificance.

They strolled up the Bow Road in the direction of Poplar Town Hall and Assembly Rooms. The impressive, gleaming white Art Deco building, finished before the outbreak of war, emerged out of the evening smog like a cruise ship.

Millie was proud of her neighbourhood and its radical roots. Beyond the Town Hall lay Bow Police Station, where the suffragettes were beaten and held on remand before being sent to Holloway. And the very ground she trod was where her old nan Nelly had marched with the rest of the match girls in defiance at their treatment by factory bosses.

'Funny, ain't it? Each generation of women fights its own war,' she mused. 'And when you think about it, the reason is always the same.'

'Which is?' Annie asked.

'Women fighting for what should be theirs by right.' Angry tears pooled in her eyes. 'Like poor Pearl. She had a right to safety, didn't she?'

'Hey,' soothed Annie, 'don't be getting yourself all upset now.'

She reached out and tried to hug Millie to her, but a second later, she was nearly knocked off her feet by the figure of a man sprinting past.

'Watch yourself,' he snarled as he flew by.

'Stop! Stop him!' bellowed a red-faced man puffing after him.

The girls watched, helpless, as the man shot past them, rounding the corner down Fairfield Road and out of sight.

'Bloody hell,' groaned his pursuer as he reached the girls and leant over, holding his knees to catch his breath.

'Sorry,' said Millie, gesturing to her tummy. 'You asked the wrong person.'

'Don't worry, love. Did you catch a look at his face?'

'Yes, youngish fella, flat cap, beginnings of a moustache . . .' Annie said.

'Could be any bloke in Bow under twenty,' he sighed.

'What'd he get away with?' Millie asked.

The chap pointed to a fleet of charabancs lined up on the other side of the street, with a queue of excited kids snaked up the kerb beside.

'The satchel with all the spending money for our beano. Toerag,' he said in despair, kicking the kerbside. 'Of all the people to rob from . . . I work for the Transport and General Workers' Union. To celebrate the Queen coming tomorrow, we'd laid on an outing to the seaside today for a load of kiddies. We'd planned the funfair, fish and chips, ice cream, the lot.'

'Oh no!' gasped Annie.

'Fat lot of fun we'll have now. I don't know what this

world's coming to. There's men dying on the beaches of Normandy as we speak, then there's scum like that in the world.'

They watched as the man walked off, dejected, back to the buses.

'Seems Mrs F was right about the crime wave round here,' Annie sighed.

Turning, they walked back past the Town Hall, when Millie suddenly remembered something.

'Are you going to the dance later?' she asked, pointing to the poster in the window advertising the Friday evening dance at the Assembly Rooms.

'No, don't think so,' Annie replied. 'I'm going to head to the allotment, make sure everything's perfect for tomorrow.'

'Oh, please come,' Millie begged. 'Curly's insisting we go, he wants to show me off and I couldn't stand it without you. Please!'

'Is it right, you know, what with Pearl and everything?' Annie asked. 'She's in all sorts of states over tomorrow.'

'We have to continue life as normal, don't we?'

Annie shrugged. Millie was having her dead lover's baby and Pearl's husband was buried in the allotment . . . What the hell was normal any more?

*

Looking around the fancy interior of the Assembly Halls, with its Moroccan leather chairs and walnut furniture, Annie secretly wished she hadn't agreed to come to the dance. All the girls were dolled up to the nines, with the young bloods out in their sharp suits eyeing them up.

She'd far rather have been back at the allotment.

Excitement was humming as the band struck up and hordes of young couples took to the sprung floor.

'Right, I've done my bit,' said Millie, returning from the bar, where she'd been chatting with Curly and his friends. 'He'll be propping up the bar now until he's unconscious.'

Annie glanced over to where Curly held court. He used the whole room like some tribal proving ground, slapping backs and receiving associates. Having his pregnant wife there was the feather in his cap. Annie realized with a jolt how much she loathed what he stood for. Three days ago, Allied troops had launched a massive invasion off the coast of Normandy. The papers were full of it, fine men being shot down in their prime to end this seemingly endless war. Then there was Curly and his kind. Millie deserved better. She looked ravishing this evening in an ice-blue gown, which set off the colour of her eyes.

'You look beautiful, Millie,' said Rose admiringly.

'You really do,' agreed Pearl.

'Behave,' she laughed, 'I look like the iceberg that brought down the *Titanic*.'

The girls were still laughing when Millie spotted William, walking near their table.

'Cooee, William,' she called. 'Don'cha look smart.'

William paused, looked their way and shifted uneasily.

'What's tugging you? Ain'cha gonna come and say hello?' Millie asked.

'I, er . . . Sorry, I'm just leaving,' he stuttered. Then he was off, weaving through the crowds and out the door.

'What's biting him?' Rose asked.

'Bit peculiar,' Annie murmured.

'Come to think of it, we ain't seen him round the allotment lately either, have we?' Millie said. 'Not since that night . . .' Her voice trailed off.

'You know what, I'm not in the mood for tonight,' Pearl said, draining her drink and getting to her feet.

'Oh, don't go,' Rose urged. 'This could be our last dance before I leave.'

'Sorry, Rose, but I shouldn't be here. It's not right.'

Then she, too, was gone, rushing for the door. It was here that she collided with a man walking in and his cap landed on the floor.

'Watch yourself!' he snapped, bending down to pick it up. As he stood back up, Annie turned to Millie in shock.

'It's him, isn't it?' she hissed. 'The bag snatcher from earlier.'

'It bloody well is an' all,' Millie agreed. 'The front of him!'

'Ought we to call the police?'

'Hang on . . .'

They watched in a state of stupor as he walked straight over to where Curly was standing at the bar and whispered something in his ear. Watched as a broad smile spread over Curly's face.

*

Annie had acquiesced to Millie's pleas to say nothing about what they had seen, but as she walked home from the dance, she felt distinctly uneasy. Millie assured her she'd deal with it, but what was happening to her neighbour-hood? To her friends? Events were spiralling out of control, and she didn't have the first clue what to do to put things right. She had set up their allotment to feel a sense of pur-pose and it had blossomed into her bolt hole, an escape from the war. Yet now, danger seemed inextricably drawn to it . . .

She paused outside the Fairfield Works, which stood like a giant fortress, their tainted allotment contained within its ancient walls. Soon the eyes of the world would be on it.

An image of his face falling into the black earth flashed alarmingly into Annie's mind with such shattering force she had to stop and hold on to the wall for support. Every detail was as clear as the night itself. The leaden weight of his body, the woodlice and spiders that crawled horrify-ingly over his lips as the first shovelful of earth rained down.

'Stop it!' she gasped out loud, snapping open her eyes and breathing deeply. The night air smelt salty and ripe as the flesh of an oyster. A lone gull wheeled over the factory walls.

By the time she reached Blondin Street, her heart rate had steadied. Letting herself in, she unpinned her hat.

'Where are you, Nan?' she called as she walked into the scullery. 'We came home early, no one had the heart for it tonight . . .'

Her words trailed off as her nan glanced up sharply. She was washing her hands in a bowl of soapy water in the sink. The water ran red, the colour of blood.

'Nan, are you all right? Have you cut yourself?' Elsie tried to hide her hands, but Annie was too quick and pulled them from the suds. It wasn't blood she was washing off, but red, rusty-coloured paint.

In that moment, Annie knew.

'It's you,' she breathed in astonishment. 'It's you who paints the statue's hand red.'

Elsie said nothing. Her eyes darkened.

'Oh, Nan, why?' Annie asked, frustration spilling out.

Annie wanted to tell her how reckless she was being, how she would be fired on the spot had Elsie been seen, but instead, all she could muster was this: 'You need to forget what happened to the match girls. They won. It's done.'

'Not to me it ain't,' Elsie said, rubbing her reddened palm. 'The years have passed quicker than I care to remember. They say time is balm to the mind, but I'll never forget the sights I saw.'

'Nan, tell me what you saw.' Annie's voice was a whisper, filled with fear as she searched her grandmother's face.

A pulse beat very briefly, very fast, in the papery lid of her eye.

'I can't, dear, I can't.' Elsie reached over and kissed her, her soft downy cheek brushing Annie's. She smelt of cinnamon and Sunlight soap, mixed with the metallic tang of paint. 'But know this, everything I do, I do for my family.'

Twenty

The day of the Queen's visit dawned, hot, blustery and belching ripe smells. To Pearl, it felt as if every factory over the Stink House Bridge was competing for Her Majesty's attention.

The smell of sugar, oil and rotted bones hung like soup in the air, sharpening her senses. Pearl had scarcely slept a wink last night, and now the moment was here, she felt like she was an actress, playing out a role.

Her Majesty was inching closer, with a small army of officials from the Ministry of Agriculture and factory bosses in her wake, the press close behind. Every kid in Bow was clinging to the top of the factory walls to get a closer look. Secretaries and factory girls hung out of the windows up above, waving Union Jack flags in a state of febrile excitement. Even the birds looked as though they had swooped down for a closer look.

The girls were lined up by the side of the allotment, next to where the runner beans had grown like wildfire. Pearl didn't see the lush lines of lettuce, radish and summer spinach bursting from the ground, nor could she appreciate the scented clumps of dahlias and marigolds. Her thoughts remained rooted to one place only – the remains of her husband, buried beneath their feet.

'Oh gawd, she's nearly here and I need to pee,' muttered Millie, rubbing her not-inconspicuous tummy.

'Hold it in,' ordered Annie under her breath.

And then she was there, petite and perfect in powder blue, extending a gloved hand towards Annie.

'I'm so impressed that you managed to get all this to grow from a bombsite,' she enthused, smiling brightly. 'It's tremendous.'

'Thank you, Your Majesty,' Annie replied, her skin flaming the same colour as the chrysanthemums. 'We used pierced dustbin lids to clear the shrapnel.'

'How resourceful,' she exclaimed. 'And these runner beans! What *have* you got in that soil? You must tell me what fertilizer you use. Is it National Growmore?'

'No, it's from me nan's compost,' Annie said, forgetting herself. 'She's always behind a horse's backside with a bucket.' Her hand clamped to her mouth.

'Pardon me, Your Majesty.'

'It's quite all right,' the Queen replied, a twinkle in her eye. 'It's obviously working, this allotment is splendid. Keep up the good work, girls.'

Mrs Frobisher winked at the girls as Her Majesty was moved off towards the cauliflowers.

A flash of deeper blue caught Pearl's eye. Two policemen were advancing up the yard, emerging from behind the giant stacks of timber. Further behind them, at the back gates on Old Ford Road, a Black Maria screeched to a halt.

Pearl's heart started to beat fiercely. It was happening, just *exactly* as she had feared. She watched, numb, as one of the officers discreetly mouthed something in the Works Manager's ear, then glanced over in their direction. Panic exploded in her chest. Her legs slid from beneath her and she was dimly aware of the commotion her collapse had caused.

'Stand back, give her some air,' rang out Mrs Frobisher's voice, followed by a muttered apology.

'Don't worry, I'm perfectly used to it,' she heard Her Majesty say. 'Poor girl, she must have worked too hard in the allotment.'

Then the royal party was ushered off quickly, away from the advancing police and the fainting match girl.

Pearl's vision swam in and out; a face appeared.

'Pearl,' Annie mouthed, her expression urgent. 'They're here about Curly!'

*

Leaving Pearl with Rose, Millie and Annie hastened their way across the yard and over to the recreation ground and the Girls' Club allotment.

As the allotment hove into sight, the first thing they saw was Curly pinned to the ground by two constables, flailing like a cat in a string bag.

'Get your bloody hands off me!' he bellowed. 'Do you know who you're dealing with?'

'A dirty great thief by the looks of it,' muttered a third constable as he emerged from behind the back of the potting shed carrying three bulging hessian sacks. Shaking the earth off, he emptied out the contents. Annie gasped as a shower of jewellery, watches, wallets and purses fell to the ground. The thing she found most shocking of all? The bundles of ration books and clothing coupons.

'I ain't never seen them in my life before,' Curly laughed.

'Yeah? We'll let the fingerprints be the judge of that,' said the constable, snapping on a pair of handcuffs.

'You know they've introduced life sentences as a deterrent against this sort of thing,' Millie remarked casually. 'After all, there's men dying for our country as we speak.'

Curly whipped his head round, his chin covered in earth and drool.

'What the . . .'

Turning and smiling sweetly to the arresting constable, she handed him a set of keys.

'That one's to his lock-up, and this one's to his club. You should find plenty of items of interest, isn't that what you fellas call them?'

Curly's eyes were full of a primal, defensive anger as he was hauled off the ground and, for a moment, Millie almost felt sorry for him.

'You bitch!' he yelled, lashing out wildly at her with his boot. 'You bloody nark bitch.'

'You always said you was going places, Curly. With any luck, prison!'

'You silly little cow,' he sneered, shaking his head. 'We could've gone places, you and me, instead you want to stay a low-life working-class match girl.'

'Exactly!' she screamed, finally losing her cool. 'I'm the class that works. It's work what's made me respectable. What work have you ever done in your life?'

He spat hard at her feet, before being hauled off in a cloud of curses and flailing limbs.

Millie sat down heavily on the bench outside the potting shed and Annie realized she was trembling.

'Millie! What . . . Why didn't you tell me?' she gasped, sinking down beside her.

'Because it was my problem to sort,' she shrugged, rubbing her tummy and breathing in gulps of warm sooty air.

'I've been planning this for a while, but I had to wait for the right time to carry it out. Soon as I realized last night Curly was involved in that bag snatch, I knew the time had come.' Her eyes shone fiercely. 'I'm sick of being the victim in this marriage. If Samuel taught me anything, it's to fight for what you believe in.'

She could have told Annie more, of course, about the dawn visit to his club, how she withdrew £200 from his desk and packaged it up before posting it through the letter box of the Transport and General Workers' Union, marked 'Seaside Spending Money'. Or about the anonymous call to the police telling them to be at the allotment by 1 p.m. How she had then persuaded Curly to meet her at the allotment so that he could take her out shopping for baby clothes. But she'd had a busy morning and was tired. So instead she turned to Annie and smiled.

'Put the kettle on. Me tongue's hanging out!'

*

The Certificate of Merit arrived three weeks after the Queen's visit. It was a handsome thing, which Mrs Frobisher had thoughtfully framed.

'You don't look very excited, girls,' she said, as she pushed it across her desk one Saturday dinnertime.

'It's smashing,' Annie lied. For what did it really matter? She didn't need a certificate to tell her the worth of her allotments.

'The inspector from the Ministry of Agriculture was most impressed with what he saw this time,' Mrs Frobisher went on.

Annie smiled weakly at the girls. Funny how he had failed them when they only had an outbreak of blight, not a body in the ground.

'And, of course, the chairman is thrilled with how the Queen's visit went.' She leant forward conspiratorially. 'I rather think he wishes it was his idea to turn those bomb-sites into allotments.'

'But it was Annie's,' Rose loyally pointed out.

'Exactly, Rose,' Mrs Frobisher smiled. 'Which is why we wanted to give Annie more responsibility.'

She leant back, eyes twinkling.

'The chairman has decided to turn over the old tennis courts to you girls, the entire plot, to cultivate as *you* see fit. It's an enormous gesture of the faith he has in you.'

'Blimey!' Annie breathed. Her mind was already roaming the possibilities – rabbits, more chickens, goats even! – when Mrs Frobisher dropped the bomb.

'I'm afraid we will need the yard allotment back, though. The Works Manager needs that space to store more logs in, and as it's closest to the sawmill . . . Don't look so worried, Annie. I will personally oversee the uprooting of every single plant and bulb to ensure everything safely survives the transferral. Anything that comes out of the ground will be treated with great care.'

'When?' Annie managed.

'As you know, on Friday, 14 July, the factory will close at noon for one week's annual holiday. If you have no other plans, perhaps you could make a start then? The diggers will be coming in when the factory reopens for business.'

Annie nodded and felt the walls close in. Two weeks away.

'Goodness, Pearl dear, why are you crying?' Mrs Frobisher asked, astonished.

*

'It's over,' Pearl said emphatically. 'I'm going to the police.'

The girls sat in silence round the flames of a bonfire at the Girls' Club allotment later that evening and let the repercussions of her vow take hold. The sun was sinking and the sky looked like it was on fire, the water tower bracketed with orange and gold.

'They'll find his body, and I'm not about to stand by and let you all take the blame,' she vowed, eyes as dark as the bottom of the canal. 'I'll go to the police, but I'll say I buried him by myself.'

'Do you think they'll believe you?' Millie asked.

'They'll have no choice,' she said shakily, looking around before settling her gaze on Elsie. 'I shan't say otherwise. All you were doing was trying to protect me. I'm not about to turn over the only people who have shown me such kindness.'

She prodded the bonfire with a stick, showering vermilion sparks into the dusk.

'The best I can hope for is a prison sentence, but maybe I deserve it.'

Rose burst into tears and buried her head in Pip's fur.

'How can you say that? He beat you for years! He . . . he would have killed you. It was just a wretched accident.'

'Maybe,' Pearl sighed. 'But in a way, it's a relief. As long as he's down there, I'll never really be free.'

No one spoke. They just listened to Rose weeping as the old ground beneath their feet seemed to groan and tick as the earth cooled.

The rank smell of the river rushed over their faces in the cooling breeze. No one smelt the summer jasmine curling round the potting shed. No one heard the figures of two men emerging out of the gloom of the recreation ground. No one except Pip, who leapt from Rose's lap barking.

'You better put that bonfire out. Warden'll be along in a bit.'

'Ted!' Annie gasped, whirling round. Elsie's head snapped up.

'How much did you hear?' she demanded.

'Everything. But don't worry,' he soothed, holding both hands up. 'I'm here to help.'

'How . . . how can you possibly help?' Elsie demanded angrily.

''Cause I have someone with me who saw everything.'

Gently he drew the figure of a younger man out of the darkness and edged him closer to the light of the flames.

'William,' Pearl gasped, eyes wide.

'This young man's been in bits,' Ted said, gripping him supportively by the shoulders. 'Don't be cross with him. I knew something was up, and I got it out of him.'

'I'm so sorry, Pearl,' he cried, twisting his cap between his fingers. 'I came back that night, to see if I could have a second crack at persuading you to go to the pictures, and that's when I saw you and him.

'At . . . at first I thought you were kissing. Then . . . then he punched you. Fists first, then this horrible big stick. He kept on and on lashing you, I thought he was going to kill you and I wanted to help, believe me I did, Pearl.' He started to cry and Ted gripped him so tight, it was as if he were holding the lad up.

'I was too scared. I should've fought him off. I'm ashamed of myself.' He wiped his eyes angrily, but tears cascaded down his pale cheeks.

To hear this young man, barely out of short trousers and tormented by the dreadful events, was too much. Annie wanted to go to him, but Pearl beat her to it.

'Oh, William,' she cried, cradling his face gently. 'What could you have done?'

'I was about to run, fetch the police,' he admitted. 'Only then Pip started attacking him. God, he was jibbed, I thought he was about to stick a knife in him and then you pushed him. He fell. There was a crack and then . . .'

'He died,' Pearl finished.

'But it was an accident,' William insisted. 'Any fool could've seen that. You never meant to kill him. If he hadn't died that night, you would've. Or Pip.'

'Why didn't you say anything, lad?' Elsie asked.

'I wanted to, Mrs Trinder. I came back the next day, expecting to see the place crawling with police, but when there was nothing, I decided it would be best to keep my mouth shut, except it's been eating me alive.'

'Which is why you ignored us the night of the dance,' Pearl said.

He nodded sheepishly. 'Every day I wanted to talk to you, but my courage failed me.'

'But it's not failing you now,' she said softly. 'You're here, aren't you?'

'Yes, and I want to try and put things right. If you go to the police, Pearl, I'll come too. Tell 'em everything I saw.' He pushed his chest out. 'Testify too in court if I have to.'

'I think the lad's very brave to admit what he saw that night,' Ted said, casting a long glance at Elsie.

'Yes, he is,' Pearl agreed. 'I'd already made my mind up, but now I'm certain.'

'Can I just ask one thing, love?' Elsie said, suddenly looking very old and very weary.

'Anything, Else,' Pearl replied.

'Will you wait until Rose leaves before you go to the police? It's only two weeks away. Let her get safely to the countryside.'

Elsie sighed and closed her eyes. 'There'll be blood on the moon if Maureen finds out.'

Pearl nodded. 'Of course.'

And with that, the group stared round at each other, stunned into silence by the enormity of what was to come.

FRIDAY, 14 JULY 1944

The noise of it all was deafening.

'*That's the wrong way to tickle Mary. That's the wrong way to kiss! Don't you know that over here, lad, they like it best like this!*' bellowed Sandra, singing so loudly she almost drowned out the machines.

'Come on, you lot, why ain't you joining in?' she yelled, without once breaking off from her packing.

Her foghorn voice carried the entire length of the floor to where Rose, Annie and Pearl were also packing matches at their machine in subdued silence.

'Shut your cakehole and get on with your work! Hooter ain't gone yet,' yelled back the foreman, before pausing by their station.

'You all right, girls? Thought you'd be demob happy by now.'

'Just tired, boss,' Annie replied, pressing down on a matchbox before moving onto the next. No one had dared voice it, but they all knew that when Pearl made her revelation to the police tomorrow, nothing would ever be the same again.

Rose would be gone, on her way to a new life. Even if Pearl were to be found not guilty of his manslaughter, the factory would never have her back. And as for Annie, she didn't care so much about the job, she could get another factory job – Compton's were hiring machinists to work on army denims – but what would become of her allotments? She couldn't bear to think of how she had failed them and Mrs Frobisher's trust in her.

'Five . . . four . . . three . . . two . . . one!' The hands on the clock ticked down, inching them all closer to their fates.

The hooter blasted out and a great cheer echoed round the tiled room.

'That's that then,' Rose smiled sadly, as the machines juddered to a halt.

'Bet you won't miss seeing these,' Annie said, picking up a Bryant & May Swan Vesta matchbox.

'All right, girls!' Sandra jumped on Rose's back, before rubbing a knuckle over her head. 'Gonna come and join us down the Bombay Grab? I'm going to get absolutely roasted on rum and black. I'll even get the first round in as a farewell to Rose.'

'Get off,' Rose giggled, pushing her away.

'We can't. We got work to do down the allotment,' Annie replied.

'God, you ain't half become dull since you started up them allotments,' Sandra grumbled, ripping off her hairnet. 'Ta-ta.'

'See you, girls,' Rose smiled weakly.

When the floor had emptied, they walked to the high windows and looked out over the yard allotment. It looked so pretty from this height, a magical green oasis, nestled in a concrete jungle. No one could ever guess at what lay beneath.

With a scorch, Annie realized how much she would miss it. The companionable silence as they worked along to the Dig for Victory broadcasts, the thrill of seeing the first shoots push through the ground, even the aching back. Creating this garden had changed her. How could she go back to the narrow life now? And how, *how* were they supposed to dismantle it, bulb by bulb . . . bone by bone?

Twenty-one

Saturday, 15 July 1944 would go down in Rose's mind as the day she left number 20 Blondin Street forever. She gazed around the cold, empty room with a feeling of unreality. What little they had had already been sent on ahead to Essex in packing boxes. Strange how their lodgings looked and felt no different empty. She had been raised in these rooms, a whole childhood spent under the same patched roof with a woman who, despite adopting her, didn't seem to have a shred of maternal love in her body.

Perhaps that was uncharitable. Maybe leaving the East End was *exactly* what Maureen needed. There had been the Depression, the Blitz, losing her job, and now these pilotless rockets had started dropping out of the sky. Life had been one long test for Maureen Riley.

Sighing, Rose picked up a birch broom and decided to give the old place one last sweep through, vowing as she worked to try to understand her adopted mother better.

'Why are you bothering with that?' Maureen's accusatory voice tore through the empty room.

'Just trying to make it nice for the next tenant.'

'There's a difference between scratching your arse and tearing the skin off,' she snapped, taking the broom out of her hand. 'Save your energy for the journey. Train leaves at 6.30 p.m.'

'Can I go to the allotment and say goodbye to the girls?'

'Very well, but don't think about trying to smuggle that dog with you! And don't be late. I'm going for a lie-down before we leave. I can feel one of my heads coming on.'

Rose watched her mother's mouth fix into a sour grimace as she stomped off to her bedroom.

Outside, it was a perfect drowsy summer afternoon and sunshine bathed the cobbles liquid gold. Washing gently flapped from lines and all the mothers of the street were out on their doorsteps shelling peas into their apron laps and chewing the cud. Could these women talk, and how!

With an ache, Rose realized how much she would miss the smells and sounds of Blondin Street.

At the factory, Rose gave a start as she walked through the back gate. With the factory closed, there wasn't a soul about, apart from Ted and his crew on practice manoeuvres.

'Hello, love. They're all up at the allotment,' he called to her across the empty yard. With no clatter of machinery from the sawmill or rumble of steam tractors, it was eerily silent. It might be one hundred years ago, with bonnet-wearing crinoline workers crossing the cobbles. A smell of history wrapped itself around Rose. Freshly felled logs, sap and woodsmoke clung to the ancient bricks.

The queer feeling of desolation continued as she arrived at the allotment. The girls were sitting on a bench, sipping tea in silence.

The ground had been stripped of every plant and the earth below lay naked, tangled roots exposed. All that remained on the plot were the runner beans, arching into the cloudless sky like a macabre signpost to what lay beneath.

Pip bounded over, tail going nineteen to the dozen.

'Here she is,' Millie said, smiling up as Rose approached. 'We thought Maureen might've kidnapped you before you could come and say goodbye!'

'Don't be daft,' Rose said with a heroic attempt at a smile, as she bent down and scooped Pip into her arms. The tears were on her before she could stop them, as Pip wriggled and licked her face.

'What am I going to do without you?' she said, burying her face in his fur, broken-hearted.

'Me and Nan will take great care of him, Rose. I promise,' Annie vowed.

'So this is it then,' Pearl said, rising to her feet and dusting the earth off her palms.

Rose choked back a sob and threw her arms around her, inhaling as she felt the sharpness of her ribs. Pearl had lost so much weight, even her wrists were stick-thin. The unfairness of it all cut deep. She had already endured years of suffering, and now her future looked set to be the same.

'I'll be back, Pearl, whatever happens,' she promised.

'Thanks, Rose. I don't regret coming here,' she wept. 'I'd never have met you girls otherwise.'

'Oh, stop it, you lot,' Millie said, pulling out her handkerchief. 'Now you've set me off.'

Soon all four girls were wrapped in a group hug, a tangle of limbs and broken hearts. The future lay ahead, unformed and utterly terrifying. The only thing that made any sense was this moment, and the strength of their friendship.

At their feet, Pip tipped his head back and began to howl into the sky.

'We know how you feel, boy,' Millie said, pulling away and rubbing her lower back. 'It's rubbish is what it is.'

Rose stilled and looked at Pip.

He broke off from his fearful howling to gaze at them, his brown eyes wide and urgent. Wheeling round, he barked once, twice, and then began to howl again.

'R-Rose, what's wrong with Pip?' Annie asked slowly.

A strong gust of wind sent an old sack gusting up the yard and the leaves of the runner beans trembled. Then came the scent of something queer and sour in their nostrils. Burning, sulphur? No, it was not like any factory fumes Rose had ever smelt. Panic crawled up her spine. Where had she last seen Pip behave like that?

The oxygen seemed to leach from the air and her head began to spin. Looking up into the cloudless blue sky, it hit her.

'G-girls . . . Doodlebug!'

All three craned their necks and scanned the horizon over the factory roof.

'I can't see nothing,' Millie puzzled.

'Believe me. Four weeks ago, when that rocket hit Grove Road, he was just the same.'

All four stood rooted to the spot, frozen in indecision.

A distant throbbing noise seemed to rise up from the bowels of the earth.

'Run!' Annie yelled.

'Where?' Millie screamed, clutching her tummy.

'The trenches, in the tennis court,' Annie said, and

taking Millie's arms, they began their stumbled race to safety.

'I can't see anything,' Millie puffed as she half ran, half staggered, clutching her back. 'This is bloody ridiculous, in my condition.'

At the end of the yard she stopped, and clung to the gate.

'I feel peculiar.'

The blood roared in Rose's ears.

'Millie, you *have* to run!'

'You go on . . .' she said and groaning she bent double.

'We ain't leaving you here, shift your backside,' Annie shouted and, grabbing her by the arm, she wrenched her up the road.

They rounded the corner into the recreation ground and it was then that they saw it. Two black specks on the horizon, like two tiny birds. The speed was astonishing. Within moments, Rose could make out a trail of brilliant flame forking from their tails. And suddenly they were no longer birds, but missiles, hurtling unswervingly in their direction.

'There's two!' screamed Pearl, but her words were quickly drowned out by the blood-curdling staccato throb of the engines.

'Get in the trench!' Annie roared, pushing them down. Rose half slithered, half fell into the darkness of the earth, limbs clashing.

The breath left her body. A whimper. A groan. Then an unearthly howl from Pip as a shadow passed over their heads.

Then all at once, perfect silence.

'The engine's cut out,' Annie breathed. And no one replied, for they all knew that could only mean one thing.

Rose felt the hairs lift on her arms and the air seemed to suck straight out of the summer sky.

The unearthly boom mushroomed all around them, and in that moment she knew. It had hit the factory.

The walls of the trench vibrated, spewing earth into the blue, and for a moment all anyone could do was lie flat on the damp earth floor. For a minute, Rose realized she was entirely deaf, but as she lifted her head from the ground, saliva spooled from her mouth and her hearing came flooding back. Pearl was screaming, Millic moaning. Rose clutched her head in her hands and clawed her way back to standing.

'Is everyone all right?' Annie gasped, staggering to her feet.

'Yes, yes, I think so,' Rose choked. 'But the factory . . . It's been hit.'

'Ted!' Annie paled. 'He was in the yard, with the firemen.'

'Quick, we've gorra get over there,' yelled Pearl.

'Come on, Millie,' Rose said, gently taking her arm and guiding her out of the trench.

But as Millie surfaced, blinking into the smoke-filled field, she felt the hem of her dress and looked up in shock.

'I think I've wet myself.'

'No,' said Annie slowly looking at her sodden dress skirts. 'Your waters have broken.'

*

'Rose, go and fetch Nan. Pearl, get Millie to the Girls' Club allotment and wait with her,' Annie ordered.

'Where are you going?' Pearl asked.

'To find Ted.'

And then she was off, sprinting hard in the direction of the factory. Annie didn't see the tiles slithering off the houses in Blondin Street, nor could she hear the crump of falling rooftops. She just knew she had to get to Ted.

Acrid debris and dust turned the sky as dark as night. Spikes of pain slashed her face and, in horror, she realized glass from the factory windows was falling like rain on her head. The walls of the gas plant split in two like a knife sliding through butter. If that collapsed, they'd be done for!

Another explosion. A shower of bricks spewed into the air and a hot wind blew Annie clean off her feet.

Crashing to the ground, she huddled amongst the debris in a ball and waited for the swirling morass to pass. Annie desperately needed to breathe, but as she lifted her head, her lungs filled with a bitter choking dust.

I'm going to die. Please, God, I don't want to die.

She thought of her nan and how outliving her grand-daughter would destroy her. In the distance, she heard the clanging of ambulance bells and whistles. She dared to lift her head a few inches off the ground. As the smoke cleared she felt the last of her breath leave her body. How could it be?

Two storage buildings had been flattened to rubble, the gas plant was cracked and tottering, but the allotment . . . It was gone!

Annie's legs felt like water as she staggered to her feet, ears ringing, and it was then that she spotted him. Ted was lying like a rag doll on the cobbles.

'Ted!' she screamed. He didn't stir an inch.

It was hard to see whether he was alive or dead. Every bit of his skin was covered with grey dust and slivers of glass. His arm fell limp and lifeless back on the cobbles, a deep stain of blood seeping over his overalls.

Ambulance, rescue workers and locals were on the scene in moments and he was placed on a stretcher.

'Please, love, let us see to you,' pleaded one.

'No, I've got to see my friend's all right,' Annie wept, running alongside his body as they carried it as fast as they dared up the yard.

Out on Old Ford, a row of ambulances were screeching to a halt and the back doors of one were thrown open as they approached.

'Stand back,' ordered the driver.

A scream sounded behind her, and Annie turned round to see her nan.

Elsie stopped when she saw Ted's body, one hand over her mouth, one on her heart.

'Is . . . is he alive?' she managed.

Annie shook her head. 'I don't know.'

Elsie's body seemed to shrink. 'Oh God, I'll never forgive myself.'

A sudden thought pierced the fog in Annie's brain.

'Nan. It's Millie. She's having the baby.'

*

Once Rose had fetched Elsie, she made to follow her but as she glanced right up Blondin Street, she felt the stuffing knocked clean out of her.

Their home was nothing but a smoking pile of rubble.

Shock and fear rooted Rose to the spot as her mother's last words came back to her. *I'm going for a lie-down.*

Pip was already tearing towards the site, and the sudden movement galvanized her into action.

'Mum! I'm coming!' A burst water main had turned the street into a slick of slimy mud and Rose crashed to the cobbles, but she pulled herself back up and carried on running.

Flinging aside bricks, she ignored the stench of domestic gas. It was a hopeless task. How could one small terrace produce so much debris and masonry?

'Get that dog off here!' yelled a voice as Pip prowled the site, tail low, ears pricked high, sniffing in every corner.

'No chance!' she yelled back.

After ten minutes, Pip stopped and began to bark, frantically scrabbling at the rubble until his paws uncovered the corner of an old horsehair mattress.

'He's found her!' she yelled.

As Rose carefully began to move old planks of wood, a whimper reached her ears and she worked faster.

First she uncovered a waxy-looking joint, then a knee, then a shoulder blade.

'Coming, Mum,' she cried, and, pulling aside wood and bricks, Maureen appeared from her coffin of debris.

'Ambulance on its way,' came a voice from below.

The plaster dust had thickened in Maureen's eyebrows, forming a claggy paste in the corners of her eyes. Carefully, Rose took a rescue worker's water bottle and handkerchief and, soaking it, gently dabbed it over her mother's eyes, then her parched lips.

The touch made her eyelids flicker open.

'What happened?' Maureen whispered.

'Hold on, Mum,' Rose urged. 'Ambulance's nearly here. You're all right now.'

But there was something about the milkiness of her gaze, the way she couldn't focus, that made Rose realize her words were without foundation.

Blasts are odd things. Maureen's housecoat had been ripped off and her torso was exposed. The skin on her stomach was mottled and covered in a spidery trail of stretch marks.

The paleness of her exposed skin only added to her vulnerability.

'Come on, Mum, let's get you decent,' Rose joked weakly, taking off her cardigan to cover her over. Then she saw it. A scar, stretched from one side of her abdomen to the other, like a grotesque smile stitched across her skin.

Maureen's focus swam back and she caught Rose staring.

'Aaah,' she sighed, before coughing. Brick dust spooled from her lips and the rubble shifted. Maureen's body plunged an inch further into the debris, as if the whole bombsite was trying to claim her body back.

'Hurry up!' Rose screamed at the rescue workers.

Maureen's tongue darted in and out of her mouth, her lips so caked in plaster dust, Rose had to moisten them three times before she could understand what she was trying to say.

'What a thing I did.'

Her eyes flickered closed, her lips mumbled in no prayer Rose had ever heard before.

*

The ambulance bumped up the pitted road containing the body of Maureen Riley and Rose watched it turn the corner in shock.

As it slid away, Annie came running behind.

'She's gone,' Rose said flatly, scooping down to pick up Pip.

'Don't say that,' Annie cried, her red hair silver-grey with dust. 'You don't know that.'

But she did. A cold sweat soaked her back as she stared up at the detritus of poverty and pain that had once been her home.

'Millie?' she murmured, turning back to look at Annie.

'A baby girl, born ten minutes ago,' Annie wept, biting her bottom lip as tears coursed tracks down the dust on her cheeks.

'And Ted?'

'I-I don't know, he's in hospital now,' she gasped, her breath coming in catches. 'The rocket missed the factory and landed in the yard, fifty yards from where he was working. And Rose, the yard allotment. It's gone!'

Twenty-two

And it was too. Completely evaporated, a giant hole in the ground with no trace of a thing – *or a body* – left behind.

Rose had stopped in at the factory on her way back from the hospital the next day to see for herself. Setting down her paper bag, she stared over the still-smoking crater in a mixture of shock and fear, unsure of what might remain. But there truly was nothing to see. Yesterday's blue skies had been replaced with a fine ghostly rain, shrouding the bomb crater in mist. The remains of the rocket had already been removed by the army and the ground tumbled into the fire-scorched, bottomless hole.

All around her was a hive of activity. Every able-bodied factory worker that hadn't gone away for the holidays had been called in and was busy clearing the tons of glass and dirt under the supervision of a team of engineers.

'I'm sorry about your mum, Rose,' Sandra called out as she traipsed past. 'I hope she didn't suffer.'

Rose shook her head, too numb to answer. She hadn't, according to the doctor she had just seen up at the London in Whitechapel. She had died of a massive heart attack in the ambulance. A blessing apparently, as she was sure to have died of her injuries, having taken the full force of the broken chimney stack.

Rose was grateful for that at least, but as she stared down into the pit, her thoughts seemed to spiral downwards, too. The suddenness of Maureen's death meant that she would never get the answers that eluded her. Worse still, her death had opened up yet more questions. She thought of all the bitten-down rages, the dark and uneasy sleeps tormented by her past, and her flesh shrank.

Rose picked up the bag at her feet, which the hospital mortician had given her, containing Maureen's belongings. She had left the earth with not much more than she had when she entered it, save for a pair of battered boots and a set of dentures.

'I didn't even know she wore false teeth,' she had said in shock to the mortician.

'Perhaps she'd been ashamed,' had been his reply. But instantly it had made her wonder, what else had her mother covered over?

Rose had been about to leave when, as an afterthought, she had turned to him. 'Was it you who laid out her body?'

To this, he had nodded.

'The scar across her stomach . . . what is that?'

'Why, a Caesarean scar, of course,' had come the shattering reply.

*

In Blondin Street, Rose pushed open the door and walked softly up the passage. Setting down the paper bag, she looked through the doorway to the parlour in a sort of awed silence.

Millie was sitting by the fire in an easy chair, feeding her daughter, with the girls and Elsie sat around her. The new mum looked exhausted. Her blonde hair was flattened to her head, her ankles were swollen and thick blue veins smothered her engorged breasts. She had never looked so happy or radiant, Rose realized.

Millie looked up.

'Rose, darlin', you're back,' she exclaimed. 'Come and sit down and meet Marigold.'

'Oh, Millie, she's impossibly beautiful,' she said, taking in the soft peachy fuzz of hair and the tiny curling eyelashes that swept over her cheeks.

'And you look like a natural!'

'Who'd have thought it?' Millie joked.

'What a start to life, though, eh,' Annie said, getting up to fetch Millie a glass of water. 'Born in an allotment. She better be green-fingered.'

'Like her dad,' Millie said, softly kissing Marigold's head.

'I'm so sorry about Maureen. How are you?' Pearl asked as she sat down next to her.

'I'm all right,' Rose lied, unable to take her eyes from Marigold's face. 'I stopped in at the yard, on the way back from the hospital. Have you seen?'

'Me and Annie just went to look,' said Pearl, clearly still stunned at the turn of events. 'I–I don't know what to think. Or do now, for that matter.'

'Well, I know what I think,' Elsie remarked, shaking her head as she looked round at them all. 'It's God's way.'

'Divine intervention, you mean?' Pearl replied. 'I'm not sure about that.'

'Pearl, you can't seriously still be considering going to the police, can you?' Millie cried, and Marigold jolted.

'Sorry,' she said, lowering her voice and gently soothing her daughter. 'But I'm with Elsie on this. What that man did to you was unspeakably wicked, and now you've been given another chance.'

'Perhaps you're right,' Pearl said. 'I just need time to take it all in.'

The question rushed out of Rose, taking even her by surprise.

'Elsie, did you know that Maureen had given birth?' she asked, wrenching her gaze away from the baby. The question had been brooding in her mind since she left the hospital.

Elsie looked up sharply. 'What do you mean?'

'The mortician at the hospital, he told me she'd had a Caesarean, and yet she told me she'd never given birth. Why would she lie?'

Elsie stared down at the floor, and when she looked up, Rose felt afraid.

'W-what else has she lied about?' she stammered. 'Is my mum – my real mum, that is – really dead?'

Elsie let out her breath in a single great sigh. 'There's a story I must tell you, dear girl, but first, I need to tell it to Annie.'

And then she was standing, reaching for her coat.

'Nan?'

'Come on, we're going to the hospital.'

'Why?'

'To see Ted.'

*

They found Ted at the furthest end of a ward crowded with the injured from the second rocket which had struck over in Stepney. It was nothing short of a miracle that the doodlebug which had landed in the yard at Bryant & May had done so when the factory was closed for the annual holiday. Had it struck at the same time two days previously, the yard would have been crowded with workers clocking off.

'He's suffering from bad burns, a broken hip and con-cussion,' the ward sister warned as she led them to his bedside. 'He's also heavily medicated, so don't expect much.'

Annie sat down at his bedside and swallowed back frightened tears. Ted looked shocking. His face was gro-tesquely swollen and covered in tiny slashes. She turned and buried her face in her nan's shoulder.

'There now, dear, he's a tough man,' she soothed.

'Why are we here, Nan?' she asked, looking up, bewil-dered.

'I need to tell you the truth, dear,' she replied quietly and with an air of resignation. 'About me. About Maureen. About our . . .' and here she stumbled, 'our pasts. Now she's dead, I owe you and Rose that much. 'Sides, tell the truth and shame the devil, ain't that what they say, dear?'

Annie felt queasy, knowing she wasn't going to like what she was about to hear.

'When I was seventeen, not much younger than you, I worked for Bryant & May.'

'You lied!' Annie protested angrily. 'You said you never worked in the factory.'

'Calm yourself, madam,' she hushed. 'I didn't lie. I *did*

earn a wage for Bryant & May, just not at the Fairfield Works.' Her mouth tightened. 'If you can call it a wage. Starvation wages they paid us homeworkers, but we had no choice except to take the work. My father was in the infirmary with consumption, so it was left to me and my brothers and sisters to help Mum make matchboxes.'

'I didn't even know you have brothers and sisters, Nan!' Annie breathed.

'Had, dear,' Elsie corrected. 'Had.'

She drew in a big shaky breath.

'Nine of us nippers there were, crammed into two rooms in Dixie Street, over in Bethnal Green. I was the oldest, and the littlest, Emily, was eight months.'

A flicker of a smile softened her face. 'We had a special bond, she and I, but I loved them all dearly.'

'What . . . what were their names, Nan?'

'Eliza was fifteen, Mary, twelve, Alfred, ten, Beatrice, nine, John, seven, Margaret, five and Marie, three,' she said, without missing a beat.

'It wasn't a childhood for us. We worked all hours making matchboxes, just to scratch a living. I still feel like I do it in my sleep.'

Her eyes flickered closed and her hands moved rhythmically over her dress skirts. Annie recognized the movement. It was the same one she did day in, day out.

'It was my job to go to Bryant & May to fetch the chip and paper. I used to take Emily's pram. Three-mile round trip before I'd even started work. There I'd join the queue with the rest of the children.'

'Children making matchboxes? Really?' Annie queried.

Elsie shot her a look that brooked no argument.

'Then sixteen hours of the same old in a dirty, dilapidated room,' she went on. 'You have machines now, of course, but back then, all we had was our bare hands. Two measly pennies for every two gross boxes made and, even then, when I took the finished boxes back, Bryant & May deducted money for paste and string. It broke my mother's heart to see her children sweating for pennies.'

Annie was taken aback at the dark hatred she saw in her grandmother's eyes.

'Those bastards got rich off our childhoods. It was 1897 and the world was waking up to workers' rights, but us homeworkers were the forgotten people. We were the lowest of the low, least in society's eyes.'

'Hang on, Nan,' Annie gasped. 'That was nine years *after* the match girls' strike. They won all sorts of improvements in wages and conditions . . .'

'And their victory came with a bitter edge,' Elsie murmured. 'The bosses were so humiliated at being forced to back down, do you think any of those improvements came the way of the forgotten homeworker?'

Annie shook her head.

'So you talk of staff welfare, of concern for the worker, and that may be true of now, dear girl, but believe you me, back then Bryant & May worked my family to death for a pittance.'

'To death?' Annie breathed.

Elsie stared bleakly at Ted in his hospital bed, emotions chasing over her face like clouds.

'It was the early hours of Boxing Day when the fire

started. Our rooms went up like tinder, 'cause of all the wood shavings and matches stacked in a cupboard.'

'Fire?' Annie whispered fearfully.

Elsie nodded.

'That's right. Fire brigade reckoned it had been smouldering unseen in the cupboard where the matches and paste were stored, and once it took hold, the fire raged from the rafters. They didn't stand a chance . . .'

Her voice trailed off, her eyes boiling with an ancient rage. 'Where were you, Nan?' Annie asked.

At this, she broke down and began to weep.

'Against my mother's wishes, I'd sneaked out to meet my young man. It was 3 a.m., we met at the end of Dixie Street. We were having a little kiss when we heard the shouts of "Fire!" Oh God, Annie . . .'

Annie watched, dumbfounded, as her nan's arthritic fingers kneaded and twisted the hem of her skirt, feverishly working the fabric into knots.

'I tried to save them, but the fire was too strong. I couldn't get near. My young chap broke down the door, but the smoke in the passage was so thick.'

Helpless tears slid down her cheeks as she opened her palms and stared at the faint scars trailing the skin.

'Again and again, I tried to crawl up the passage floor, but dear God! The heat! My hands and legs got burnt, but all I could think of was my brothers and sisters, little Emily was just a baby . . . *Just a baby . . .*'

She pressed a knuckle into her mouth as a heartbroken sob escaped. Annie didn't dare speak as her nan tried to compose herself.

'I didn't even hear a single scream,' she whispered,

shakily plucking a handkerchief from the sleeve of her blouse. 'Save for the roar of the flames, it was as silent as the grave.'

The tears slid down her nan's face, dripping from her jawbone and seeping into the fabric of her skirt. She made no effort to brush them away.

'I had enough tears for a hundred years,' she said in an awful kind of a whisper.

Annie was speechless with horror.

'W-where were the fire brigade?' she managed eventually.

Elsie stared at the floor, as if searching for the fallen threads of her story. She shuddered, collecting her thoughts once more.

'John, our neighbour, he went off to raise the alarm but the fog was so thick that night, he had difficulty finding the post. Ten minutes had passed by the time he had guided them back.

'By the time they'd got it under control, there was no question of there being survivors. They tried to stop me, of course, but all the king's horses couldn't have held me back.'

'Oh, Nan!' Annie cried, trembling. 'What did you see?'

'There wasn't much left to see,' she admitted. 'Mum and two bodies on the bedstead, three under the bed and the rest huddled in a group by the fireside. Blackened beyond recognition. Their bodies were so charred there was no way to tell who was who. Except for Emily . . .'

Elsie squeezed her eyes closed.

'Her little body was untouched by flames. She'd suffocated with not a mark on her.'

'How?' Annie gasped.

'Because my mother had shielded her in her arms. Amongst such gruesome sights, her face was pink and untouched. Every time I close my eyes, I see my baby sister's face.'

The image roared through Annie's mind so intensely that for a moment she too felt as if she might be suffocating.

'It was felt best that my father was not to be told in his delicate condition. Not that it mattered. He must have felt it somehow, for he died the very next day.

'My whole family gone in the space of one night, and I was to blame.'

'You can't really think that, Nan,' Annie choked.

'Can't I?' she said sharply. 'You're telling me if I hadn't sneaked out, I couldn't have helped my mother to get them out? I was her eldest child. I failed her.'

She shook her head despairingly. 'I've tried to wash their blood off my hands for the past forty-seven years, but I must hold myself accountable. As must Bryant & May.'

Annie's mind flickered to the red-handed statue near the factory and then to the night of the fire, when her nan was struck dumb with fear in the face of those leaping flames, and, suddenly, so much made sense. The visceral truth was so much worse than she could ever have imagined.

'The funeral caused quite the spectacle in the East End,' she went on. 'Thousands lined the streets to watch all those coffins pass by, and do you know what stopped my family being buried in a pauper's grave?'

Annie shook her head.

'The generosity of all those East Enders, who donated their hard-earned pennies and farthings . . . A tragedy on such a scale moves hearts and unties purse strings, you see, my dear.'

She laughed suddenly. A hollow, painful sound that echoed up the hospital ward.

'History doesn't recount whether Bryant & May made a donation, but as they didn't pay us a living wage, I doubt whether they'd offer anything in death.'

Annie reached out from the edge of the hospital bed and held her grandmother in her arms, wishing she could ease the old woman's impossible suffering, soothe away the years of pain and guilt, but she knew this would not be possible. Some wounds could never be cauterized.

'So where does Maureen come into all this?' she asked as she broke away.

'The fire was so notorious, I just wanted to escape. My chap proposed, right in the middle of a hospital ward where I was being treated for my burns. He wanted us to move to Kent and start afresh, but I didn't deserve second chances, so soon as I was discharged, I left him.

'I started using my middle name of Elsie, instead of Polly.' Here she paused, stumbling on her grief. 'I-I buried that girl along with my family.

'Over the years, I papered over the wounds – reinvented myself, you could say. In time, I met your grandfather and got a job in a rag factory, down Cable Street. I was a grafter, too,' she added proudly. 'Worked my way up to being a forelady. I remember that day in 1924 when Maureen came to the factory like it were yesterday. She begged me for a job, scrap of a girl she was, terrified . . . '

'Maureen? Terrified?' Annie scoffed, thinking of the hard-nosed woman she had known.

'Bitter experience turned her into the woman you knew,' Elsie replied. 'Back then, she was eighteen and her mother had turned her out on the streets. Her father, a bare-knuckle boxer, was hunting for her . . . vowing murders!'

'Why, what had she done?' Annie asked, intrigued.

'She was caught with a babby and not a ring in sight. It caused no end of a stink.' Elsie shook her head. 'Bad enough, but the father was a Lascar seaman. Brown as Bovril.'

Annie's eyes widened.

'But Maureen used to cross the road if she saw anyone who wasn't as white as she was.'

'Well, she didn't back then, dear.'

Elsie stared out of the window, at the sea of smoking chimney pots.

'So what did you do, Nan?'

'What could I do?' she replied, wrenching her gaze from the window. 'Turn her away? No, dear. I gave her a job, found her lodgings and a way out of her scandal.'

'But why? Why take her under your wing like that?' murmured Annie, who already knew the answer.

'Because, dear girl, I saw something in her that I recognized,' Elsie replied. 'Fear. Guilt. Shame . . . Call it what you like, she was as lost and scared as I had been at the same age.

'I had to win her trust, mind you, so I told her about the fire and my part in it all.' She shrugged. 'After that, we were bound by our secrets.'

'So what happened to the baby?' Annie asked.

'Why, nothing, dear. Rose was born and when Maureen brought her home to lodgings next door to ours in Blondin Street, we told the neighbours she'd adopted her.'

'Maureen was Rose's real mum?' Annie cried. 'B–but that's preposterous.'

'It's more common than you might think, dear,' Elsie replied wearily. 'When women get caught out, they have to resort to . . . to alternatives.'

Annie's head was reeling. Alternatives? Like Millie pretending Curly was the father? Like burying a body? Elsie's decisions suddenly made sense in light of her brutal past, but did it make them right?

'Don't be so judgemental, dear,' Elsie remarked, reading her thoughts. 'Don't judge Maureen – or women like her – until you've walked a mile in their shoes. At least she didn't get rid of her or give her up.'

'B–but she made life a living hell for poor Rose.'

Elsie exhaled deeply.

'Sadly, Maureen's shame turned to poison. It wasn't Rose she was angry with, it was herself. And in her own way, all she wanted was to protect Rose from the shame she'd experienced. Keep her on the straight and narrow.'

'In a straitjacket, more like,' Annie scoffed.

'She did what she did out of love,' Elsie insisted.

Annie sat in silence, digesting what all this meant for Rose, for her, for the future, when Elsie reached over and gently tucked back a lock of her red hair.

'So now you know my story.'

Annie's head was spinning, but there was a fragment of the story as yet untold.

'No . . . no I don't, Nan,' she blurted. 'The boy you were with the night of the fire. What happened to him?'

Elsie shifted creakily, looked to where Ted lay in his hospital bed, almost forgotten in the unfolding drama of her tale. A sudden flush infused her bloodless cheeks and, to Annie's astonishment, her aged face was transformed by love. Every feature softened, as if a great weight had come off her heart.

'Dear girl, I couldn't believe it when I first saw him in the yard at the allotment,' she replied. 'My heart fair flew into bits . . . I imagined him to be dead.'

She touched her chest lightly with her fingertips.

'I'd already buried him in my head and heart. To see him like that, and him a fireman, after all these years . . .' She shook her head. 'I was scared. It was easier to pretend I didn't know or recognize him, but of course he saw straight through me. He always did.'

She reached out and touched his hand.

'I never stopped loving him you know, Annie. Even after I met your grandfather.'

Ted stirred, moaning softly. His eyes were too swollen to open, but Annie could tell he could hear them.

'You took your bloody time, old girl,' he whispered. 'But then you always was a stubborn thing.'

Twenty-three

The shame that Maureen and Elsie had experienced had been like a bright silk thread, which had kept on unspooling over the years, tangling them in knots until neither had known what the truth felt like. Misplaced guilt had been the bond that had tied them together, and it had taken Maureen's death to finally free Elsie.

Rose's forgiveness of her mother was born of understanding. Once she knew *why* Maureen had been so wretched and controlling, her painful childhood made sense. There was nothing to be gained in hating her mother for lying and manipulating her, otherwise all she would be doing would be perpetuating the mistakes of the past. She needed to look forward, not back, like the rest of the country.

God willing, this painful war would soon be over. German armies were surrounded in the Ruhr and the horrors of the Nazi concentration camps were being revealed to the world. Rumours were already circulating that Hitler had topped himself in a secret bunker. A nation needed to celebrate *and* grieve, before finding its place in this strange new world.

Rose was about to take her first tentative steps into a new life too. She checked her bag for the fiftieth time that morning, to make sure she still had Tom's letter, telling her which train station to get off at.

'He'll be there,' laughed Millie, shifting little Marigold on her hip. 'Are you excited?'

'Nervous,' she grimaced, reaching out to tickle Marigold behind the ear. The little girl giggled and pumped her chubby legs out, until she squirmed her way out of her mother's arms. Rose watched the nine-month-old girl as she shuffled her way across the grass on her bottom, little pink fists stretched out towards where Pip was snoozing in the spring sunshine. Rose often marvelled at the pathos of Marigold entering the world, just as her own mother was leaving it.

'I'm going to miss Marigold like anything,' she admitted. 'But I think Pip's going to love his new life in Devon.'

After Maureen's death, Rose had written to Tom, to explain why she had ignored his letters; she felt she owed him that much at least. His response had been instantaneous. The Lend a Hand on the Land scheme he suggested she sign up for had seemed a perfect way for Rose and Tom to rekindle their friendship. She had lodgings lined up and Mrs Frobisher had agreed her temporary release from the factory. A long summer working on the land alongside Tom stretched gloriously ahead.

'Just spare a thought for Billy no mates in Bow here,' Millie grumbled, but the girls knew she was teasing. 'I still can't believe you're all leaving me.'

For Rose wasn't the only one leaving Bow that very afternoon. Annie had won a six-month apprenticeship scheme with the Women's Farm and Garden Association, with a grant from Poplar Council, to train to become a gardener in food production. Pearl was going too – finally returning home to Liverpool to be reunited with her mum and dad.

They were holding a small party at the Girls' Club allotment to mark the end of an era. A trestle table groaning with sandwiches made with cucumbers fresh from the allotment, hard-boiled eggs courtesy of their chickens, sweet, juicy tomatoes and jellies made with their own fresh raspberries, had all been laid under the shade of the sycamore. Even the blackbird who'd made her nest in the branches above seemed to have taken flight, Millie realized sadly.

'Where has Nan got to?' Annie asked, smiling as she watched Marigold use the edge of the table to haul herself up and poke an exploratory finger into a jelly. 'I'm not sure how long we can hold this one off.'

'She'll be here soon enough, love,' Ted replied from where he was thinning the onions.

'Where is it you're going to be based again, Annie?' Pearl asked.

'Woodyates Manor, near Salisbury,' she replied, cocking out her little finger. 'I'll only be living with a Lady Lucas, no less.'

'Sounds posh,' Millie remarked. 'Don't come back all hoity-toity with a plum in your mouth.'

'Sod off!' Annie grinned, picking up a clod of earth and

hurling it at Millie, who dodged it, shrieking with laughter.

'Don't be using language like that at the manor house, or they'll take that grant off you,' rang out a voice.

Ted's face lit up when he saw his wife striding towards them, with a pail clanking in each hand.

'Oh, hello,' he said, taking out a hankie and mopping his forehead. 'She's been at it again. Don't you think we've got enough horse shit on that compost?'

'When it comes to composts, you can never, ever have enough horse shit,' Elsie puffed, setting down the steaming buckets. 'Look how many plants we have now. We'll not run out.'

Elsie was right and together, she, Ted and the girls surveyed the burgeoning allotment. It was a magnificent sight that thrilled Annie to her core. What had started out as a single allotment had spawned into five ten-rod plots stretching out across Bryant & May's recreation grounds and tended by a rotating team of factory workers, firemen, locals and schoolchildren. It truly was a community affair now.

Thanks to donated seeds shipped in by the American Red Cross, the field was a sea of luxuriant leeks, carrots, sprouting broccoli, potatoes and even something called sweetcorn, which Annie had never heard of before. And all planted under a full moon, just as Samuel had requested.

Annie felt proud that they had tilled this small corner of England into something worth fighting for. The words of her nan's – and the nation's – favourite gardener, Mr Middleton, rang through her mind.

The very essence of gardening consists of rooting out and destroying all the evil things, and cultivating and developing all that is good and beautiful in life.

He was right. Their allotments had helped them to live through some very dark days. The yard allotment was long gone now. The crater from the rocket was filled in, and the spot where John Brunt had made his violent return into Pearl's life was now covered in a giant stack of logs, which would end their lives as matchsticks. Pearl would never recover from the trauma of that night, or the years of sadistic violence, but at least back home with her mother, she could begin to rebuild herself again.

'Well, we ain't rested on our spades, have we,' Elsie remarked.

'No, love,' Ted smiled, sliding his arm around the old woman's shoulder. 'We certainly haven't. We've a few more years of digging for victory ahead, though, old girl.'

Elsie groaned.

'What don't ache, don't work,' Ted chuckled. 'Besides, you've a few good years left in you yet.'

'Your lips to God's ear,' she bantered back.

Annie felt comforted to know that in her twilight years, Elsie had finally found peace and acceptance in Ted's arms. His love and steadfastness had rescued her from the horrors of her past. It made leaving Bow that much easier to bear. And leave she must. She would miss the factory, but she owed it to her nan to find out what more she was capable of beyond packing matches. The war was not yet won, and if the Government was to be believed, food shortages were set to become even more urgent. She intended to put her training in food production to good use. Which just left Millie . . .

'What are you going to do after we go, Millie?' Annie asked, turning to the platinum blonde, who was looking particularly ravishing in a pair of dungarees, mud-encrusted boots and cherry-red lips, courtesy of her pal at Yardley over the Stink House Bridge.

'Well, I thought I might find myself a GI with deep pockets and head up the Palladium for a few pink gins,' she winked, plumping her hair.

Annie's mouth dropped open.

'Behave!' she laughed. 'What do you think I'm gonna do? I'm going to go home, give Marigold her bath, read her a story and then we'll both fall asleep.'

'You could always come and stay with us over the summer,' Pearl ventured. 'Especially when Curly gets released from prison.'

'That's kind, Pearl, but I'm like a hardy perennial. Takes more than a bad man to uproot me from an area I love,' she joked. 'Besides, I have a feeling he won't be coming back to Bow in a hurry. Did you know he was also charged under the Essential Work Order? Once he's released, they're shipping him straight into the army, so he can do a real job for a change.'

'Just as well,' Ted remarked. 'Rumour has it, the Transport and General Workers' Union are waiting to flatten him with a bus.'

'Right, how about we get tucked into that spread?' said Elsie. 'You girls can't go on a long journey without food in your bellies.'

'You better listen to the lady,' Ted grinned.

'More than our life's worth not to,' Millie agreed.

Under the shadow of the giant, smoking factory, and surrounded by nature's harvest, the girls sat down to eat.

As Annie took her place at the table, it struck her that the full cycle of human experience had played out in their wartime allotment – *birth, death and renewal* – in life, as it was in nature.

*

After staying behind to clear up the tea and lock up the potting shed, Millie looked at her daughter's jelly-smeared face and chuckled.

'Look at you, you grubby little mite. Shall we go home?'

Scooping Marigold into her arms, she nuzzled the top of her head, savouring the warm, biscuity smell of her, before tucking her into her pram and pushing her out through the factory gates. The nights were worst. That was when her loneliness and grief sliced the sharpest. Samuel would have made the most devoted father. One day, she would tell Marigold about the golden-haired man who flew twenty-ton bombers, but who only knew true happiness in the garden. She carried the ache of his sudden death permanently, constantly suppressing the anger that, at times, felt like it might swallow her whole. No one ever talked about grief or anger in this war, as if to admit to feeling it was unpatriotic.

Lost your dad, brother, husband, lover? Never mind. A stiff upper lip, keep calm and carry on. Well, sod that. Millie *needed* to mourn, otherwise how would she even know their affair had existed?

It was a perfect spring evening. The sky was softening to a deep, luminous shade of blue. The apple trees at the back of Clay Hall Road were bursting into bud, and a gentle wind scattered tufted dandelion seeds like confetti over the cobbles.

Millie paused at the end of Parnell Road and, on instinct, kept walking. The thought of another night sitting by the wireless alone was too depressing for words. The lonely night could wait.

There was one place she wanted to be, the place she felt closest to him. By the time she'd pushed the pram over the doorway of the ruined church, Marigold's eyes were growing heavy.

Parking the pram by the moss-covered altar, Millie put the brake on and sat down on the crumbling remains of a pew. Locals steered well clear of bombsites. But Millie loved the peace and solitude she found here in the ruins of the abandoned church.

The fragrant smell of herbs was pungent in the warm, still air. A noise rustled somewhere at the back of the church, starlings building their nests, most likely. She gazed up at the soft light flooding through the ruins of the stone archway. The sun was bending to the horizon. The vegetation had run rampant since she had last been here with him, all those years ago. Willowherb, dandelion and chickweed coated the aisle like a carpet, with golden rod pushing through cracks and draping doorways.

In its own way, it was beautiful. Samuel had taught her that. In fact, he had taught her to view a lot of things differently. And perhaps that was his greatest legacy, that and the beautiful little girl fast asleep in her pram.

Gently, Millie tucked Marigold's blanket up under her chin. She loved her so much, it hurt. She thought of all the things Samuel could have taught her. Now it fell to her, somehow, to be mother, father, protector and provider. She would have to go back to work, of course – the £100 in her secret bank account was dwindling – but Elsie had assured her she would look after Marigold. She would muddle by, somehow.

'I won't let you down,' she whispered into the dying light.

'I know you won't,' said a voice from the doorway.

Millie froze, the hairs on the back of her neck prickling. She turned, and her heart punched in her chest.

A man was standing in the entrance, caught in the shadows.

Even in the gloom, she could see the frailty of him. His cheekbones protruded painfully and his eyes were dark and haunted, almost too big for his face.

He stepped out of the shadows and Millie stumbled back in fear. This was madness. No. It couldn't be.

'Please . . .' He stretched out his arms. 'Don't be afraid. I tried to get word to you . . . I didn't want it to be like this . . . I wanted to write to you, but . . . Curly, I wasn't sure . . .'

'H-how?' The words rushed out in a shudder. 'How is this possible? T-they told me you were dead!'

He ran his hands through his hair, blinking back tears.

'Millie . . . please . . . I escaped . . . I bailed out . . .'

'B-but your navigator,' she stammered, fearful she had completely lost her mind and was talking to thin air. 'H-he said you didn't make it out.'

'I can see why he thought that,' he replied. 'It was dark, so much chaos, there were aircraft exploding all around us . . . it was . . . hellish . . .' He broke off, as if recounting the memory was too much for his frail body.

'When I landed I was captured straight away, then held near the Polish border before I escaped. With the help of the Resistance, I was able to hide out until it was safe to be on the move.'

Millie stared dumbstruck at the man before her, frozen in her own skin.

'And here I am,' he whispered fearfully.

She clutched the handles of the pram, a queer cry echoing through the church. This was not real. It was her mind playing cruel tricks on her.

'I was reconciled to death, Millie,' he went on, moving slowly towards her through the deserted church, as if any sudden move might cause her to bolt. 'It was only the thought of you that kept me moving through all those nights. You . . . you alone have kept me alive.'

Her heart contracted. She longed to rush to him, to touch him, to see if he was really real, but she did not dare. He was so painfully thin, as if the flesh had melted from his bones.

He stepped closer and held out a hand. She smelt the soft, warm scent of him and choked back a sob. And then she was in his arms and she felt blind, beyond logic. Her lips found his with scalding relief. Tears soaked their cheeks and as his chest pressed against hers she felt his frail body tremble with emotion. He pulled back and, gripping her face in his hands, he planted urgent kisses all over her cheeks, her forehead, the sweep of her brows, shuddering with relief. At the touch of his lips, the damp saltiness of his tears, little by little, he came back to life.

'It's you,' she laughed, clinging to him, patting his shoulders, running her hands down his arms. 'It's actually you!'

'Yes . . . yes!' he cried, pulling her back into his embrace.

And there, standing in the empty church, they clung to one another, speechless with joy, overwhelmed with love.

'And, Millie,' he wept, his voice soft and unbelievably, wonderfully, ecstatically clear in her ear. 'Is she mine?'

Gently, she pulled back Marigold's blankets and placed her in his arms. A look of love, so pure and powerful, transformed his features. Now it was his turn to feel disbelief as he gazed down on his daughter's face. Holding her like she was made of glass, his tears fell like summer rain.

They talked until night fell like a velvet curtain over the roof of the church, filling each other in on the surreal events of the past eighteen months, plotting an uncertain future, but a future nevertheless.

Samuel had to return to his base. There was no end of paperwork, medicals, red tape to be waded through, but Millie didn't care. They had the rest of their lives together.

They kissed again, neither wanting to part, until Samuel pulled back.

'I nearly forgot,' he said, pulling a faded packet from his breast pocket. 'This is what kept me going. Your marigold seeds, minus a few. I planted some in France.' He hesitated. 'I thought maybe, when this war is over, we can go there, see if they've blossomed?'

Millie smiled and rested her head against his chest. 'Maybe, but perhaps for now we can rest a while, on British soil.'

The Match Girls

One explosive summer that changed the course of history

The fire that killed Elsie's entire family sounds like something from a penny dreadful, but, tragically, it is based on a true story that devastated the East End 121 years ago. Today, all that remains to mark the high cost of such a painful human tragedy is a solitary gravestone in Plaistow Cemetery, East London.

During the early hours of Boxing Day 1897, a fire broke out in a cupboard at 9 Dixie Street, Bethnal Green, East London. In the two small rooms of the first-floor slum, eleven members of the Jarvis family lived in abject poverty. They scarcely scraped a living by making matchboxes for Bryant & May.

On the night of the fire, Sarah Jarvis and her nine children – Hannah, aged sixteen; Mary Ann, fourteen; Thomas, twelve; William, ten; Louisa, eight; Alice, five; George, three; Caroline, two; and baby Elizabeth, eight months – were asleep, huddled together for warmth on a freezing, foggy night.

Unlike the plot of this novel, there were no survivors. They were all dead by the morning. When the firemen entered the house, they were faced with the unrecognizable remains of the family. In a primal act of pure maternal instinct, Sarah had clasped her eight-month-old daughter close to her, shielding her, so that, while she was badly burnt, her baby's body was almost untouched by the flames. Sarah could offer her daughter very little in life, but she could protect her in death.

The father, Thomas, who had entered the workhouse infirmary the previous week, died of consumption a few hours after the rest of his family, never knowing of their fate.

And it is here that the heartbreaking story takes an extraordinary turn. East London, in common with so many other working-class communities, was bound by a strong code of honour. It was a community that very much looked after one another through good times and bad. The deaths of so many children would have been felt deeply by all. Rather than having them buried in paupers' graves, East Enders, many of whom were probably on little more than starvation wages themselves, donated their farthings, halfpennies and pennies, and made possible one of the saddest-ever processions through the streets of the East End.

The funeral caused a sensation. Thousands lined the streets in their Sunday best as the cortège made its way to the cemetery. Over the sea of black, you could have heard a pin drop. Shops closed, shutters were drawn and people stood in perfect silence as the dead passed, only moving to lift their hats as a mark of respect. Thousands more waited at the cemetery and the police were deployed in large numbers to control the crowds.

The gas workers' band led the four carriages with the

coffins pulled by horses with plumes and velvets. These were followed by coaches and omnibuses with family and friends. Other vehicles joined en route, and bringing up the rear were those on foot. Street vendors carried on a busy trade in the sale of memorial cards, and three omnibuses shuttled passengers to the burial place and back for a shilling each way.

At the cemetery, a hushed crowd watched in horrified fascination as ten polished elm coffins were gently lowered into the earth. In a final note of pathos, baby Elizabeth was not separated from her mother in death, and they were buried together in the same coffin.

'This catastrophic event has now been generally forgotten, but their deaths serve to remind us of the poverty and appalling conditions that were part of London's East End workers' everyday life,' says Peter Jarvis, who is related to the family and told me in detail about the horrifying event.

'The Jarvis family's world was similar to many of London's poor – eking out a meagre living as matchbox makers. Although the whole family was engaged in assembling matchboxes, their wages were so inadequate, they were left starving. Life would have been a little better if they had entered the workhouse.

'Sarah and Thomas were children of the Nichol and the workhouse but they were fighters, fighters for survival. It is their struggle that makes their tragic end bearable for me – just. But nothing can make the deaths of all those children bearable.'

I wanted to weave this event through *The Allotment Girls* as part of Elsie's story, to illustrate the brutal poverty that working women of the Victorian era lived through. Elsie might come across as a woman quick to bury bodies and scandal, but she is also a product of her generation. Tough, embittered by experience and forced to endure miserable living and working conditions.

It was these same conditions, forced upon workers at Bryant & May, that instigated the famous match girls' strike in the summer of 1888, when 1,400 women walked out of the Fairfield Works in Bow and into the history books. The strike has been depicted in countless books, plays and films, with the women always cast as vulnerable victims, living in grimy, soot-encrusted slums, forced to work for a pittance and falling prey to the infamous phossy jaw, the grisly disease caused by white phosphorus that caused the sufferer's jaws and teeth to crumble and putrefy.

The exploitation by greedy factory bosses is real, but the match girls' role as meek, waiflike victims has been misunderstood. It is a commonly held belief that the women were led out on strike by a middle-class socialist by the name of Annie Besant. But a book written by Louise Raw challenges that. In *Striking a Light: The Bryant and May Matchwomen and their Place in History*, which I read as part of my research, the author puts together a compelling argument to show that the strikers needed no outside help and were far from downtrodden victims. Using strong bonds of working-class solidarity and female resourcefulness, these courageous women, not Annie Besant, organized themselves and instigated the strike.

'Always hold your head up. Remember you're as good as anyone,' urged Mary Driscoll, a key figure in the strike. This is a self-belief I felt sure my character Millie would have shared!

With bold swagger, this tough tribe of women marched defiantly from Bow to the Houses of Parliament in their velvet, feathered hats, forcing their bosses into an embarrassing climbdown, in which they ceded to the strikers' demands.

This strength of character and robust pride in themselves and their communities put them firmly in the same category as many other East End women I have interviewed over the years.

Ted Lewis, whose grandmother Martha worked at Bryant & May at the time of the strike, recalls a tough woman whose life was a continual fight against poverty.

'Martha was a child when she started work making matchboxes for Bryant & May. Her day would begin at 5 a.m., when she would clear the grate and light a new fire, before walking to the factory to join the queue with many other children for work,' he recalls. 'At the age of thirteen she left school to begin work for them full time. By the time the First World War broke out, she was married with five children. Her husband, James, enlisted as a rifleman. By now she was a woman of standing in the community, respected and entrusted to deliver babies and lay out the dead.'

It would have taken all that strength of character to survive what happened next – the notification that her husband was missing, presumed dead. But she carried on, and in 1916, she was asked by the army to help identify local soldiers who had been badly wounded. Walking the wards, she was drawn to a man who was bandaged head to toe. Looking into his eyes, she just knew it. 'Jim, is that you?' she gasped, at which he broke down in tears. She promptly fainted as her husband came back to life.

This sounds like something from a film, but the reality of caring for a badly wounded man with no medical or financial assistance, as well as raising their children and making matchboxes to scratch a living, makes this far from a fairy-tale ending.

'She had enormous strength of character and was devoted to her family,' says Ted with obvious pride. 'She kept the whole family fed from a large stew pot permanently simmering. I would be dispatched down to the butcher for "two penn'orth of bones and leave the meat on".'

Channelling the same esprit de corps as her fellow workers, Martha could always be relied upon to hold her own.

'In later life, when she had a fractured hip and walked with a stick, I used to take her down the pub. She was fond of a drink or two,' chuckles Ted. 'If it ever got rowdy, she'd say: "If it kicks off, prop me in the corner and I'll take 'em on with my stick!".'

It's this 'take 'em on' attitude that forced the shareholders at Bryant & May to finally start to think about the welfare of their staff. The match girls' victory brought about unimagined improvements in the lives of future match workers. To erase the shame of the strike, the bosses set up a welfare scheme that was second to none.

By the time of the Second World War, workers enjoyed on-site medical care, a dentist, library, pension fund, a generous savings and hospital fund, and social and sports clubs – including the Match Girls' Club, which organized pottery, needlecraft, keep fit, dressmaking, debating and singing lessons as well as an annual beano and dance.

'Oh, it was a plum job,' says eighty-two-year-old Ann Simmons, who worked there in the 1950s. 'My nan hated me working there, mind. "You'll get phossy jaw," she used to say. A lot of the old East End women could never forget, or forgive! But by the time I worked there it was smashing; everyone wanted to work there! There was such camaraderie and friendliness amongst the girls. It taught me to be strong, work hard and to appreciate the value of friendship. I enjoyed the best years of my life at Bryant & May.'

All that organization placed upon so slight a thing as a match, but history had shown it to be explosive if workers were exploited. I visited the imposing factory, its enormous red-brick water towers still looming large over the skyline, hoping to get a sense of the turbulent history of the place. I felt somehow that if I could stand in the place where Sarah Jarvis's children queued outside for the matches that would ultimately go on to kill them, their stories would resonate more deeply. Perhaps I might feel the reverberation of the strikers' hobnail boots echoing off the cobbles as they marched, or maybe if I listened hard enough I'd hear the distant sound of laughter and song drifting down from the top floor of the factory. Surely the robust spirit of the match girls would sing from the ancient walls.

Sadly, the past is dead and buried. No ghosts remain. Today the factory has been developed into a giant luxurious housing complex with names like Manhattan and Lexington (the East Enders who remain in Bow call it the Yuppie factory).

The top match floor is now a string of split-level loft apartments offering a metropolitan dream, a far cry from when girls packed matches there for twelve hours a day as the Luftwaffe tried to bomb them. The place where the rocket struck in the yard is now a luxury leisure complex and gym, and the site of the old allotments is concreted over, proving that you can't inhabit the past. But I hope you can perhaps get a sense of it through reading this book. I also hope you are as moved as I was to learn about the fierce maternal love of doomed Sarah, and matriarch Martha who raised her family with dignity and humour. Women to be admired. Women who were the heartbeat of their communities. *Women worth writing about.*

Do you have a family member whose story
you are proud of? Please do get in touch on:

katharinethompson82@gmail.com
@katethompson380
https://www.facebook.com/KateThompsonAuthor/

For more information on the Dixie Street fire and
for a pamphlet, contact DixieStreetFire@gmail.com

Acknowledgements

As ever, enormous thanks to my editor, Victoria Hughes-Williams, and all the incredible team at Pan Macmillan, who throughout all my dealings with them prove just why they have been named Publisher of the Year 2017. Their imagination and talent knows no bounds.

A heartfelt thanks to Diane Banks and Kate Burke at Diane Banks Associates, whose enthusiasm, talent and expertise I have come to rely on.

My writer pals Dani Atkins, Ella Harper and Kate Riordan. Warm, wise and witty women who never fail to make me laugh, give great advice and pour generous measures! What more can you ask for from a friendship?

To my research sidekick, Sarah Richards, for trekking up towers and pounding pavements with me and for organizing my life with such skill. I treasure our friendship and my pencil case!

The inimitable Anita Dobson and Carole, for the offering of such wonderful support, friendship and bubbles. What a joy to have met you both.

To historian and tour guide Rachel Kolsky for bringing to life some truly dazzling women with her infectious energy and passion. I so enjoy our walks, never knowing quite where they will lead!

Huge thanks to the Bow Geezers, an Age UK supported men's social group. This lively lot regaled me with tales of the history of Bow over sausage rolls and beer. I learnt far more from the Geezers about their vibrant East End community than I could in any archive. Thanks, fellas.

Their female equivalent, the Bow Bells, were also incredibly warm and welcoming and full of rich tales of the old days. Huge thanks must go to Ann Simmons for describing her working life at Bryant & May, and Kate at Age UK East London for helping to arrange these interviews and more.

Grace, Violet, Vera, Joan, Iris and Rene who remember with humour and exceptional detail their rich childhoods in wartime Bow. Thank you, ladies!

Enormous thanks to George Donovan, the schoolboy turned wartime pig farmer for filling my head with stories. They broke the mould when they made you, George!

June at the Bow Quarter for just being so thoroughly lovely.

Ted Lewis, who sadly died in August 2017, and his wife Bett, who welcomed me into their home and shared the unique history of their proud and strong East End families. Ted was a true gentleman. RIP.

Peter Jarvis and Richard Gregory for sharing with me the heartbreaking story of the fire which killed their ancestors and the painstaking research into their lives. It was truly humbling to learn of Sarah Jarvis's strength in fighting for her children.

Ursula Buchan, historian and author of *A Green and*

Pleasant Land: How England's Gardeners Fought the Second World War, for ensuring there were no howlers.

Jane Sill and Ray Newton of the Cable Street Community Gardens. This tranquil and magical garden is sandwiched between the busy highway leading to Tower Bridge and the Commercial Road, one of the main routes into the city, and yet it might be in the heart of the countryside. Men, women and children of all ages, cultures and faiths come together to share an appreciation of the natural world and cultivate their own small piece of the East End. Jane helped me to understand what gardening can give to the soul. http://www.cablestreetcommunitygardens.co.uk

Linda Owens Fogg, thank you for your kindness and support as always.

Jim Burton and Bradley Snooks, huge thanks for your help! What these boys don't know about Bow ain't worth knowing!

Finally, enormous thanks to Malcolm at Local History Library & Archives in Tower Hamlets for his unrivalled knowledge of the East End, and Elizabeth at Hackney Archives for unearthing box after box of Bryant & May archive material. I'm very grateful to you both. I also visited the Imperial War Museum archives, which has a fantastic collection of material relating to the Dig for Victory campaign and the fascinating Ragged School Museum in East London. https://www.raggedschoolmuseum.org.uk

What incredible and free research resources we have in this country.

Further Reading

Striking a Light: The Bryant and May Matchwomen and their Place in History, Louise Raw. Continuum Books. Paperback edition, 2011.

The Match Makers, Patrick Beaver. Henry Melland Ltd for Bryant & May Ltd. 1985.

Bomber Command, Max Hastings. Pan Books. Pan Macmillan. 2010.

A Green And Pleasant Land: How England's Gardeners Fought the Second World War, Ursula Buchan. Windmill Books. 2014.

Dig for Victory: The Wartime Garden, Twigs Way. Shire Publications Ltd. 2015.

Allotment & Garden Guide, Twigs Way. Sabrestorm Publishing. 2009.

How to Grow Food: A Wartime Guide, Doreen Wallace. Batsford. First published 1940. Reprinted 2012.

Bow and Bromley-By-Bow, Gary Haines. The History Press. 2008.

If you enjoyed *The Allotment Girls*,
then you'll love

The Wedding Girls

In one corner of London, it's forever Hollywood . . .

It's 1936 and the streets of Bethnal Green are grimy and brutal. Herbie Taylor's photography studio is a sanctuary, nestled on bustling Green Street. All life passes through its doors, each person wishing to capture that perfect moment in time.

Stella and Winnie work in Herbie's studio; their best friend Kitty works next door as an apprentice dressmaker. Kitty creates magical gowns for the brides-to-be, wondering with each stitch if she'll ever get a chance to wear a white dress. Stella and Winnie sprinkle a dusting of Hollywood glamour over happy newly-weds, assisting Herbie to capture memorable portraits of their special day.

But as the clouds of war brew on the horizon, danger looms over the country. The community of Green Street has always been strong, but can it survive the ultimate test? Will the Wedding Girls find their happy ever afters, before it's too late?

Secrets of the Singer Girls

1942. Sixteen-year-old Poppy Percival turns up at the gates of Trout's clothing factory in Bethnal Green with no idea what her new life might have in store. There to start work as a seamstress, and struggling to get to grips with the noise, dirt and devastation of East London, Poppy can't help but miss the quiet countryside of home. But Poppy harbours a dark secret – one that wrenched her away from all she knew and from which she is still suffering . . .

And Poppy's not the only one with a secret. Each of her new friends at the factory is hiding something painful. Vera Shadwell, the forelady, has had a hard life with scars both visible and concealed; her sister Daisy has romantic notions that could get her in trouble; and Sal Fowler is a hardworking mother who worries about her two evacuated boys for good reason. Bound by ties of friendship, loyalty and family, the devastating events of the war will throw each of their lives into turmoil, but also bring these women closer to each other than they could ever have imagined.

'A poignant and moving story of the friendship of women during wartime Britain' **Val Wood**

Secrets of the Sewing Bee

Orphan Flossy Brown arrives at Trout's garment factory in Bethnal Green amidst the uncertainty of the Second World War. In 1940s London, each cobbled street is strewn with ghosts of soldiers past, all struggling to make ends meet. For the women of the East End, their battles are on the home front.

Flossy is quickly embraced by the colourful mix of characters working at Trout's, who have turned their sewing expertise to vital war work. They fast become the family that Flossy has always longed for. Dolly Doolaney, darling of the East End, and infamous tea lady, gives her a particularly warm welcome and helps Flossy settle into wartime life.

Things aren't so easy for Peggy Piper, another new recruit at the factory. She's used to the high life working as a nippie in the West End, and is not best pleased to find herself bent over a sewing machine. But war has the ability to break down all sorts of class barriers, and soon Peggy finds the generosity and spirit of her fellow workers difficult to resist.

Dolly sets up a sewing circle and the ladies at Trout's play their part in defending the frontline as they arm themselves with their needles and set about stitching their way to victory. But as the full force of the Blitz hits London, the sewing bee are forced to shelter in the underground tube stations on a nightly basis.

In such close quarters, can Dolly manage to contain the secret that binds them all? And how will Peggy and Flossy cope as their lives are shaped and moved by forces outside of their control?